Books by Richard A. Lupoff

CIRCUMPOLAR!
SUN'S END
GALAXY'S END
COUNTERSOLAR!

COUNTERSOLAR!

Richard A. Lupoff

ACE BOOKS, NEW YORK

This Ace book contains
the complete text of the original hardcover
edition. It has been completely reset
in a typeface designed for easy
reading, and was printed from new film.

COUNTERSOLAR!

An Ace Book/published by arrangement with
the author

PRINTING HISTORY
Arbor House edition/January 1987
Ace edition/August 1989

ISBN: 0-441-11791-0

Ace Books are published by The Berkley Publishing Group,
200 Madison Avenue, New York, New York 10016.
The name ''ACE'' and the ''A'' logo
are trademarks belonging to Charter Communications, Inc.

PRINTED IN THE UNITED STATES OF AMERICA

10 9 8 7 6 5 4 3 2 1

Now we have gone to the moon! For sixty years I have lived for this day and for the realization of this dream.

Someone asked me, *Could we have done this sooner?* To this question, my answer is, *Undoubtedly yes!*

As early as the 1930's we possessed sufficient knowledge to build at least a simple space-flier. We had achieved all necessities of airframe design, powerplant development, and navigation and control systems.

Also we had acquired the concept of combining these elements for flight beyond the stratosphere. Workable interplanetary craft were described in detail by, for instance, Otto Willi Gail and visualized precisely by draughtsmen like the immortal Frank R. Paul.

If only the will to do so had been present we could have ventured into space sometime between 1935 and 1940. Certainly by 1942 at the very latest.

—WILLY LEY
July 20, 1969

This Side

Indian Ocean

Africa

Sumatra
Borneo
Asia
Arabia

Australia

Russia
Europe

Great
Scandinavia Britain
Iceland
Greenland

Japan

Atlantic Ocean

New Zealand

Canada
Hawaii
U.S.A.

Latin
America

Pacific Ocean

That Side

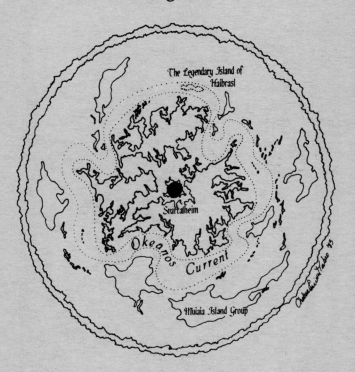

The Legendary Island of Haibrasl

Svartalheim

Okeanos Current

Muiaia Island Group

CHAPTER
1

Outside the *City of Santa Barbara*'s curved Plexiglas windows, heavy, moist flakes of sleet swept down, illuminated against the night sky's blackness by the giant craft's aerial running lights. Massive blobs that struck the Plexiglas were melted by the huge skyliner's skin heaters. They slid across the streamlined surface, making brief streaks, then disappeared into the cold slipstream.

The soft sound of the sleet against the leading edge of the transatlantic skyliner was shut out of the combination ballroom and dining salon, as was the whine of the *Santa Barbara*'s four gargantuan, magnetic-powered pusher props, by the flying wing's insulated skin. The *City of Santa Barbara*, headed eastward from New York's Roosevelt Field to the Harriet Quimby Aerodrome near London, was by far the most luxurious craft on the transatlantic service.

With a rated speed in excess of 200 miles per hour, it was also the fastest. Leaving Roosevelt on the evening of December 31, 1941, the skyliner would meet the New Year 1942 a thousand miles at sea, shortly before passing over the old steamer, *Titanic*, once the unsinkable pride of the transatlantic fleet and still the favorite of tradition-minded travelers unwilling to accept the coming obsolescence of surface liners in this bright morning of the age of aviation.

1

It was arranged that the *Santa Barbara* and the westbound *Titanic* would exchange a salute of flashing lights as their paths crossed.

Aboard the *Santa Barbara* the Glenn Miller orchestra was performing a selection of popular tunes. As the musicians swung into "Tuxedo Junction," the band's female vocalist, a dazzling honey-blond, stepped up to the microphone. Her daringly cut black gown set off her creamy skin. A glittering bracelet worn over one of her long black gloves caught the glare of the spotlight and sent a rainbow of colors flashing over the diners as the singer gestured.

Although the sumptuous dinner had been completed and its remnants long since cleared from the salon, every table remained full. The sole exception was the captain's own table, where a seat had been left free.

The captain himself was decked out in his formal dinner jacket, replete with brass and braid of the airline's insignia, a gracefully stylized swallow silhouetted in black against a chrome-yellow disk. The *City of Santa Barbara* itself bore out the motif. The 172-foot wingspan was constructed of a light, strong alloy tinctured yellow and marked with black swallow silhouettes.

Every male in the dining salon was attired in dinner clothes, most in civilian garb, some in the attire of their nation's military or naval services.

The women were comparably gowned. Bare shoulders, elbow-length gloves, upswept hairdos. Glittering necklaces drew the eye (unnecessarily) to hardly concealed bosoms.

As the empty seat to Captain Irwin Jarrold's right was the sole vacancy in the great room, so the occupant of the chair beyond the empty one provided unique contrast to the formal dress otherwise universal. He was a slight man, his deeply lined face showing every one of his sixty-two years. His white hair, worn unfashionably long, stood like a halo around his head. An unkempt white moustache held a few stray crumbs from the evening's meal. His gray sweater showed several holes, and one cuff was unraveled, yet the gnarled hands with which he gestured as he spoke were clean.

The man to whom he was speaking listened carefully, drinking in every word. He was younger, a vigorous, muscular man with sandy-colored hair, sun-bronzed skin, and the squint lines around his eyes that showed his years working in the California desert, building and testing his brilliant, revolutionary all-wing aircraft. The *City of Santa Barbara* was the triumph of Jack Northrop's career and the vindication of his theories.

Yet he hung on every word spoken by his seatmate. Northrop knew that Albert Einstein was not a garrulous man; when the greatest thinker since Newton spoke, one did not interrupt.

The other two seats of Captain Jarrold's table were occupied by a man and woman whose conversation held the captain's attention. A retired naval officer with a long-held interest in aviation, Captain Jarrold had built the Black Swallow Line into the world's leading airline.

While the company's president, Eugene Bullard, sat in his San Diego office suite setting policy, Jarrold traveled tirelessly, supervising training, evaluating aircraft, grilling flight crews, and occasionally piloting a skyliner himself.

But this was New Year's Eve, the great flying wing was performing magnificently, the occasion was gala.

Jarrold's immediate seatmate was a tall, thin dark-haired woman. She wore evening attire, but her bare shoulders and arms showed sinews like steel cables. The set of her jaw marked her as one who could set the highest goal for herself and, having done so, would let nothing stop her from attaining her goal.

The captain and the woman were engrossed in a three-way conversation with the man seated to her left. He was immaculate in white jacket, wing collar, and bow tie, his rounded, balding head and black skin contrasting with their snowy surroundings.

"It's a thrill to have you aboard," Jarrold was saying. "What a wonderful gift for my grandchildren—baseballs autographed for them by Babe Didrikson and Josh Gibson, the greatest battery in baseball!"

Babe's eyes flashed at the captain. "Do they know they're getting them?"

Jarrold shook his head. "Their birthday is next week. We'll make our return flight after we debark our passengers and unload the *Manta* at Quimby Aerodrome, then board a new complement of passengers. I want to surprise them."

"I didn't know you carried freight on this wing, Captain," Josh Gibson put in.

"We don't normally. But you know the flying wing was developed to be a military bomber should we ever need one again. There are bay doors and we loaded the *Manta* through them. It's—"

He was interrupted by the arrival of the honey-blond singer. The captain sprang to his feet, followed by Gibson and Jack Northrop. Einstein, puzzled, followed suit. His expression was abstracted until he saw who it was whose hand the captain was taking. A steward held the beautiful vocalist's chair for her. The captain introduced her: "Miss Beejay Diamond." He named each of the others at the table.

The singer shook the hand of each person at the table, starting with Babe Didrikson's. Einstein was the last, and held her velvet-gloved hand in his two. "Your singing was lovely, Miss Beejay," he said. "As you are yourself, if I may make such a boldness."

The vocalist reddened. "Why, thank you, Dr. Einstein."

"I love music," Einstein said. "I think in it God reveals himself to us most clearly. The beauty of all creation, the beauty and simplicity of all truth, he shows us in music. Perhaps someday you would let me play for you my violin."

"I would be honored." She noticed a shadow behind her, turned to see another steward place a silvered ice bucket near the table. He lifted a champagne bottle and presented its label for inspection by Captain Jarrold.

Jarrold nodded his approval, then checked his watch. "You'll be due back on the bandstand in a few minutes?"

"Oh, yes! Glenn is a real stickler, you know. Some of the fellows call him a slave driver, but that's why we're the best in the business."

"I understand entirely. That's how Jack Northrop became the greatest aircraft designer in the business, and I'm sure that's how Babe Didrikson and Josh Gibson rose to the top of their field. It's the only way!"

"You'd be surprised, Cap!" Didrikson's southeast Texas drawl was a surprising contrast to her rapid, powerful movements and her determined manner.

"I thought you were a perfectionist, Miss Didrikson."

"Well, I am. I'm just sayin' it isn't the only way. It's my way, but it isn't the only way."

To Didrikson's left, Josh Gibson had lifted one hand to cover his mouth and was chuckling softly.

Didrikson gave him an elbow in the ribs and his laughter doubled.

"What are you so happy about?" Didrikson demanded. "What's so golly-whanged funny?"

"You're right, Babe," Gibson said. "I was just laughing because you made me think of the 'riginal Babe."

"You played against him, didn't you?" Captain Jarrold put in. "The greatest pitcher of all time. Some say he could have been as great a hitter, too, but pitching was his true love."

"It wasn't his true love, Cap'n! He'd rather pitch 'cause then he only had to work twice a week, 'stead of every day! George Ruth was the laziest man the Lord ever put on this disk. He trained on hotdogs and whiskey. And he did, he surely did like the ladies. Pardon me, Miss Beejay. But he surely did. So he could just smoke cigars and drink whiskey and eat hotdogs and sleep in the mornings and pitch twice a week.

"I asked Babe once—we were barnstorming together in the off-season, playing in Cuba—what he could do if he cut out cigars and booze and floozies and ate proper 'stead of hot-dogs. I remember that night like it was yesterday, sitting in a nightclub in Havana, living like kings. Babe looked around the table. It was me and the Babe, Cool Papa Bell was there, Bobo Newsom was there, and we were surrounded by some gorgeous Cuban women—you wouldn't believe it. Pardon, Miss Beejay.

"And Babe just downed a Cuba libre and puffed on his stogie and he looked me straight in the eye and he said, 'Josh, if I cut out cigars and quit the booze and left the fast women alone, I couldn't play baseball at all, because if I did that, it would have to mean I'd be dead!' "

Beejay Diamond lifted a crystal champagne glass. "I won't be here at midnight so I'll wish you all a happy 1942!" She took a small sip, put her glass on the white linen tablecloth, smudged Captain Jarrold's cheek with her crimson lipstick, and headed back for the bandstand.

Albert Einstein turned toward Jack Northrop. "You truly

built this wonderful skyliner, eh? I so admire those who can do things practical. *Ach*!'' He shook his head slowly, a faraway look in the deep blue eyes. "When I was a patent clerk in Bern, *ach*, my dear friend Grossmann got for me the job. Poor Marcel, dead now—he died the same year as my poor wife. Oh, but the things they try to patent, you could laugh or cry. You could laugh or cry. Practical genius, Mr. Northrop, practical genius. I so admire that. And what next, if I may ask? What will you build for us to exceed this magnificent craft?''

Glowing, Northrop said, "Another generation, sir. You know there was a government backing for the development of the flying wing. It's been such a success, we wish to move on. You know, we built a series of mock-ups before we built the full-scale wings. First wind-tunnel models, then radio-controlled miniatures, then a quarter-scale crew-carrying mock-up. That is the *Manta*.

"The new generation of skyliners will be built to fly through the highest stratosphere. We've built experimental engines that will apply magnetic power directly to the movement of the aircraft. No propellers. No need for atmosphere. They will be fully sealed, fully self-contained, capable of flying anywhere. And at speeds that will make these flying wings look like sailboats!''

Einstein had reached into the sagging pockets of his loose trousers and extracted a long-stemmed, slim pipe. He packed the bowl and sent a small cloud of smoke rising above the table. "So, magnetic propulsion.'' He rubbed his chin with a gnarled thumb and finger. "In 1902 Grossmann got me that job. Technical expert, third class. Three years I worked there. Promoted to technical expert, second class. Above that I never rose, until I left the job, above second class I never rose.''

"We're taking the *Manta* to England for evaluation by His Majesty's government. Then on for tests in North Africa. When we unload at Quimby, I would be happy to show you the *Manta*.'' Northrop had the eagerness of a schoolboy mechanic showing off his car to Barney Oldfield. "If you could spare the time to look at the craft, that is.''

Einstein had drawn a puff of smoke through his long pipe and released it. Where the first had disappeared into the air, this new cloudlet floated above their table. A faraway look was in those eyes again. The white-maned head was cocked to one side as the scientist studied the movement of the cloud.

The gnarled hands dug through baggy pockets, reemerged. Einstein picked up a swizzle stick and began drawing mathematical symbols on the linen tablecloth.

Northrop watched for a few seconds, then found a pen inside his dinner jacket: one of the new solid-ink type necessitated for high-altitude use. He pried the swizzle stick from Einstein's fingers and substituted the pen; he unfolded a clean linen napkin and spread it beneath Einstein's hand.

A huge clock mounted behind the bandstand pointed its hands straight up. Glenn Miller, spotlight glinting off his rimless glasses, polished trombone in hand, wished the audience a happy New Year.

At the captain's table, Babe Didrikson planted a brief kiss first on Captain Jarrold's cheek, then on Josh Gibson's.

A subdued cheer swept the room—the passengers on the *City of Santa Barbara* were not a boisterous lot.

On the bandstand Glenn Miller turned to face his musicians. "Happy New Year, boys and girls." He raised his trombone, used it to signal a beat to the orchestra, then led them into his theme song, "Moonlight Serenade."

The *City of Santa Barbara* continued to slice effortlessly through the thinning sleet. The sky was no less black, but the swirling flakes were more sparsely scattered; a few breaks were appearing in the storm.

At Captain Jarrold's table, Albert Einstein blinked. He closed the pen he had been using and shoved it into a trousers pocket. He turned toward Jack Northrop and said, "I am going to play some Mozart with my friends Menuhin and Joseph Szigeti. And then a little trip I take to Vienna. Some medal I am supposed to accept I think. From the Emperor Karl at Schönbrunn."

He laughed and shrugged his gray-clad shoulders. "Emperors! Palaces! Medals!" He laid his hand on Northrop's white sleeve. "Silly! So silly! But I will tell you a secret. I go really to walk the streets where Mozart walked. To stand before his house in homage. On one trip I will visit the house of Isaac Newton and that of Mozart! Only I wish my wife could also come."

He stood up, muttered, "I have a little to think," and walked absently away from the table.

Jack Northrop leaned over and studied the napkin on which Einstein had made his notes. He folded it carefully and slipped it into his jacket, the writing side concealed.

"That old man made off with your pen," Josh Gibson said to Northrop.

"And he left me this." Northrop tapped his jacket with a tanned thumb. He smiled. "I think I got the best of the bargain."

"I think you did," Gibson said.

A heavyset officer came huffing between tables, headed toward Captain Jarrold. His uniform bore the insignia of chief signal officer, blazoned beneath the Black Swallow Line crest. His sparse faded hair lay flat on his head, and a neatly trimmed moustache could have been borrowed from a much older Adolphe Menjou.

He slid between two dowagers, barely avoided colliding with a steward, waving his hands toward the captain. When he reached the captain's table, he leaned over and whispered in Captain Jarrold's ear.

Jarrold turned to him, asked, "Are you sure?"

The signal officer nodded vigorously.

Jarrold slid his chair from the table. "Jack, can you come with Mr. Sterling and me? To the bridge. . . ." He stood up. "Miss Didrikson, Mr. Gibson. I'm very sorry."

The three men hustled away from the table.

Jarrold said, "Jack, you haven't met our signal officer. Mr. Sterling knows more about radio than anyone I know. Morris, this is Jack Northrop."

"I recognized you, sir. A pleasure." They exchanged a hasty handclasp.

"All right, what happened?" Jarrold asked.

"We were monitoring the bands, Cap. Routine stuff, you know. Looking out for distress cries. We've been holding an open link with *Titanic*. She's right on course; we should cross in just under forty minutes."

"Yes, yes. And . . . ?"

They had reached a bulkhead, entered a short companionway that would lead them to the signal bridge.

Sterling halted, out of breath. He wiped perspiration from

his forehead, took a deep breath. "You know the transmissions that have been coming in. Uh, Mr. Northrop, I understand your work, sir. But, Captain, uh, how much information does Mr. Northrop—there is a security aspect."

Northrop said, "I've been cleared by the secretary of the navy personally. Your captain knows my credentials."

"That's right, Morris. Mr. Northrop is to have full access to all information that we have. Anything you can tell me, you can tell him also."

Sterling nodded. "Let's go on to the signal bridge, then. Everything is recorded there."

They clustered around the radio signal clerk's desk. They kept their voices low. The signal clerk had of course been investigated and cleared as well. Although the *Santa Barbara* was a civil craft, she carried government signal gear and was on standby for conversion to military use in case of emergency. Crew members with access to advanced equipment or sensitive information were all sworn reservists, subject to navy discipline.

Sterling seated himself at the operator's station. He shuffled among papers on the desk. "Here it is. We've been getting these fragmentary transmissions, sir. I've kept you posted, Captain Jarrold, but Mr. Northrop—"

"The secretary has kept me up to date," Northrop said.

"Yes, sir. You know, then, that the transmissions seem to be coming straight from the sun itself. But of course that's impossible."

"Certainly. The only other explanation is that the source is directly in line with the sun. Either between us and the sun, or directly beyond it. And it must be moving at a speed to keep it in that straight line or the source would seem to move. It would move, relative to us."

"Very well," Captain Jarrold snapped. "We can have a full review later on, complete with history. What is this newest transmission, Mr. Sterling?"

The signal officer read from the gray sheet that the clerk had prepared. " 'Situation growing desperate. Cannot last more than a few days. No replies received to prior transmission. Please reply. Anyone. Please reply.' " He dropped the gray sheet onto the desk. "That's it, sir."

"And we can't reply, eh?"

"I don't know of any transmitter powerful enough to penetrate the distance and all the electrical activity going on inside the sun. And we've eliminated every source between us and the sun. It isn't the planet Venus or Mercury. There's no sign of a stray asteroid or other source. So it has to be something opposite us, beyond the sun and directly opposite us. The other transmissions have all been fragmentary, but they were all consistent with this latest. A couple of times they've identified themselves as planet earth calling. How can that be?"

Jarrold exchanged a glance with Jack Northrop. The two men had known each other, had worked together on advance projects for years, going back to Jarrold's days in the navy and Northrop's early efforts as an aircraft designer for Lockheed before moving out to start his own company.

They had sat up many nights over coffee and brandy, discussing their work and speculating on the challenges that might lie ahead for scientists and engineers, aviators and astronomers.

As if they had rehearsed the answer to Sterling's question, they nodded and spoke in unison: "Counter-Earth!"

Sterling looked around as if uncertain of his reaction. "Counter-Earth?"

"That's right."

"But I thought that was a myth. A fancy they wrote about in cheap magazines. I even saw a movie about it once, but nobody really believes in that!"

Northrop said, "We've considered every possible explanation. Nothing else will suffice. The only answer is another planet like our own, circling the sun in the same orbit as our own. Don't know if you ever heard of Charlie Avison, a brilliant worker. Developed a whole theory of Counter-Earth. He says if the other planet started with the identical composition of our own, then everything would have evolved there just as it did here on earth."

He let out a gust of breath, as if his excitement were simply too much to contain.

Sterling asked, "Even to the development of the English language? And of Morse code? And even their name for their planet?"

Northrop nodded.

Sterling still seemed unconvinced.

Captain Jarrold said, "The evidence is before you, man! Trust your own eyes!" He reached for the gray sheet, rapped it against the deck with hard knuckles.

"But—what can we do about it?"

Captain Jarrold and Jack Northrop had been standing all through the conversation. Now Jarrold drew a swivel chair toward Sterling's and sat down. Northrop followed suit.

Once again they exchanged glances; Jarrold nodded almost imperceptibly.

"The N-M1," Jack said softly. "The Northrop Magnetic-drive, model One. *Manta*."

"I thought that was just a flying test bed for the new engines, Mr. Northrop."

"It's intended for that. But it's our prototype. It's fitted with high-altitude suits. It can glide or fly in atmosphere, but it should function in a vacuum as well. Without propellers, we don't need air for thrust. We can direct our power with the engines. The cabin is sealed and we have air and supplies."

Sterling blanched. "You seriously intend to undertake a flight to this so-called Counter-Earth?"

"I intend exactly that."

"You'll fly out from Quimby, then? We'll off-load *Manta* and you'll take on a crew then, and fly out of England? You never really intended to test the N-M1 in Africa?"

Northrop said, "We intended all of that. But this is a new circumstance."

Captain Jarrold put his hand on Northrop's arm to stop him. "Let me tell him this, Jack. Mr. Sterling is absolutely reliable. There's no need to hold anything back from him."

He leaned forward earnestly. "Mr. Sterling, we have reason to believe that others may be receiving these signals as well. Just so long as they were fragmentary—so long as the whole enterprise was subject to question—we could afford to take a cautious, orderly approach to this situation. But now, we have to move fast.

"Jack, I have sealed orders for you from the secretary of the navy, approved by President Cordell Hull himself. They're locked in the safe on the command bridge. I haven't read them myself, but the secretary told me that they authorize you, in case of an emergency, to select a special crew and launch at the earliest opportunity. I am authorized to declare that emergency, and in Mr. Sterling's presence, I so declare. Whom do you want to take? How soon can you launch?''

Northrop put his hand to his chest. Feeling the folded linen napkin in his inside pocket, he opened it on the message desk. He studied it briefly, then looked up at Jarrold. "Do you know what this is, Irwin? Dr. Einstein was plotting a course to Counter-Earth.''

Jarrold nodded. "He has been apprised of the situation throughout. The President personally appealed to him, and Dr. Einstein has agreed to participate as the President's personal representative and observer. Who else is on your list?''

"*Manta* will carry four comfortably. Two more. We know that Dr. Einstein is a great scientist. I can handle more practical engineering jobs on board, and I'll be chief pilot. I want two people who are young and strong, quick and smart. I'm going to ask Didrikson and Gibson, Irwin. I know that will seem strange, but they're my choice.''

An hour later the bomb bay doors—or main cargo hatch—of the *City of Santa Barbara* slid majestically open. A miniature flying wing, a perfect replica of the giant skyliner, was lowered gingerly.

A midair launch had never been intended. The attempt was an unexpected contingency. Mildred "Babe" Didrikson and Josh Gibson, attired in unfamiliar aviators' high-altitude suits, sat tensely in their assigned places. The request to serve on *Manta* had been a surprise to both of them, but the urgings of Jack Northrop and Captain Irwin Jarrold had quickly convinced them to go along.

Albert Einstein, rapt in thoughts of his own, sat calmly beside Northrop.

Jack Northrop clutched the control yoke in both hands. Through the crew bubble he watched the operations of the launch crew.

The sleet storm was blowing out its last energies.

Manta dropped.

Before Northrop could feel the miniature flying wing's control surfaces take hold, a sudden gust in the slipstream lifted *Manta* a few feet too high.

She cleared the ventral surface of the parent craft with inches to spare, but *Santa Barbara*'s right outboard pusher prop crashed into *Manta*'s wingtip. The smaller craft was impaled on the propeller blade, swung horizontally, then thrown behind the *Santa Barbara*.

Spinning wildly, *Manta* plunged headlong through the black night, toward the black Atlantic waves.

CHAPTER
2

The early-morning sky was a sparkling blue marked with tiny white puffs of cumulus. Although the midsummer heat that had prostrated much of Buenos Aires was expected to return later in the day, January 1, 1942, began with a cool and invigorating feel.

A brisk breeze was even blowing off the Rio de la Plata's estuary, carrying a marine tang into the heart of the city and reminding the sophisticated *porteños* of their heritage: sea-farers, explorers, and cognoscenti. Let the rough-riding gauchos and the poverty-stricken *piedras negras*, Argentina's own *peónes*, give themselves to the land and its exploitation. Let the *estancieros* manage their great rural baronies. The *porteños* were more concerned with culture and politics, the great games upon which their lives were founded.

The broad Plaza de Mayo hummed with the passage of Mercedes and Lancias, Humbers and Renaults and Pierce-Arrows. Nattily dressed Argentines filled the plaza's side-walks: shopgirls hurrying to their jobs, office workers pausing on their own way to study the latest fashions from Paris, from Bond Street, or to gaze longingly at a Viennese torte or a platter of German *Küchen*. The temptation was great but a trim-figured *porteña* would resist.

Although the first day of the New Year was officially a

holiday, industrious *porteños* would still put in a few hours of diligent striving, adding to their wealth and enabling themselves to make the extra purchase, the little extravagance upon which Argentines doted.

One end of the plaza was dominated by Buenos Aires's great nineteenth-century Cathedral.

At the other end of the plaza stood the Casa Rosada, seat of Argentina's Presidential power.

A nation that had maintained peace with her neighbors for some eighty years, whose democratic institutions were strong and stable, whose health and prestige grew with each passing day, Argentina was a country of great ambitions and few problems. Chief among these latter was that of retaining her independent position *vis-à-vis* the contending powers of Europe and Los Estados Unidos, the Colossus of the North. Germany, Italy, Spain, even old Austria-Hungary, renascent under the young Emperor Karl, sought to influence the rich and burgeoning Argentina.

Britain owned much of Argentina's industry, including the vital national rail system.

And always the Colossus loomed with its notions of Manifest Destiny, its Monroe Doctrine, its obnoxious Roosevelt Corollary.

Happy and prosperous, Argentina could not afford to become smug.

Atop the Casa Rosada's tall flagpole the Argentine flag snapped its blue and white and its golden sun, as high above the Plaza de Mayo as the crucifix atop of the Cathedral's highest spire.

Within the Casa Rosada a small staff of functionaries stood to duty. Office staffs were at minimum levels. Even the smartly liveried servants and Presidential majordomos were reduced in number and relaxed in mien.

At the heart of the palace lay the great Salón Blanco. This was the White Room, where diplomatic credentials were presented and official receptions sparkled with the cut glass of chandeliers, the jewels of beautiful women, and the bubbles of champagne imported from Chile and from France.

The room was sealed and darkened. Two men sat on silk-cushioned Chippendale chairs. One of them, elderly, digni-

fied in wing collar and morning suit, was none other than
Pedro Ramírez, distinguished President of the Republic.

The second, seated to the President's left, was a younger
man, his thick, black hair combed straight back and close to
his head, belying his forty-odd years of age. His face was
broad and handsome, with the slightest touch of bronze,
speaking of an Indian great-grandparent. He wore the neat
powder-blue uniform tunic of an army officer: white shirt,
black tie, dark trousers, and brilliantly polished boots.

Rapidly moving images danced in reflection on the officer's
large, rimless eyeglasses.

The images were those of Gene Autry, the splendid singing
cowboy, and Dorothy Christie, the gorgeously gowned and
sexy queen of the phantom empire of Murania, 25,000 feet
beneath the hilly *pampa* of Autry's *Estancia Radiograma*.

The projector, threaded and operated by the Presidential
military aide himself, stood behind the two men. A sparkling
screen had been erected and a loudspeaker concealed behind
it to blare out the hoofbeats and dialogue of the motion picture.

Muranian robots and Thunder Riders had captured Gene
Autry and dragged him before the ruler of the underground
kingdom. The singing cowboy stood to lose the ownership of
his precious ranch if he did not return in time for his daily
radio broadcast. His ranch hands, rallied by the plucky young
Betsy K. Ross, were racing across the plain to rescue Autry.

A strip of brightness appeared and widened as the great
doorway of the Salón Blanco was opened. The black-and-
white images on the screen paled to an indistinguishable gray
as a flunky hurried into the room. He touched the military
officer gingerly on one shoulder with a white-gloved hand,
bent, and whispered in his ear, "*Mi mayor*, pardon, a most
urgent telephonic communication."

Major Perón hissed angrily under his breath, asking the
President of the Republic if he might be excused.

"Go ahead, Juan. And close the door. This is exciting!"

Perón scuttled from the Salón Blanco, following the liveried servant. "What's the matter with you, breaking in on a
Presidential meeting like that? I would have had your hide
then and there, only the President would have been even an-
grier! Now, what's this all about?"

The servant cringed as if expecting to be struck. "Pardon, my major. You told me that you wished to receive communications at any time from the lady. I thought—"

"Never mind. Just get back to the Salón Blanco and stand by in case the President wants you! But leave the doors shut! Keep an ear tuned. Respond at once when the President summons you! Now disappear!"

The servant obeyed.

Major Perón lifted the handset of the elegant pale blue and white telephone. He spoke into the mouthpiece, "*¿Cómo?*"

The answering voice identified its source as Radio Belgrano, a call coming in from the combined studio and engineering center in the Buenos Aires suburb of that name. "Stand by, please. A call for Major Perón from Señorita Duarte."

Perón could not keep the smile from his lips as he thought of the little actress, his Evita. He had not married until past the age of thirty—a common enough practice in Argentina— but his bride had died young, leaving the major a widower before the age of forty. He had thrown himself into his career, studying and teaching history, representing his country in its embassy at Rome, studying the methods of warfare of the Old World powers. He had even written a book on the Eastern European campaign of 1912, an important if little-remembered theater of the world-shattering *Einjahrkrieg*, the One Year War.

The book had been published in time to make Major Perón a minor celebrity among the senior faculty—mostly German—of Argentina's Colegio Militar.

He had come to the attention of the President of the Republic and had become the President's personal military aide.

And then he had met the aspiring young actress. Evita could do anything, play any role—the schoolchild in *Los Inocentes*, Catherine the Great in *Heroínas del Historia*, even a female rocketeer in the space fantasy *Oro Blanco*! Within days she had arranged to move into an apartment adjacent to his own on Calle Posadas and obtained a key to the connecting doorway. She called herself *una grasita*, a greaser, a poor country girl from the village of Junín, one hardly fit to mix with the *porteños* of Juan Perón's acquaintance. But she soon proved to be more than a match for any rival, a generous and remembering friend to any who helped her and an implacable and unforgiving foe to any who opposed.

At last she picked up the telephone instrument at Radio Belgrano. "Juanito, Pocho," Perón heard. Evita's voice could be cultured and dramatic when the role demanded; only rarely did it revert to the harsh mispronunciations of Junín. "I'm sorry to phone you at the Casa Rosada. Were you with the President?"

"Yes. What is it? Quickly, Evita."

"It's the English. He called me here from El Palomar. He said you told him not to contact you directly."

"Right, I did. But what did you tell him?"

"I told him to stand by. That I would relay his message to you and your reply to him."

"Are you on the air, Eva?"

He could hear her contemptuous snort. "Use your brain, Pocho! How could I be speaking with you if I were on the air? We had only a rehearsal today, an early rehearsal. We were working on the next installment of *Oro Blanco*."

"Of course." She was right, as usual, but Perón didn't care for her readiness to show her scorn when he erred. He would have to speak with her about this. But for now: "How much more information did the English give you? Who else is there at Belgrano with you?"

"Just the rest of the cast. That *ramera* Libertad Lamarque, damn her. Some reporter for *Antena* magazine. And the scriptwriter Hector Blomberg."

"Ah, Hector! He's good when he can stay upright at the typewriter! Is he sober this morning?"

"Barely! I've never seen a hangover like Hector's."

"But the English, my dove. What else did he say?"

"He said that Herr Horten is with him at Palomar, that Herr Richter has arrived from Río Gallegos."

"Yes, yes, and . . ."

"And what, my Pocho?"

"Did he bring anything with him from Patagonia?"

He heard her intake of breath. "Yes. He said that Richter had brought a jar of fireflies and that they could have a ride today on the bat."

Perón stiffened. He said, "Wait there. I'm coming right over. Can you get a car?"

"I have none here."

"What about Blomberg? What about that plutocrat Yankelevich? Doesn't he keep a car at the station all the time?"

"He does. But he'd be angry if—"

"Never mind Yankelevich. Tell Blomberg that he's going to have to put Libertad in your role."

"*Libertad*! I'll kill her before I'll give her my role! I'm about to be ravaged by a tentacled Venusian! It's my juiciest scene!"

"*¡Grasita cabeza-vacante*! Empty-head! You have no idea what's important in this world! Do as I say! I'm coming over!"

He slammed the receiver down, severing the connection without awaiting an answer. Let her settle her problem herself! And let that fool Ramírez watch Gene Autry and Betsy Ross and all the robots in Murania to his heart's content. If all went well, Perón would surpass his mentor, and the name of Perón would live in the history of Argentina when that of Ramírez was forgotten.

He strode from the Casa Rosada using a rear exit invisible from the Plaza de Mayo. In the palace's car park he trotted to his reserved place. He opened the saddlebag that he kept strapped to his big BMW motorcycle, exchanging his rimless spectacles for a pair of aviator's goggles ground to his personal prescription. He pulled the decorative chin strap down from the visor of his military cap, settling the high-crowned cap and chin strap in position.

He kicked the BMW into life, jack-walked it to an alleyway leading from the Casa Rosada, and roared off through the streets of Buenos Aires, headed for Radio Belgrano.

Where traffic was heavy, he hit the Klaxon button on his motorcycle. What point was there in being an officer of the army, nothing less than the military aide to the President of the Republic, if he had to wait for traffic jams to clear?

He crossed a drawbridge over the slow-moving tributary that cut off Belgrano from the fashionable Barrio Norte, cruised now through half-empty streets, pulled up beside the radio headquarters.

Inside the station he threaded familiar corridors. In Studio A the unctuous Father Hernán Benítez was addressing a microphone, delivering one of his tiresome daily homilies. How could that priest find so much to say, and every syllable of it utterly banal!

In Studio B a staff announcer was rehearsing his delivery of the news that would be broadcast at the half hour; the sponsor's message, promoting the products of the Guerrero Soap Company, was a standing script that needed no more practice.

Oro Blanco, White Gold, the action-filled adventure of the future, emanated from Studio C.

Juan Perón halted outside the studio. Through the sound-proof double-pane window he could see the cast assembled, with clarifying evidence of Evita's anger against her co-worker Libertad Lamarque. The two women wore identical hair-styles, swept up and arranged on the crowns of their heads. Evita's hair was blond, Libertad's jet black. Evita wore a dark purple blossom in her hair, Libertad a yellow one. They wore identical tailored suits with padded shoulders, pointed lapels, pleated skirts.

The writer Blomberg held a master copy of the script. It was unclear whether the pained expression on his face was the result of difficulties in the studio or the souvenir of the previous night's carouse. His pudgy face was unshaven and gray; his thin pale hair was unkempt, as was his rumpled suit.

At a table nearby a sound-effects technician sat with clappers and horns, trays of pebbles and sheets of cellophane that could simulate the crackle of flames, pitchers and cups and a rotary drum whose canvas coating could simulate the rushing of the wind or the whoosh of rocket engines.

The technician looked up as Perón signaled through the window. Perón gestured toward Evita. Aspiri nodded, stood up, spoke to Blomberg.

The writer's mouth opened in an agonized expression. His gray face reddened and he threw his script through the air. The loose pages scattered and floated to the floor.

Evita smiled tightly and headed toward the exit, exchanging a final cold glare with Libertad Lamarque.

Moments later Perón and Eva Duarte sat in a control room, cut off from any eavesdroppers.

"You're sure you got that message right?" Perón badgered. "It's of the highest importance. When the President notices that I've left the Casa Rosada, he's going to ask a lot of questions!''

''I told you exactly what the English said!'' Evita snapped. ''If you doubt my word, phone him yourself. He's waiting at Palomar to hear from you anyway.''

''I know that, *cabeza-vacante*! Don't you understand the danger of this affair?''

''I don't see what's so dangerous about fireflies and little bats. I don't see why such matters should require the attention of the Casa Rosada anyway! I'm your little slavey doing your stupid errands and never complaining—''

''Ha!''

''—and you don't see fit to explain anything to me. Well settle your own petty problems if you don't think I'm reliable. I have a career of my own! I'll have you know that Radio El Mundo is after me. I can have a five-year contract just for the taking, with guaranteed time off to make films, too! Bugs and bats, pah!''

''All right. Never mind.'' Perón made an effort to control himself. It was true that he had not explained the situation to Evita. The obtuse language was necessary to protect the work he was engaged in, but to Evita it would seem foolish.

''Come, *querida*. You have been more than helpful. Come with me to Palomar and we will meet the English and see what he has to show us. You said that Yankelevich keeps a car here, even when he is not at work?''

She nodded.

''Then we'll take it. You are not dressed to ride double on my motorcycle. If Jaime has any complaints about our taking his car, let him bring them to President Ramírez's ears. He'll learn a lesson when Radio Belgrano's license comes up for review!''

With Evita in tow, Perón obtained the keys to the station owner's car from his private office. They climbed into the car and Perón started the powerful engine. The car was a Hispano-Suiza Boulogne, designed to be driven by a chauffeur. Perón handed Eva into the front seat and took the wheel himself.

He roared out of the Radio Belgrano parking lot and headed for the air base at Palomar, some thirty miles away.

When they arrived at the air base, Perón's uniform brought

him a salute from the *guardia* and a clear path to the sealed hangar where Reimar Horten carried on his researches.

Perón's knock brought a scraping sound from inside the hangar. A peephole in a small door opened, then the door itself. Ushering Evita before him, Perón stepped inside. The hangar was dark; he blinked while his eyes accustomed themselves to the gloom. The air inside was musty, with the smell of machinery, oil, rubber, ozone generated by electrical discharges.

A clumsy fifteen-year-old Heinkel 20 biplane stood near the hangar's main doors. The plane was covered with dust and its engines dripped oil, both symptoms of recent use.

Behind the relic, painted in olive drab and brown camouflage colors, stood a smaller craft, whose clean, rakish lines almost screamed of graceful, powerful motion.

A crew of overall-clad mechanics were busily working over the smaller craft.

Leaving the mechanics under the supervision of a man whose scrawny physique was belied by his military bearing and harsh, commanding voice, a taller man strode rapidly toward Juan and Evita.

The two men shook hands. Perón said, "*Querida*, may I present Sir Oswald Mosley. You have spoken with him before, but you have never met."

Turning toward the other, he said, "Sir Oswald, Señorita Duarte."

Evita examined the Englishman as he bent over her hand. He was tall and elegantly groomed. His moustache was full and neatly clipped, a good strong earth color, not the washed-out shade so common among Anglo-Saxons. His eyes were clear. His teeth were good, if a bit on the horsey side. He managed to wear an outfit somewhere between that of a workman and that of an aviator, yet give it the appearance of a fencer's costume.

Even as he murmured banalities, she decided that she found him satisfactory.

She smiled as she withdrew her hand.

Perón spoke to Mosley. "Richter delivered as promised, Oswald?"

Mosley motioned with his head, characteristically using the movement to indicate the streamlined aircraft that was mostly concealed by the clumsy, aged Heinkel. The movement whipped Mosley's lanky, high-crested hair toward the airplanes. "Horten is inside the cabin, monitoring instruments. Richter personally flew the nuclear fuel up from Río Gallegos in that relic. I don't see why he refused to ship it by rail—it would have been so much safer."

"You know the reason," Perón contradicted. "You Britishers own the Argentine railroad system—how do you put it?—lock, stock and keg."

"Barrel."

"*¡Exactamente!* Just so, thank you. He is barely willing to work on this project, solely because of your presence, Sir Oswald. He considers you half a traitor to your nation, which makes you half a decent man in his eyes."

Mosley scowled blackly. "I am loyal to my nation. I flew for His Majesty in the One Year War. I served in Parliament after peace returned."

"*Por supuesto,*" Perón soothed the Englishman, "of course you did. And lately you have been calling for the overthrow of the entire system of social organization, have you not?"

Whether the remark was intended as a question or not, Mosley agreed that he had. "But not out of traitorous motives. Capitalism has obviously seen its last days. Socialism is a dead-handed and unviable alternative. Only the organized state, the disciplined society, offers a way out for England."

"As you say." Perón had taken Evita by the arm and was walking her slowly past the old Heinkel biplane, toward the streamlined ship. "You see, *querida*, why we referred to a bat in our communications."

"I do. But what was the nonsense about fireflies? This airplane looks like a bat about to take flight, but I see no bugs!"

Mosley, at her other side, laughed loudly. "A metaphor, Señorita Duarte."

"You may address me as Eva." She fluttered long eyelashes at the fool, watched for and observed the expected intake of breath that followed.

Mosley grinned, showing more teeth than ever. "My thanks! By fireflies, señorita, we refer to the fuel which powers our little green bat. Herr Horten was one of the great aircraft designers of the German Reich. But after the unfortunate incidents of 1927—of course you are too young to remember such things, but I hope you have heard of them—"

"You refer to the circumpolar air race, Sir Oswald."

"I do."

"I personally saw the *Spirit of San Diego* as it flew over my village of Junín. I was a little child, but my father, the town's *caudillo*, you would say—"

"Mayor?"

"Yes, and more than that. He left his office in the town hall and held me on his shoulders to see the wonderful airplane. But I understand that the German competitor—"

"Herr Udet's *Kondor*, a wonderful aircraft, years ahead of its time!"

"Yes. But *San Diego* triumphed and won the prize money offered by an Englishwoman."

"An American by birth, but a British subject, yes."

"Yes. And the German team was disgraced and the aircraft industry of that nation blighted as a result. Am I not correct?"

"You are. Which is why the brothers Horten transferred their enterprise to Argentina. And why Herr Ronald Richter has been at work in Patagonia on his atomic fuel. The Horten brothers and Richter are the managing directors of AIA— Argentina Instituto Aeronáutica. Please forgive me if I fail to give the proper Spanish values to the words."

"And what are they doing now?" Evita gestured toward the streamlined aircraft.

Perón stepped back into the conversation. "I have permitted the institute to establish its laboratories on my family *estancia* in Río Gallegos. There is a certain element of danger involved in some of Herr Richter's work. Some of the materials he hopes to use as a power source. And also, there was a certain element of, let me say, privacy. We would not want prying eyes to see everything that was going on."

"And now?" Evita demanded.

"Now," Perón said, "we have the most advanced aircraft in the world, designed by Herr Reimar Horten and his brother, Herr Heinrich Horten. We have the most advanced fuel in the world, developed by Herr Richter. Together"—he clapped his hands proudly—"we will show the world what we can do."

He patted the streamlined ship's needlelike prow. "I have taken the liberty of naming our craft *Patrilandia*."

Evita looked at him scornfully. "And where will this wonder plane fly? To the North Hole? To the other side of the world? It has been done!"

"Better than that, *querida*. Better than that."

"There is nowhere on earth that man has not visited. Well, the mountain peaks of Tibet. Some of the more remote islands of the other side of the disk."

"Still better. Think, my *grasita*, of your roles at Radio Belgrano. Think of your role in *Oro Blanco*!"

"As the rocket flier!"

"*¡Así!*"

"To the moon! To another world!"

"*¡Así, mia querida!* To another world indeed!"

CHAPTER
3

Flung by *Santa Barbara*'s huge pusher prop, *Manta* spun madly through blackness. For a moment, as the miniature wing hung upside down, she was both behind her mother ship and above the greater wing.

Through the transparent crew bubble, Jack Northrop could see the *Santa Barbara*'s aerial running lights; in addition, the Plexiglas windows of staterooms and salons showed a dim yellow glow through the still-falling sleet, while the great magnetic engines emitted a ghostly bluish radiance.

Then *Manta* tumbled. *City of Santa Barbara* disappeared into the blackness. *Manta*'s radio crackled with frantic calls from *Santa Barbara*'s bridge but Northrop had no time to respond.

The miniature wing flipped again. The world was spinning around the skyship. Northrop thought for a moment that he had spotted *Santa Barbara*'s lights again, then realized that this was another craft, another ship. Something far larger than even the huge flying wing *Manta* had left seconds earlier.

What had seemed for a moment to be an aircraft thousands of feet above *Manta* was in fact an ocean liner thousands of feet below! A great set of running lights glimmered upward through the gloom. Running lights, and more. Huge search-lights blazed up through the night.

26

With a start, Northrop realized that the radio before him was still active. A voice—he recognized it now as Sterling's—was frantically calling, "*Manta! Manta!* Respond! Urgent!"

Even in this moment, Northrop yielded up a grim laugh. Urgent, yes. At *Manta*'s fluttering, irregular rate of descent there might be two to three minutes' time, at most, before she smashed into the icy waves of the North Atlantic.

He managed to thumb his transmitter button. "*Manta* here."

"*Manta*, can you make *Titanic* below?"

"I see her."

"Try to level off. Do you think you can level *Manta*?"

Before Jack could respond, he heard another voice, one with a Scots burr to it: "*Manta, Titanic* here. D'ye see our spotlights?"

"Yes."

"Can ye glide in, *Manta*?"

The jolt of *Santa Barbara*'s propeller had killed all power from *Manta*'s own engines, but Northrop had been wrestling with the miniwing's yoke and pedals. He had managed to stop the vertical rolls that the huge propeller had caused in *Manta* and was struggling now to control the craft's new problem: a flat spin.

He grunted some response to the radio voice, concentrating on his own aircraft. He pushed *Manta* into a steep dive, wrestling the elevon controls to halt the spin. If he failed, the result would be a fatal spiral dive. If he succeeded—and if there was time to level off again before *Manta* smashed into the murderous Atlantic seas—the miniwing might yet glide.

For a moment Northrop released the yoke with one hand and tried to restart *Manta*'s engines, but the effort was futile. Even if the engines remained in good order—a dubious prospect at best—they could not be brought up through their starting sequence before time ran out for the little skyship.

"*Manta! Manta!*"

Even as the voice penetrated Jack's awareness, the wing's cabin was flooded by a brilliant light from below.

"We've got ye! Our searchlights are on ye! Now ye're steady, we can see ye!"

The voice was right. Northrop could see the world outside *Manta*, the swirling sleet and the lights of *Titanic*, steadied.

He eased back on the yoke, balanced the elevon pedals. He couldn't level *Manta* entirely: a stolen glance at the airspeed indicator warned him of the danger of a glide stall that would surely be fatal at this point.

"Can you pick us up if we ditch?" he radioed.

"We'll do better if ye can handle it, *Manta*! Home in on our searchlights. If ye can land slow and ground-stall, ye can settle on the pool cover! D'ye think ye can do that, *Manta*?"

For the first time the expression on Jack Northrop's normally jovial face showed the fierce, wolfish grin of the competitor called to confront the ultimate challenge: win or die.

"We're coming, *Titanic*!"

He managed to guide *Manta* to an approach from behind *Titanic*. The great ship's funnels, which had once belched orange sparks and black smoke from gigantic coal-powered boilers, now showed the same eerie blue magnetic light and threadlike magnetic discharges that *Santa Barbara* had done.

Jack Northrop brought *Manta* around *Titanic*'s great stacks. There was not room enough to drop to the level of the pool deck if he approached over the stacks.

Manta's controls were sluggish, gummy. The craft made unexpected jogs in the air, as if a giant had chosen to reach up and punch the skyship with random blows.

Looking through the bubble, Northrop saw his own craft illuminated by *Titanic*'s giant searchlights. The right side of *Manta* was complete and apparently undamaged.

But Northrop's heart sank as he looked to the left. *Manta*'s port wingtip hung, a shredded mass of yellow skin and exposed structural members.

Such was the damage done by the unexpected gust that had swept *Manta* into *Santa Barbara*'s pusher prop.

"Ye look fine," the radio voice encouraged.

Northrop blinked away stinging perspiration that dropped from his forehead into his eyes.

He could hear the scream of the atmosphere now.

He could see *Titanic*'s plank-covered swimming pool, huge searchlights marking its four corners.

He could see passengers in New Year's Eve finery milling about as stewards and crew tried futilely to keep them away from the deck.

Titanic's master was risking dreadful damage to his ship

and hideous injury to his passengers by letting *Manta* attempt this landing rather than ditch in the ocean.

Scores of lives, perhaps hundreds, depended on Jack Northrop's skill and *Manta*'s performance in these final fateful seconds.

The miniwing swept lower yet. There would be no waveoff and second approach. *Manta* was acting the role of a pure glider; she would land or fail now, on the first and only attempt.

As the wing slipped between the two great searchlights marking the stern end of the pool, Northrop applied full flaps to cut his speed, full elevons to make the miniwing nose up into a stall. His landing gear was already down, his airspeed indicator and altimeter spiraling toward zero.

Sleet swirled in the searchlights' brilliant beams like cones of falling feathers.

Manta thudded onto the heavy pool cover, rolled a few yards, yawed into a fragmentary ground loop, then halted.

For a few moments there was total silence. Jack realized that his hands were gripping the yoke, his skin was clammy, his knuckles were white. He heard a single almost explosive sound and realized that it was himself: he had been too busy even to breath, so great had been his concentration. Now he exhaled, felt his heart thumping in his chest, drew gratefully on the cabin's sweat-tanged air.

He looked around him, realizing for the first time since *Manta* had left the *City of Santa Barbara*'s belly that he had three passengers.

From outside *Manta* he heard cheering: *Titanic*'s midnight revelers had got a treat this New Year's that they would never forget.

Inside the miniwing's cabin, Babe Didrikson and Joshua Gibson were climbing from their seats. Gibson reached forward and took Northrop's sweating hand in his own huge and muscular grip. He said, simply, "God bless you, man. God bless you."

"That goes triple for me," Babe Didrikson put in.

Titanic's seamen were surrounding *Manta*, pushing formally clad passengers away. Men in proper black and white, women in gowns and jewels, equally wore dustings of sleet; they seemed unaware of the cold and wetness in the excitement of the feat they had witnessed. Someone in an officer's cap and heavy mackintosh was making his way through their ranks, headed toward the circling sailors and the damaged miniwing.

In *Manta*'s copilot seat, Albert Einstein sat gazing through the transparent bubble, oblivious of his surroundings.

Northrop said, "Are you all right, Dr. Einstein?"

Startled, the scientist looked at him. "I was just thinking," he said, although in his customary accent it came out, "I vas choost dinking."

Northrop asked again, "Are you all right?"

"I was just thinking, you see the flakes in the lights there, how they might act like molecules of gas in a vacuum. Now, if the molecules are freed from resistance of air but subject only to the attraction of gravity still . . ." Abstractedly, he ran his fingers through his undisciplined hair.

"He's okay," Gibson said. "I can see that."

The mackintosh-clad officer had reached *Manta*. He stood facing the crew bubble, signaling to Northrop and the others.

Northrop hit the bubble release. A hydraulic lifter opened the transparent panel. Northrop and the others climbed from *Manta* and onto the sturdy pool cover of the mighty *Titanic*.

"A remarkable landing, lad," the officer said. He clasped Northrop's hand, gestured to the others. "Come along now. We'll get ye all warmed up below, and we'll have to figure out what to do with your remarkable aircraft here."

"Let's get *Manta* below, too. Do you think you can, Captain?"

The officer peered at the skyship appraisingly. "I think we can fit her, lad."

Northrop grinned—this time his normal, warm expression, not the hard, wolfish grin that he had worn throughout *Manta*'s frantic struggle to survive. All he said was, "Thank you, Captain. And my three passengers will appreciate the hospitality. Especially Dr. Einstein."

"Aye, the famous scientist! It's an honor to have him aboard my ship."

As they made their way through curious passengers, body-guarded by uniformed seamen, Northrop mulled over the notion of being called "lad" by the officer. He was far on the downslope side of forty, secretly dreading the approach of the half-century mark in his life. Lad indeed! Well, enjoy it while you may.

Inside the captain's stateroom they were treated to hot drinks and comfortable chairs. Northrop introduced Mildred Didrikson—she was so often called Babe that her real name was often forgotten—and Josh Gibson.

The ship's master introduced himself as Captain Davidson. "Of the Scots Davidsons," he emphasized. "Not that I've anything against the more numerous Davidsons of the Hebrew persuasion. Dr. Einstein, ye'd be most welcome to take bed and board any time on my ship."

A steward appeared and replenished the hot coffee all around. Sandwiches, too, were provided.

"If ye'd like to add a wee nip of something festive to the java," Captain Davidson offered, "I've the water of my homeland at your service."

His offer was taken up.

"What I'm concerned about," Northrop said, "is *Manta*. I'm most grateful to you, Captain. I'm sure we all are. But we only attempted the midair launch as a matter of urgency."

"Aye," Captain Davidson assented. "I've spoken with my friend Captain Jarrold aloft and with his Mr. Sterling. We understand your unusual mission—at least to an extent. But I don't quite understand just where ye're going, and why in such a hurry."

The old Scots officer, service marks on his captain's uniform showing the decades of service he had given the merchant fleet, brushed a huge gray moustache.

"We've reason to believe that Prussian revanchists have teamed their efforts with some Latin Americans of unbridled ambition. We are in a serious competition, almost a race. That's why I'm so worried, Captain. It's urgent that we have *Manta* refitted and launched at once. Within a matter of hours, if possible!"

"I've the finest mechanicians in any fleet aboard *Titanic*, Mr. Northrop. If your craft can be mended, my lads will do the trick, and they'll do it lickety-split! But I'm still a wee bit puzzled, lad. Where are ye going in such a terrible rush?"

"We're headed for another world, Captain Davidson. We're headed for another world, and I fear that the fates of both that world and our world are at stake!"

Captain Davidson snorted. "Ye haven't been at the water of life too much, have ye, Mr. Northrop? D'ye mean to visit the red planet and have at Mr. Wells's octopussy Martians?"

Northrop said, "Laugh, Captain. But your joke isn't as far from the truth as you think."

"No?" The seaman raised eyebrows the color of steel shavings. "I didna mean to poke fun at ye, sir. I know your name; ye're world famous and famously respected. But ye don't truly intend to fly away from the earth and flitter off to another planet? Isn't this one disk enough for ye?"

"I've probably said too much already, Captain Davidson. It wouldn't be too good for either of us for me to say more." He peered into a Spode cup so thin it was translucent, swirled his whiskey-laced coffee in its bottom. Despite the midwinter seas, the heaviest that the North Atlantic could produce, *Titanic* rode as steadily as a streamliner on its rails.

"I will say this. We're not going to Mars. I'm sorry I can't tell you more than that. But you'll have the undying gratitude of the United States government, as well as the Black Swallow Line and myself, if you can get *Manta* repaired pronto."

"In that case, sir, if ye'll come with me right now, we'll hie us to the ship's machine shop and see what we can see. I think ye'll be happy when ye see the work my lads can do."

Northrop heaved a sigh of relief. "And if you could have your signal bridge get word back to the *City of Santa Barbara*—if we can let Captain Jarrold know our status . . ."

"Of course, of course. It's been done already, Mr. Northrop. Ye don't take me for a neophyte, do ye?" He stood up and moved toward the hatch.

Northrop followed.

Captain Davidson turned back for a moment. "Your friends, Mr. Northrop. While we tend to your craft, they're to feel free—they've the run of *Titanic*. They're our honored guests."

He drew Northrop closer by one elbow, tilted his head as a gesture. "Perhaps the old gentleman would like to have a leetle nap while the younger folk move about."

But Einstein had already settled on a lounge chair, a blanket over his legs. He had lit his pipe but it lay now growing cold. His eyes were closed and he snored gently.

• • •

Babe Didrikson and Josh Gibson left the captain's quarters and followed Jack Northrop and Captain Davidson to a ship's elevator. They exited while the others continued down into *Titanic*'s bowels, headed for *Manta* and *Titanic*'s machine shop.

When Babe and Josh left the elevator, they found themselves in what appeared to be a hotel lobby. Chandeliers glittered overhead, an orchestra played, celebrants who had welcomed the New Year in formal finery seemed determined to dance and drink the night away.

They wandered through milling crowds. Their casual dress drew stares from lords and dowagers, but word had clearly passed among the ship's crew that they were to receive every courtesy. Technically, they were distressed passengers rescued from a damaged ship; they were not expected to possess proper dress.

The main ballroom opened onto a mahogany-paneled bar room. Drinkers who didn't want to wait for stewards to tend to their needs bellied up to the wood, leaning polished pumps on a glistening brass rail. Josh stopped to order a drink. Babe, still caught up in the bustling crowd, was carried into the next room.

Here the younger set, the scions of Britain's noble houses and her *nouveux riches*, escaped the watchful eyes of their parents. A quartet of black musicians, immaculate in tuxedos, played hot jazz tunes.

Tables were covered with white linen, every one of them bearing one or more bottles, every celebrant's place marked by a glass. Cigarettes of various colors smoldered in ashtrays. The men wore their hair in uniformly short, pomaded styles. The women's lipsticks were dark and vivid, their hair upswept, their dresses—rather than gowns—seemed the subject of competition as to which could be cut lower at the bosom, flare wider at the hips.

When not dancing, the women remained in their seats, while their escorts wandered from table to table, seeking out new partners for dancing. Couples disappeared from time to time, heading out of the room for parts unknown.

Babe decided that she didn't particularly care for the clientele, but the music was fine. She settled against a back wall to listen. These were the kind of tunes she liked, the kind she had played as a child in Texas and loved to hear when her baseball team got a night off on their travels. She found herself humming along, subconsciously playing an imaginary harmonica. One of the musicians was in fact playing mouth harp; the others played drums, banjo, trumpet.

A blond-haired man with a slightly mottled complexion and a wispy moustache wove toward her, a bottle in one hand, two glasses tinkling ice cubes in the other. In front of Babe he lurched. She caught him by one shoulder, saving him from a crash against the wood-covered deck.

"I say, miss!" He stuck out his lower lip and blew thin hair from his eyes. "The captain ought to be whipped for that! Can't keep his bloody ship on an even keel! Kill his passengers if he doesn't watch out."

"I didn't feel anything." Babe shook her head.

The blond man leaned to one side, grabbed Babe's arm with the same hand that held his whiskey bottle. "There, you see? Done it again! I think I'll register a complaint when we make port. Have the fellow's job, lift his ticket, whatever. Who's he think he is?"

Babe reached up and disengaged his fingers from her arm.

The blond man looked into her face. He struggled to gain a clear focus. "Do I know you?" he slurred.

"I doubt it greatly."

"Say, though"—he grinned crookedly—"you are just awfully pretty. But you speak so deucedly odd. Say something else."

"What do you have in mind?"

"Ah, ah, that's a naughty question. Say a little more, won't you? I don't think you're even British!"

"I'm from Texas."

His eyes opened and he leaned backward. Babe was tempted to let him topple over, but she caught the front of his jacket and set him upright again.

"A cowgirl! Remarkable! And how did a cowgirl ever wind up on His Majesty's seemstip, uh, steamship *Titanic*?"

"I'm not a cowgirl. I'm a baseball player." Babe was getting annoyed. "Don't you think you'd better join your friends, mister?"

He made a clumsy grab for her. "I want you to be my friend, cowgirl. I've never known a cowgirl before." He sloshed some whiskey into the glasses, got more on his tuxedo. "Come on." He winked, started to lose balance, opened both eyes again.

For a moment Babe had thought he was a serious masher. She was ready to handle that—she'd dealt with enough of them in her career, starting with a leering English lord she'd encountered at the Olympic Games of 1932. Her first exposure to big-time athletic competition, and her first encounter with the so-called elevated classes.

She had burst upon the world scene with her gold medals for everything from high jumping to the javelin toss. When it became known that her true love was baseball, that she was the best pitcher in her section of east Texas, she'd been invited to a major league training camp.

The press had treated the incident as a publicity stunt. They'd been willing to play along with it, as long as Babe made good copy and provided eye-catching photos. With her sharp tongue, her Texas drawl, her harmonica playing, and her ever-ready grin, she had been a newshawk's dream.

With her blazing fastball and her astonishing repertoire of inshoots, outshoots, and change-ups, she had won the support of manager John McGraw and actually made the team. She was proud to be the first woman to play in the big leagues, but she was prouder to be rated on her won-lost percentage and her earned-run average than on her gender.

Now she slipped past the drunken Englishman. She caught the eye of one of the musicians, muttered an excuse, and made her way to the bandstand.

The harmonica player had a row of instruments lined up before him. He gestured as Babe reached the bandstand. She nodded gratefully and took a harmonica, caught the tune they were playing, and joined in. Soon the rest of the band stopped and listened while the two mouth harpists harmonized.

They played sad blues songs by Walter Jacobs, Robert Johnson, Blind Willie McTell. At first the audience complained, then they settled in and listened.

Babe hadn't had such a good time in years.

They were just finishing a tune by Sonny Boy Williamson when Babe spotted Jack Northrop and Josh Gibson poking their heads in the door. Gibson signaled to Babe. She returned the borrowed harmonica—or tried to. The musician thanked her and said it was a New Year's present.

She joined Northrop and Gibson. "What now?"

Northrop grinned. "The captain was right—they're first-grade mechanics. *Manta*'s being repaired now. We can take off at dawn. But I'm not sure I've been entirely fair with you. I've got us the use of the captain's cabin. I think we should talk."

They returned to Captain Davidson's quarters. Einstein had finished his nap and was seated at a chart table. He had a huge sheet spread on the table. It was covered with diagrams and symbols.

He looked up. "While you were gone I took a little think." He patted the chart paper. "The course I figured is no good now. No good at all." He shook his head. "Hours later it is, and from a different place we will leave, it is so?"

Northrop started to speak, then saw that Einstein wasn't waiting.

"So a new course I have worked out." He ran a fingertip over rows of figures. "Only what time we will fly, I need to know."

"Dawn," Northrop said. "We fly at dawn." He cast his glance around the cabin, grabbed for an ephemeris, flipped pages. "The first dawn of 1942." He smiled to himself. "Sunrise at six-thirty-five A.M."

"*Ach*, good." Einstein fingered a stubby pencil, entered a number in the top row of his computations.

Northrop watched in amazement as Einstein worked his way down the sheet of figures, filling in the blanks that he'd left before. He seemed to be moving with careful deliberation, yet he took just seconds to complete his work. "And so," he said, "all correct." He smiled.

Northrop shook his head. He slid into a chair. "I've been having second thoughts," he said. "I kind of recruited you three in a hurry, up there." He gestured skyward, toward the course the *City of Santa Barbara* had traversed hours earlier. "I'm not sure I was really fair. Especially to you, Babe, and to Josh. Dr. Einstein is a scientist. I know he wants to go on this journey. But you two are athletes. We can use you—your quickness, your strength. We don't know what emergencies we'll be facing on this journey, but I'll be grateful to have you along."

He stopped and cleared his throat. He wasn't accustomed to making speeches. He was an airman and an engineer. But he went on. "The secretary of the navy believes that a potential foe of our country is mounting an expedition to the planet that we call Counter-Earth. We must—*must*—get there before they do, or at least in time to stop them from working mischief. If they gain power on Counter-Earth, they'll not only establish tyranny there, they will be in a position to build up their forces and return to our own world with an invading army!

"We must stop them!

"We should build a fleet of skycraft for this job, and outfit them with trained soldiers and marines, and take on this mission. But Washington believes that time is even more urgent, and I think so, too! That's why we'll be leaving"—he looked at his watch—"in less than an hour.

"But you two are neither scientists nor soldiers. You stand to risk your lives, nothing less. You are under no obligation to go. *Manta* could stay on board until *Titanic* reaches New York and the government can assign replacements for you. All it would cost would be a day or so."

He paused and rubbed a suntanned muscular hand over his face. He looked weary—and he was. "But if you're willing—if you agree to go—we can save that day. And who knows? It just might make the difference between victory and defeat!"

"Why you making so much fuss, Mr. Northrop?" Josh Gibson shook his head. "Pennant race is over. We're just barnstorming. Sure we'll go. Least *I* will. Babe?"

Mildred grinned. "Never turned down a challenge since I was a kid. Not gonna start in now!" She thought about it some more. The more she thought about it, the more she liked it. She jumped out of her chair. "Wow! I love it, I love it! Let's go!"

CHAPTER
4

Save for its exterior finish of mottled olive and brown, *Patrilandia* bore a superficial resemblance to *Manta*. The craft was a monoplane, but more than that it was a flying wing. Every possible function had been combined into the airfoil so there was no distinguishable fuselage or tail, no externally mounted engine nacelle—only a smoothly faired crew bubble and smoothly retractable landing gear.

As Juan Perón and Oswald Mosley accompanied Evita to the craft, Evita noted that Mosley walked with a distinct limp. "You have injured your leg, señor?" she asked.

"It's nothing. An old war wound." But Mosley paused for a moment, using the occasion as an excuse to take Evita's arm and place part of his weight upon her for a few seconds. "It does still smart now and then. Huh! But we must grin and bear it. I've managed very well, I hope."

Perón responded to perfection. "Sir Oswald is far too modest, *querida mia*. He trained his way back to health and led his nation's fencing team in the Olympic Games."

"That was long ago, Juan!"

"Perhaps. But we still practice at foils, do we not? And you hold your own, Sir Oswald. You hold your own and more, I should say. With a whole leg, you are one foeman I should not like to meet, I assure you!"

"But a war wound? *¿Es verdad?* Is it truly so?" Evita clung to Mosley's arm now, noticing that he bore her slight poundage with no difficulty.

They stood beside the newly christened *Patrilandia*, Evita gazing from one man to the other. "More an embarrassment than a badge of heroism," Mosley said.

"It is too painful, then, to discuss?"

How did this Argentine wench get her eyelashes to do that? Mosley wondered. He said, "If I must, then. I was just a boy at Sandhurst when the Kaiser started that silliness. Couldn't wait to do something shining, so I took leave and applied to go to active service. Lots of the boys did, you know."

He had stopped leaning now, released her altogether. He was getting ready to use his hands as airplanes; she had seen this so many times before, but they were always grateful for an audience and a grateful man was a useful man. She looked up at him admiringly. She touched his sleeve gently. "You were just a child. A child at war." She thought of a good scene in *Heroines of History*. Yes, Clara Barton at Valley Forge. She brought a tear to her eye, she could feel it. Good!

Mosley reddened a trifle.

She would not overdo.

"The war was just getting under way. It was my very first flight over enemy lines. I was flying a little Bristol Scout. Such a plane!" He shook his head. He wiggled one hand in front of Evita. Clearly, to Mosley it was a Bristol; to Evita, a hand.

"The aircraft weren't even armed, you know. That came later. We used to carry sidearms aloft. Sit there and potshot at each other! *Ha-ha!*"

The man has laughter to match his teeth, Evita thought.

"Well, don't you know, this Kraut came at me. Flying a Rumpler. A Taube. Good aircraft, best the Kaiser had that early on. I'd never seen one before. Funny-looking thing, monoplane, like the Scout was. Funny how they went to doubles and triples after that and now everybody's building monoplanes again. . . .

"Well, Jerry comes at me—"

"Jerry?" Evita interrupted.

"Just our name for the Kaiser's men. Jerry." Mosley cleared his throat. Evita detected Perón shifting uncomfortably from foot to foot. He must have heard this story a hundred times. He can just hear it again, she decided.

"So, there we were, lined up, head-on, must have been a thousand yards apart." Mosley was using two hands now. *¡Por cierto!* Of course he is. One is himself, the other must be Jerry.

"I had my pistol out. Jerry had his. We flew at each other like jousting knights. Pointed our weapons. Let fly. I think I got a piece of his fuselage, but no serious score. I know he missed me—felt the bullet whiz by my skull and a half tick later I heard the report.

"Well, by now we'd flashed by each other." He swished his hands through the air. "I'd just started to swing my Bristol about to have another go at it when I felt this devilish wallop in the old lower limb, eh? Didn't hurt a bit, just then. Hurt like the deuce later, I'll tell you, but I hardly felt a thing straightaway, just a bloody hard socko and then not much more.

"But I looked down and there was ruddy all over my flying trousers. Tried to move my hoof but I couldn't feel a thing in it. Made the pass back anyway, and then I saw that the Taube was a two-seater. Never'd seen one before, you know! Good old joke was on me! Jerry's backseat man had done the deed after we were past. Turned around and shot me from behind! Medicos confirmed that later on, but I didn't need any confirming, I knew what he'd done, the blackguard!

"Well, I wanted to keep up the fight but I couldn't hold my eyes open. Felt so sleepy I just couldn't do it! Nauseous, too. Banged down in some Frenchy's vineyard and woke up in hospital. Surgical dressing all over. Nurses hovering— *Sister Jane to take your temperature, sir,* and, *Sister Margaret to change your bandages, sir.* All that rot.

"And I just a boy. All that rustling poplin! Thought I'd go mad. Fell in love with a hundred nurses, one after another, some all at once.

"Doctor came by, said they'd try to save the old gam for me but he couldn't make'ny promises. Did it, too, the old sawbones did. But they don't quite match now. Hard on my tailor, you know. But I don't complain, I don't complain. Grin and bear it, that's what I say. Grit the old molars and hold thy silence, don't the Good Book say that somewhere? Eh, Perón?''

"I think Herr Horten is ready for us now, Sir Oswald," Perón mouthed sourly. He lifted the hatch of *Patrilandia* and leaned inside. *"Mein Herr!"*

"Ja! Bist du Perón?"

"Und Mosley auch."

Evita heard the sound of scrambling from inside the sleek skycraft. A wizened figure in oil-stained coveralls levered himself through the hatch. He flashed a quick, tight smile to Perón; an icy one to Mosley.

Then he caught sight of Evita and his manner changed.

Perón said, "May I present Miss Eva Duarte, the famed actress."

"Enchanté, mademoiselle." To Evita's astonishment he reached into a pocket and extracted a pair of spotless white gloves, pulled them onto his hands, and bowed to take her hand and lift it to his lips.

"What is the status of *Patrilandia*?" Perón asked Horten.

Evita watched the coveralls-clad German as he answered. Her first impression was that he was a hired mechanic, but his manner of speaking to the others—to Perón as one would to an equal, to Mosley as to a barely tolerated interloper—quickly dashed that image.

Horten was shorter than Evita's five feet five inches as Mosley was taller than Juan Perón's full six feet. Despite his stained coveralls, his bearing was stiff and more than correct. He wore graying hair cropped close to his head in the Prussian manner. He switched from language to language, as did Perón and Mosley in the course of their conversation, with ease. But his Spanish and English, the two languages known to Evita, had a harsh and unpleasant accent.

Horten said, "The fuel has been delivered from Patagonia by Herr Richter. Together we have loaded it onto my ship. All tests confirm that everything is correct. We need merely load supplies and we are ready to depart."

Perón nodded. *"¡Bueno!"* To Mosley he said, "You are ready to depart, Sir Oswald?"

Mosley nodded. "My gear is aboard."

"As is yours, Herr Horten?"

"Of course."

"The weapons also are installed. We will need to check on the ammunition level. Food and water." He consulted his wristwatch. "We should depart within the hour, if we are to follow the course as planned." He turned . "*Querida*, are you prepared for the grand adventure?"

She felt herself growing red. "You have not consulted me about this, Pocho." She saw Perón wince at the use of his nickname. He knew that she used it only in the most tender of moments—or when in a fury. And he knew that she was not being tender. She was too angry to stop and savor his discomfiture.

"But I told you at the radio station. We are to depart this very morning."

"You told me nothing."

"I told you, another world. I reminded you of your role in *Oro Blanco*, your rocketeer's adventure. We will bring reality to the dream."

"And what am I to do, travel to the planet Neptune in a suit and heels?"

"*Patrilandia* is equipped with quilted flying suits, almost like the ones Blomberg conceived for *Oro Blanco*. In fact, we received our inspiration from those flying costumes."

"And did you see what they looked like? Did you see the publicity stills that Blomberg made us pose for, wearing those absurd getups? Did you see the spread in *Sintonía*? I wouldn't wish that costume on Libertad Lamarque, and you know what I think of her! Besides . . ." Evita didn't give Perón a chance to interrupt; she saw the others, their expressions, as she berated her major. Let them see. Let them see how she treated the military aide to the President of the Republic! Junín was far behind her, Junín and its provincialism, its outdated customs of women deferring to men, Junín and her mother's guesthouse and her command to the daughters to be nice to the male diners.

Nice, indeed!

"No change of clothing! I suppose you are well supplied with uniforms and decorations and proper suits and hunting costumes. My major! ¡*Mayor Pavo Real!* Major Peacock! Peacock Perón!"

"No, no, no!" He made placating gestures with both hands. Evita could see Horten and Mosley behind Perón,

Horten tense and expressionless, clearly horror-stricken at her outburst, Mosley hiding a grin behind a carefully manicured, long-fingered hand. His eye flashed to Evita's—he comprehended more than either Perón or Herr Horten. Let him.

"Evita mia, you'll see, it isn't like that at all. While you were away, Blomberg sent your dresser to the house. To your apartment. She packed a wardrobe for you. It's aboard the *Patrilandia*. And we won't be gone that long anyway. Besides, there will be shops, couturiers; you can get whatever you wish when we arrive."

"Perón!" He blanched. As she never called him Pocho except in tenderness or in anger, he knew that she never called him Perón except in moments of public adulation or private scorn.

"Perón! You tell me there will be shops? You tell me that we are to travel to Neptune—"

"I did not say Neptune."

"Mars! Who cares? Pluto! Mongo! To See Emperor Ming! You tell me there will be boutiques on another planet? I expect swamps and monsters, deserts and spider men. Boutiques! Pah!"

From Perón there was an angry exhalation. Evita knew the sign. He was close to his limit. She could push him a tiny fraction farther, but she had better stop then. He barked, "The world we will visit is exactly like our own. You can shop in Buenos Aires or in Paris if you wish. You can see your picture in *Antena* and *Sintonía*. You must stop complaining."

She shook her head. "You are hopeless, Perón. Never mind. Never mind. Just show me how we will perform this marvel."

Perón indicated the little German with a movement of his head. "Herr Horten is our technical expert. Two brothers, Reimar and Heinrich, and their colleague Herr Richter. Herr Heinrich Horten has remained in Río Gallegos. Herr Reimar will explain, please."

To Horten he said, *"Bitte, mein Herr."*

The spiky-haired dome snapped down and back again in something more than a nod but less than a bow. "If mademoiselle will accompany me to the skyship, I will be pleased to explain."

The interior of *Patrilandia* was not unlike that of a large automobile, with elements, perhaps, of a private railroad car. Evita was familiar with private railroad cars—or rather, with one private railroad car, in which she had traveled just once, the flat, comfortable ride from Junín to Buenos Aires. The click of iron wheels against sections of track, the flash of vegetation-covered countryside, the sense of adventure and anticipation: to a child of thirteen, that journey had been the experience of a lifetime.

There had been some disappointment involved in that journey as well, and the aftermath had been nine long, hard years of struggle, during which Evita had worked her way up from extra and occasional chorine to become a star of radio and motion pictures. She had vowed that she would live to travel in her own private car, and she was close to such status now—as well as being the companion of Juan Domingo Perón, military aide to the President of the Republic, and a rising star of another sort himself.

"If mademoiselle will seat herself," Reimar Horten was saying. Evita managed a gracious smile; she had drifted into a reminiscence and lost the moment. That was dangerous. One must retain control of one's situation.

She slid into a seat like the driver's seat of the Hispano-Suiza.

"You see, mademoiselle, the controls of *Patrilandia* are in essence standard aircraft controls. It is a bit like driving an automobile—we speed up, slow down, turn left and right." As he spoke, he manipulated the controls. "However, we are able to move in three dimensions rather than two. *Patrilandia* will rise or descend as we wish. The craft requires controls also for what we term attitude. Bank, roll, yaw. In order to—"

"Por favor, Señor Horten." She interrupted him and he spun toward her, eyes glinting. "You do not expect me to fly this craft, I hope. In *Oro Blanco*—"

"I have not had the honor to hear your broadcasts, mademoiselle."

"—our ships are powered by huge rockets. Is this how the *Patrilandia* will fly?"

"No, no! The great contribution of my colleague Herr

Richter is the power of the element uranium, directed toward the energizing of our craft.''

"And how is our course determined? The heroic rocket captains of Radio Belgrano seem to have no difficulty in finding their objectives—except when it suits Señor Blomberg's convenience to have them get lost, of course. Do you use maps?''

"Ah! That is my own contribution to our cause. Here you see the device that I have developed from the Muvian earth compass brought back by the *Spirit of San Diego* years ago. That could tell us a position anywhere on the face of the earth disk. But my invention—the *Hortenmekkanopantograf*—will function similarly for any location in the solar system. Mademoiselle, behold!''

He uncovered a transparent case some eighteen inches square and four inches deep. Within it, as if projected by a motion-picture device, there shone a miniature sun and a compressed representation of the planets known to science. The earth and its moon were visible, as were the myriad glittering dots of the belt of asteroids.

In the orbit of earth but directly opposite the planet's position lay an identical planet and moon.

Evita said, "Which is our world?''

Horten indicated it.

"And its twin?''

"That is but recently discovered, you see. And that is our destination.''

"So that was your meaning, my Juan!''

Perón grinned the grin that had won him the nickname of *Teniente Toothpaste* in the days when he was a fresh young officer.

"And if that other earth is exactly like our own, why should we bother to go there?''

"Because, *querida*, we have received radio transmissions from the other earth, the Counter-Earth. Some of us—I myself included—have doppelgängers on this other world. Think of it: two Peróns! We shall make an alliance. I shall help the other Perón to win his cause upon Counter-Earth. And he shall return with me, and we shall have our triumph here!''

Eyes widened, she said, "And there is another Evita?''

Perón shrugged. "I don't know. It seems there is not, although we have far too little information. You would like to
find out, would you not?"

Her expression changed. "If not Evita, it must be that *puta*
Lamarque who has won my position. I'll kill her! Very well!
I will go along with you! How soon can we depart?"

Perón and Horten exchanged glances. "We are all here—
Sir Oswald, Herr Reimar Horten, you and I, *querida*. Herr
Heinrich Horten and Herr Richter will remain our support on
earth. Are we ready, Herr Horten?"

The creaking Heinkel biplane was wheeled out of the way
of *Patrilandia*. The hangar doors had been rolled back, and
now *Patrilandia* was towed onto the restricted runway by a
donkey-tractor.

Within the sleek craft, Reimar Horten and Juan Perón sat
side by side at the controls. Sir Oswald Mosley and Eva
Duarte occupied the passenger seats.

Patrilandia's crew bubble was raised. The air was heating
up now as the summer day progressed. Evita drew a delicate
handkerchief from the cuff of her jacket, dabbed at her brow,
and put the handkerchief away.

At the end of the runway the tractor left the monoplane
and chugged back to the hangar. Reimar Horten lowered the
bubble; *Patrilandia*'s own air supply came into play, cooler
than that blowing from the Plata estuary but tainted with a
metallic tang.

"All strapped in," Horten ground. "Ready then."

The engines had already begun their low moaning. As Horten studied the dials upon the control panel, he eased the
engines up to a higher pitch. They were whining like eager
animals wanting to be fed.

Perspiration broke out on Horten's brow, not from heat but
from tension and excitement.

The engine whine rose still higher, became a scream.

The scrawny pilot kicked in a control.

The craft leaped across the runway; to Evita it was as if
she had been thumped on the back by a giant hand, then
shoved backward and downward into her seat by another.

She glanced through the bubble. She was astonished to see
that *Patrilandia* had leaped from the tarmac like a wild crea-

ture fleeing a predator. The hangars and runways of Palomar had shrunk to half their size and were shrinking still as *Patrilandia* tore the hot January air.

The broad boulevards and graceful buildings of Buenos Aires spread themselves beneath her gaze. For an instant she could see the transmitter tower of Radio Belgrano, then as *Patrilandia* tilted and continued to rise, the broad expanse of the Plaza de Mayo, the Cathedral lifting its spires at one end and the shimmering pinkness of the Casa Rosada at the other.

"Let me take the controls," she heard Perón say to Reimar Horten. "There's a little message I have to deliver before we really get under way."

The scrawny German protested briefly. Evita could not understand his words, but his gestures and tones made clear the message *he* was delivering to his seatmate. Then he yielded. He folded his arms angrily over his narrow chest and stared stonily ahead.

Perón leaned forward, peering through the transport bubble. He sent the bat-winged craft careening toward the Plata estuary. The flagship of the Argentine navy was in port, her sailors freed on shore leave for the New Year's celebration.

The estuary itself was dotted with shipping and pleasure boats. Across the estuary, Montevideo was visible as a black bulge on the horizon.

"Our brothers in arms have been influenced too much by France, and by the Colossus. We'll give them something to think about." Perón dropped *Patrilandia* into a low, roaring course close to the choppy gray surface of the estuary.

The bat-winged plane screamed across the wave tops, so low that salt spray splashed off the transparent bubble. The gray hull of *Malvina*, the Argentine flagship, loomed in front of the craft. From her seat Evita could make out the numbers and the name of the ship painted on her hull.

The monoplane was so low to the water that *Malvina* towered above it. A wave slapped *Patrilandia*'s underside, knocking the monoplane into a crooked dance. With consummate skill learned handling every form of locomotion from horses to powerboats, Perón fought the bucking craft back under control.

He swept *Patrilandia* up, firing the craft's wing-mounted

weapons as the aircraft came above rail level of the ship. Rows of pockmarks appeared in the ship's railing.

Sailors scattered around *Malvina*'s deck, diving for cover as *Patrilandia* swept overhead. The bat-winged craft swept between *Malvina*'s two great funnels. The passage was so close that the startled faces of sailors were clearly visible through the bubble.

Perón gave a whoop of triumph. "Better than Gene Autry! Old Pedro should see me now!" He clutched the flight yoke in one hand, reached behind him with the other to clutch Evita's. "We'll live in the Casa Rosada someday! You'll see!"

Patrilandia climbed at an astonishing angle, something close to forty-five degrees. Perón kept the craft in a gentle spiral, rising above the Río de la Plata. Even as *Patrilandia* climbed, she continued to accelerate. The airspeed indicator crept past 400, then 500, and still *Patrilandia* accelerated.

"Can we just continue like this?" Evita demanded.

Reimar Horten turned toward Evita. He had put on a pair of wire-framed eyeglasses with thick lenses. The correction must be opposite for each lens: one eye appeared to waver and bulge out to several times its natural size; the other, to have shrunk to half the size of a centavo coin.

"That would be possible, señorita," he said. "But we will do far better than that." He tapped the *pantograf* with a fingernail that was well manicured despite his mechanical work.

Horten moved control levers set into the side of the *pantograf*. The sector showing the earth grew to fill most of the tank. A tiny dot of dark crimson glowed like an angry ember.

"Our ship," Horten gritted. "We have a very long journey ahead of us—almost two hundred million miles. But look here." He sketched a line from the earth to the lunar disk suspended near it in the *pantograf*. "Our timing was such that we would pass near the moon in any case. Instead of this, we will pass through the central cavity of the moon." He looked from the *pantograf* tank to see if she was following.

She concentrated on the silver bridge of his spectacles, a trick she had learned to give the illusion of rapt attention. If she let her gaze stray to his own mismatched eyes, she might be unable to maintain her composure.

Horten cleared his throat pedantically. "I have calculated

that the moon's rotation creates an immensely powerful magnetic field within the hole. Mineral deposits within the lunar crust act as an electromagnetic armature—but there is no core! We will pass through the cavity, acting as the core. We will pick up the energy of the magnetic charge. It will hurl us onward at many times our speed of approach. This technique will be one of the gems in the crown of my achievements!''

Evita looked immensely impressed. She glanced at Mosley, realizing that the atmosphere within *Patrilandia* had changed, almost palpably thickened.

Mosley was looking outside the craft. The sky had evolved from its January brightness to a dark blue approaching that of sunset. Behind the bat-winged craft, Buenos Aires had disappeared. All of Argentina and most of South America could be seen beneath scatterings of cloud cover. The land mass was shrinking. The glittering whiteness of the South Rim's ice wall was visible to the south of Patagonia.

Ahead of *Patrilandia* the sky grew darker than ever. Stars began to appear. The moon was visible, approaching full disk. From the surface of the earth its central hole appeared little more than a black dot against the creamy whiteness of the moon. From *Patrilandia* it was a clearly visible circle of darkness centered like a bull's-eye within the satellite.

Hours passed. Perón yielded the controls to Mosley. ''More fun than a wood and fabric flivver! Not as much to do, either!''

Reimar Horten remained in the pilot's seat, monitoring the performances of Perón and Mosley. Evita, bored, found herself wishing that she had taken flying lessons, but when these others had been learning to fly these wonderful contraptions of metal and glass, she had been busy learning to keep a roof over her head and a piece of sausage on her dinner plate.

''Here we go!'' Mosley said. They had changed their orientation—the moon now appeared to be beneath them, the earth a tiny representation of itself shining a luminous blue far overhead.

Patrilandia's feel was different, too. Instead of fighting the pull of earth's gravity, the ship was now accelerating along with the tug of the lunar mass. The ship's engines had been cut back to little above an idle, and the speed continued to increase.

Ahead of *Patrilandia*, the moon's central hole no longer appeared a black disk. Thin atmosphere swirled within it, and magnetic discharges ignited glowing masses of ball lightning, startling displays of crackling electricity that shot from one side of the opening to the other.

Mosley gripped his companion's shoulder. "Are you sure we should be doing this, old top? We could still swerve around. That looks like a mighty dangerous place for an aircraft!"

Reimar Horten shrank from Mosley's touch. He did not answer.

Patrilandia flashed into the electrical murk. Mosley's hair stood on end. Instruments read crazily. A globe of ball lightning the size of a melon appeared on the control panel and rolled back and forth.

With a roar and an audible electrical hiss, *Patrilandia* sprang from the cavity, rocketting above the far side of the moon, the side that had never been seen from the earth.

Even in the instant that it took *Patrilandia* to rise high above the moon's surface, the four space travelers had time to register shock at the sight of the pyramids and temples, the obelisks and sphinxes surrounding the fissure.

CHAPTER
5

Rays of winter sunlight glinted off a far calmer Atlantic Ocean this morning. The revelers crossing to America aboard *Titanic* were not to be seen now: the only ones to appear for early breakfast were those who had celebrated through the night and stopped for a meal before retiring.

Jack Northrop personally supervised as *Manta*, her shattered wingtip repaired and her yellow skin gleaming, was loaded onto the freight lift that had carried her below hours before. This time the lift rose to the liner's pool deck. Sailors and mechanics had worked through the night; they had had no time to celebrate the arrival of 1942.

Captain Davidson stood by as *Manta* was rolled into position at one end of the winter-covered swimming pool.

"Ye're certain ye can rise safely in this distance?" he asked Northrop. "Landing here was a grave emergency, and even so I might more safely had told ye to ditch instead. Well, all's well as ends well, Mr. Northrop. But now we've an option before us."

"Please, Captain. Rest assured." Northrop patted an engine covering. "I'll admit that a few of my early models took a lot of runway to get airborne. But that was because they were underpowered. Since we've put in the Muvian power plants, that's all changed. I'll tell you, every time we build one of these, there's a royalty to pay, but it's worth it!''

Davidson rubbed his chin. He'd been up all night with Northrop and the mechanics belowdecks, giving orders, hearing problems, talking them over with the great aircraft designer. Despite his years, he took the strain easily. Only the gray stubble on his cheeks and jaw, matching the color of his thick moustache, betrayed him.

"Very well, then. And if your journey is so terribly urgent that it cannot wait till we reach New York and depart from good old Roosevelt Field, ye'll have my permission to fly away from us.''

He saw Northrop's emphatic nod, shook his hand heartily, and stood away from *Manta*. Einstein and Didrikson and Gibson were standing by, waiting to board the flying wing. Now Jack Northrop waved them aboard. The two athletes clambered into the craft, then reached back to help Einstein.

Northrop followed hem. He dogged down the bubble, waved at Captain Davidson and the *Titanic* crewmen standing nearby. "I'm going to give you folks some flying lessons," he told the others. "This is too long a trip to make with one pilot. Besides, we need to have others able to take over, in case I'm unavailable.''

The normally taciturn Gibson asked, "Why would that be?''

"Let's get on our way," Northrop said. "Then we'll talk about it.''

He took a final look around to assure himself that no crewmen were standing dangerously close to *Manta*, then began setting controls and switches.

The chart that Einstein had worked out in Captain Davidson's quarters to replace his computations from the *City of Santa Barbara* was spread beside Northrop.

Jack strapped himself into his seat. Josh Gibson sat beside him, the others behind.

Manta's engines hummed softly.

Northrop eased the throttle in, holding back on the craft's wheel brakes. When the engines had reached the level he'd waited for, he eased off the brakes. *Manta* leaped forward, her wheels rolling across the pool cover for only a short distance. Then the flying wing seemed to vault into the air.

In seconds she was airborne, climbing from the deck of *Titanic*. Northrop banked and circled the great old ship once, dipping his wings as he did so. The yellow of the craft shone like a golden luminescence in the morning air.

Manta's climb was more like a sailboat's tack than a continuous spiral. Northrop had schooled himself through decades of pioneering aviation design to make the most of available resources. His commitment to the flying-wing principle was not merely an aesthetic one, for all that his views harmonized with Einstein's in praise of the beautiful and the simple in all things. Northrop knew that the pure airfoil was the most efficient form of aircraft, the closest theoretical approach to perfect flight. And he flew skycraft with the same dedication with which he designed them.

While Jack Northrop flew *Manta* and Josh Gibson watched his moves, studying the instruments before them, Mildred Didrikson had other things on her mind.

One minor annoyance was the tipsy Englishman she had fended off in *Titanic*'s jazz bar. She didn't even know the man's name; she would almost certainly never set eyes on him again. But he had managed to annoy her at a personal level that drunks and lizards seldom achieved.

Only the kindly musician—and the fact that Babe was a devoted player of blues and jazz tunes on the harmonica—had helped her avoid an ugly incident. The masher wouldn't have got anywhere, Babe knew that. But she had been tempted to land a fist on his drooping blond moustache, and that was out of character for her. She knew she was tough. Growing up in the poor east Texas region where she had, voluntarily forsaking the safe role of the tame house-ridden girl that had been offered her and competing with one and all, boys and girls alike, had made her as strong and as feisty as anything could.

But she was not one to get into fistfights, hadn't been since she was in her early teens and had won her place as an equal in every sport and enterprise she had set her heart on.

Why had she come so close to punching the masher?

She shook her head. There were other matters to consider, matters of much more immediate concern.

She leaned forward, studying Einstein's chart. The scientist himself was sitting with eyes half closed, fingering a cold

long-stemmed pipe. Doubtlessly he was pondering some scientific problem that had baffled thinkers through the ages.

"I don't understand something here." Babe wasn't sure
which of her companions she was really addressing. Northrop
was busy with the controls of *Manta*. Einstein seemed abstracted, mentally absent from the little ship. And Josh Gibson might be the world's greatest homer hitter, but he was
hardly a scientist.

Nonetheless—

"If that Counter-Earth is directly opposite us, then if
they've been sending us radio signals, how do they get through
the sun? I mean, I know the sun isn't a solid object like a
planet, but still, with all the flames, all the terrific activity—
they say that even sunspots can kill radio for a few hours at
a time—how do their, uh, beams get through to us?"

Einstein had given no indication of hearing what she said,
but now he raised his chin and opened those deep, startling
eyes. "A very good question, young miss. We tried to send
messages back to Counter-Earth, you know."

"No, I don't. Nobody told me about this."

"No, of course. But we did. This has been going on a
while. This is not something that just happened yesterday.
You have heard of cosmic rays, no doubt."

"A little."

"Indeed a little. Well, you know about as much as anyone,
then. The Counter-Earth signals were mixed up with them.
Only when we realized they were not all the same, did we
clarify these signals and begin to understand them as messages."

He reached into a pocket for his tobacco. "This is permitted, Mr. Northrop? It is not dangerous, we will not
emulate the sadly recalled *Hindenburg*?"

Jack Northrop looked over his shoulder. "It's all right, Dr.
Einstein." Then, "Josh, let's leave off for now. I can lock
the controls and *Manta* will fly herself for a while. Let's hear
what Dr. Einstein has to say."

"Eh? I thought that all of this was familiar to you." He
loaded his long-stemmed pipe and lit it carefully, scraping a
wooden match on the bottom of his shoe.

"You see, as radio waves are transmitted, they spread, like
an ice-cream cone. The farther from the source, the wider

are those waves dispersed. From Counter-Earth to our own planet, you see, the waves must travel ninety-three million miles first to the sun, then the diameter of the sun itself, fighting their way through all that fiery activity, atomic nuclei bouncing around, elements changing into one another. *Ach!* The center of the sun! What a wonderful and terrible place that must be! And how can that little weak signal, that radio wave, survive such a battle?''

He waved his hands expressing his wonder.

"And yet it does it. It does it. Or it seems to do it, yes?'' He drew on the pipe, let a tiny cloud of gray smoke into the cabin, and watched it disperse. "And then that little signal travels still another ninety-three million miles from the sun to us. How can this be? I could not see this happening. It did not seem possible. And yet it was happening. The signals were arriving.

"Well, such an old fool as I, it took me too long to observe the obvious. Suppose we take two ice-cream cones, two very big ice-cream cones. Each is ninety-three million miles long—that's a very, very big cone.

"We place one cone with its tip at the radio transmitter of our friends on Counter-Earth and its broad end marking a circle around the sun. The other cone we place with its tip at our own earth and its broad end also at the sun.

"Now, suppose those radio waves, instead of continuing to spread like an endless ice-cream cone, could be made to come back together, the way these two cones are arranged? You see? Part of the signal may indeed be destroyed by the sun. I am sure that part of it is so lost. But most of it is saved; it spreads around the sun just as the ice-cream cone does, and then it comes back together and—behold!—we receive our message!''

"But—but wait a minute!'' Babe shook her head. It all *seemed* to make sense, but there was something the matter, something missing. "Look, uh, *why* does it come back together? Why doesn't the, uh, why don't the waves just keep on spreading?''

"Good!'' Einstein smiled happily. "You have perceived the need for further thought on the subject. And a little thought I have given it. So, I will ask you another question, Miss Babe. You know that our sun has its many children—

our own world, Mars, Jupiter, and so on. We children all
circle our mother in a ring, or a series of rings, but all of
these rings are flat, you see? They are all at least approximately in what astronomers called the plane of the ecliptic.''

He drew a series of concentric circles with his pipe, revolving around his other fist. ''But why are not some of them
differently arranged?'' He drew a circle over the top and then
beneath his fist. ''Why is this not so?''

''I have no idea. I never thought about it!''

''Of course not. You have been too busy doing other things,
Miss Babe! You and Mr. Joshua—millions worship you. My
grandchildren, they want to grow up, the girls to be like you,
Miss Babe, the boys like Mr. Josh!

''*Ach!* But an old fool like me, an idle old film, I have had
time to think about this nice puzzle. Suppose there is a field
or layer of force, a kind of influence that holds all these planets and asteroids and moons and comets in the plane of the
ecliptic. Like two cookies holding flat the nice sweet filling.
These layers—one above the plane of the ecliptic and one
below, although which is which is your own choice—keep
these children dutifully circling in their plane.

''And this same layer, or pair of layers, also does the same
for radio signals. Our friends on Counter-Earth send out their
messages. They are dispersed until they reach these barriers,
then they bounce back and reconverge.''

Jack Northrop slapped a hand on his knee. ''Like the
Heaviside layer around the earth!''

''Yes, yes. You see, Jack, you had not heard all of this
before.''

''Bits of it. Bits of it only. Now I see. Do you see it, Babe?
Josh? Do you?''

''I think so,'' Babe said.

Josh said, ''I don't really worry about that part. I'll help
with the flying. That looks pretty easy. Let me have a try at
it now. Will that be all right?''

Northrop unlocked the controls. ''I'm all for that. Keep
her going as she is for starters, Josh. Just get the feel of the
controls.''

Gibson nodded. He took the yoke at the copilot's seat.
Northrop released his own. ''Feels nice,'' Gibson said.

''All right. Now we're going to bank and turn. Like a race

car on a tilted track, only we have to provide our own tilt. If
we tried to turn without banking, we could go into a flat
spin—like a car turning too fast on a flat roadway.''

"Got it.''

The sky was darkening as they rose.

Behind them the earth continued its endless, complex motions—revolving about the sun, rotating about its own North
Hole, and turning like a flipped coin as it moved through its
orbit around the sun. Each of the known planets followed
somewhat similar patterns of motion, although in some the
rate of revolution was so slow that the seasons were as long
as earth's years, while others kept one side perpetually turned
toward the sun, making for a world with one surface searingly
hot and the other perpetually frozen.

The moons of the various planets followed similarly varied
plans. Earth's own moon was one that kept a single side
turned forever toward its parents. Its patterns of craters and
rilles, mountains and dry-bed "seas," had been observed for
ages. The far side of the moon was a world as mysterious to
earthly observers as earth's own reverse side had been to the
occupants of Jack Northrop's world prior to the great circumpolar air race of 1927.

Now, as *Manta* climbed the deep gravity well of earth, the
planetary disk behind her turned so that the white gleam of
the South Rim pointed toward the skyship. With earth in full
edge, the whiteness glittered brilliantly with reflected sunlight. It stood like a huge, broad line in the sky, then slowly
tilted to reveal the legendary features of the earth's farside.

Exploration and commerce between the two sides of the
planetary disk had been initiated just fifteen years earlier. The
magnetic-powered Muvian engine and earth compass were
the two most important bits of technology imported to the
familiar side of the disk. Others had followed, as near-side
products and know-how were exchanged for them.

Now Muvia, Svartalheim, Yu-Atlanchi, Okeanos, and Hai
Brasil were becoming familiar terms on the near side, just as
Britain, Mexico, Egypt, China, and Quebec were becoming
known on the farside.

And behind *Manta* those farside localities were becoming
visible.

Babe said, "There goes our world.'' She slapped the pockets of her flying suit and found the harmonica she had brought with her from *Titanic*. She played a few notes, almost making a tune, then slid the instrument back into her pocket.

"A music lover," Einstein commented. "It pleases me to find myself in such company."

Babe glowed at the compliment. She had no understanding of Einstein's scientific work, but she had an idea who he was. A notion that he was one of the great minds of all time. For the first time in a dozen years she felt herself blushing.

"Hey, Mr. Northrop!" she said.

"Just call me Jack."

"Okay. How long we going to be gone? I hope we can get back in time for spring training. We're going to be in a hot pennant race this year, and I guess I can afford to miss a little barnstorming money, but I have to get my arm in shape for opening day."

Northrop smiled. "I don't really know how long we'll be gone, but I'm in a little bit of a hurry myself. This year is the four hundredth anniversary of the discovery of my town by Spanish explorers. They were there in 1542, and there's going to be a big celebration in Santa Barbara. I don't want to miss it!"

"That's very nice. But spring training starts next month!"

"I can't promise, but I think we'll be back before that. I don't think we'll be away very long. It's just that—"

"Whoa!"

Josh was the one who yelled it but they were all startled. The ship's lights and controls went dead, her engines quit. "What happened?"

Northrop's voice sounded in the darkness. "I don't know. Just hold steady. I think we can—"

He got no farther. The ship quivered once, then the engines came back on with a low, moaning sound that rose quickly to the familiar, almost subaudible hum. The lights shone dimly, then recovered their usual brightness. The instrument needles jumped and wavered, then settled to their proper positions.

"I don't know what happened. I'd better take back the controls."

They were well past the halfway point in their trip from the earth to the moon. They had emerged from earth's gravity

well and were now accelerating as they toppled into the
moon's.

Babe Didrikson felt her head grow momentarily woozy as
the orientation of up and down reversed. It was a sensation
she had felt many times when she had been engaged in competition diving. You go off the board, she told herself, climbing, reaching for the clouds. If you do it right and you have
the right spring coming off the board and if you have the right
kind of mind, you feel as if you were falling up into the sky,
as if you could go on falling and falling forever, past the
clouds and past the blue and on forever into heaven.

And then you tip over and you don't stop falling, you *keep*
falling, only instead of falling into the sky you're falling
through the sky, falling toward the water, and you can do
anything, you can do anything you want. And then you hit the
water and it's over and there's nothing you can think about,
nothing, except that next dive, that next fall up into the sky.

Only now *Manta* was falling. She had sprung from the
earth and fallen up into the sky and kept falling until she was
past the clouds and past the blue and there was nothing there
but heaven. And now *Manta* was still falling, falling into the
moon.

And ahead of them, through the crew bubble, Babe could
see the moon and its familiar pasty off-white surface with no
ice ring marking its outer edge and no continents or oceans,
just cream-colored features in sunlight and shadow.

But the center of the moon, the central cavity that from
earth had always appeared a simple black dot, wasn't a simple
black dot at all. There were fuzzy clumps of light moving
around in the cavity, and flashes and streaks of lightning,
like a summer storm coming in off the Gulf of Mexico.

Only it was happening in the center of the moon, which
Mildred Didrikson's schoolteachers had always said was an
inert and airless place that had never known the tread of any
foot or the sound of any voice. A place that had not changed
when Adam walked in Eden, when Noah built his ark, or when
Pharaoh ordered the Children of Israel to raise the pyramids.

Somehow it seemed that the unexpected activity in the lunar cavity must have caused the blackout of *Manta*'s systems.
Had a brilliant flash preceded the blackout? It seemed to Babe

that it had, but it was so unexpected and so sudden she couldn't be sure. She asked the others.

Josh had been concentrating too closely on *Manta*'s controls and her instruments to notice much about the moon. Jack Northrop had been rhapsodizing about his hometown and its planned anniversary celebration. And Dr. Einstein, having explained his theory of the layers that bounced radio signals between Counter-Earth and earth, had now withdrawn into himself to "have a little think." In such moments he was as oblivious to his surroundings as if he were a million miles away.

She leaned forward. "Jack, what now?"

Northrop shook his head. "We'll take a look at the lunar cavity. We can whip through there—it's on our flight plan anyway—and get a glimpse of the far side."

Josh said, "What you expect to find there?"

Northrop shrugged. "Probably just more of the same. Craters and plains. But we'll take a look anyhow."

What had been up was now down. *Manta* had changed her attitude when Northrop executed a perfect Immelmann at the point where gravity flipped between earth and moon.

Now *Manta* dived into the lunar cavity.

The crater-pocked region surrounding the opening rushed up at them, then they were within the cavity.

The 1927 expedition had reported earth's cavity lined with ice, filled with roaring whirlpools of brine, inhabited by immense monsters of ancient origin. Later expeditions had documented those reports with photographs and motion pictures.

Now the crew of *Manta* had the opportunity to compare the lunar cavity with its terrestrial counterpart.

The walls were bare, roughened, and pitted. Streaks showed the paths of ancient lava flows caused by the moon's primal volcanism and by the heat generated in later ages when giant meteorites created great craters.

There was, surprisingly, a mistlike atmosphere. That and the unceasing electrical activity turned the region into a mad fairyland.

Fuzzy blobs of ball lightning accumulated on the skin of *Manta*. Sizzling, jagged lines of electricity wove among the blobs, wrapping the ship in a coruscating cocoon of pure electricity.

Handling the controls, Jack Northrop felt his skin prickle, his hair stand on end. The sharp reek of ozone filled the air. A realization of danger swept across him and he reacted with the reflexes of an engineer who had test-flown his own designs for two decades and lived to tell the tale.

He punched the master power control, plunging the ship for the second time into silence and darkness. Perhaps it was the earlier, unexpected blackout that had planted the idea in his mind. Whatever the reason, he later came to feel that this move had saved the ship from a major catastrophe.

The electrical cocoon surrounding *Manta* sizzled and writhed, then the occupants of the ship felt themselves flung forward, arms of pure energy hurling their ship through the cavity.

Manta emerged on the far side of the moon.

Again, up became down and down became up.

The ship tumbled.

Northrop punched the power systems back into life. The lights glowed, the engines moaned.

They were accelerating away from the moon at a startling rate.

Northrop heard Einstein muttering about the fascinating particle-like behavior of the energy within the cavity.

Manta sped away from the moon, belly-first beyond the misty atmosphere of the cavity and unimpeded by friction in the vacuum of space.

Jack Northrop looked through the top of the bubble; what was directly overhead for him was a view straight down at the far side of the moon.

He gasped aloud.

Even as *Manta*'s course carried her away from sight, even as the moon—and the disk of earth beyond—shrank visibly, he could see what surrounded the cavity.

It was a scene from a Cecil B. De Mille spectacle.

It was a vision of ancient Egypt.

And something was rising from the Avenue of Sphinxes.

At first it was a mere speck, black against the whiteness of the lunar surface and the flat stones of the Egyptian roadway.

Northrop stabilized *Manta*, holding her in position to see

the speck continuing to rise and to grow. It became a line, then a boomerang, then a bat.

A bat rising from the Avenue of Sphinxes?

Was it a living thing? Was it an Egyptian deity? He tried to remember the gods of Egypt. He was not a student of the subject, but ever since the Carnarvon expedition and the discovery of King Tut's tomb, every magazine in the civilized world had picked up the theme for articles, Hollywood for films, clothing designers for new fashions, cultists and racketeers for inspiration.

Was it Bast? No, that was the cat goddess. Anubis? No, he was the jackal god. Set? Horus? Ptah?

He couldn't remember and there wasn't time and it didn't matter.

The bat-thing was closer and he could see that it wasn't a living bat at all; it was a skycraft a little bit like *Manta*. It was painted in a mottled pattern of browns and greens. It had a crew bubble like *Manta*'s and distant sunlight glinted off the Plexiglas.

Glowing exhaust trailed behind the craft.

A speck of red blossomed from its nose and almost instantaneously *Manta* bucked and tumbled. Jack spun in his seat.

He could see the gaping, ugly hole in his skycraft's yellow wing.

CHAPTER
6

As *Patrilandia* was thrust from the lunar fissure, her electrical systems underwent a total dropout, but her nuclear-powered engines continued to function. Before Reimar Horten was able to take any corrective action, the lights glowed and the indicator needles quivered back to life.

Horten frowned. "That was not expected. However, it seems to have done no harm. We shall continue as planned."

"Continue as planned! Not so, *mein Herr*!" Oswald Mosley's noble drawl disappeared as he grew excited.

"But of course we shall continue. Why should we not?"

"Didn't you see, man? Didn't you see the wonders surrounding the fissure? We shall be famous. Howard Carter and Lord Carnarvon's discoveries shall be as nothing compared to this! Think of what treasures we shall find, think of what it means! The ancient Egyptians, of all peoples, were on the moon! Why, Lindbergh and Earhart and Hughes's discovery of the Avenue of Sphinxes in the South Polar ice rim will be as nothing compared to this! We shall have the key to human history!"

Reimar Horten made a disgusted sound. "You English! One moment I hear you crying for the green hills of your beloved Staffordshire, the next you are *en route* with us to

Counter-Earth. And now you want to stop and wander in the ruins. An old English custom, that. We shall continue!''

"No, Reimar." Perón seemed to expand in his seat. Without rising, he was able to dominate the others physically. "We should land. Sir Oswald is right—but for the wrong reason."

Mosley's eyebrows rose. "Wrong reason?"

"Exactly. If we were merely going to wander through the ruins, I would agree with Reimar entirely. We haven't the time for little jaunts of pure exploration. We must join our comrades on Counter-Earth before things take a wrong turn there—or before anyone else arrives, perhaps to work against our cause."

Horten carefully lifted the curving metal arms of his glasses from behind his ears. As he took the lenses away from his face, his weirdly mismatched eyes were suddenly the same size.

"And who else would be going to Counter-Earth, Major? I was not under the impression that commerce took place between these worlds on a regular basis."

"If we received those radio signals, others may have as well."

"I thought your precious Radio Belgrano was the only one with equipment such as is necessary for this job."

"We don't know that. Others may. The French, the British, the Colossus. We don't know."

"Well, then. All the more reason to continue."

"But we don't know what we'll find down there. The Egyptians worked wonders that the modern world by no means comprehends. How did they carve the great sculptures for their temples? How did they move the huge stones for the pyramids. They had the power to seal poison in tombs so that it would kill desecrators after thousands of years. They had the power to preserve bodies so they would last forever!

"What weapons, what tools did they have, that we may find? The least we can do is spend a few hours to see if we can learn anything useful!"

"No. We have not time." Horten's muscles tensed.

Evita said, "The power to preserve bodies forever. I have seen photos of queens, as if alive, six thousand years old! We must land, yes!''

"Then it's three against one, old top." Mosley grinned his horse-toothed grin.

"This ship is not one of your milk-toast democracies, Sir Oswald." Horten put a harsh edge on Mosley's title. "We shall take correct action. That is not determined by voting."

Perón laid a muscular hand on Horten's wrist. His fingers tightened. "Land this ship."

Their eyes met. Perón increased the pressure on Horten's wrist. Although they wore flying suits, Perón had transferred the holster and sidearm from his uniform, but he left the holster buttoned closed.

Horten gave an almost imperceptible nod.

Perón released his grip.

The scrawny Horten turned back to the controls and swung *Patrilandia* into a great arcing curve, pointing the bat-shaped craft back toward the lunar surface.

He circled, permitting the others to survey the great structures below. The buildings and monuments seemed to be in a perfect state of preservation. No Napoleon had arrived here to desecrate the temples, no greedy builders had stolen the pyramids' facing stones to build commercial roads, no priests of Jesus had defaced sphinxes to show their scorn for older gods than theirs.

"We can land there." Perón pointed.

Horten nodded his grudging assent. He guided the bat-winged *Patrilandia* between rows of towering statues with the bodies of lions, the faces and breasts of women.

Patrilandia rolled smoothly to a stop.

The travelers had seen no palm tree, no cattle, no human. This Egypt boasted no crocodiles or ibises: there was no Nile. There appeared to be no life at all.

"Is there air?" Evita's face was pressed to the Plexiglas of the crew bubble. Her eyes shone with excitement, her breath came in spurts.

"There seemed to be some atmosphere in the fissure," Horten said. "But I doubt that there is enough here to breathe. I would advise extreme care."

The four of them doublechecked their flying suits and their heavy boots and gloves. The suits were fitted with thickly quilted leather helmets, goggles, and oxygen gear that had been developed for use in stratospheric flight. Here it would serve to provide vital air where nature offered little or nothing to sustain breathing.

Evita examined her image in the surface of the crew bubble before stepping from *Patrilandia*. She looked like an alien being, a monster from an episode of *Oro Blanco*, a publicity photo of an actress in a grotesque costume. No sight of her flawlessly smooth complexion, as rounded and dewy as a schoolgirl's, no wisp of her silken blond hair.

She turned away.

"We must stay together," Perón said. "If any of us become lost, the result could be fatal. And one of us ought to remain with *Patrilandia*."

Horten, his sparse frame broadened by his thick altitude suit, made a disparaging gesture. "Who is going to interfere, Major? Do you suspect enemies are lurking, prepared to steal our skyship?"

"I saw no one. I expect no one. But we must not take useless risks, *mein Herr*."

"Very well. And who will be the guard?"

They looked at one another. Horten nodded toward Evita. "The young lady, perhaps."

"Evita should not be left alone. She must be protected."

"You, then."

"I will be with her!"

"Very well. I will stay. Go, you three. You Argentines are half English at heart anyway. Go with your Sir Oswald. I shall remain behind."

Mosley's laugh was muffled by his flying suit and oxygen apparatus. "Not a chance of that, my dear fellow. Not a chance."

Horten looked up at him. "May I ask why not?"

"Consider what you have just said, Herr Horten. If you hold the three of us in such low regard, what's to stop you from just flying off and abandoning us? You didn't want to land here anyway; you wanted to continue on."

"You truly believe that I would abandon you?"

Mosley nodded.

"Then, Sir Oswald, you are your own candidate. Major Perón, Señorita Duarte, let us get this over with as quickly as we may."

Mosley held up a gloved hand. "Impossible. I cannot let

this opportunity pass. I have to see what lies outside. I'm willing to trust Herr Horten. Let him remain behind.''

''Go, then!'' Perón exploded. ''Sir Oswald, on your honor as an English gentleman, you must give your utmost protection to Señorita Duarte. If I have your pledge to that effect, I will stay with Herr Horten. You will make note of everything relevant that you see. Later on we can mount a full expedition to exploit this site. Will you do this?''

Mosley assented.

''Your faith in me is touching,'' Horten spat. ''It shall be returned in due course, I assure you. Well, Major, shall we settle in for a friendly game of cards while the two brave explorers visit sites of local interest?''

Evita and Mosley climbed from *Patrilandia* to the paving stones of the Avenue of Sphinxes. Mosley said, ''Are you comfortable?'' His voice was muffled by his breathing apparatus, and the attenuated atmosphere that clung to the vicinity of the lunar fissure thinned it drastically.

Evita could barely make him out. ''I am well, thank you, Sir Oswald.''

''My friends usually call me Kip. I should be pleased if you did so.''

''Kip. Yes.'' Behind her breathing apparatus she smiled her small, flawless smile. ''And now, let us explore.''

She took the lead, almost trotting down the Avenue of Sphinxes. It stretched for miles, but *Patrilandia* had set down within a few hundred yards of one end, and the avenue terminated there at the pillars of a great temple.

Evita halted before the steps that led into the building. She sensed Mosley behind her and to one side.

''Flawless,'' he said. ''Magnificent.''

She looked back over her shoulder. ''How long do you think this has been here? How did the Egyptians reach the moon?''

Mosley's shrug moved the heavy shoulders of his suit. ''There's so little air here . . . no water . . . no wind . . . no life. It could have stood forever like this. Relics are perfectly preserved in Egypt for six thousand years. This could have been here for sixty thousand. Six hundred thousand. Who knows—six million?''

''But Sir Oswald—Kip! How old is life on earth? In Junín,

the Church discourages too much curiosity about such things. One is led into error, into sin, when one inquires too much into antiquity. But surely the world is less than six million years old. A few thousand, since Adam and Eve. . . ."

He laughed again. "Surely the earth is far more than six million years old—but Adam and Eve, or their Egyptian equivalents, lived a lot more recently than that. You've a good point, though. This settlement must be more recent than the pyramids we know of on earth. Unless—by Jove, I just wonder about all that! Come along, Evita! Let's get a look!"

She let him take her wrist and tug her along, up the steps, past statues of Egyptian deities, under a lintel and between pillars magnificently carved with symbols she did not understand. She was not unconscious of the fact that he had called her Evita, however.

Their altitude suits were fitted with tools and emergency kits. Oswald Mosley and Evita Duarte tested electric torches, then advanced once more.

They passed through an antechamber, halted in an immense pillared hall. The floor was of polished obsidian. A thin coating of moondust lay undisturbed on it.

Their padded boots, the thin coating of dust on the obsidian, the attenuated atmosphere—all silenced their footsteps. Evita half expected them to echo like the footsteps of travelers in a radio drama, carefully furnished by a sound technician.

They approached a high altar. Above it loomed a magnificent statue in obsidian and lepis lazuli and gold. It was the divine mother, Isis.

"So lovely," Evita breathed. "Lovely, and immortal! Do you know her, Kip?"

Mosley identified the goddess. "She was the chief goddess. Her husband was Osiris. He was murdered, and Isis raised her son Horus in secret so the killers would not know of him. When he came to manhood, he avenged his father's death."

Evita knelt before the statue. The goddess held a sistrum. She seemed to be blessing Evita. "I was raised to be a good Catholic, Kip. This story is so like the Christian story, and yet different. I could worship this goddess. I always venerated the Virgin. But this goddess I could worship."

She inched forward, approaching Isis' altar on her knees. The thick flying suit made her movements clumsy. The breathing apparatus obscured her voice.

She half felt, half heard a click as she shifted her weight on the polished stone. The rectangular altar pivoted, revealing a blackness against the blackness of the floor. Evita shone her electric torch into the opening. Stairs led away into the depths beneath the goddess's statue.

Evita edged forward. She sat on the top step, shining her torch into the gloom.

"Don't do it!" Mosley said.

She looked up at him. "Do what?"

He moved his head. "Don't go down there. It's too dangerous. It's too unknown. We shall have to mount an expedition later on. We'll come back with proper equipment, more workers. We need trained archaeologists."

"I'm going, Kip."

"Think of the deaths after Carter opened Tut's tomb! The Egyptians had powers we cannot even imagine! Don't go!"

"I'm going!"

"I forbid you, Evita!" He moved to take her shoulder, but she moved first; before his hand reached her, she was no longer there, but halfway out of sight.

She continued down the staircase. She had had enough of taking orders. She had shed Junín. She had catered to men, but only for her own purposes. At Belgrano, at the offices of *Antena*, at *Sintonía*, at Pampa Films. But always to suit her purposes, to achieve her goals. The fools thought of their little pleasures of the moment—she thought of the years of her immortality!

And now she thought of the millennia of her immortality!

She shone her torch around her. The long staircase was walled on both sides, each wall bearing hieroglyphic inscriptions whose meaning was sealed to Evita.

But she continued.

The walls ended and the staircase continued. The air grew thicker. Evita pulled the breathing apparatus away from her face. The air had a musty odor to it and an oily taste, but it was better than breathing only the characterless gas provided by the apparatus.

She halted and pressed the back of one gloved hand to her

eyes. She had shifted her goggles to her forehead when she
removed her breathing mask, but now specks were dancing
before her eyes.

Was she growing dizzy? But she felt well. In fact, she felt
better than she had since leaving Palomar. Her skin tingled.
The glowing specks, scintillations in the thickening air, must
then be real.

The air itself was like a black fog, punctuated by dancing
sparks of green and blue, purple and orange.

She felt radiant. As if her whole being were glowing with
a new and magical energy. As if she were becoming the pos-
sessor of wondrous powers lost to humankind for thousands
of years. Powers that the queens of Egypt must have possessed, powers granted them by Isis and lost to womankind
since women had ceased to worship the goddess.

What could she do now that no other woman could do?
What wonders could she perform?

Shocked, she realized that she had reached the bottom of
the long staircase of stone. She was wandering through the
murky atmosphere. Her electric torch worked correctly, but
its beam revealed nothing: it penetrated the blackness to a
distance of a few yards, then faded, revealing nothing more
than thick, dark atmosphere.

She began to run.

She was able to continue indefinitely, punctuating her
strides with great, gliding leaps. She who had been a sickly
child, a scrawny woman, never the least bit of an athlete, was
running like a lioness of the Andes.

But where was the staircase she had descended? Where did
this catacomb lead, and how could she find her way back to
the temple of Isis, to Oswald Mosley, to *Patrilandia*?

Stop, then!

She halted, panting, her face and her body moist with perspiration. She shut off the torch and attached it to the belt of
her flying costume.

The scintillating points continued to dance around her.

She must be calm and she must solve this problem for
herself. She sat cross-legged on the stone floor, rested her
forehead against her palms. She held her eyes shut to keep
out even the tiny brightness of the scintillations; she waited
for her pupils to open to their maximum.

When she was ready, she raised her head slowly, then opened her eyes with equal slowness. She revolved slowly, still crouched on the stone floor.

A dim radiance, eerily green, penetrated the darkness. So faint was it that Evita was not certain it was there at all: an illusion, a chimera, a will-o'-the-wisp.

She rose slowly and moved toward it.

With each pace she took, the radiance became more distinct. It was upright. It was motionless. It was as tall as a woman but it loomed over Evita, perhaps as much as four feet off the floor.

She approached it.

It was another altar, another representation of the goddess. But now Isis was illuminated by no external light: she glowed from within.

Evita was struck by her beauty. She stood before the altar. She felt tears of adoration and of joy rolling down her cheeks. She was drawn.

She climbed carefully upon the altar. She was as close to the goddess as she could be. Dared she touch the figure?

She reached to touch the goddess's gown, but her hand met no resistance, only a sense of tingling and of warmth. She inhaled sharply, set her jaw, stepped into the goddess, and turned. The goddess's body was her body; the goddess's accoutrements were her own.

She wore the Hathor crown of bullock's horns, the sun disk of Ra, the falcon's wing headdress and cobra-headed decoration. Her necklace and bracelets were of lapis lazuli and gold; her gown was of white linen, so fine she could tell it was transparent.

She had become one with the goddess, and the goddess had given to her some part of the divine power that she wielded. Evita grinned her triumph.

Perón and Horten eyed each other suspiciously. It boded ill for their mission, Perón considered, that so much distrust had appeared. Horten, his brother, and the nuclear researcher Richter had emigrated happily enough to Argentina when Germany's situation in the international community had worsened.

As military aide to President Ramírez, Major Perón had

played a vital role in welcoming the immigrants, in making their enterprises successful and beneficial to Argentina as well as to themselves. But Horten seemed bent upon making enemies of the other three.

As for Oswald Mosley, Perón had suspicions of his own. He disliked the amount of influence if not downright control that the English exercised in Argentine society. And while relations between the two countries were generally cordial, there was the long-standing dispute over *las Islas Malvinas*. What maddened about the islands was that they were of little economic or strategic worth. They had no practical value to either nation, but such commitment of national honor had been made on both sides that neither Britain nor Argentina could bring herself to relinquish her claim.

Oswald Mosley was in disfavor with his country's government and he had befriended Perón readily enough. But he seemed smitten by Eva Duarte, and Perón was in no frame of mind to accept Mosley as a rival suitor for Evita's favor. Perón had not liked the idea of Mosley going off with Eva Duarte to explore the ancient structures they had found on the moon, but no other arrangement had worked either. And in their bulky altitude suits, romance was likely to remain unbudded.

So here sat Major Juan Domingo Perón and Herr Reimar Horten, glaring at each other in mistrustful silence. Horten had climbed from *Patrilandia* after Mosley and Eva Duarte had left; he checked the condition of the craft, returned satisfied to the crew compartment, and settled in to stare endlessly at the ship's instruments. Perón had even less to occupy him. He settled finally for a sketch pad and pencil, cartooning his impressions of the buildings and the alien landscape that surrounded the ship.

The engines had been shut off. The cabin lights and instrument illumination were low. Ambient light flooding through the bubble was ample for their needs. The luminous mist within the lunar central fissure glowed nearby like a city's lights in the night sky, viewed from just beyond the horizon.

Now Perón's eyes were dazzled by a flash from the fissure. When he recovered, the lights of *Patrilandia* were slowly recovering from a blackout. Reimar Horten was fumbling for his wire-rimmed spectacles. He pulled their metal arms around his ears.

Both men stared straight up. An object had been flung through the central fissure by the same electrical discharge that had knocked out the lights of *Patrilandia* and dazzled the eyes of her two occupants.

Without waiting for discussion, Horten hit the controls that would seal the crew bubble and start *Patrilandia*'s nuclear engines.

Perón caught one clear sight of the brilliant yellow ship that had plunged upward from the fissure. He did not know who had built the yellow craft or who had been aboard. He did not need to know.

What he understood—and realized that Reimar Horten understood as well—was that the die had been cast. Someone—whether in England or France, in Austria-Hungary or in the Colossus of the North—had picked up the radio transmission from Counter-Earth. That someone, whoever he or she was, had arranged for the construction of a skyship comparable to *Patrilandia*, had launched that ship just hours behind *Patrilandia*.

And because the bat-ship had detoured from her original flight plan to explore these strange relics on the moon, her yellow-winged rival had surpassed *Patrilandia* and was on her way to Counter-Earth ahead of Perón and his companions.

He found himself pressed back in his seat as Reimar Horten gunned *Patrilandia* down the Avenue of Sphinxes. The ship came to speed, leaped from the paving stones into the attenuated atmosphere that surrounded the central fissure. She banked, nosed up, followed the yellow-winged interloper at a steadily accelerating pace.

The rival ship left no visible wake, but her exhaust was a dancing, ever-changing glow. Horten, one eye huge and the other the size of a .22-caliber slug behind his thick-lensed glasses, pressed forward in hot pursuit.

Perón took charge of *Patrilandia*'s guns. The ship was fitted with .50-caliber machine guns and a 37-mm cannon fixed in her nose. The armament was adapted from fighter aircraft of the world's most advanced air forces.

Testing the weaponry, Perón fired a short burst from the .50s and a single high-explosive round from the cannon.

They worked to perfection.

He looked past Reimar Horten's shoulder, watching the flight path of the yellow ship. He couldn't tell whether *Patrilandia* had been spotted by her prey. Certainly radio silence was no problem, and no ordinary sounds could carry in the near-total vacuum this far above the moon.

Perón fired a burst from the .50s.

The yellow ship swerved, then regained her course.

Horten followed with deadly tenacity, slowly narrowing the gap between the two craft. He matched the yellow ship move for move.

The yellow ship tried a sudden maneuver, a swerving inside loop.

Horten flipped *Patrilandia* in a dangerous corkscrew.

For a split second the yellow ship lay directly in Juan Perón's gunsights. He pressed the firing button. The 37-mm cannon coughed its heavy high-explosive round.

An eyeblink later the yellow ship bucked like a wild animal. The ship twisted. An ugly black opening appeared in one wing.

The ship went spiraling away.

CHAPTER
7

Jack Northrop was not a combat flier and *Manta* had not been designed for military use. The ship was a test model, planned and built to try out design features and power systems meant for incorporation into full-size aircraft, like the *City of Santa Barbara*, and their military counterparts.

But Northrop was a certified test pilot. Despite his age— he was well past forty and had the sprinklings of gray in his dark hair to prove it—he'd kept his reflexes fast and his skills sharp.

And he knew *Manta* to the last spar and rivet. He had designed the ship, he had worked in coveralls alongside the mechanics who built her, he had been the first pilot to take her aloft.

Manta's top power output might be less than that of her olive and brown pursuer, but her maneuverability was unmatched.

When *Manta* shuddered and Northrop spotted the gaping damage to her yellow wing, he spun the ship in a quick evasive maneuver. He had no weapons. He couldn't outrun his attacker. He could outmaneuver the bat-winged craft, but that would merely buy him time: sooner or later he would wind up in the other craft's cross hairs again. Only sheer luck caused the first direct hit on *Manta* to occur in a nonvital spot.

The next might knock out a control system or a power plant. It might smash directly into the crew bubble and kill all four occupants of *Manta* in a single explosion.

Could he get behind his attacker, land on the lunar surface, possibly dive back through the moon's central fissure, and find a hidey-hole in some deep crater or shadowed mountain lee?

He flipped *Manta*, swerved. But the drably marked pursuer stayed on his tail. He saw the deadly trails of tracer rounds wing past *Manta*. He glanced back and saw the deadly flare of the other craft's cannon fire again. This time the round missed *manta*, but another hit would come sooner or later.

The enemy was too fast; he flew too well for Northrop to dodge past him and return to the moon.

There was only one other course open.

He sighted in on the searing disk of the sun. He held his arm in front of his eyes, protecting them from the glare. He looked back at the other craft. Unless the two ships were very close, *Manta* would shrink to an insignificant dot. She would be lost in the brilliance of the sun, would disappear totally as far as the other ship could tell.

Then it was a contest of wits: if the enemy could guess quickly enough what had happened, he could match courses with *Manta*. The bat-winged craft could overtake *Manta*, could pass her. Then the enemy could turn back and attack once more, diving from the blinding sun as the legendary Baron von Richthofen and his Flying Circus had done in the One Year War, decimating the fliers of Britain and France and America.

But the enemy seemed to have missed his guess.

Northrop looked over his shoulder. He could see the bat-winged craft quartering the sky in a search pattern. He'd never find *Manta* that way, and every second that passed made it less likely that he would locate the yellow ship even when he did discover his mistake.

Soon Northrop saw the other craft drop away, heading back to the lunar surface. He heaved a sigh of relief.

Babe Didrikson said, "What was that all about? Was that the moon air corps attacking us?"

Northrop shook his head. "I don't think so. Those buildings that we saw—they were surprise enough! But they looked deserted. There was no sign of any life or activity there. I think they've been deserted for a long time—I don't know how long."

"Then who was it?"

"I think our rivals. Whoever they are. They got here first, they spotted us using the lunar fissure to boost our speed. Probably they landed to investigate the same buildings that we saw. When we whizzed past, they didn't want to let us get ahead of them, so they attacked."

"And you don't know who they are?"

Northrop shrugged.

"Should we head back to earth? To spread the alarm, find their base, and do something about it?"

Northrop hummed cogitatively. "I think our duty is to press on. If they're that eager to stop us, they must be up to something very serious and very dangerous. We ought to get to Counter-Earth first, and try to prevent their mischief."

No one quarreled with that.

Jack Northrop turned to studying Einstein's chart, setting *Manta*'s controls to take her to the remote planet in hopes of arriving before their rivals.

Manta's equipment included no weapons, but a full complement of astrogational tools, including a swiveling telescope.

Northrop alternately consulted the chart, set controls, sighted in on the sun and other stars, returned to Einstein's sketches and computations. He wiped sweat from his forehead. Josh Gibson maintained a steady hand on *Manta*'s controls between Northrop's resettings. Gibson had picked up flying skills with amazing rapidity. He held *Manta*'s course smooth and even.

But Northrop was becoming increasingly distraught. He was sweating more heavily. There was a slight tremor to his hands. He turned to Einstein and consulted him, pointing to the diagrams and computations the savant had performed.

Gibson said, "We not going to fly straight there, are we?"

"Of course not!" Northrop snapped.

"Didn't think so. Can't fly through the sun, right? So we got to swing around her. That it?"

Northrop ignored the question.

"Even so, I like to know a little more, Jack. Where we going?"

Northrop hissed in exasperation. "All right. Just a second." He turned back to the control panel, locked *Manta*'s controls so the craft would not drift off course while Gibson's attention was elsewhere.

He rattled the chart, trying unsuccessfully to make it lie flat. "Look, here is earth, here's the moon. As of the time we left *Titanic*. Okay?"

Gibson grunted affirmatively.

"Now"—Northrop pointed—"a straight line from earth to Counter-Earth would pass through the sun. We have to avoid that; we can't get much closer then the orbit of the planet Venus. Maybe later on we'll design larger ships. Build them with heat and radiation shielding. If we develop commerce with Counter-Earth, we'll want that—we'll want to pass as close to the sun as possible to save time and supplies on the trip."

He looked up at Josh. "So far so good?"

"That's fine. Go on."

"So Dr. Einstein plotted this course for us."

Northrop ran his finger along a line, a long, curving line that led from earth, passed through the moon, swung wide of the orbit of Mercury and close to that of Venus. Then it curved back and closed in toward Counter-Earth. The line passed through Counter-Earth's moon before settling on the planet.

"You want to pick up more speed here?" Josh pointed to Counter-Earth's moon.

Northrop shook his head. "Just the opposite. We can use the lunar fissure to brake our speed as well as to increase it. It will require a trick maneuver—we'll have to swing past Counter-Earth when her moon is on the far side."

"Not so." Einstein's wiry white hair hovered over the chart. "If we pass through the fissure that way, we will even faster wind up going. No." He shook his bushy head. "This we must do."

The savant fumbled through his pockets, found a stubby pencil and sketched another line on the chart. "You see? Up through the moon, we gain energy. Down, we lose. We give it back. But down, we are for Counter-Earth headed so we must be careful not to crash. If too fast we arrive, we maybe will want to loop around and come twice through the moon."

Northrop held his hands to his head. "I would have done it backwards!"

Josh Gibson looked from the black sky to the chart, back to the sky. He shook his head. To Northrop he said, "This is wrong, Jack."

Northrop snapped to alertness. "What?"

"Looky here." Gibson pointed. "Now this chart shows us going like so." He retraced the course Northrop had indicated. Then he pointed through the bubble. "We not going there. No." He shook his head again. "We going *there*." He pointed into the darkness.

Northrop sat before the ship's telescope, following Gibson's pointed finger.

"You believe me, Jack. You don't, then just ask Babe here. She knows. I got the sharpest eyes in the National League. I can look at a pigeon flying over the ballpark, I'll tell you it's a boy or it's a girl."

Babe said, "That's the truth. Nobody has eyes sharper than Josh."

"And I say, we not going where we supposed to be going."

Northrop sank into his seat. "All right. I knew something was wrong. I couldn't find the error. This is Einstein's work. *Einstein*'s. The greatest mind in the world! Where did we go wrong?" He stared through he telescope again, then back at the chart. "We're not headed for Counter-Earth. We're headed for . . ."

He laid a variant course on the chart.

". . . the asteroid belt. We're headed for Ceres. But how can it be? How can it be?"

Einstein jotted a few numbers on the bottom of the chart. He turned his stubby pencil and erased a number in his earlier computations, inserted a new value.

"Well, you see—" he laughed, embarrassed—"a little mistake I made. Four times three, you see it here? Four times three, it should be twelve, you see, not twenty-one. A little trouble with arithmetic I always had. Transposing figures, you know. Fractions, too. I had always a little difficulty with fractions."

Babe Didrikson said, "What do we do now?"

Northrop leaned over the chart. "I don't know. I'd like to make a course correction right now, but that isn't as simple as it sounds. Especially with a hole in the middle of one wing. The craft is off balance. We don't have all our capabilities. I think we'd do better to go on to Ceres. We can land there. We can make repairs again and relaunch. I don't like it much; it'll take more time, put us back behind the others in all likelihood. But I'm afraid we'll have to do it."

Babe shot a glance at Josh. "What do you think?"

"He the boss. I sure don't know how to do better."

"Okay," she said. "Let's just do our best."

Northrop nodded. "There's nothing else we can do." He gave a sigh. "We'll have more time for flying lessons. Josh is doing well. How about giving it a try also?"

They spent the journey busily.

Northrop never ceased checking *Manta*'s instruments, never could keep himself from staring forlornly at the ship's damaged wing.

Josh Gibson and Babe Didrikson took turns sitting beside Northrop, learning the operation of *Manta*.

Only Albert Einstein did not participate. He had brought his violin with him, his only personal belonging on the ship. He would sit staring into the void, his eyes fixed on some distant point, "having a little think" for hours on end. What thoughts passed through that great mind, the others were never to know.

Only, at times, he would open his violin case and fix the instrument under his chin and play from memory: Mozart, Bach, Haydn, Vivaldi, Scarlatti. But most of all, Mozart.

He played well. He seldom spoke, only occasionally muttering, "Wolfgang, only God could have told you this. And you have given it to us."

Northrop, worried and nervous, turned on the savant. "What do you mean? God told him what?"

Einstein smiled. "I do not play as well as I would like. The music—it is God's word."

"But what? Do you mean there's a secret message in the music?"

The smile broadened. "Such a charming notion. But it is not so secret. We must listen, only. God speaks to us in all things. Just listen, listen, listen. And none has ever listened as well as Mozart. That is all."

Northrop turned away, took the telescope, looked at Ceres.

The asteroid was now visible to the naked eye as a bright dot. In the telescope it showed as the largest of a cluster of asteroids. These in turn stood against a band of irregular fragments tumbling in a toroidal orbit beyond that of the planet Mars.

He wanted to kick himself.

He ought to have checked Einstein's computations. He knew that Einstein was the greatest physicist of the age, but the old man had always stated openly that his major insights were all the fruit of intuitive illuminations. With his reliance on intuition and his talk of God, Einstein was regarded by much of the scientific community as a phenomenon, more mystic than scientist.

And Einstein had never quarreled with the designation. He merely retreated to his cottage and smoked his pipe, played his violin, or went fishing, and had his "little thinks." And the results turned in by the experimenters in their laboratories and the astronomers at their telescopes bore him out.

But the old man had never claimed to be much good at simple arithmetic—that was one of the world's standing jokes. And he could be vague; he could go for a walk and get lost. He resembled the holy fool more than the white-coated scientist of popular imagery.

And Northrop had looked at Einstein's chart and the figures that went with it and followed them blindly, without checking the math. And they were going to find themselves hundreds of millions of miles off course, at best delayed disastrously in their race with their mysterious (and deadly!) rivals, at worst lost forever in the deeps of space!

The asteroids . . .

More properly, planetoids, for they were little planets rather than little stars. Ceres and a few others showed in *Manta*'s telescope as perfect miniature planets: flattened doughnuts was the simile used in elementary schools, or half-deflated inner tubes, or life rings. The central fissures were generally smaller than those images would suggest, and the topography of the planets was, of course, far more complex and far more varied than those of doughnuts or inner tubes. But basically the shapes were the same.

And in the asteroid belt the shapes to be seen were every possible variant on the basic toroid. Some were partial toroids, resembling the letter C. Others were squashed or distorted shapes, ranging from straight lines to figure eights to solid lumps of matter as round and apparently as solid as golfballs. (But no one had been there. What if they were hollow! What might be inside? No one knew.)

From behind Northrop came strange music.

He turned to see a trio: Einstein playing his violin, Didrikson with a harmonica, Joshua Gibson playing an impromptu drum on the chart-board. They would play a little, then halt, then Einstein would speak, hum a sample part, then the three would resume playing.

Northrop said, "What's that?"

Einstein said, "We may call it a three-part variation on Haydn's Piano Sonata Number Forty-nine."

"I suppose he heard the voice of God, too."

Einstein smiled. "Anyone may hear the voice of God. It is hard only to clear our ears and our minds of such clutter as the world provides."

"I'm going to try something. Going to try and talk to Moe Sterling back on earth."

He flicked the switches on *Manta*'s radio, slipped a headset over his ears, and lifted the microphone from *Manta*'s panel. When the radio warmed up, it produced a steady stream of static. Northrop maneuvered knobs on the radio, aligning the steerable antenna as best he could with earth.

When he was satisfied, he spoke into the mike, listened, spoke again, patiently fining up the signal. There was no obstacle between *Manta* and earth, no need to bounce a signal off any hypothetical Einstein layer. It was just a very long distance, and he wondered if the signal could be picked up.

At this distance, also, he couldn't see the earth in detail. It appeared as a bright point in space; in the telescope it was a larger, brighter point. But he couldn't tell which side of the planet was facing him. *Manta* carried an ephemeris. With some work it should be possible to compute the answer to that question: he'd do it himself if it came to that, not ask Dr. Einstein to do it.

But—

"This is *Santa Barbara*. Communications Officer Sterling speaking. Please identify yourself, caller."

"Moe!"

"Who's this?"

"Jack Northrop! I'm calling from *Manta*. We're—"

"*Manta*! Your signal's weak. Can you crank it up any?"

"This is top power."

"Where are you? We heard from Captain Davidson that you got off *Titanic* all right. But then there were two huge flares in the lunar fissure. Nobody's been able to raise you. The world is going gaga, Mr. Northrop! We thought you were lost, that *Manta* was destroyed.

"Besides, if one lunar flash had destroyed *Manta*, what was the second flash? And something else is brewing. President Ramírez has clamped a blackout on all news from the Argentine. Before that happened, there was a broadcast in German proclaiming somebody named Richter as the new Chancellor of the Argentine Reich. No shipping is permitted in or out of Buenos Aires, but refugees have been reported crossing the Plata estuary to Uruguay in small boats."

"Look, your signal is breaking up."

"Repeat. Can't hear you, *Manta*."

"I said, your signal is breaking up, *Santa Barbara*. We're at extreme range and it's impossible to keep the antenna aligned."

"Where are you? Can we help?"

"*Manta* is off course for Counter-Earth. Approaching asteroid Ceres. We were attacked and damaged over lunar far-side. We hope to refit at Ceres and continue our journey."

"What happened over the moon?"

"That may be your Argentine angle, Sterling. Ask Captain Jarrold to get word back to Washington, to the secretary of the navy, to President Hull himself if he can. We were attacked by another skyship. This whole thing is bigger than anyone realized. The stakes keep climbing!"

• • •

Ceres loomed large in *Manta*'s telescope. Northrop had sat with his eye glued to the instrument until points of light in the sky began to dance.

Behind him the impromptu concert had ended to mutual applause by the musicians.

"What I want to do," Northrop said, "is land on Ceres. It's large enough to have an atmosphere. We'll find out soon whether it actually has one or not."

Gibson peered through the Plexiglas. Ceres was now clearly visible to the naked eye. Its toroidal shape was clear. Its axial rotation was just past full edge; one of the asteroid's sides was turning majestically toward *Manta*.

"Got continents and seas like earth. I guess we can land this thing all right."

Northrop said, "We could land even in a vacuum—but it would be a lot tougher. We'd have to reverse the engines' thrust and try to stall in. This way, we'll be able to make a proper flying entrance and land the way we'd like."

"Look there. Ice at the hole and a shining rim. Like earth!"

Northrop pressed his eye to the telescope again. His hands began to tremble with excitement. "This is amazing! Amazing!"

Babe said, "Come on, Jack! What is it?"

He pulled back from the instrument. "See for yourself."

Babe peered through the telescope, then turned it over to Josh.

"Glory be! They ought to see this back in Georgia! The land of Egypt! Wouldn't all those preachers be amazed! I hear about this all my life, but I never thought I'd live to see it! You think the Pharaoh there, Jack?"

"I don't know what to think."

"Look," Babe put in, "there were pyramids and temples on the moon, too. Are they all over the place? I didn't know that the Egyptians had spaceships."

"There's a very big difference. The moon is a dead world."

"Even though someone flew up and attacked us." Babe's tone was sardonic.

"I don't think they were moon people—or Egyptians. I think we were attacked by another craft from earth, one that probably left shortly before we did and that took off from the moon to pursue us. But that—" Northrop pointed at the asteroid—"that is a living world. The moon has only a thin, misty bit of atmosphere. Ceres has enough air to breathe, to sustain life. Look! Even with the naked eye we can see clouds, storm systems, forested land masses. Through the scope we can see pyramids.

"There's life there! And soon we will be with that life!"

"Huh! Monsters, I suppose. I saw those in Texas, at the Crown Bijou. Saturday matinee, a western, a space movie, three shorts, and a serial. Will they have tentacles or fangs? Or both?"

"I think they'll be very human. If they built the pyramids of Egypt, they're as human as you or I. And if they built them here as well, they should be very much the same."

"Would they have radios?"

"Huh?"

"I said, would they have radios?"

Northrop shook his head. "I'm sorry. I didn't mean that I couldn't understand you. I just—uh . . . you surprised me. Of course they should. The least we can do is try to signal them."

He looked at Dr. Einstein as he warmed up the radio set again. But the savant sat with his eyes slitted, ignoring the others and their excitement, having a little think. A little, little think.

Northrop aimed *Manta*'s steerable antenna at Ceres. Although the target was only a fraction the size of the earth, the distance was an even smaller fraction of the distance to earth, and it was shrinking steadily. It seemed simple enough to beam in on the asteroid, but there was no response to his efforts.

"I don't know." He shook his head. "Either they don't have radios, or I'm on the wrong wavelength, or they just didn't receive my message, or maybe they don't want to answer."

Babe shrugged. "Maybe they haven't invented radios."

Northrop shrugged. "I suppose that's possible. Space travel but no radio? So far ahead of us in one regard, so far behind in another."

"They might not have all the same interests."

"You're probably right. Well, let's just take a little survey of their world. *Manta* seems to be bearing up all right. I can't help worrying about that wing, though.''

He reversed the skycraft's engines. The yellow ship slowed as it approached the asteroid. Soon Northrop could feel the grip of atmosphere on *Manta*'s wings.

Babe poked his shoulder. ''Say, this atmosphere . . .''

Northrop looked at her.

''I mean—how do we know it's air? How do we know they, uh, breath the same kind of air that we do?''

''We don't know that. But I expect that they do. If they lived on earth and they can live here also, they'd have to breathe the same air that we do. If they're human—and we know they are!''

The Cereans didn't make them wait very long before they got the answers to their questions.

Manta dipped into Ceres' atmosphere, slowed, climbed into vacuum, and dipped again, enough times to reach a comfortable speed. Northrop was spiraling through the atmosphere, cautiously searching for a good landing field, when the Cereans rose in a swarm of ships to greet the newcomer.

They were tiny—each must carry a single occupant.

They were sleek—like needle-nosed darts with glossy black exteriors and trim of a different color on each.

They may or may not have been fitted with radios. If they were, they didn't use them; one pilot matched course with *Manta* and made a clear hand signal through his transparent canopy, and Jack Northrop obeyed without hesitation and started down toward the surface.

And they may or may not have been armed. No one was eager to find out.

CHAPTER
8

"Gott in Himmel!"

"They're gone!"

"My fault! My blunder!"

Despite Horten's words of self-culpation, his tone was one of anger and suppressed violence rather than humbleness.

Juan Perón asked, "Where could they have gone? I'm sure I scored a hit. Then they disappeared."

Horten gestured using his thumb. Although he pointed it upward, the jerking motion was not that of gladiatorial mercy. *"Die Sonne,"* he gritted. "A trick as old as war in the air. They were above us to begin. They climbed. In the glare of the sun they disappeared."

"What about going after them?"

"Nein, nein, nein. Already they are gone. They could anywhere be, by now. If they have weapons, they could lie in ambush. No, this encounter is completed. There will be more!"

Perón shielded his eyes and tried to penetrate the glare. He wiped away tears that were caused by the unbearable brightness. "I suppose you are right. We will return for the others and then go on. We've lost time already."

"As I warned! This was not my doing, Major! I was the one who wished to pursue our original plan. I was the one who argued to proceed directly. It was your English and you two half-English Argentines with your romantic notions of repeating Lord Carnarvon's feat who caused this trouble!''

"Please, *mein Herr*. Nothing will be gained by our quarreling now. Turn back. Land again. We will pick up Evita and Sir Oswald and be on our way. Perhaps we can overhaul those yellow interlopers.''

"We will save more time if we simply continue!''

Perón was aghast. "Continue?''

"*Ach! Fortsetzen. Continuar.* My usage is not correct?''

"I understand you. Or do I? You propose to leave Evita alone with Sir Oswald? With no supplies, no water—while we go on to Counter-Earth? You want to maroon them here? Leave them to their death?''

The wizened Horten laughed aloud. "Your heart bleeds for the two poor castaways, eh? No food, no water. How will they survive?''

Perón's face whitened with rage. He waited for Horten to go on.

"Perhaps I think another motive is involved. The lovely, so lovely Señorita Duarte. The English baronet with his country estate and his high connections. How can a poor Argentine officer, a mere major, compete? You cannot even get your paramour into the Jockey Club, can you, Major Perón? The Casa Rosada is open to you but the Barrio Norte is closed. An irony.

"While Sir Oswald—ah, even with the glamorous limp and the so modestly narrated heroism, so very, very English, my Major—Sir Oswald provokes dreams of Parliament, Downing Street, maybe even—who knows!—Buckingham Palace!

"What romance may blossom on the moon! Wh—''

Perón cut Horten's speech short. He lunged at the other man's throat. He tightened strong fingers around the scrawny neck.

Horten managed a single gasp.

He made one attempt to pry Perón's fingers from his neck, then dropped his hands. His face grew red. His eyes, one huge and one tiny behind the thick-lensed glasses, bulged.

Perón jerked his hands away from Horten's neck and sprang back from the other. He stared in amazement.

Horten stood panting, his face slowly regaining its normal

color. Before him he held a German military dagger. Intended for ceremonial use, its hilt worked with black and silver symbols and decorations, its blade thin and seemingly not strong, but its edges honed to razor sharpness and its point like that of a needle.

Horten wiped the reddened tip of the dagger on his flying suit and returned it, through a flap in the suit, to its sheath.

Perón looked at his belly. There was a very small patch of red on his own flying outfit.

Horton said, "The wound is trivial. I would advise you to take a patch from the repair kit for your suit. In case you need it to act as a seal, Major."

He turned away from Perón and gave his attention to *Patrilandia*'s instruments. "Still—" he sighed—"I suppose that we would be short-handed with just two of us on board."

Perón, seated now at the gunner's post, stared ahead. He wore a sidearm. He could draw it and dispatch the wiry German. But Horten had had the chance to kill him, Perón. He had held his dagger to Perón's belly and pressed it into his flesh just far enough to sting, just far enough to bring blood. He could have shoved forward and up into Perón's heart. He had not. And Perón would not draw his sidearm and kill the other in cold blood.

Patrilandia swung through a banking, leisurely turn. Perón saw the moon below them, and the earth farther beyond.

Their brief dogfight with the yellow skyship had brought them to a new angle before the earth and moon. The lunar disk had spun so that it was fully edge-on to *Patrilandia*.

The rocky outer edge of the moon, lacking earth's ice rim, showed naked, pitted rock. There were craters there, some of them so deep that their floors were lost in shadow. Perón wondered if all of them even had floors. Perhaps the moon was hollow, as some theorized the earth also to be. Like the flattened inner tube, with immense and mysterious caverns hidden forever from the eyes of those who dwelt on the surfaces.

Beyond the brilliant lunar edge that cut diagonally across *Patrilandia*'s Plexiglas bubble, lay the earth. The planet was in full disk, the ancient far side now exposed to Perón's eyes. He saw—or imagined that he saw—the outlines of Trapalanda, Uttarakuru, Yu-Atlanchi. Certainly he saw the great

River Okeanos winding endlessly around the equator of the far hemidisk. He wondered if the fabled forces of the nation of Svartalheim were at work, slowly spreading their influence through land after land.

Beneath *Patrilandia* the broad edge of the moon grew huge and bright. The craft skimmed low over the edge of the disk. Horten piloted the ship skillfully until the pyramids and sphinxes appeared against the yellow-white pumice. *Patrilandia* dropped softly onto the Avenue of Sphinxes.

Two figures stood side by side on the steps of a temple overlooking the roadway.

Patrilandia rolled to a stop.

Juan Domingo Perón climbed from the craft, Reimar Horten behind him.

Perón looked back for a moment, exchanging glances with Horten. Their conversation since the fight had been minimal, formal, banal. They had exchanged information only concerning the operation of the ship and its navigation back to the lunar fissure.

No reference had been made to Eva Duarte, Sir Oswald Mosley, or the former conversation. Out of their silence had arisen a tacit agreement to make no mention of the fight.

Perón's suit had been neatly patched. He could feel the wound near his sternum as a sore point. There had been little bleeding. Now even that had ceased.

Oswald Mosley raised a bulky arm in salute. The four figures advanced toward each other, two and two.

Watching Mosley and Eva Duarte, Perón blinked. Perhaps he was still suffering the effects of the aerial chase, of his attempt to make out the yellow ship as it lost itself in the sun's glare. Even so, Eva Duarte seemed to glow against the backdrop of Egyptian architecture.

He shot a glance at Mosley, then looked sideways at Reimar Horten. If either of them noticed anything strange about Evita, he did not indicate it.

"I say, that was a splendid chase, Herr Horten." Mosley was nodding and gesturing. "Went after that yellow-winged bugger, did you! Come up under his belly—a tough maneuver, that! 'Minds me of the great aerial tussles we used to have over the trenches during the One Year War. Einjahrkrieg don't you fellows call it; odd lingo, pushing all the words together like that.''

They were close together now, standing like a conversational grouping at a cocktail party. Mosley mouthed on. ''Gen'rally like to be on top, of course. Easier to get the jump that way, easier to hide out in old Sol, eh? Learned that little trick from the Baron himself! Lord rest his soul! Bugger got away, though, did he? Wonder who he could be? Don't suppose he followed us all the way from old terra firma, do you?''

''Into the ship!'' Horten ignored Mosley's blather, gestured the three into the *Patrilandia*. Perón stood beside Eva Duarte, peering into her face. She wore the breathing apparatus and flier's goggles that went with her altitude suit. He could not make out her expression, could hardly see the color of her skin. It seemed, perhaps, that there were a few small lines at the corners of her eyes. Squint marks, he inferred.

They clambered aboard *Patrilandia*.

''At least that struggle as a test flight served.'' Horten had sat in the pilot's seat again, although both Perón and Mosley were qualified pilots as well. *Patrilandia* was Horten's design, his brainchild. His attitude toward the craft was proprietary, and toward the others commanding. For the moment they gave to this arrangement their tacit consent, but later events might bring about a dramatic alteration to that balance.

The Plexiglas bubble was sealed and flying gear was removed. Horten appeared once again in his mechanic's white coveralls; Perón, in military garb; Mosley, in a casual outfit of whipcord breeches and tan raw-silk shirt; Eva Duarte, in slacks and blouse retrieved from the luggage her dresser had prepared.

''I say, Miss Duarte and I had quite an adventure while you chaps were off playing warbirds with that yellow chap. Got separated for a bit. Evita gave me a bit of a scare, I'll have to confess.''

Horten said, ''Please hold your story until we are on course. Once that is achieved, we will have much to discuss.''

He turned his back to them, switched on *Patrilandia*'s systems, revved the nuclear engines. Once more the bat-winged craft leaped from the Avenue of Sphinxes. Horten consulted the *Mekkanopantograf.* He adjusted the ship's course. He studied the *'graf* at length, then gave a grunt of satisfaction.

Evita had sat silently since boarding the ship.

Perón turned to give her a smile of reassurance. She was more beautiful than ever, he thought, more lovely in these informal clothes than she had been as a powdered and be-wigged *aristo* in a costume drama of the French Revolution. Even though the squint lines around her eyes were definitely present. Her hair was lovely, silken, blond. Perhaps there was a tiny wisp of gray at the temple. But no, that was an ab-surdity: Evita was just twenty years of age, a young woman in the first bloom of her maturity. It was a trick of the irreg-ular light.

Oswald Mosley strode to the bat-ship's small larder and returned with drinks for them all. Horten held his hand up and received his silently. Perón took his, muttered his thanks. As Evita reached for hers, the drinking implement slipped in her hand. It began to tumble.

But her hand was beneath the drink. She grasped it and thanked Mosley.

How did she do that?

The others had all observed the phenomenon.

How did she do it? She had reached for the drink, it had slipped, and then her hand was beneath it and she caught it, not spilling a drop.

How?

Behind his metal-rimmed glasses, Horten's eyes widened. Oswald Mosley's jaw dropped. Perón knitted his brows. He was amazed at his own thought processes, at the way his attention strayed to Evita's softly coiffured hair. No, it was not an illusion caused by *Patrilandia*'s lighting—there were definite wisps of gray at her temples. Probably the fault of her hairdresser.

"Ah, we investigated the Temple of Isis," Mosley said.

The others snapped from their separate realities when he spoke.

"Marvelous architecture. Been to Luxor, Thebes, Mem-phis, you know. Seen the real stuff. Valley of the Kings, all the right ruins.

"Absolutely authentic." He shook his head. "Magnificent workmanship, quite perfect. And looking new, you see.

Quite, quite remarkable. Don't suppose there's much weather to grind it away, no marauders. Quite spectacular preservation. 'Course, Miss Duarte here, showed more pluck than this old warbird.''

He crossed his legs, using his hand to help the weaker one move.

''Quite gave me the slip. Disappeared into the vaults beneath the Temple of Isis. I tried to follow and find her but got nowhere, figgered I'd do better to fetch help than wander off and have the two of us lost, eh?

''And then I saw that you two chaps had gone off in *Patrilandia*. Well! Imagine my state of mind, eh? Skyship gone. Horten and Perón gone. Miss Duarte disappeared into the bowels of an ancient Egyptian temple. What to do? What to do? Eh?

''Well, at this juncture what should I see but an apparition of the goddess herself—or so I thought! Flowing robes, crown, sistrum—that's what they call those rattle things, you know—the works. And quite breathtakingly beautiful, I must say that. And her costume quite revealing, I must say that, too!

''But of course it wasn't the goddess at all, it was our very own Miss Duarte. Don't know how she found her way back out of that temple. There I'd been imagining all sorts of dire and terrible fates overcoming the young lady, but she emerged all by herself, quite unharmed, and here she is, back among us safe and sound!''

Juan Perón looked sourly at Mosley and Evita. He made no comment.

Behind *Patrilandia* the earth and moon had shrunk to two small disks, slowly whirling in blackness.

Evita had said nothing during Mosley's narrative. She appeared uncomfortable. No one had commented on the oddity of her dropped and recovered drink. She ended an uncomfortable silence by raising a different topic. ''This Counter-Earth we are seeking—what's this all about?''

The others exchanged glances.

Evita said, ''I know of other worlds. We use them in *Oro Blanco*. Mars with its red deserts and green men. Venus with its immortal steaming swamps, giant amphibians, endless storms. But what is this Counter-Earth?''

Horten growled, "A world like earth."

"But exactly like? No other planet is exactly like ours."

"No. This one only."

"We have seen it, then?"

"No." Horten shook his head.

"Then how do we know it exists?" demanded Evita.

Horten refused to continue the conversation.

Perón said, "It has long been theorized. We cannot see it because it lies beyond the sun, directly opposite our own earth. As we move, so does Counter-Earth. So we can never see it, nor its inhabitants, us."

"And the wireless, you know," Mosley added. "Now we've heard their call. So we know they exist. And their planet, you see. Could hardly be people there without a world."

"Just like earth. With a moon, I suppose. And they speak what language?"

"Several. Several, all of which are very familiar to us." Perón had resumed speaking.

"I see." But the expression in her eyes indicated that she harbored serious doubts. "And this Counter-Earth, this other earth, it is exactly like our own?" she persisted. "Exactly? Edward is king of England, while his morganatic wife sits stewing for a crown? Karl reigns in Austria-Hungary with his Empress Marie? The fool Ramírez sits in the Casa Rosada watching North American cowboy films by the hour, while Argentina suffers?"

Perón and Mosley exchanged uncomfortable glances. The Englishman spoke. "As far as we know, yes. But—we aren't quite, ah, absolutely—that is, it would seem so, ye-es, but, ah, we might find a tiny difference here or there."

"So we might." Evita strode to the edge of the Plexiglas bubble and peered into deep space. "So we might."

She turned to face the others. "And just what difference might we find? That Parliament has relented and granted Wallis a crown? That Pedro Ramírez might decide that he would rather watch Humphrey Bogart than Gene Autry? *The Maltese Falcon* instead of *The Phantom Empire*?"

"Who knows?" Mosley spread his hands. "That's what we'll find out pretty soon, I should think. A bit of patience. When the right time comes, we shall ask our questions.

"Ah, but meanwhile, Miss Duarte, our very own major has given thought to just such questions, you know. You have read his book?"

"I have looked at them. Military history. Theories of warfare. Subjects for men to read—or boys."

"Then you have not read Major Perón's analysis of the One Year War—his theories of errors on the Kaiser's part."

"Germany was betrayed," Reimar Horten inserted.

"Doubtless," Mosley said sardonically.

"Give then your theory," Horten told Perón.

Perón drew his large, rimless eyeglasses from his uniform pocket. When he wore them, his face changed. From the hearty, aggressive military man he seemed instantly transformed into a professor—slower, more thoughtful, yet less certain.

"The war was coming for some time, yes. Germany was preparing to fight. Consider, Austria-Hungary was a great empire but weak, divided by internal rivalries, too concerned with culture and not enough with strength. France and Britain were stronger, but they too were concerned with their own affairs, Britain with her many colonies, France with her own empire. Cochin refused to acquiesce. Quebec demanded freedom. Morocco flirted with the Kaiser himself.

"Why did the Kaiser go to war in 1912? If he had waited another two or three years, kept building his army, kept building his fleet so he could have stood up to Britain, he might have won the war."

Perón stood like a professor who had made his leading point, hoping that his students had been convinced.

Evita remained noncommittal.

Oswald Mosley cleared his throat. "Don't mean to differ, you know. Read your book several times—brilliant work, Perón. But don't you think Teddy Roosevelt had something to do with it? I mean, when he was elected President again, he made it very clear that he'd sniffed out Willie's game. Teddy was on to him, and if Willie'd waited any longer, he'd have had doughboys breathing down his collar. So he had to start his fight, ready or not. Don't you see?"

Perón shook his head up and down. "Precisely my point, yes. But I ask you, why was Roosevelt elected in 1912?"

"Why?" Mosley giggled. "Because the States are a de-

mocracy, that's why. Why, with his silly grin and his bully-
this and bully-that, those fools just couldn't resist. Not against
a sourpuss schoolman like Wilson.''

"Huh! You follow the politics of the Colossus closely, my
lord.''

"I follow politics, Major.''

"Just so! But do you remember that Roosevelt had already
been President—that he left office and made his party place
that balloon Taft in the White House?''

"Yes.''

"And that Roosevelt chose in 1912 to return and displace
his own man, resume the Presidency—and that Taft refused
to yield?''

"Surely.''

"And what then? Pardon me, *querida*, are we boring you?
Sir Oswald and I get carried away. Our political debates are
sometimes quite heated.''

Evita hesitated.

Mosley didn't wait. "As I recall it—I was just a boy in
England at the time, you know, just a cadet at Sandhurst—
Taft offered Roosevelt the vice presidency, and to the aston-
ishment of all concerned, Mr. Roosevelt accepted.''

"Yes.'' Perón nodded. "And then Taft went on a campaign
tour. He sat on a burro wearing a cowboy's sombrero, posing
for his photograph on the rim of their Cannón Grande. Taft
weighed three hundred pounds. The poor beast could not hold
his weight. The animal's limbs buckled on one side. Taft was
thrown into the *cañón*, the burro stumbled the other way. *El
Presidente* fell a full mile—straight down. The burro simply fell
to the ground, uninjured.''

Evita laughed heartily. *"¡Que maravilloso! ¡El Presidente
Gordo—una milla entera! ¡Maravilloso!''*

"Ye-es.'' Mosley brushed his moustache with the first fingers of his hands. "Yes, I do recall. So those American To-
ries put Roosevelt back up on top, and he won the election
over Wilson. But what connection has that with the One Year
War?''

"My theory is this.'' Perón removed his glasses, pinched
the bridge of his nose between forefinger and thumb, and
rubbed. He slid the glasses back into his tunic. "If Wilson
had won the election, he would have fumbled and hesitated

to act. The Kaiser would have had time to prepare his forces. He would have won the war in Europe.

"Even if Taft had won, the result would have been similar, with Roosevelt fuming and stamping but unable to take any action.

"But with Roosevelt elected, Wilhelm was driven into a state of panic. He went to war unready to fight—and he lost!"

"So, Pocho," Evita said. "A brilliant lesson in history of the Colossus. But what has this to do with Counter-Earth?"

"*Querida*, only this: but suppose one pebble had been misplaced. Suppose that *Presidente* Taft's burro had stumbled to the other side. Then the burro would have fallen *una milla entera*. *El Presidente* would have fallen the other way, dusted off his clothing, put on his sombrero, and walked away unhurt. Wilson or Taft, but surely not Roosevelt, would have been President. All history would have been changed!"

"And all because of one pebble, Perón?"

"That is precisely the truth."

Evita pondered. "Tell me," she said at last. "Is there, on Counter-Earth, a Radio Belgrano? Is it run by Jaime Yankelevich? Does he employ another Hector Blomberg to direct *Oro Blanco* in his interludes of sobriety? Does the cast include another Libertad Lamarque and another Eva Duarte?"

Perón shrugged. He looked at Mosley, then shrugged again. "*¿Quien sabe, querida?*"

Sparks leaping from her eyes, Evita exploded. "This you have kept from me until now! Now I *must* go there! I will see about such things. Another Libertad! Another Evita!"

Patrilandia nosed over. Perón, Mosley, Eva Duarte, grasped whatever objects were at hand to keep from toppling.

Mosley was the first to recover. "I say, Herr Horten! Was that an air pocket we hit? Didn't know the dashed things even existed up here!"

Horten grinned. "We have now left the plane of the ecliptic. If you will be so kind as to attend to the *Hortenmekkanopantograf*."

The black tank showed the two earths and their moons, the planets Venus and Mercury, and the sun. A glowing dot represented the *Patrilandia*.

By lowering one's eye level to that of the sun and planets in the *'graf*, it was clear that *Patrilandia* was out of the topographical disk that included the natural bodies. And it was dropping, with the slowness of the minute hand of a clock, away from that disk.

"We will be lost!" Evita cried. "What is wrong? Why are we falling?"

Horten laughed his grating laugh. It was a sound without mirth, and spread no happiness to its hearers. "We are not falling. I have directed the engines to propel us in this direction. Since the danger of passing too near the sun must be avoided, we will dip beneath and reemerge when we have passed. Then our passage to Counter-Earth we will resume."

"But—*under* the sun? *¿Debajo del sol?*"

"Under or above—it makes no difference. As the *Judeglanzend* Einstein has proven, all is relative."

"But what will keep us from falling forever?"

"*Mademoiselle, s'il vous plaît.* It is a mere convenience of speech to say that we are beneath the sun. Or above it. If you are more pleased to consider, then consider the plane of the ecliptic to be vertical." He placed his hand flat on the *'graf*, turned it ninety degrees so its flat plane was perpendicular to the tank.

"Then we are merely dodging aside, so as to avoid such heat. We are perfectly safe. We shall return when we wish to do so. Nothing can possibly imperil us."

Silently, *Patrilandia* slowed, then stopped. It was as if a child's sled had run gently in a snowbank. Horten jumped to examine the craft's instrument panel. Even as he did so, the instruments flickered and died. The roar of *Patrilandia*'s nuclear-powered engines, so constant a sound that the four had blotted it from their conscious minds, faded into silence.

Patrilandia lay motionless, silent and dark.

CHAPTER
9

The gleaming black needle-ships formed a ring with *Manta* at its hub. The space before and behind *Manta* was clear, but needle-ships aligned themselves above and beneath the yellow craft, as well as on both sides.

They approached Ceres at an angle, dropping from above the side of the disk that was in shadow.

"We'll have to make a night landing." Northrop handled the controls smoothly. *Manta*'s damaged wing caused little problem in vacuum. "I'd sure like to know what's on the daylight side—it looked exciting in the telescope!"

"I think that's the side we're going to land on." Babe Didrikson pointed ahead. "The planet's been turning. I think the other side is in sunlight now."

Northrop ran his hand over the top of his head. "You bet! I'm not thinking straight."

Josh Gibson's voice was reassuring. "Got to keep cool. Like Cool Papa Bell, right, Babe?"

Babe laughed. "You ever see Cool Papa, Jack?"

"Sure I have. Outfielder for Chicagos. A speed merchant."

"Right." Gibson grinned. "Papa 'n' I played in the minors together. He could handle anything. Some old-fashioned

99

towns, they still don't like the idea of blacks and whites playing on the same team, staying in the hotels, you know.

"Some of the boys, they either want to fight it out or else tuck tails 'n' run. Not Papa. He stays real cool. He keeps 'em cool. I never once saw him run from a fight in all the years I know that man, but I never saw him have to fight, either. He just so cool, so smart, so fast, he goes into any situation. Next thing you know it all worked out and there's Cool Papa on the other side, just sittin' and smilin' away."

Once on the night side of Ceres, the black needle-ships disappeared momentarily, then became visible again as ghostly running lights appeared, outlining them against the blackness.

Northrop switched on *Manta*'s own running lights.

Beyond Ceres the asteroid belt stretched like a miniature Milky Way Galaxy across the night sky.

On the surface of the planet, lights glowed as well. They crossed over cities that gleamed like clusters of gems. There was a demonic glow above a volcano. Red flames danced within the caldera, clouds of steam and smoke writhed above the cone, illuminated from beneath by glowing lava. Lightning flashed between the clouds and the volcano itself.

Manta and her escorts flew low over a sea where ships made luminous wakes.

All the time Northrop had been maintaining *Manta*'s flight path and conversing with Didrikson and Gibson, Albert Einstein had maintained a thoughtful silence behind the others.

Now he said, "I think it is time to land."

Northrop looked to the nearest needle-ship. The pilot had turned on cabin lights and was gesturing.

The central fissure of the planet lay dead ahead. Unlike earth's North Hole, with its deadly maelstrom, or the moon, with its electrical vortex, Ceres' central fissure appeared to be lined with titanic machinery.

But *Manta* would not investigate on this approach; the four travelers would not discover what lay in the center of Ceres. Not now.

The escorting needle-ships indicated emphatically that the *Manta* was to descend now.

Beneath the yellow craft lay desert land—dunes and oases. Although this was the night side of the planet, the desert was

illuminated by sunlight reflected off thousands of other asteroids that shared its wandering orbit far beyond that of Mars.
The light that impinged on the pale sands was like that of a
myriad miniature moons.

Manta moved so low that her shadow was visible beneath
her, or rather her multiplicity of shadows, cast by as many
sources as sent their light to the night side of Ceres.

A river wound its sluggish way beneath the craft: if Ceres
were a ghostly, alien Egypt, then this was the equivalent of
earthly Egypt's Nile.

A triangular peak loomed against the blacklit night sky.

"We in the land of Pharaoh now," Josh Gibson said.

"It's fantastic." Northrop had been babying *Manta* along.
Here, in normal atmospheric flight, the hole in her wing
caused by the shelling above luna, that had mattered little in
the vacuum of space, mattered a great deal.

Babe Didrikson stared through the bubble. *Manta* had
slowed. Northrop guided the craft around the pyramid—
Manta's altitude was lower than the peak of the structure.

"It's impossible," Babe whispered.

"Nein." Einstein patted her on the hand. "Impossible?
Ach, dear Miss Babe, you should try to avoid saying that.
Unlikely, yes. A strain on the poor human imagination with
its petty, petty limits. But not impossible. For you see it, do
you not? It is there."

He gestured.

More pyramids rose as *Manta* coasted slowly past them.
Her engines made a low, electrical whining sound. A few of
the massive structures showed tantalizing lights near their
bases, but it was not possible to tell who, or what, was there,
what was taking place.

"Oh, if only the reverend could see this." Gibson hummed
a soft passage from some hymn learned long, long ago.
"Reverend Riley, that was his name. Used to joke that he
was Irish, the original Black Irishman. Used to talk about
Pharaoh all the time, told us wonderful stories. Wonderful,
wonderful Bible stories. Daniel and his coat, and Moses in
the bullrushes and Pharaoh's daughter. Children of Israel in
bondage and the plagues and the parting of the Red Sea.
Wonderful, wonderful stories."

Manta slanted down onto a modern airstrip lined with standard beacons. The flying wing rolled to a stop, spot-lighted by brilliant beams.

Ground carts rolled across the tarmac, skidded to a stop on either side of the skyship. Uniformed troopers scrambled from the carts, surrounded the ship with weapons drawn and at the ready.

Jack Northrop powered down *Manta*. He looked at his companions. "They don't seem eager to come for us, but I don't see that we'll gain anything just sitting here. And I don't think they want us to leave."

He gestured through the clear bubble. Several of the black needle-ships, their shapes visible thanks to their running lights, circled overhead.

"Let's face the music," Babe said.

They clambered out of their flying wing. As he turned away to face the armed troopers, Northrop gave the ship an affectionate pat on its yellow skin. "Hope we'll see you again, baby. And get that bum flipper fixed."

The commander of the troopers—one they assumed to be the commander, based on his bearing of authority as much as the markings of his costume—stepped forward.

He didn't speak, but gestured toward the nearest ground cart.

They were driven to a low structure, taken inside, ushered to a comfortably furnished apartment, and left inside.

When the guardsmen left, Josh tried the door. "Locked." The others nodded.

They sat in a modern living room. Babe and Josh had located a well-stocked kitchen and rustled up a hot meal for them. They had discussed briefly the question of what meal it should be, settled on a post-midnight breakfast, and fixed bacon and eggs, toast and coffee, hash browns with onions.

Jack Northrop munched a piece of toast and sipped his coffee. The four of them had no formal organization; he was certainly not their commander in a military sense. But he was *de facto* captain of *Manta* and that made him, in effect, the leader of their expedition. Also, his connections in Washington placed him in a position to direct the group. But still . . .

"I'll have to admit that I'm baffled."

No one quarreled with that statement.

"Forcing us to land and locking us up like this is hardly a friendly act."

The others worked on their food, Didrikson and Gibson with gusto, Einstein with an air of distraction. The three seemed quite willing to let Northrop work on the problem while they listened and nodded and ate.

"On the other hand, they could have treated us a lot more harshly than they did. They could have destroyed us in the air, I think. Those black ships—gorgeous design, clean, efficient, I'd love to get at the controls of one—they look pretty deadly. I'm not certain that they're armed, but I'd bet a cartwheel that they are."

He grunted, "Huh," ran his hand over his head, poked at a bit of egg with his fork, and put it in his mouth. "They might have something else in mind for us."

Josh asked, "What?"

Northrop shrugged. "Who knows? Interrogation, perhaps. Some kind of hostage deal." He pushed his legs straight out in front of him, stretched his arms and rotated his neck to loosen up stiff muscles. He suddenly realized how weary and sore he was after the long journey that had started in the ballroom of the *City of Santa Barbara* so many miles and so few hours ago.

"Maybe," Babe put in, "they don't know what to do with us. And they're just stuck with us while they figure it out."

"What—what do you mean?"

She frowned in concentration. "We never knew these people were here, right?"

"Right."

"But they must have been in touch with our world. Look— just look!" She lifted her cup and saucer. "Just like home, right?"

Northrop nodded. The furnishings could have been thirty years old.

"And they're people just like us. Not Martians or anything." She stood up and walked to the window. The curtains were drawn but she pulled them away and stood looking out. Their quarters were on the side of the building away from the landing strip.

She looked onto the eerie scene of pyramids and sand dunes, a few scattered palm trees. Even in the moonless night the desert and the pyramids were lighted by a thousand asteroids and a million stars. "So desolate," she whispered. "Yet so beautiful."

She turned back to face the others. "They've been here all these years. And we saw their work on the moon, didn't we?"

"We did."

"Well, why? If they've been on earth all along, and nobody even knew about it, maybe they don't want us to know. Look at this stuff! That kitchen could have been my mom's back in Texas when I was a little girl. Big wooden icebox, iron stove, the coffeepot, and the frying pans." She waved her hands in frustration, heaved a great sigh. "Maybe we just got here by accident. You said we were off course, that something was wrong with our chart."

"My fault, Miss Babe." Einstein, silent until now, acknowledged.

"Well, whatever. I'm not blaming, Doc. I'm only saying, if we just kind of blundered in here uninvited and they don't want anybody to know about 'em, maybe they don't know *what* to do with us. Maybe they're, oh, keeping us cooled while they try and figure it out!"

"Then maybe we ought to make our move first," Northrop said. "Although I'm not sure what it should be."

Josh Gibson shook his head. "Think of Cool Papa. They taking nice care of us, got us fed and warm. I say, let's take showers, get a good sleep, and see what they got to say in the morning."

Northrop admitted that might be a good idea.

"Then you go ahead, Jack. You help the doctor, okay? Babe and I, we'll clean up the dishes."

They were summoned a few hours later.

Sunlight pouring into their quarters came from a tiny, remote sun almost a quarter billion miles away. It appeared weak, and the illumination it provided was not much brighter than moonlight; on Ceres, day and night were not very different. How life survived with so little nourishment was a puzzle, but they had more immediate concerns to occupy their attention.

They were ushered into an office and confronted by a swarthy individual wearing an old-fashioned suit of black wool, a white shirt, and striped necktie. He wore his gray hair cut short, his gray moustache neatly trimmed.

He looked up as they stood facing him.

His jaw dropped in amazement and he pulled his round, tortoiseshell glasses from his face.

"Dr. Einstein!"

He rushed around his desk, pulled a chair from its position near the wall, and slid it to Einstein. "Please, please."

The scientist allowed himself to be guided into the chair.

"Such an honor! I never dreamed—even when I was on earth—the famous Dr. Einstein!"

Flustered, the man backed away. He caught himself against his desk. He fumbled for his glasses, put them on again, then looked from Einstein to the others. "Uh, please, uh, do have seats."

He stood gazing at Einstein the way a schoolboy would look at Red Grange or Benny Goodman.

Then his face grew red. "Do forgive me, please. Ah—I am Colonel Selk. I welcome you to Khem-Ceres. I hope my people have been treating you with consideration. Are you comfortable? Is everything satisfactory? Have you had enough to eat? I didn't send anyone in to cook or serve. I thought you'd be happier if we didn't intrude, but if you would prefer—no? Good! Then, if you would please introduce yourselves—except for Dr. Einstein, of course."

The others gave their names, then Jack Northrop said, "Colonel Selk—is that it, Selk? Good. Colonel, I hardly know where to begin. We left earth on an urgent mission. We went off course and discovered we were heading for this planet. We had hoped to land here and make repairs on our ship—"

"Yes," Selk interrupted. "My people have looked over your craft. Very nice little design. The damage to the wing is fairly simple—whatever happened, you were very lucky. It should prove easy to correct. But you say you were off course, Mr. Northrop?"

Northrop explained the computational mistake.

"Ah, I see." Selk sat behind his desk, his elbows on the arms of his swivel chair, fingers laced beneath his chin. "But to come directly here? Of all the places in the solar system? Is this not a remarkable happenstance? Why not some unoccupied disk—there are enough of them around us!"

He laughed and gestured around the room, as if he were gesturing around the sky, indicating the thousands of bodies in the asteroid belt, as well as the planets and comets in their orbits. Then he leaned forward and fixed Northrop with a serious gaze. "Perhaps this is what Carl Jung would call a synchronicity. What do you think?"

Northrop was taken aback. "Jung?"

"C.J. Jung. Yes. Do I have it right, the name?"

"I—I've heard of him. But what—I mean . . ." He stopped to gather his thoughts.

Einstein said, "Colonel Selk, I was the one who made the error, yes, that brought us here. A Jungian synchronicity, perhaps. But no ill intentions were involved."

The colonel leaned back. "That's good enough for me, Doctor. All that it takes to satisfy me is your word."

"But, wait a minute." Northrop, more composed now, studied Colonel Selk. The man was older than he, closer to Einstein's age in fact. But despite his civilian garb, the military bearing was present in his every gesture. "I'm glad that you accept our *bona fides*, Colonel. But what of your own?"

"Eh?" Selk's steel-gray eyebrows rose.

"Your aircraft—apparently military aircraft—forced us down. We are an unarmed civilian expedition. We were taken into custody, locked up overnight, then brought in here as, in effect, prisoners."

"And—?"

"Why—at the very least, we demand an apology. We want to repair our ship and leave."

"Okay, I apologize." He grinned in self-congratulation at the idiom. "Your vehicle is already repaired."

Northrop relaxed in his chair.

"But before you leave, I think we will have to talk for a while. At the very least."

"That's fine with me. We're in a hurry, but there must be time to find some things out. For starters, what's going on here?"

Selk smiled. "You're surprised to find us here? To find what you would call an Egyptian nation on the asteroid Ceres? Our Khem."

"You bet."

"I have to admit that it's a bit of a puzzle to us as well. You see, we are a very old civilization."

"I know that!"

"Yes, of course. But have you any idea *how* old?"

"Six, seven thousand years."

"Yes, Mr. Northrop. You say it so easily. But have you any real grasp on what that means? How old, may I ask, is your own nation?"

"Let me see. It's 1942, take away 1776, that's . . ."

Selk laughed before Northrop could complete the mental computation. "Mr. Northrop, three thousand years ago my people were sending archaeological expeditions into the Nile Valley, to the edge of the Sahara Desert, studying sites that were already ancient three thousand years before. Can you comprehend?

"Please!" Selk held up his hands. "Please, don't treat these periods of time as mere numbers. Think about them. Think back. The discovery of your continent, the Renaissance in Europe, the period that your historians call the Middle Ages. What would you call that—from the sack of Imperial Rome to the new birth of enlightenment in Italy? How long was that period? Almost exactly a thousand years, I recall. *One* thousand years.

"Egypt was old, Mr. Northrop, *old* on the day that Caesar was murdered. Old when Romulus suckled at the wolf's teat. Old when Pericles spoke in Athens. Old, thousands of years old when Philip of Macedon strode the mountains of Greece.

"Old." He turned toward Einstein, the expression in his eyes changing once more from stern authority to almost worshipful respect. "Old when you people, sir, were our captives. We wronged you then."

"I wasn't there," Einstein said softly.

"Even so. Is time not an illusion, however stubborn a one?"

Einstein's craggy face showed a network of wrinkles as he chuckled. "You know my work!"

"I study it."

"I am flattered. Then perhaps you would answer for me a little question or two."

Colonel Selk bowed his head.

Now Einstein's manner lost its vagueness. Now he was not the dreamer, although he was no less the thinker.

"We seek consistency in the universe," he said.

" 'I shall never believe that God plays dice with the world,' " Colonel Selk quoted.

"Yes." Einstein stood and started pacing, his hands clasped behind his back. "We have, circling the sun, various planets: Mercury, Venus, Earth, Mars, and so on. Next comes the belt of asteroids, so-called. More correctly planetoids we should call them, but the other name is established. And so forth."

Selk nodded, made a vaguely encouraging sound in his throat.

"Whence came these asteroids? Do you know?"

Colonel Selk shrugged. "The familiar theories, Doctor—either an ancient planet that was destroyed, perhaps by warfare or some cosmic disaster. Or a planet that never was—the bits of primal debris, as they accreted in each successive orbit to make the planets—in this region, they failed. Your computations regarding gravitation might explain what happened here."

Einstein shook his head ruefully, his long hair flying. "Not yet. Not yet by far. Perhaps someday there will be an explanation." He slumped into his chair, fumbled in his pockets for his long-stemmed pipe and his tobacco. He concentrated on lighting the pipe, then gazed from the window of Selk's office.

Selk said, "Was there another question?"

Einstein was having a little think, perhaps trying to work out a gravitational explanation for the existence of the asteroids. But he looked at Selk, startled. "Eh?"

"Pardon. You said a question or two. Was there another?"

"Hmm. So we see the planets, yes. Many of them with their own families of moons, rings, you see? And each is unique. Mercury is alone in its orbit. Mars, in its. The planet has its moons, yes, but there is no other object that we can see in the Martian orbit."

He held his pipe by the bowl, gesturing with its stem, a small cloud of bluish smoke rising from the bowl. "Why is it that we now learn of Counter-Earth? The planet, we are told, resembles ours in every way. It has its own moon. It is populated. The people there have built radios and call to us, they know somehow of us, and they send us messages.''

He gestured for emphasis. ''In our own languages!'' He paused. ''Now, how can this be? Why is one planet treated so specially? Why has only one world a doppelgänger? If all planets had them, one could devise easily a theory to explain this doubling. Several such, in fact.

''But only one.'' Now he looked and sounded wistful, like a child baffled by some minor and inexplicable tragedy in its life. ''Why only one?'' he asked, and again, ''Why only one?''

Colonel Selk nodded solemnly. ''Yes, I can answer that question, Doctor. And in the course also answer Mr. Northrop's questions about our presence here. Some he failed to ask but I am certain''—he faced Northrop—''he was sure to ask in time.

''Dr. Einstein, Mr. Northrop, Miss Didrikson, Mr. Gibson—we do not know where we originated. You know the Egyptians on earth. Have you seen pyramids and sphinxes on the moon—on earth's moon?''

''We sure have!'' Josh told him.

Selk went to the door, spoke softly to an aide, returned to the others. ''We should have refreshments,'' he said.

''We don't know our own origins! That, Mr. Northrop, is why I made such a point of the age of our civilization. We have lost our own antiquity! Did we originate on earth, then colonize the moon and this planet? Or did we originate here and colonize the earth? Or elsewhere altogether, on a planet circling some distant star?''

He gazed out the window. Even in Khem-Ceres' morning brightness, such as it was, the sky was dark and the stars were visible.

''Our scholars love to quarrel over this, but no one really knows. Perhaps ten thousand years ago, perhaps two or three times that—no one knows—our ancestors may have landed here from their true home. We built well on earth, on Ceres, on luna. We have long chronicles, but they are not long enough. Somewhere they fade out.

''Why is that? No one knows.'' His voice was a litany of old grief, a loss so ancient that even the memory of it was nearly gone. Nearly.

"Did we destroy ourselves in war? Was the desert of Africa once a fertile valley? I think it was. I fear that our ancestors are responsible for the terrible wastes that now exist. My people, Dr. Einstein.

"This I do know—this we recall. I recall personally. We withdrew from the affairs of the world. An elite, an inner elite of the people of Khem. We left the earth. The people who live in ancient Khem, which you call Egypt—these are Semites. Arabs. Some Nubians. But we are a different people.

"We withdrew to our base on the moon. There we could live, and here on Ceres, Khem-Ceres. We did this centuries ago, but we felt a responsibility for the people of earth. We had given them much of their civilization, and we were horrified by the march of their history.

"Finally we saw what we believed was the supreme menace to the planet. You know of a land called Svartalheim?"

Northrop nodded. "We don't like the reports that came back from there in 1927. There isn't much commerce yet, between the two sides of the planetary disk. But Svartalheim is a frightening nation."

Selk nodded. "Yes. We believed we had found a weapon that could end the threat. We did not want to destroy them. We had built a machine that we could train on their land from here—from Ceres! It would be focused, amplified, and aimed by a great electronic lens we had created."

"Created? Where?" Northrop asked.

Selk shook his head sadly. "We used the central fissure of luna."

Northrop pursed his lips. He asked, "With what result?"

Selk sighed. "It was intended to . . . neutralize weapons. Calm dispositions. To make peace."

"What went wrong?"

"I don't know. It was a very advanced weapon. If 'weapon' is even the right term for it. It would respond to neural codes. It—we were too eager, Mr. Northrop! They had allies, the Svartalheimers. Ancient relatives elsewhere. In Europe. The world was imperiled. We hurried our testing. We used it too soon."

"What happened, man? Come on!"

"It somehow—it isn't my field, I'm not a specialist—it

somehow failed. It created a submolecular vibration. Doubling and halving, doubling and halving. The energy was titanic. It was . . . Instead of having the effect we intended, the earth absorbed the energy we poured into it and—and replicated itself. Everything! Continents, oceans, ice caps. The crust, the magma, the very core of the earth.

"And the people, every last one of them. Every piece of paper. Every bit of clothing. Every house. Airplanes, even as they flew. And every living thing. Fish a mile beneath the sea, birds soaring above mountains, every tree, every veldt, every bacterium living in the belly of an earthworm buried in the soil. Everything. Instantaneously. Flashing one hundred eighty degrees to the opposite position. The earth, the moon, everything upon them. Suddenly there were two instead of one.

"What had we done? What cosmic balance had we ruined? We didn't know. We still don't. Two identical earths—only now you wish to travel from the one to the other. Dare we permit you? Dare we prevent you?

"We do not know!"

Silence. One could hear the breaths drawn in the room. A clock ticking away on a mantelpiece was suddenly audible in the hush. Tick-tick-tick-tick.

The silence was broken by Einstein's question. "Colonel Selk, when did this happen?"

Before the other could respond, the refreshments he had ordered arrived. The door opened to admit an aide pushing a cart with coffee and rolls.

No one spoke until the aide departed, but no one took anything from the polished silver trays before hearing the answer to Einstein's question.

Colonel Selk looked at the savant with great dark eyes, eyes marked with grief and ancient guilt. "It was October 4 by your calendar. By ours, of course, another date, another time, another whole system of measuring time. But by your calendar I remember clearly, more clearly than I wish I did. October 4, 1912."

CHAPTER
10

" 'Nothing can possibly imperil us,' " Evita mocked the German. "I'm happy to see *Patrilandia* functioning so well!" Her eyes flashed with anger.

Horten flicked toggles and turned knobs without effect.

"Well, Herr Inventor, Herr Genius?"

He ignored her but she continued to taunt him. A line of red crept from Horten's collar toward his hairline.

Evita continued to taunt.

Finally Horten whirled with a hiss of breath and swept a bony backhanded slap to Eva Duarte's face.

Her eyelids flew open, her mouth gaped. She lifted her hand to feel her cheek, where an angry redness began to appear.

Horten's body was propelled backward as if an invisible hand had crunched into his belly. He struck the inside of the crew bubble with a thump and fell to the floor. He pushed himself to his hands and knees, shook his head, muttering, then climbed back to his feet. He glared at Evita, then turned his back.

She slumped into her seat, breathing in short, shallow gasps, the aftermath of the incident. She held her hand to her face. She felt as if she had just come through the kind of dusty free-for-all she had fought a decade earlier as a barefoot child in the streets of Junín. She had always held her own in those rough-and-tumble encounters, and she had given better than she got today. A warm feeling of satisfaction crept through her belly. It was a better sensation by far than she had ever experienced after a sexual encounter.

The grin on her face concealed more than it explained to the others.

Patrilandia was brightly illuminated by the sun shining through her transparent bubble, so it was of no concern that the ship's own lights had failed along with her engines and instruments. Nor would there be an alternation of day and night in this situation—if anything, there was a danger of overheating if the ship were stuck for very long. But that was of no immediate concern.

More puzzling was what had happened—and what could be done about it.

The ship was unmoving and unworking, but there was no visible sign of damage and no indication of what had stopped her.

"Perhaps one of us ought to take a little look outside," Mosley offered.

Perón looked out. "You will fall."

Mosley stood beside Perón. "The ship is not falling."

"What's holding it up, then?"

Perón shrugged massive shoulders.

Mosley raised his eyebrows. "I don't know either, old boy. But whatever it is, if it can hold a skyship, it can certainly sustain the weight of one old warbird. Game leg and all!"

"You are volunteering, then, Sir Oswald?"

Mosley hesitated. It had not been his original intention to, but it looked as if he'd put his foot in it now. His good foot, at that! "I'm certainly willing, Major. But I wonder if Herr Horten might not do a better job of it. I'm just an old kite jockey, don't you see? More than willing to give it a peep, but Herr Horten is the engineer. I suspect he might do a better job of it, eh?"

Horten had recovered from his thump against the bubble. His face had gone from crimson to ice-white, but had now returned to normal. A fleck of foam appeared at one corner of his mouth; he leaned against the panel, his knuckles white, his face expressionless. "There is nothing to see. There is nothing to investigate. The *Patrilandia* is in perfect order. There is nothing wrong with this vehicle. Nothing.''

He turned back to the control panel and continued to work at it. The results—or lack of results—remained unchanging.

Perón and Mosley exchanged significant glances. They retreated to a far corner of the cabin. Eve Duarte remained in her seat in a posture of fatigue. She dozed lightly.

Perón nodded toward Horten. ''I suppose he is correct, Sir Oswald. To all indications, *Patrilandia* is undamaged. But if she refuses to respond, we remain stuck here, no?''

Mosley moved his head. ''Yes. Precisely so.''

''In that case,'' Perón said, ''one of us had better investigate. Since it was your idea, Sir Oswald, I will defer to you.'' He extended his hand toward *Patrilandia*'s hatch.

Mosley checked the condition of his flying suit. Everything was proper; he would be warm and dry outside *Patrilandia*, protected from minor impacts should there be any. But the breathing apparatus was not functioning. He could go for a while with the air he had in the suit itself, but not for very long.

He looked at his wristwatch, then held it to his ear. It had ceased to function.

Perón checked his own watch. It, too, had stopped.

Dropping to one knee, Perón opened a supply chest at the rear of the cabin. He extracted a rope ladder and carried it to *Patrilandia*'s hatch, attaching it to the outside of the bat-ship's mottled skin.

''Climb down this,'' he suggested to Mosley. ''See if you can breathe outside. I would have expected a vacuum here—''

''So would I,'' Mosley agreed.

''—but now, who knows? There could be anything.''

Mosley swallowed, crawled over the edge of the hatch and part of the way down the ladder. He looked beneath his feet and saw the blackness of space and the unblinking brightness of the distant stars. Holding to the ladder with one hand, he opened his altitude mask with the other. He inhaled. ''Amazing, Perón! It's perfectly good air! A trifle damp, almost like a Staffordshire mist, but perfectly good.''

''And can you see anything? What is the ship resting on?''

Mosley descended farther. As he approached the end of

the rope ladder, he seemed to encounter a mushiness. It wasn't as if he were standing on a solid surface—more like that same Staffordshire mist. The deeper he descended into it, the more it seemed to thicken and compress beneath his feet, until it held his weight in a spongy, springy sort of way.

As he lowered himself, the mistiness thickened visibly as well as tangibly. He fancied himself a character in a Conan Doyle novel, crossing a fog-shrouded moor, waiting for a hound with blazing eyes and dripping fangs to leap upon him.

He shuddered, then shook himself back to reality.

He looked back up at the bat-ship and Juan Perón leaning over the edge of the hatch, watching him.

"I'm going to let go and take a few steps now," Mosley called up to Perón.

Alarmed, Perón said, "No! You will fall and be lost!"

"No, I won't. This will hold me."

"There is nothing there!"

Mosley halted momentarily. He looked up again. "What do you see beneath me, Perón?"

"Nothing. There is nothing."

"But I see it."

He let go of the rope ladder. For a moment his muscles tensed as he sank more deeply into the spongy mist, but then he regained his balance and stood looking at *Patrilandia*. "I'm all right, Perón. I'm going off to explore a bit. Don't worry."

He had to force himself to take the first few steps. It was a frightening sensation until he became accustomed to it, but soon he got the knack of it and found it exhilarating. He could bounce in the stuff, jump into the air and sink into it up to his knees, then spring back and walk around. He tried to pluck a handful but came away with nothing in his hand.

He had to keep *Patrilandia* in sight: that was vital! There were no landmarks in this stuff, no signposts. He might count paces if he walked in a straight line, then reverse his course to return to the ship, but that was a risky business, one that he did not wish to attempt. A miscalculation, a slight error in direction, and he could become hopelessly lost.

Yet something did seem to loom nearby, a shape so vague in the mist that he wasn't even certain that it was there. He peered at it, leaning toward it. It might be a structure, something with broad walls and pointed towers. He took a few steps toward it but it wasn't there.

He retreated toward *Patrilandia*. His foot slipped, or seemed to. It was his game leg, though, and he'd had occasional problems; maybe this was just the leg acting up because of the odd, springy footing. He knelt, tried to feel a solid surface, something that might have felt slippery. There was nothing. He pulled the glove from one hand. In the mist his fingers felt cold. And, yes, there was something. Or he thought there was. Something cold, slippery. He couldn't get a grip on it. He crouched down, lowering his face, trying to get a look at whatever it was.

Only whiteness.

He lay belly-down. The mist was chilling, moist, heavy in his lungs, but not unpleasant. He moved his arms and legs. Stranger and stranger. He could swim in the stuff. It would be pleasant to doff his altitude gear, to strip to his shorts and swim freely, but the mist was too cold for that.

He turned his face.

Something had brushed against him in the whiteness.

Something had—that is, he thought something had—brushed against him in the whiteness. He was sure it had. No, he was almost sure that it had.

He shut his eyes and shook his head, then opened his eyes again. He was able to roll in the mist, roll over on his back, see the vague olive shape of *Patrilandia* looming above him, the rope ladder hanging over her side.

He backstroked a few yards, rolled again, drew himself up, and sat cross-legged in the mist. It was really very pleasant. It would be even pleasanter to sit like this at a campfire with good companions at his side, a hot brandy in his hand.

Something stalked past him, a figure he was almost certain was human. Shrouded in white, vague at the edges, but upright, human. "Perón?" he said.

But it was gone.

Something touched him. He stared at the thing. It was almost formless, yet not formless. It was made of strands and organs that he couldn't make out; it writhed. When it touched him, touched his cheek, it was cold and slimy. But he put his hand to his cheek; it came away dry. There was nothing there.

He thought he heard a whispering. He couldn't make out

the words, or even the language. The sound was mixed with
a kind of slithering, as of wet creatures moving against one
another. He couldn't see them, only the white.

He thought he'd better get up and walk again, but he found
it more natural to resume his swimming progress. The mist
wasn't any less cold, but somehow this bothered him less
than it had; he shucked his second glove and his boots. Yes,
he could swim more easily this way, and more pleasantly.
The feel of the mist against his skin was pleasant. It was very
pleasant.

But feeling it on his hands and feet wasn't enough. Not
nearly so. He tugged his flier's helmet off, then his jacket,
his heavily padded trousers. He was completely naked, and
the mist felt wonderful against his skin.

He tucked his head down to his chest, hunched his shoulders over, plunged his hand downward. He was back in Staffordshire again, learning to swim in the brook. At the deepest
point he had loved surface diving, holding his breath and
swimming straight for the bottom and exploring for old coins
and cups in the silt.

His father had told him that the family estate had once been
a Roman outpost, and he had actually retrieved a Roman
denarius of solid silver; it hung, matted and framed, in his
childhood room to this very day.

Now he plunged straight down into the delicious white
mist, pulling with his arms, kicking with his strong leg, letting the weak one rest.

He heard himself scream as the mist gave way to blackness. He emerged headfirst, saw the distant stars beneath him.
If he continued a few feet farther, he would tumble away,
tumble forever into the infinite cold and dark.

But it wasn't so. He stopped, panting, pulled himself to
one knee again. He was disoriented. He was on the white
surface. Above him blackness stretched away forever, blackness sparkling with stars and galaxies, nebulae and streamers
of cosmic plasma.

There was no sun.

There was no *Patrilandia*.

There was no Staffordshire.

He experienced an overwhelming urge to weep.

He threw himself back into the whiteness. He began to

swim, but the consistency of the white stuff was thicker than ever, and he had trouble moving his—he couldn't remember their name.

It was hard to breathe.

He found that he could move more comfortably by simply wriggling, sending waves of muscular contractions along the length of his body. He could make his progress through the . . .

He could make progress by thrusting himself forward, segment by segment. It felt good around him. All around him. He could move. That was his only thought. Forward. Forward. Inching forward. Moving forward in the comfortable, the . . .

It wasn't there.

The . . . wasn't there. He tried to probe forward, but it wasn't around him anymore, not there, nothing there. He probed, groping for it to one side, to another. Somehow he found it, felt a great sense of relief pass through him.

He could extend his body forward, extend a pseudopod, draw himself forward, reabsorb the pseudopod, become fully himself again. Then the process recommenced. Laboriously, he moved. He was not bothered by the slowness of his pace, the laboriousness of his progress. He simply moved forward.

When he encountered more places where there was nothing, he simply changed direction, moving at random, extending, moving, reabsorbing.

When that became too troublesome, he simply lay in place, letting the chemistry of his molecules maintain itself, maintain himself, simply lying where he was.

"How long has he been gone?" Juan Perón asked even as he looked at his wristwatch. He cursed when he realized that the watch had stopped—he had known that, but forgotten.

He started over. "He has been gone too long. Something has happened. I should have made him wear a lifeline, like a diver."

"Too late for that now." Reimar Horten had finally come away from *Patrilandia*'s controls. "Mosley is gone. British trash, good riddance to him. He was a defective specimen anyway."

"He is our associate!"

"Kaput."

"He is out there."

"Lost."

"We must find him."

"Tod und weg. You understand me? Dead and gone. We have another problem. *Patrilandia* is in perfect condition. We are caught in a zone of disruption, of mechanical stasis. Your wristwatch is conclusive proof of that. Nothing works here— no machine, no mechanically powered process. So, how are we to leave?"

"Sir Oswald may help." Besides, Mosley was important to Perón. Britain was too influential by far in the affairs of the Argentine Republic. The governments of Monckton and Baldwin were too friendly with the Colossus for Perón's Taste, and by far too demanding in their attitude toward Argentina. The fool Ramírez and his predecessors for the past half century had been too soft on Britain and the extension of British influence. All else aside, the festering problem of the Malvinas poured slow poison into the veins of the Republic. And Chile, across the Andes, remained an ever-present threat.

A government in Britain headed by Sir Oswald Mosley would attend more toward Britain's own problems at home and leave the other nations of the world to settle their own problems. And such a government would be most friendly to a future Argentina ruled by Juan Perón.

What lay on Counter-Earth could be exploited, an alliance could be struck, but Oswald Mosley was an important instrument in the hands of Major Perón. He must be controlled. The obvious attraction held for him by Eva Duarte—and for her by Oswald Mosley—could be used for that purpose.

But certainly, so useful a tool as Oswald Mosley was not to be abandoned simply because a German *revanchista* harbored a dislike for all things English.

"He is my friend," Perón said to Horten. "A hero of the One Year War and a dedicated champion of his people. I will never abandon a friend. We must find him."

Horten made a sound of disgust. "Go, then. Find him if you can. Tie a lifeline to your own waist if you wish."

He turned away to study the *Mekkanopantograf,* but the low, rectangular chamber was vacant and dark. He opened a drawer beneath the box and removed a binder. He spread it on his lap, turned from page to page studying his own blue-prints and technical instructions concerning *Patrilandia*.

Perón faced away. "Evita," he said. *"Querida. Favor."*

Eva Duarte had been dozing. He touched her arm and she wakened with a start. Her neck was stiff and her muscles did not feel well. "What do you want, Pocho?"

Perón knelt beside her and spoke softly. He explained the situation with Mosley. Evita's eyes widened when she realized that the Englishman was lost outside *Patrilandia*.

She pushed herself erect and started toward the still-open hatch. She felt lightheaded and weak. Slowly she regained her strength. This had never happened to her before. She was frightened by the sensation.

She leaned over the edge of *Patrilandia*'s hull, following with her eyes the rope ladder that Mosley had used. She could see, but her vision was lacking the precise clarity to which she had been accustomed all her life. She was developing a problem with her eyes. Perhaps this was what astigmatism was like. She thought of Reimar Horten's ugly wire specta-cles, their thick lenses, the repulsive appearance that their distortions gave to his face. She shivered.

"Do you see the same as I?" Perón asked her.

"I see only darkness. Blackness, emptiness, and stars." She turned away. "The sun above. Or would Engineer Horten say, beside us?"

The German ignored her jibe.

"Evita," Perón said. "One of us must look for Sir Os-wald. I would go, but after what happened"—he shifted meaningfully—"you must not remain alone with our Horten. And we cannot both search for him." He dropped his voice to little above a whisper. "In case he gets the engines started. We might all find ourselves abandoned here."

Evita drew back, looked him full in the face. "There is nothing there!" She pointed down. "Nothing! One would fall, be lost."

Perón shook his head. "The ship is sustained. It is far heavier than a human."

"Different. Different. Where is Sir Oswald? Falling for-ever!"

"No! No, he is not! I saw him with my own eyes. When he left *Patrilandia*, when he reached the bottom of the ladder.

He felt around with his foot. I saw him. There is some invisible medium outside, beneath us. He leaped about like a child. Then he started away. I lost sight of him—he went too far— but he is somewhere nearby. This will hold you up.''

She hummed to herself. ''But you cannot go alone. Or with me. Evita must take this risk.''

''It is no risk! Look, *querida*, my dove, we will tie a lifeline to your waist. If you become lost, you can follow it back. Or tug. We can arrange signals, like a deep-sea diver. One tug means all well, two tugs to mean you wish to return. Just wait then, and I'll haul you in like a big fish. You know how strong I am.''

He flexed his biceps, took her hand and placed it on a straining muscle. ''I will be your protector! Nothing can possibly imperil you! My pledge! My sacred oath!''

She rubbed her cheeks with the palms of her hands. Her skin felt dry to her, like the skin of her mother as she remembered her. Her mother, who still lived in Junín, still ran her guesthouse there. Something wonderful had happened to her in the Temple of Isis, but something terrible also.

''Look at me, Perón. Look at my face.''

He obeyed silently.

''Am I the same?''

''Of course, Evita *mía*.''

She shut her eyes. ''You are a terrible liar. Something is wrong.''

''Nothing is wrong.''

''You wish me to go after the English?''

''Please.''

''You will tire of me. You will desert me.''

''Never, I swear.''

''I will do as you wish.''

He began to rummage for a lifeline to attach to her flying costume, but she stopped him with a movement of her hand.

She clambered over the lip of the hatch, made her way down the rope ladder. As she descended, she felt the springy texture of the mist and saw it thicken about her ankles. She swung from the bottom rung of the rope ladder. Although she wore the heavy costume of the space flier, she felt as light as a bit of fluff carried on a breeze.

When she held her hand aloft, she could see two images

of herself. One was that of the flier, jacketed and gloved, bulky, heavy, clumsy. The other was that of the goddess, slim and graceful, weightless, her skin glowing with beauty and strength beneath her nearly transparent gown.

She turned to wave at Perón. He stood in *Patrilandia*'s hatch, looking after her with worry on his face. He blew a kiss after her.

She glided away. The mist swirled around her heavily booted ankles; her lightly sandaled feet barely touched the top of the mist.

The whiteness thickened.

She came to a hole in it. Through the hole she could see the blackness of infinity marked by the pinpoints of distant suns.

Heavily booted as she was, weighted down by her padded flying suit, she was barely able to jump across the opening.

Thinly sandaled as she was, gossamer-light in her thin, caressing gown, she floated across the opening with ease.

As she progressed, *Patrilandia* shrank to a miniature, then to a speck, then disappeared. She was unworried. She knew that when the time came to return, she would find the ship without difficulty.

She crossed unmeasured distances of whiteness, uncounted openings in the thick mist.

When she found Oswald Mosley, he was lying motionless. He had managed somehow to gather shreds of the white mist into a nest for himself, and had curled into it like a sled dog in the highest reaches of the snow-peaked Andes. His eyes were shut, his hands clasped around his shoulders, his knees drawn up against his chest. His breathing was shallow and slow, like that of a creature in hibernation.

She tried to lift him in her clumsy gloved hands, but he was by far too heavy for her.

She lifted him in her naked arms, cradled him to her bosom as a mother would cradle an infant. He sighed and snuggled against her.

With easy, gliding steps she moved across the face of the mist, carrying Mosley in her arms. When she came to gaps in the whiteness, she floated gracefully over them, moving with slowness so she could gaze down into the blackness and feel the greatness of the distance involved, the beauty of the stars streaming away and away into the dark.

Blomberg had told her that as light traveled from its source to the eye, it moved at a definite speed. He had told her that all of the stars, even the nearest, were so distant from the earth that it took years for the light to reach us. That the farthest star was so distant that its light had been traveling for hundreds of thousands of years, that it had left the star when giant mylodons had roamed the plains of Patagonia and Tehuelche Indians nine feet tall built campfires of driftwood to light the long wintry nights of the Tierra del Fuego.

She handed Mosley up into *Patrilandia*'s bubble, then followed.

CHAPTER
11

"Marvelous! Marvelous!"

The ordinarily sedentary Einstein paced the cabin of *Manta*, long-stemmed pipe in mouth, hands clasped behind his back, eyes half closed and raised to the stars above *Manta*'s transparent bubble.

"You're right about that, Doctor." Josh Gibson agreed with the savant. "I've been in the land of Pharaoh! I'll tell 'em everything when I get back home. Won't they be amazed? Won't they be astonished?"

Einstein directed a thoughtful glance at Gibson. "Perhaps there will be more time, someday. I would like to return to the land of Khem. I would like to learn more of the machine that turned one earth into two earths. Creating matter from energy! Such an achievement!"

He turned a seat on its swivel and sat down, gazing through the side of the bubble. "And now we know when the two earths began to diverge. On October 4, 1912. Before you were born, Joshua. Or Miss Babe. But I was already a man of thirty-three years. And Mr. Northrop was how old? A young student at the *Gymnasium*, not so?"

Northrop turned from *Manta*'s controls. The damage to her wing had been repaired on Khem-Ceres; the ship was performing perfectly. Northrop said, "I was sixteen years old.

Dreaming around the campus at Santa Barbara High School. A few of the teachers were interesting, but mostly I couldn't keep my mind on my work. Much too busy dreaming about airplanes.''

''Just so! If you were as poor a student as I, you must have been a trial.''

''I was!''

''But look,'' Babe broke in. ''I'll admit, I didn't pay too much attention to that Colonel Selk. Or maybe I didn't understand him very well.''

Einstein nodded.

''I'm not sure about some of what he said,'' she continued. ''He claims that there was only one earth until 1912, is that right?''

Einstein grunted assent.

''And they *made* the second one?''

''Well, you could say that. Yes. They were trying to control the Svartalheimers with a kind of energy beam. Something wrong they did. The energy they poured into the earth—it took on the molecular configuration of the planet. And the moon, too. And—ping!—Counter-Earth.''

''Huh! So the other earth is just a sort of copy of ours, is that it?''

Einstein cocked his head to one side. ''Maybe.''

''We're not sure?''

Einstein smiled. ''Maybe the other earth was the original, no? And our earth is Counter-Earth. How can you tell which is which?''

Babe sputtered. ''Look at me!'' She plucked at her sleeve with her other hand. She stood up and went to Einstein. ''Here! You see?'' She held her hand in front of him.

''Oh, you are as real as I am, Miss Babe. As real as this wonderful machine in which we are riding. As real as the other Miss Babe on the other earth. But which is the original? Hmm?''

The savant's brow wrinkled in contemplation. ''But, in fact, I let myself forget that you were born after 1912.'' He shook his unruly mane. ''A foolish *Alte* I have become, silly and forgetful.'' He looked up. ''No. You must forgive me.''

Babe waited for him to continue.

''You are the original Mildred Didrikson. You were born.''

He turned to address Joshua Gibson. "And you also, my brother. Is that not so?"

"No sir," Gibson said. "I was born December 21, 1911. Got it in the family Bible, right there. My mama showed me that."

"Aha! That is even more interesting, then, if we could but know Miss Didrikson's birth date."

Babe stuck out her jaw. "We were poor folks in east Texas. We were a big family. My mama and papa always tried to keep a record."

"*Ach*, yes. And the year? It is not polite to ask this of a lady, I know, but you will forgive me, I hope."

Babe's truculence dissolved in laughter. "Who said I was a lady? June 26, 1914, that'll do as good as any date for me. My mama does say that it was summertime."

"Very well. That is very good, and most interesting," Einstein resumed. "You see, since you were born after October 4, 1912, we know that you were actually born. You are not just a duplicate, however real."

"I don't get it," Babe protested. "What's the diff? Are you saying that some people are real and others aren't?"

"*Ach, ach, ach*. I say things sometimes not simply enough. The truth is always simple, and we only confuse ourselves when we do not see it clearly."

He paced the cabin the way he sometimes paced a classroom. He halted and gazed at the stars, the expression in his eyes as far away as the shining points themselves.

He turned back to face the others. Northrop had locked *Manta*'s controls. With Gibson and Didrikson, he made a trio of students. Einstein smiled, thinking of Bern, of Zürich, of Prague, and of students he had addressed in those cities. Always the minds eager to be filled and to be stimulated, always the challenge of seeing the beauty and simplicity that lay at the heart of God's work, always the task of grasping the patterns and expressing them so others could comprehend!

"How do we know," he began, "how old the earth is? Do we know? We used to think it was a few thousand years old, is it not so?

"But as we studied our planet, we learned better. We learned a little how rocks are made. We found some old bones, we discovered how to measure their age by carbon.

We wondered how the sun could burn and burn and never burn out, so we had to figure out a thing or two about nuclei.

"Always this." He tapped his forehead. "Maybe the beasts are better off. They live only in the moment; they think only of their surroundings, their food, their mates, their homes."

He heaved a sigh. "*Ach*, but the good God, he gave us such brains in these noodles, we wonder, and we think, and so we have to try and figure things out. So . . ."

With the knuckles of one hand he rubbed the bottom of his jaw. "So," he resumed, "by examining the physical evidence, by making measurements, by computing, you see, we figure things out. Is that not so, Mr. Northrop?"

Jack nodded. He didn't want to interrupt this private lecture by the world's greatest mind.

"So, the bishops and the roughnecks who say they know the age of things exactly, and it is just a few thousand years—we leave them to themselves. But we know that the earth is many, many millions of years old. Do you see this?"

He waited for them to nod. These were more like his students at Pasadena or at Princeton, not so much like the ones in Europe. All right.

"You see? We do not know this because a bishop told it or because the Bible says it. Pardon me, Mr. Gibson. We know things by an examination of physical evidence and the use of mathematical proofs."

He stopped and raised a finger.

"But suppose, as one preacher suggested, God had planted all the evidence just to play a little trick on us. He made an iceberg in Siberia and put a mammoth inside it. He planted trees in the redwood forest and made them with rings for a thousand years. He stuck sharks' teeth in the desert to make us think this once was ocean. He buried dinosaurs' bones in Canada to make us think monsters once walked here.

"Why?" He shrugged. "Just a joke, *ja*? But if God did this, put everything in place to make us think the world is very old, but he really made it just today, how could we tell? We remember our lives. But God created us with memories already. We go to the library and see old newspapers. But God put them there. You see? Whatever proof we seek, we can find. But God can fake anything. So we have to assume that God does not play such tricks on us. We have to believe the evidence of our senses. And we know how old the world must be—at least approximately.''

Einstein paused and Josh Gibson spoke up. "But if the world is really all that old, and Pharaoh's machine made another one just like it, then everything'd be there, too! Old newspapers, dinosaurs' bones, everything! People there'd be brand new but they'd think they been there all along!"

Jack Northrop said, "What about the ephemeris? All the tables would be wrong. All the planets would be one hundred and eighty degrees out of position!"

"Ach, sicherlich!"

"And all our ephemerides are correct."

"So we know which earth is the original one." Einstein glowed. "You have solved the problem, Mr. Northrop. I congratulate you! And Miss Didrikson, you now can rest easy. You are the original Miss Didrikson. If there is another of you on Counter-Earth, though, you must understand, she is also real. Her world was created on October 4, 1912, but it was created already as old as ours—and identical to it. But any changes there, you see, can only have started with that date."

"There are changes," Northrop volunteered.

"Ja?"

"There have to be. If their ephemerides are wrong, they'll know something's phony. They'll have to try and figure it out. My guess is, that's why they've been radioing us. But I wonder—is there another Jack Northrop on the other earth? Is there another *Manta* in space, on its way to our earth?"

He closed his eyes to help him concentrate. Then, "I don't think there is. They radioed because there's something wrong and they're calling for help. That's why we're headed for their world. There was no reason for anybody on our world to suspect Counter-Earth was there. Even Charley Avison's ideas were just a sort of intellectual conceit. Our ephemerides are right, everything looks right to us. So we didn't try to call them, and they didn't send a ship to visit us."

Babe said, "What about those stinkers on the moon?"

"Those stinkers on the moon—I wish I'd got a better look at their craft. I only caught a glimpse of it—everything was going on so fast. It looked familiar to me. If I could just get another look at it. . . ."

"But you're sure they're from our world, Jack? You don't think they came from the other earth?"

He shook his head. "I'm sure they didn't. Maybe there's a Jack Northrop on Counter-Earth and maybe he's still working for the Lockheed brothers, designing airplanes. And maybe Cordell Hull is back in Virginia practicing law and Alf Landon is still President. But that bat-winged baby—no, it wouldn't have been waiting at the moon to ambush us."

He gazed through the Plexiglas, scanning the sky ahead of *Manta*, looking for the blue and white of Counter-Earth. "I'm almost certain that the ship came from our world. Almost certain."

Josh Gibson also stood looking through the Plexiglas. But he wasn't just looking for Counter-Earth. "You wanted another look at that bat thing, Mr. Northrop. I think you gonna get it."

He pointed behind *Manta*.

Northrop moved to follow Gibson's pointing arm. He drew in a quick breath. "Everybody strap in, fast!"

He dropped into the pilot's seat and unlocked *Manta*'s controls. He swung the yellow skyship through a roll so she was again moving on the same course she had been, but inverted in attitude.

It only took a moment for Northrop and the others to reorient themselves. Briefly they felt that they were flying upside down, strapped into their seats, hanging from the ceiling, which had previously been the floor, in imminent danger of crashing through the transparent deck and plunging into blackness.

Then they were right side up, the transparent bubble over them, the solid deck beneath.

There was no hiding in the sun for them, not this time. The blaze and glare were the remote terminus of an acute triangle; *Manta* and a fast-closing speck represented the triangle's base.

"It's that same bat-thing that almost got us before!" Josh Gibson's fingers curled in frustration: one of the world's great athletes and great competitors, but there was nothing he could do in this situation.

Jack Northrop swung *Manta*'s telescope toward the distant ship. A growling noise came from his throat.

Babe asked, "You recognize it? You know who that is?"

Northrop nodded, made more grumbling sounds. "I can't see who's in there, but I know that ship by its outlines. Some of the finest aircraft designers in the world—especially the Horten brothers. They were working in Germany. Ernst Udet sponsored them, and young Herbert Bismarck."

He looked away from the telescope. "After 1927—you two were just kids then, weren't you?"

Didrikson and Gibson exchanged a look. "But we both remember," Babe said. "Lindbergh and Earhart and Hughes. And Jax Bullard. How they won the big circumpolar air race against the Germans and the Russian princess. It was in all the news. They were everybody's heroes."

Northrop nodded. "After the uproar quieted, German aviation got a bad name. Too many dirty tricks, too much political double-dealing. And we remembered the One Year War. Nobody wanted to face another war like that, with Germany stronger than ever and better prepared to fight."

He turned to Einstein. "I'm sorry, Doctor. I don't mean to condemn all Germans."

Einstein's eyebrows rose. *"Ich komme aus New Jersey."*

The others laughed.

The savant said, "I was stripped of my German citizenship when Ernst Röhm became chancellor. So strange it was. Years earlier I had become a Swiss citizen instead, but after 1912 the German government invited me back, and I accepted. Then when Röhm and his bullies took over, I was very lucky. I was visiting then in Belgium. Giving a paper, I was. Never have I gone back. You know how my dossier is marked in the ministry? *Noch ungehängt.* They have a rubber stamp with that. *Noch ungehängt.* In English, that means, 'not yet hanged.' "

Gibson said, "Just because you're a Hebrew?"

Einstein looked into space. "Because of that. And because of my ideas, Röhm and his bullies dislike my ideas. And also I choose my friends badly. Madame Curie, Gandhi, Niels Bohr, Oppenheimer, Krishnamurti, Fermi, Lise Meitner. A bad crew. A dangerous crew. All of them, I am sure, have dossiers stamped *noch ungehängt.*"

Northrop said, "That looks like a Horten design all right."

Didrikson said, "I thought German aviation was squelched after '27."

"The Hortens left Germany. They're in South America. Keeping their heads down, but we think they're located in Argentina. At least the aeronautical institute there became very active shortly after the Hortens dropped out of sight in Europe. I suppose I should be flattered—they have a standing order for copies of my patent applications. After I filed for the N-M1, we even got a letter asking for all sorts of technical data, questions that had to come from studying the patent drawings."

"From the Hortens?"

Northrop shrugged. "From the Instituto Aeronáutico. Signed by a secretary. We sent back some press-release material. I think they got the message. But Heinrich and Reimar Horten are smart. What I won't tell 'em they'll figure out soon enough."

He peered at the pursuing craft, worry lines appearing on his forehead. "I can't figure out how they get that much speed. We're using Muvian magnetic engines. But they outpaced us at the moon—if we hadn't been able to dodge 'em, we'd be finished by now. And here they come like Barney Oldfield!"

A series of tracer rounds came from the bat-craft. In the vacuum of space they made no sound as they whipped past *Manta*'s yellow wings, but the red tracery of their flight was vivid against the black of space.

"Can't we do anything, Jack?" asked Didrikson.

"Not much." He was sweating. "I'll try and dodge 'em again, but the sun trick won't work this time, our position is all wrong."

Didrikson peered back at the pursuer. "They're painted such a dull color, too. And we're up here like a bright yellow rubber ducky!"

A burst of flame showed the position of the bat-ship's cannon. The round that it fired whipped over *Manta*'s crew bubble trailing a thin line of smoke.

Northrop shoved *Manta*'s steering yoke forward, tipping the craft into what would have been a dive, but in the three-dimensional arena of space it was merely another form of turn.

"Won't that expose our belly?"

Northrop kicked the elevons once, the ship swung dizzyingly. He kicked them again, reversing the action. Even though the medium of space would not respond to aerodynamic controls, the *Manta*'s steering verniers swung the ship accordingly.

"We're showing 'em a narrow profile now," Northrop shouted. "I don't know how long we can just keep dodging, but there's nothing else we can do!"

Manta's maneuvers were carrying her out of the plane of the ecliptic. Northrop was vaguely aware of this, aware that if the ship's power or steering systems were knocked out, she would tumble forever through space, until her passengers died of starvation or cold.

But as long as the ship had power and steering, he could always take observations and locate her position. Einstein was capable of plotting a course for *Manta* from anywhere—Northrop's confidence in the older man was not shaken. He would simply have to recheck the computations.

Another line of tracers whipped past *Manta*'s bubble.

Another lurid flare marked the firing of the bat-ship's cannon.

Northrop maneuvered frantically.

Manta had taken a number of hits from machine-gun bullets, but the craft had been fitted with a self-sealing double skin as protection against high-altitude pressure loss. That system served now to seal punctures resulting from hits by the bat-ship's machine guns. But a strike by a cannon shell, especially if it hit the Plexiglas bubble, could be fatal.

Again and again Northrop dodged. Now back toward the plane of the ecliptic, now away from it. Now toward the orbits of the outer planets, now back toward the sun.

With a silent rush the bat-ship overtook *Manta*. Northrop's craft, though less powerful than its attacker, was more maneuverable. *Manta* spun, dived, headed away from her attacker once more.

Without warning *Manta*'s engines, previously keening at their peak output, whined down to a low moan, then fell silent. The ship's lights and instruments flickered and went dark.

The four occupants felt a surge and a strain as the ship decelerated and rocked to a halt.

"Why you do that?" Gibson asked Northrop.

"I didn't!"

"What's the matter?" Babe asked.

"I don't know. We just stopped."

Einstein gazed out of the bubble. "You did nothing to stop our progress, Jack?"

Northrop said he hadn't. "The ship just died on me!" He seemed amazed, more let down by the failure of his creation than alarmed at their increased vulnerability.

Einstein looked into darkness. "Very beautiful. Like walking in mountains. When earth becomes too crowded, we will have to look elsewhere for the solitude that restores our souls and refreshes our thoughts."

There was a silent moment.

"I want to know what stopped us," Gibson said.

"That I must ponder."

"You said some layer here bounced off radio beams, Doctor."

"I did, yes." He unbuckled his restraining belt. "This is all right, Jack? Good. Sometimes I have to pace—a foolish habit, yes."

Didrikson pointed straight up through the bubble. "What are they doing now?"

The bat-ship was circling above them. Even as they watched, it tipped into a dive. Glowing lines marked the course of tracer rounds. Spurts of flame punctuated the darkness each time the bat-ship's cannon fired.

With a rattle like Texas hail against a corrugated tin shed, bullets bounced off *Manta*'s wings. A heavy cannon shell slowed as it approached *Manta*'s crew bubble for what would surely be a direct hit. Before the shell reached the Plexiglas bubble it had almost halted. It struck with a thump, bounced onto *Manta*'s wing, then rolled off the yellow surface and lay motionless beneath the skycraft.

Gibson stared. "What's it layin' on?"

Didrikson and Northrop joined him. "Nothing. There's nothing there. It's lying on nothing."

Einstein, oblivious, hummed a tune. "This maybe will require a big think," he mumbled. "Maybe a very big think.

Hmm. But if something is here that can bounce radio waves, the same thing can hold up our ship, I suppose. But it stops our engines also. It makes dark our lights. This I must ponder."

Before the others could stop him, he had opened *Manta*'s hatch and started down the ship's exterior rungs.

Jack Northrop shouted, "Stop!" But it was too late. Einstein was already gone.

"It should be a vacuum out there. We should all be dying now, exploded by the pressure drop, choking in a vacuum, freezing."

Gibson smiled. "None of the above, Jack!"

Northrop exploded—but only with laughter. "You're right. God protects madmen and fools. We can sort ourselves out at our leisure. But . . ." He ran to the hatch, peered after Einstein. "Where did he go? Did he just fall? No—I . . ." He collapsed into his seat. "At this point we should be in free-fall if we have no power. What was our momentum? No"—he shook his head, disagreeing with himself—"we lost our momentum when we plowed into this invisible field. This—"

Didrikson said, "This Einstein layer."

"As good a name as any." Northrop stared at the instruments, thinking. "I'm afraid we're in serious trouble."

"Why? Look there!" Gibson pointed at the bat-ship. It had circled above *Manta* before diving to attack. After firing machine-gun bullets and cannon shells to no effect, the ship rose again. But now it banked away and disappeared. "Where you think they going?"

"Counter-Earth," Babe said. "That's for sure. And we're stuck here, and Dr. Einstein has disappeared."

"Don't worry 'bout that man. What did Jack say about madmen and fools? That Dr. Einstein is a genius and a fool. And I hear him talk about God. God takes care of his own. Doc be all right."

"We'll have to find him," Northrop said. "But we have two problems—Dr. Einstein is only one."

"And the other?"

"It looks as if nothing electrical or mechanical can work in the Einstein layer. Maybe that's why radio waves bounce off it. I don't see why solid objects don't do the same, but apparently it just cushions them. Absorbs their momentum. That's why our rivals' firepower didn't destroy *Manta*. The layer soaked up all the momentum they were carrying. Uh, just as it soaked up ours, so we just sit here.''

''But how are we going to get out of here?''

Josh Gibson, Babe Didrikson, Jack Northrop, looked at one another. No one had any suggestions. Not as to how they could get *Manta* flying again.

But maybe if they could find Albert Einstein, that great mind could solve the puzzle.

CHAPTER
12

Reimar Horten watched as the flaccid form of Oswald Mosley was shoved through *Patrilandia*'s passenger hatch. Juan Perón grabbed the Englishman's wrists and pulled him in while Eva Duarte—Horten could see her thickly padded figure behind Mosley—hefted the man's torso.

Perón dragged Mosley to an open area and laid him on his back, arms and legs spread, breathing mask pulled away from his face to permit the circulation of fresh air. Or of what passed in *Patrilandia* for fresh air.

"A remarkable feat," Horten commented.

Eva in the meanwhile had clambered halfway into the ship. Now she halted, panting. *"Perón,"* she muttered, *"ayudame usted."* Perón abandoned Mosley and leaned over Evita. He helped her back into the ship. Perón tried to lead her to a seat, but she waved off the attempt. Instead, she let him half carry her to the side of the cabin.

She leaned against the bulkhead, clutching at his arm, while she slid slowly to the floor. She sat there, her legs stretched out in front of her, her back against the bulkhead. She tried to remove her flying helmet and breathing mask, but she dropped her hands to her lap and instead simply sat, watching.

Perón knelt beside her. He removed her helmet and mask,

working gently and carefully. She was pale and haggard but seemed otherwise to be uninjured.

Behind him, Perón heard the sound of Mosley's struggles. He was stirring and moaning. Perón snapped, "Horten! Make yourself useful! See to Sir Oswald!"

"He is your friend, Major. Not mine. And a lot of use he has been to us. I would have left him here. We must concentrate still upon making *Patrilandia* fly again."

Perón's eyes narrowed. "*Mein Herr*, if only in view of whose pounds have paid for this craft, we had better care for this man. We may need more."

Evita opened her mouth and attempted to speak. Perón brought a cup of water. She accepted it eagerly, letting him hold it while she drank.

"You found him—you carried him back, unaided?" Perón said.

Evita nodded.

"But he must weigh twice what you do!"

She ignored the comment. "Must move *Patrilandia*," she gasped.

Perón suppressed a bitter smile. "We all agree. But how?"

From behind Perón, Horten spoke. "We are in a force field of such nature that no machinery can function. Not even wristwatches."

"There are holes."

"Hey?"

She gestured feebly, moving her hand to point vaguely outside the ship and at the layer where it had made its unpleasant landing.

"Holes in a force field?" Horten persisted.

"Whiteness. Mist, like fog."

"I see nothing outside our craft."

Perón, still kneeling beside Evita, turned toward the German. "We have not been outside. Only they have."

Evita nodded feebly. "You can see it. From here you cannot see it, but out there you can. Like raw cotton. And there are holes. I swear it, Perón."

"I believe you, *querida*. Horten, you hear what she says? If there are holes in this stuff, then we can escape. We can get our ship started if we can get to a hole."

"To believe that, I must see it first!"

Perón leaped angrily to his feet. "Go, then! Seal up your suit. Go out and see! If all this is true, then your wristwatch will work."

Horten considered this. At last he said, "This idea has merit. But what happened to these two? The señorita is recovering, but she has suffered. And as for the English—what? I do not wish to take needless risks."

"All right. I'll put a line on your waist. If you signal, I'll haul you back in. Decide how long you wish to be gone. If you signal neither all clear nor danger, I'll haul you back anyway."

Horten pursed his mouth. He removed his glasses, rubbed his eyes, then pulled the glasses back on. "I will do it, then. Very well. But every two minutes, all clear, or back I come. Agreed?"

"Agreed."

While Horten was gone, Perón gave Evita some food and brandy. She recovered her strength. She told him of finding Mosley and bringing him back to the ship. She said nothing of her own strange experiences, of her sensation of herself as the goddess Isis as well as Eva Duarte.

"But I still do not understand, Evita. How could you lift him in your arms and carry him back here?"

She looked at Mosley. "We never know what we can do in moments of extremity."

Mosley had struggled to his knees. Now he managed to rise to his feet. He gazed about himself, around the cabin of *Patrilandia*. When his eyes came to rest on Evita, they opened wide.

He began to mutter. His words were unintelligible. They had the sound of chanting rather than normal speech.

Perón shook him. "Sir Oswald! It is I, Perón! Pay attention!"

Mosley stared at him.

"What happened to you out there?"

Mosley started to turn from Perón, back toward Evita, but Perón caught his chin between thumb and fingers and held his face. "No! You must tell me!"

Mosley seemed to gather himself inwardly. "Yes, yes, Major. This is a bad place. We have to get away from here. A bad place."

"What happened, man? Be specific!"

Mosley stared, as if staring into the immediate past, as if seeing what he had seen outside *Patrilandia*. "I was slipping. Slipping, you understand?"

"You mean you could not stand? As if on ice?"

Perón felt the tug on Horten's safety line that meant that Horten was proceeding.

Mosley said, "Slipping into bestiality. As if I were—were devolving. Into lower forms. A fish. No, first, myself, as a child. Then I swam. As myself, I swam, but then I became some kind of lower creature, a fish, a worm. Then some sort of one-celled creature—I pulled myself about by extending a pseudopod, like an amoeba. Then I wasn't even that. Just some sort of organic molecule, something only half alive."

"Hallucination."

"I stripped off my clothing. I breathed the mist. It must be something in the mist that made this happen."

"It never happened. Evita found you lying still, unconscious. She brought you back here."

Mosley held his face in his hands. His shoulders moved with dry sobs. "Is that all we are? Inside ourselves, the product of these billions of years of struggle? Paramecia! Viruses!"

The voice from *Patrilandia*'s hatch was muffled by a breathing mask, but still it was harsh and authoritative. "Attend to me! Help me in!"

Perón moved to oblige. He sensed Mosley, behind him and to his side, walking unsteadily.

Reimar Horten stepped into *Patrilandia*. He sealed the hatch behind him. "Your plan will work, Perón. Once one stands in this field, it indeed becomes visible. And there are indeed openings in it. I visited one. Beyond, the firmament appears, I held my arm into the breach and my wristwatch resumed its functioning. "I reconnoitered the area. An opening is moving toward the *Patrilandia* from two o'clock, dead on. We must be prepared. When it passes beneath the ship, we will start our engines and run up to maximum power as rapidly as we can. If we are not out of the field by the time the opening has passed, we will be stuck here again!"

Above the force field, gathering speed, heading toward their goal of Counter-Earth, they spotted the yellow-winged skyship that had escaped them near earth's moon. A lucky break!

They resumed their attack. The yellow ship was obviously unarmed. Its performance showed it to possess less power and consequently less speed than *Patrilandia*.

But the pilot was skillful and his craft could perform wonders of astrobatics.

Patrilandia pursued the yellow ship. The enemy dodged, swung through complex maneuvers, doubled back.

Always it managed to escape *Patrilandia*'s fire, despite Horten's skill as a pilot and Perón's as gunner.

But Horten exclaimed, "No matter! We shall conquer anyway!" He shot a quick look at Perón.

The Argentine officer was puzzled.

"Fool!" Horten exulted. "We have them between us and the force field. We'll dance them down there. They don't know the field exists. Once they hit it we can simply pick at them until they are destroyed!"

Minutes later he cursed. "The field is absorbing the energy of our fire. It's no use, we're just dumping dead rounds on them."

He put *Patrilandia* into a slowly ascending spiral. "No matter. They're stuck there. They may never escape. In any case, we'll continue. We'll reach our goal long before they do, and if they ever arrive, they will find a welcome they will not enjoy!"

He kicked the controls out of their setting, kicked *Patrilandia* out of her spiral.

"Herr Horten."

He turned. It was Oswald Mosley, recovered now. "Herr Horten," he repeated, "your vehemence intrigues me. Is isn't a feeling one would have toward a stranger, even a rival."

"So? Is this your business, my dear Lord Mosley?"

"Do you know them? Do you know who that is?" He motioned back toward the force field, where the yellow ship now lay unmoving.

"I know."

Mosley waited for more of an answer.

Horten held his silence a beat beyond the norm; finally he said "I know that yellow ship. It is the work of John Northrop."

"You recognize the design? It looks rather like *Patrilandia*'s. You don't think this Northrop fellow got wind of what we're doing? I should hope not! Is he actually flying that ship?"

"I don't know. Probably he is."

"Alone?"

"I don't know all his friends. For all I know, he has the great charlatan with him. The madman who would destroy all order in the cosmos."

"Who is that?"

Horten's face was growing red. "*Der Wunderrabbiner von Berlin*! Our great leader Röhm made only one great mistake. He failed to order this Einstein's execution before the madman escaped from Europe. He betrayed the Kaiser in the One Year War and he slandered the young Bismarck and Ernst Udet in 1927, and now he is working for the aggressor Hull and the United States. Yes, I would be unsurprised to learn that Einstein and the engineer Northrop are in that ship. Who else might be with them, I cannot guess."

Perón had listened to Mosley's dialogue with Horten. Now he said, "If they are truly marooned, we can leave them. If they escape, they will pursue us. They must be headed for Counter-Earth, just as we are. You are sure, Horten, that they cannot overtake *Patrilandia*?"

"Totally! Nothing can imperil our mission. Nothing!"

Perón turned away, unsatisfied.

Counter-Earth loomed ahead of *Patrilandia*, blue and dazzling white, turning majestically to present first one face, then its glaring white edge, then its other face.

As the bat-ship approached the planet, Counter-Luna was hidden by the larger disk, but even now the satellite made its appearance, a tiny sliver peeping from behind the planet, then a full disk, turning and changing as did its primary.

Eva Duarte sat in the copilot's seat, beside Reimar Horten. She had not forgot the blow he had struck her—nor would she. But for the moment he was performing a useful task. He was both the chief engineer and the best pilot aboard their ship, and he could pay for his offense at Evita's leisure.

"Will you land at Buenos Aires?" she asked.

"We will not land at all just now. I intend to reconnoiter

this other earth's moon. I want to see if the same structures are to be found there as we found on the earth's moon.''

''But they must be.''

''You are so certain, señorita?''

''But the worlds are identical.''

''Yet Counter-Earth has signaled to us, not we to them. And two ships, that yellow crudity and *Patrilandia*, have traveled from our earth in response. None has traveled from Counter-Earth to our world.''

Mosley, subdued and thoughtful after his experience in the mist but otherwise recovered, asked, ''How do you know that, *mein Herr*?''

''Know what?''

''That no signal was sent from earth. That no ship has departed Counter-Earth.''

Horten did not respond at once. After a pause, he said, ''We should have known.'' But as he said this, the iron ring of certainty that often marked his speech was absent. ''Even so,'' he resumed, ''we will be wise to be cautious. Also, you will recall the burst of acceleration we received by passing through the lunar fissure. We need to slow down as we approach Counter-Earth. We can use the same electromagnetic field effect to reduce our velocity. This will require a precise maneuver—a most precise maneuver. When the time comes, you will all remain silent and alert at your posts. I will monitor the controls.''

By the time they were near enough to Counter-Earth to observe the outlines of the continents with clarity, Counter-Luna stood between *Patrilandia* and the planet.

The moon was in disk and the planet's motion at this moment brought its South Rim of gleaming white ice into alignment as well. From this distance the closer moon and the more remote planet appeared, illusorily, to be of the same size.

The turning of the moon's yellowish, cratered edge and the planet's brilliant white suggested the movements of an immensely huge, slowly milling pair of twin-bladed, counter-rotating propellers.

Horten swung *Patrilandia* into a course that would bring the bat-ship across the lunar surface and send it coasting

earthward at an angle almost tangent to Counter-Earth's atmosphere.

Unlike its acceleration through earth's moon, *Patrilandia*
this time would pass from the lunar face unseen from the
planet's surface.

Counter-Luna loomed huge in *Patrilandia*'s bubble, as well
as in the *Hortenmekkanopantograf*. The ship plunged toward
Counter-Luna's rough surface. The moon bulged and spread
to fill the entire sky in front of the ship.

The same Egyptian-style constructions that had been on
earth's moon were present on Counter-Luna. There was a
fleeting moment in which they were clearly visible as *Patrilandia* flashed low overhead. The ship crossed above the Avenue of Sphinxes, then roared over the lunar fissure as
lightning crackled and danced beneath her hull.

Now *Patrilandia* lurched up sickeningly, then dipped again
as Horten, disdaining to fly at a safe level above the surface,
guided the bat-ship up and down over craters and rilles.

Patrilandia sped away from Counter-Luna. Behind the
ship, Counter-Luna's ever-revolving mass altered its appearance from that of a solid rectangle to an ovoid, its central
fissure in contrast to the surrounding terrain like the hole in
the center of a Chinese coin.

Ahead of *Patrilandia* loomed Counter-Earth.

Horten swung the bat-ship into a course that would have it
glance off the uppermost layer of the planet's atmosphere. His
eyes flickered from the planet itself to its image in the '*graf*,
then to *Patrilandia*'s instruments, then back to Counter-Earth.

It appeared identical—identical—to earth. A moment of
disorientation swept over Horten. He pressed his hand to his
brow. This was Counter-Earth, not terra. He knew this. He
had traveled 200 million miles to get here. He shook his head
like a dog freeing itself of unwanted water. He must keep
control of himself, keep his grasp on his surroundings.

Patrilandia swept low over Counter-Earth's far side.
Through thick-lensed glasses Horten caught a glimpse of the
ziggurats of Muvia; then the ship flashed above them and the
structures disappeared in the mists of distance. In a while
Patrilandia barreled over the battlemented castles of Svartalheim. There was no time even to waggle the ship's batlike
wings.

Horten passed over the Nordhohle. He would not risk subjecting *Patrilandia* to the murderous air currents that stormed through the opening. Instead, the ship continued across the farside, running high over storms that battered the harbor at Hai Brasil.

Horten blinked. It was true, he realized. All true. Until now it had seemed a mad notion, a seductively facile conceit but one with no corresponding reality.

But it was correct after all. Here was earth. Here were Europe and Africa, Lemuria and Cíbola. The River Rhine and the River Okeanos. Another earth, perfect and complete, every sea and island and mountain in place. In fact . . .

For a moment he felt dizzy, as if he were suffering from an embolism. He gasped, felt *Patrilandia* swoop beneath his control. As his ears rang, he found himself uncertain of his own location. Was this in truth a second earth? Had he in fact seen the faces of two identical moons, two identical planets? Or had he undergone a seizure of unknown nature, an assault upon his brain that left him incapable of orienting himself to reality?

Earth's South Rim—Counter-Earth's South Rim!—loomed ahead. Horten pulled *Patrilandia* into a steep climb. The batcraft cleared knife-edged ramparts of gleaming whiteness. He swung the ship into a nearly vertical course, heading for Counter-Luna. The planet swung behind *Patrilandia*; ahead, the satellite grew.

The pyramids of Counter-Luna appeared identical to those of earth's satellite. Horten brought *Patrilandia* low over the Avenue of Sphinxes—a rock-paved path that was totally familiar to him even though he had just completed a journey of nearly 200 million miles to reach it.

He was all the more amazed, then, to see figures scuttle for the edges of the avenue at *Patrilandia*'s approach. There was even a small vehicle making its way along the road. He managed to lift the bat-ship a few extra yards and avoid smashing the ground vehicle.

Patrilandia dropped again, her landing gear making contact with the paving stone just at the moment she lost airspeed. It was a perfect landing. *Patrilandia* rolled to a halt.

Now two of the ground vehicles rolled across the stones toward *Patrilandia*.

Eva Duarte stood at the edge of the bubble. For a moment she saw herself reflected. She was as beautiful as ever, or nearly so. But she was disturbed by the wispiness and paleness of her hair. Like her rival Libertad Lamarque, she was a natural brunette. But where Lamarque chose to darken her hair even more, to emphasize the contrast of her patrician, milky complexion, Duarte had bleached her hair and tinted it blond to win a role at Pampa Films, and had kept it blond ever since.

Her protectors, of whom Perón was the latest, had preferred her as *una rubia*.

But her hair was growing out, it appeared, and beneath the blond tinting, the roots were not brown but white!

She cringed.

"Your lady is refreshing herself. She will be attended by servants, made comfortable. She will rejoin us when she feels ready. She stated that she was fatigued by the journey here. As for your mechanic, he is tending to your skycraft."

The speaker wore his hair cut in pseudomedieval bangs. His costume was of soft leather and earth-tone cloth. At his waist he wore a ceremonial dagger.

Juan Perón and Sir Oswald Mosley sat opposite him in low chairs of antique design. They had been escorted here by armed soldiers, the same soldiers who had swarmed from the vehicles that met *Patrilandia* on the Avenue of Sphinxes.

The soldiers' costumes had been cut in the same antique style as the outfit of the man now facing Mosley and Perón. Their weapons had been a combination of the archaic and the modern—halberds and heavy straight-bladed swords, and modern firearms and pistol-like devices that seemed designed to fire something other than bullets.

The four travelers offered no resistance. Reimar Horten alone had been inclined to exert a haughty authority, but the others convinced him that they would do best to cooperate for the time being.

Now two of them confronted still more anachronisms: an office furnished in the dark and ornate manner of the late

Victorian era; a man dressed like some figure out of a pre-Renaissance tapestry.

And all of this within the confines of an Egyptian temple situated on the moon of earth's twin—or almost twin—planet.

The man resumed his speech. "We're most gratified that you showed up here. And I will admit that I'm very surprised. We heard the messages going out. We would have stopped them if we could, but there was no way—it was simply beyond our control. So, here you are. I hope you're here to make an alliance with us. I suspect that you are. I know who you are, my lord. And you, Major."

He gestured expansively. "Your counterparts on our world are known to us. But since you do not seem to know me, let me tell you that I am the commander of this installation. I am the Prinz Nikolauz von Svartalheim. I had hoped by this time to possess a more elevated title, but"—he laughed bitterly—"things didn't quite work out as I had hoped. And so here I am, commanding a boondocks garrison again. It seems to be my fate."

He ran his fingers through graying hair. His face bore the lines of bitterness and of dissipation. He might once have been handsome, and the body that might once have been powerfully athletic now ran to flab beneath his soft outfit.

Perón's thoughts were distracted by his worry about Evita. When the soldiers had approached *Patrilandia*, she had first demanded to stay with Perón, but she had been weak and had agreed quickly to rest instead.

Ever since her excursion on earth's satellite with Oswald Mosley, she had shown periods of amazing and incomprehensible power. But also there were signs of frightening weakness and premature ravages of age. As Perón sat, mind on the absent Evita, he heard the drone of conversation between Mosley and Nikolauz.

"We received only fragmentary transmissions, don't you see? We'd never suspected there was a planet here at all, Your Highness. But when our receiving stations picked up the transmissions, a few of us on earth, a courageous few already at work for the establishment of a new order for mankind, were determined to act. We are here to make alliance with like-minded forces. We can help you here on your earth—and

then you can help us on ours. Two worlds—twin earths!—
with a single philosophy, a single civilization! Twin glories!''

Nikolauz grunted his approval of Mosley's ideas. "Your
world, then, is identical to ours?''

"Not quite—and that's part of the charming little mystery,
Your Highness. Y'see, on our moon, for instance, there's nobody there.''

Nikolauz's eyebrows shot up in surprise, disappearing into
his graying bangs. "No Nikolauz?''

Mosley shook his head. "There may be a Nikolauz on
earth itself. You said, Svartalheim . . .''

The prince nodded. "My nation. For only a dozen years
we have had this little outpost on the moon. For that long I
have not seen the blue sky of earth, have not walked beneath
a tree, have not bathed in a stream.''

"Then your people didn't build all of this.''

"Nein!''

"Why is it that I'm not surprised by that? Well, never you
mind, Your Highness.'' Mosley slitted his eyes. More and
more he was feeling his old self. His strange adventure in the
white mist had been a terrifying experience. But the more
time that passed, the more he was able to understand and
assimilate that series of transformations. Man was nothing
but a beast; ultimately, nothing more than a complex chemical phenomenon.

One who knew this could act upon it, could act to gain his
own ends. Any fool who thought that Man was a spiritual
being, a moral being, could be manipulated like a puppet.
Even a wicked fool, although he might be less helpless than
the other sort, was easy prey for a man such as Mosley could
feel himself becoming.

"Tell me, Your Highness, how did your people get here to
the moon? And . . . who built these huge structures?''

"We have many wonderful devices, my lord. Some we
devised ourselves. Others we obtained from lesser nations
after we conquered them—as the strong shall always conquer
the weaker and less worthy. Of that, I am sure, you will have
no doubts. So we came here.'' He steepled his fingers beneath his chin. "We used flying platforms, which we obtained from an ingenious but decadent race, neighbors of
Svartalheim. They are propelled by magnetic rays. We came

to the moon in search of new prey, and here we found''—he gestured, turning his hands palm upward, fingers extending outward toward his shoulders—''all this. Built by the people of ancient Khem? And abandoned—why? They were not conquered, they did not fall prey to plague, at least not that we can find. No remains were here. No destruction. Simply . . . gone!''

''And on earth?'' Mosley asked. ''What conditions obtain there? What differences from *my* world?''

Nikolauz shook his head. ''How am I to know that, my lord? Is Otto the Unqualified king of Svartalheim in your world? Is Sun Pu-yi emperor of China? Is William Dudley Pelley president of the United States of America? How am I to know? I have never been to your earth.''

CHAPTER
13

"We'd better go after him," Didrikson said.

"How long he's been gone?" Josh Gibson faced his fellow athlete. Jack Northrop's back was turned to them; he continued despondently to study *Manta*'s instrument panel.

"How long?" Babe echoed. "How the hell do I know? My watch stopped. Just like everything else."

"Well, he just picked up his fiddle and went. Did you see that, Babe? Took his fiddle in one hand and stuck his pipe in his face and off he went. But he be all right, I'm sure of that. I never knew a man like that doc, but he's all right."

"You haven't seen the newsreels about him, then? Or read all the stories, all the magazine pieces?"

"I mainly read my Bible."

"He's a genius but he's like a baby sometimes. He gets so wrapped up in what he's thinking about, he's helpless. They say that he gets lost just taking a walk. All the children in his town—they know that if they see Dr. Einstein and he looks lost, they take his hand and lead him home. He wasn't so bad while his wife was alive, but since she died it happens all the time."

"And you think he's lost out there?" Josh nodded toward *Manta*'s hatch, toward the blackness outside the ship.

"I don't know if he's lost. I wish we could see him." She peered through the Plexiglas, shook her head.

"Hey, try the telescope."

She placed her eye to the instrument. "There he is. How can that be? He's walking along . . . on nothing. Look!"

She relinquished the telescope to Josh Gibson. He peered through it. "See, he's okay. That's a holy man, Babe. You don't know about them, do you? I knew one of them back in Georgia. He was sanctified. He wasn't a reverend, he never went to school, he didn't have any money. But he was sanctified. He had the holy spirit in him. I tell you, that doctor, he's got the holy spirit. He be okay."

Gibson stepped away from the telescope and Babe put her eye to it once again. Einstein was walking slowly, eyes raised. He stopped once and bent over. He still carried his violin case in one hand. With the other he made a gesture as if petting a small animal. Then he placed the violin case on the nothingness beside his feet and petted two invisible things.

From them he looked up, then stood and—

Babe Didrikson turned away from the telescope. Gibson started toward it, but she swung the instrument sideways, stood with her back to it, keeping her body between Gibson and the telescope. "No," she said. Her normally sharp-edged, aggressive tone was absent. "Don't watch." There were tears in her eyes and she covered them with her hand. "Don't watch, Josh. We mustn't, not now."

He nodded.

Jack Northrop said, "It's hopeless. We'll just have to wait for him to come back. Or go after him if we must. I can't do anything with the ship."

He made his way to the rear of the cabin and lay down. He rolled an extra article of clothing into a makeshift pillow and placed it under his head. "I'm going to take a nap. Call me if he comes back or if anything happens." He shut his eyes.

After a while Gibson pointed. "He comin' now."

Gibson and Didrikson arranged their flying suits and their breathing masks. Even though Einstein had not worn the gear, they were taking no chances.

Northrop still dozed.

"Let's help him." The two athletes climbed from *Manta*.

As their feet plunged into the seeming nothingness beneath the ship, they felt a spongelike support. The blackness had become a white, misty cloud.

Einstein was walking toward them slowly, his pipe in his mouth. He carried his violin case in one hand and the instrument itself in the other, along with his bow.

His eyes were fixed on something distant. The expression on his deeply seamed face was tranquil, yet exalted.

Josh and Babe took him by the elbows and helped him to climb back aboard *Manta*. Inside the ship, his eyes slowly regained their focus, his expression became less abstracted.

Einstein nodded to Babe, then to Josh.

Babe started to speak but she felt Gibson's hand clamp down on her wrist. He shook his head fiercely. She nodded and he released her. They would wait for the savant to speak. Clearly he was all right; he would speak when he was ready.

Einstein sat with his violin lying across his lap, the bow held in one hand. He raised the instrument to his chin, placed the bow across the strings and drew a tentative note from the violin. He shook his head and lowered the instrument again. He smiled gently at Babe and Josh.

In a low voice Josh said to Babe, "He a sanctified man. Maybe he going to preach the word now."

She looked at him unbelievingly.

Einstein said, "My dear Elsa—I was not so good to her. Not so kind as I should have been." His eyes were sad, but then they brightened. "And my good Chico and my dear little Tiger—I saw them again. Good Chico. You know we named him for the funny Marx brother. My good little dog. And my poor cat. How upset the rain and thunder would make him. But he would crawl onto my lap and I would try to explain to him that it would go away, but he couldn't wait, he wanted me to turn it off right now, right now. *Ach*, the old fool that I am." From a pocket he dragged a huge faded bandanna and dabbed at his eyes and nose. "An old fool. But I saw my Elsa. God let me see her."

He looked at Babe and at Josh. His eyes brightened. "You know that the world is filled with wonders. The firmament is filled with wonders. Why such a blessing for an old fool like me? But the good God showed me some of his wonders; He let me hear a little of His harmony. *Ach*, that an old fool such as I should receive this blessing!''

"Can you tell us what it was like?''

Einstein looked upward, pondering. He lifted his violin and bow, and played softly for a few minutes. The music had a lightness to it; although the violinist's technique did not display great virtuosity, it had truth and sweetness.

Jack Northrop stirred and sat up, smiling. "I recognize that music. Wait—it's Mozart's Sonata in F major.''

"Yes,'' Einstein said. "He heard it long before I. The sublime—other composers labor to create their music, but that one, he merely listened, and he heard God's music and gave it to us. There is such unity in creation, such coherence. Our task is merely to discover.''

"Doctor, do you understand this layer? Do you know what's keeping us here? Why no machinery works? Can we escape from here, or are we trapped?''

"*Ach*, machinery. If mankind had never invented machinery, we would be better off. Think of the creatures that live in perfect harmony with nature. When a condor soars, I believe he sees God. When one sails a little boat, one can find God.''

He shook himself. "Well, and here we are, *ist nicht so*?'' He fumbled for a pen and paper, began to sketch. "It is all very easy. You see?'' He slid the paper toward Northrop. The engineer picked it up. His eyes popped.

Josh Gibson said, "You see, Babe? He's sanctified. I knew it. I told you. This is a holy man. The Hebrews have always had holy men. I learned that when I was a little boy.''

Northrop slid back into the pilot's seat. With one hand he held Einstein's scrap of paper. With the other he adjusted *Manta*'s telescope. He looked at the paper again. "It's amazing. It's so simple. And beautiful!''

"*Ja*. God's handiwork is simple and beautiful. So you understand, Jack. *Gut*.''

Northrop opened *Manta*'s instrument panel. He laid the covering aside, reached into the wires and switches. He made some changes, shaking his head all the time.

He closed up the panel again. "Here we go. Everyone ready, please.'' He switched on the magnetic engines. The four travelers heard the engines' characteristic low sound.

Northrop increased the power. *Manta* slid forward, rose from the invisible layer, accelerated.

"We're on our way."

"Now what?" Didrikson asked.

Northrop looked at her.

"Are they going to be waiting for us?" she asked. "They've attacked us twice now. We didn't get away from Ceres with anything very useful; we've been stuck in the Einstein layer for nobody knows how long. How do we know they're not waiting to jump us again? And if they do, three strikes and you're out! Who are they? Can't we attack 'em back, or at least do something to protect ourselves?"

"As for who they are, they're our rivals from earth. As for what we can do, just push on and be ready for any emergency."

"That sounds great, Jack. But . . . ready *how*? We're unarmed; *Manta* has no defenses. That bat-ship has machine guns and a cannon. We're a sitting duck."

Northrop was beginning to show his exasperation. It wasn't that Babe Didrikson's questions were unfair—the problem was, he had no answers for them. *Manta* in fact *was* a sitting duck. But there was nothing they could do about it. Nothing at all.

"I tell you, Babe, we be all right." Josh Gibson came to Northrop's rescue. "We got a holy man with us, *Manta*'s a sanctified ship. They can't beat us. They can't! You'll see."

The yellow craft sped on. Northrop turned it from time to time, spreading the sun's heat evenly.

Behind him, Josh Gibson said, "How much longer we got to go on this trip? And what are we going to do when we get there?"

Northrop was sitting relaxed now. He had turned the controls over to Gibson. "Not much longer. Let's try the radio again."

He switched on the craft's two-way device. He picked up a burst of crackling as he swept the sky ahead of them with *Manta*'s steerable antenna. "Getting something." He concentrated on adjusting the antenna. "I think we can pick up Counter-Earth."

The radio sputtered. A voice could be heard, but the message was indistinguishable.

"No good. Soon, I think."

"Jack," Babe said, "do we really have a plan? What are we going to do when we get there? You picked us up in the middle of this mission, you know. Josh and me. We're just a couple of ballplayers, not explorers."

"It's too late now to back out!"

"I have no intention of backing out. I just want to know, what's going to happen? Do you even *have* a plan?"

"Less of one than I'd like."

"Well, you'd better share it with us. As much as you do have. What do we know?"

Northrop heaved a sigh. "You were on Khem-Ceres with me. You heard Colonel Selk. We have to visit the second earth."

"Oh, yes. But we're not just explorers."

"We are not. You're right." He squeezed his eyes shut.

Before he could speak again, Didrikson resumed. "You're not just an airplane designer, either, are you?"

He shook his head. "Really I am. That's all I want to be anyway. But once you work with the government, you can't get unstuck from it."

"And . . . ?"

"I'm not a secret agent, if that's what you're expecting. It's just that, the secretary of the navy is an old friend of mine. And I've met President Hull. Look here . . ."

He stood up and walked around the cabin. They had traveled a vast distance in a tiny volume of space. He was starting to develop cabin fever, and he knew that Babe and Josh, both of them young athletes accustomed to exercising strenuously every day, must be in far worse shape than he was, emotionally.

"*Manta* is not a military craft. This isn't officially a United States expedition of any sort. We're traveling as private citizens. We even launched from international waters, not from the U.S."

"Well?" Didrikson asked.

"Washington has been worried since 1927 over the alliance of Svartalheim on the farside and German revanchism on our side of the disk. Now we have to add a South American angle, and that's bad enough."

"How does that connect with this flight?"

"If conditions on Counter-Earth are the same as on earth—and if the schemers get together and combine their forces—we might wind up having to fight an interplanetary war."

Josh Gibson said, "Oh, come on, Jack. We see those Flash Gordon movies when we on the road. And that big radio scare a couple years ago—you take that seriously?"

Northrop shook his head. "I don't think there are any Martians, if that's what you mean. Although now that we can fly in space, I expect there will be expeditions to other planets and we'll learn what's there.

"But Counter-Earth is unique! Of all the planets circling the sun, this world was created less than thirty years ago—at first as a perfect duplicate of our own. We'll see whether it's changed since 1912."

"Okay. If we got to fight the Kaiser all over again. We be gettin' there soon, I hope."

Without warning, *Manta* shuddered. It was only the smallest of movements, as if the ship had struck an obstacle no larger than a snowball, but Northrop was at full alert instantly.

Babe Didrikson, at his side, peered through the Plexiglas. "What was that? Is it the ship?"

Northrop checked all the instrument readings. "I can't find anything. It might have been a tiny meteorite."

"What? A shooting star?"

"They make shooting stars when they hit the earth's atmosphere. Out here they're just lumps of flotsam, leftover debris that have been floating through space since the solar system was created."

"You mean—you don't know where they are? We could run into more?"

"I don't know. There are swarms of the things, like swarms of insects, running through space in fixed orbits. Almost like comets. But unless they come into the atmosphere, they're invisible. Too small, too dark. They could be anywhere."

The ship shuddered at another impact.

Babe started. "Look at that!"

The meteorite had scratched a line along the side of *Manta*'s bubble.

"Can they damage us?"

"Uh, that all depends." Northrop wiped sweat from his

forehead. "Tiny ones—they can be as little as pebbles, even smaller, even like dust—they won't do any harm. They'll just bounce off, or, if they're a little bigger and they pierce the ship's skin, the self-seals will take care of that."

"But how big can they get?"

"Tons! Bigger than *Manta*! Big as a small asteroid!"

Babe moaned.

"All right, chances are we'll be all right." Northrop switched on *Manta*'s landing lights. "Maybe we'll be able to see if there are any big ones."

"Why didn't you warn us, Jack?" Gibson demanded.

"I didn't think we'd encounter this. The chances seemed so remote—but it happened."

"And what was it you said they are?" Babe demanded. "Just rocks?"

"Rocks, some metal alloys, and probably some water. Of course, the ones that reach earth don't have any water left. It all boils before they reach the surface."

"Nothing that's alive, though. That right?"

"Absolutely impossible."

"You sure?"

"There's no way that anything could live in space. Absolutely impossible. There have been bits of organic matter found in some, but those are just crude molecules. Certainly no life in space."

Gibson stood watching *Manta*'s wing.

Ahead of the ship the meteorites showed up as black specks briefly illuminated against the dead black of space.

Babe leaned toward the Plexiglas. "Can't we go around the swarm?"

"Not now." Northrop clutched the flying yoke, struggling desperately to avoid the flying specks. "If we'd known in time, we could have plotted a course around them. But we're in the swarm now. We'll just have to make our way through them. They cover hundreds of thousands of miles of space in all directions!"

"Jack!" Josh Gibson grabbed Northrop's elbow. "That's not just no rock, Jack! Don't try and tell me that's just a rock!"

He pointed through the Plexiglas.

The meteorites were small, and almost all of them that

struck the *Manta* bounced off the yellow wing surface or the transparent bubble. But a few remained on the ship.

They were hard-shelled but they moved.

One was advancing along the wing toward the bubble.

Horrified, Northrop turned a spotlight on it.

The thing froze for a few seconds, then began its inexorable advance toward the Plexiglas.

"My God! What is it?"

"I'll tell you what it *ain't*—just a rock!"

The thing had reached the edge of the bubble. Its exposed portion *looked* like rock. It had to be a shell, something like the hard coating of a barnacle.

Behind it, the skyship's yellow skin showed a complex grouping of scratches. The thing must be propelled by clawed legs emerging from the lower side of the shell.

"I don't understand how such a thing can be. How could it have evolved in space? How can it survive here? What is its nourishment?"

"I think its nourishment going to be us, if we don't do something about it first."

The thing had pulled itself onto the side of the bubble. Through the transparent Plexiglas they could see its legs. They were razor-sharp and razor-tough.

It was scratching frantically, rapidly boring a hole through the bubble.

Northrop recovered himself. "Okay, first thing, everybody into altitude gear, pressure and breathing apparatus. If that thing gets through the bubble, we're going to lose air and pressure."

"Can't we stop it?" Babe whispered.

"How? We're just not equipped!"

"It sure does look like a barnacle," Didrikson said. "We see 'em on the Gulf Coast all the time. Attach themselves to ships' hulls, live on harbor detritus. You got to be careful scrapin' them off—you can get cut up real bad on the things."

Gibson was circling the cabin. "Don't we got anything we can use on the things? No weapons, no tools?"

"We have tools!" Northrop refused to leave *Manta*'s controls but he pointed to the ship's tool compartment.

In seconds Gibson had it open. Even though he was now wearing heavy gloves, his hands flew over the tools inside.

He came away with two crowbars. He handed one to Didrikson.

A light gleamed in Babe's eyes. "Okay." She nodded.

Outside on *Manta*'s wings the creatures were increasing their numbers. Wherever one managed to gain a hold, it dug in and offered a target for more of its kind.

There was a terrifying pop, then *Manta*'s cabin air whooshed through an opening. The first of the barnaclelike creatures to bore through the Plexiglas had created a pressure differential and a channel through which the differential could equalize itself. The air rushing from the cabin had knocked the barnacle loose, sending it tumbling off the bubble, off *Manta*, and drifting through space once again.

Northrop checked his passengers. Einstein was safely bundled into protective gear. Didrikson and Gibson were scrambling for the hatch, crowbars in hand, eager to get outside *Manta*'s cabin.

Babe Didrikson emerged first. *Manta*'s aerodynamically clean design offered few projections for handholds, but she grasped one of the steerable spotlights. With her free hand she used her crowbar to pry at the nearest barnacle.

The tip of the bar was flattened and split, made for drawing heavy spikes. She struggled to get it under the parasite, then bore down with all her weight on the free end. The barnacle resisted briefly, then pulled away from *Manta*'s yellow skin, leaving deep, ugly gouges to show where it had attacked the ship.

Now it clung to the tip of the crowbar.

Babe turned to see Josh Gibson, who had made his way from the hatch to *Manta*'s opposite wing. Babe shouted at him, then realized that in the vacuum of space her voice would be lost. She leaned toward him, hoping to jab him and get his attention, but she didn't want to risk the parasite's transferring itself from the crowbar to his padded suit—the bar was solid iron and could resist the barnacle's razorlike claws, but the soft padded suit would offer no resistance to its attack.

Gibson swung around.

Babe gestured at him.

He nodded.

They stood facing each other across the rear fairing of the crew bubble. Babe held her crowbar so Josh could see it. The parasite, she realized, was slowly making its way toward her gloved hand.

Josh saw her situation and gestured with his own crowbar.

Babe held hers toward him, raised like a fencer's épée.

Josh swung his own iron. He made contact with the parasite. Its shell exploded under the impact, its internal parts flew through the vacuum, some of them bouncing off *Manta*'s hull, others simply disappearing into the void.

The two athletes returned to their work, prying loose barnacles from *Manta*'s skin.

The ship was still moving through the meteor swarm. Fortunately, the things were so sparsely distributed that few struck the ship, and of those, fewer than one in ten managed to establish a hold. Even so, it was hot, backbreaking, exhausting work.

Babe and Josh would work separately, prying loose the barnacles. Then they would rendezvous, raise their crowbars and swing them. The parasites were destroyed, but each impact sent violent tremors along Babe's arm and through her body. The more massive Gibson, she knew, would be better able to withstand the impact, but would still be suffering similarly. They would emerge from this job bruised and aching.

A black object bounced off Babe's shoulder, then a second struck her full on. Through her pressure suit she could both feel and hear the horrid scrabbling noise as sharp claws worked against her padded suit.

She gagged in horror, stared in fearful fascination at the ugly, rocklike thing adhering to the center of her chest.

She shook herself to action, grabbed her crowbar in both hands, pried at the thing. With a pop it released its hold. She twisted at it and managed to get rid of it, sending it tumbling away, without its having attached itself to her crowbar.

Bile filled her mouth, and a shocked ringing sounded in her ears. She breathed deeply, relieved to find that her suit had not been holed, that her air supply and breathing apparatus remained intact.

She felt herself twisting slowly and saw blackness, then the disk of the distant sun, then *Manta*'s yellow boomerang shape sliding gracefully away from her.

She opened her mouth to scream, but the sound only died inside her padded outfit.

She revolved again slowly, helplessly.

She shouted and waved futilely; the movements of her body sent her spinning more violently and more helplessly than ever.

The broad yellow vee of *Manta*'s wings tilted and dipped in another maneuver, and the ship disappeared into blackness.

With a sound like a soft snowball plopping against a child's playsuit, another parasite struck Babe's body.

CHAPTER
14

"Major Perón," Nikolauz said, "this is a great pleasure. You would be surprised how few of my officers have any skill at the sport, or any desire to develop the skill."

Perón said, "It was my duty initially, sir. But a country such as Argentina requires every possible skill in the warrior's repertoire. We have tropical jungles in the north, seacoast in the east, pampas in the interior, and the Andes to the west. It was my pleasure to study mountain warfare in Europe when I was attaché in Rome."

"And you skied with King Humberto himself?"

"I did, sir."

The Prinz pushed off with his poles and started the straight run down the side of the crater Jotunn. The skis used on the moon differed from those Perón had learned to use in the Italian Alps and brought back with him to use in the Chilean border country of Argentina, and the medium on which they were used was even more different. Instead of snow, lunar skiing took place on a bed of ancient dust, dust kicked up by millennia of meteorite impacts.

The Prinz was bundled in thick clothing, but against the light gravity of the moon he moved with the easy grace of an experienced mountaineer.

With a push against the powdery dust, Perón followed the

Prinz down the slope. Occasionally rocks projected through the powder. To negotiate the slope safely the skiers had to stay on the alert, swerving and dodging to avoid dangerous spills.

At the bottom of the slope they turned back and surveyed the trail they had left coming down Jotunn's outer edge. "Our trail will remain like that, Your Highness? There is no new snowfall here to cover it, no summer thaw to remove the pack?"

The Prinz laughed. "Someday I am going to develop a great vacation resort here on the moon. Think of the possibilities, Major. *Visit the Pyramids! Unravel the Secret of the Sphinx! Ski in the Mountains of the Moon!* I'll show them! Otto may have beaten me out for the throne, but I'll be rich! I'll be richer than a king!"

Perón made a sound of agreement. "But so far, all you have done on the moon is establish a small garrisón, is that correct?"

"Oh, no! We've done far more than that!" The Prinz glanced around, assuring himself that no one else was within earshot. The thin atmosphere of the moon did not conduct sound well, but there was no point in taking needless risks.

"Major Perón, my own people have seen fit to send me here to this backwoods post. But a leader will make the most of any opportunity, and I have made the most of this one. I am going to send you to my allies on earth. *Our* earth, you understand."

He pointed at the blue-white planet that dominated Counter-Luna's sky. The planet was in oblong, showing its icy rim and one face, the flattened disk angled away from Jotunn so that its near features were clearly illuminated; its farther ones, lost in the blurring mists of its atmosphere.

Near Nikolauz and Perón stood their lunar vehicle, an ugly tracklaying device that could crawl up and down steep slopes with little likelihood of overturning. When Perón had mentioned his experience as the chief of Argentina's mountain warfare school, the Prinz had invited him for the skiing expedition and Perón had accepted at once.

Eva Duarte, Mosley, and Reimar Horten had remained behind, each of them pursuing a different interest with members of Nikolauz's military court.

"Your country of Svartalheim is in close alliance with the
Prussian Empire, is that not so?"

Nikolauz nodded. "And we have friends in Argentina,
Major."

"Yes. There are similar convergences of interests on *my*
earth."

"But our best friends are elsewhere. They have but recently come to power. They have yet to consolidate their hold.
Their situation is perilous—but if they can gain full control
in their own country, we shall eventually control all of earth.
All of our earth. And then, together, Major Perón, we shall
mount our expedition. We shall construct a fleet—an ar-
mada!—and bring the other earth under our sway! With your
assistance, of course."

Perón found himself holding back his feelings. He was
relieved that the warm skiing outfits included knitted masks.
He would not wish the Prinz to see his expression at this
moment.

He said, "What opposition do you face? I would expect
that Muvia would be a problem, based on her conduct on my
own world. But what of the Colossus? Bullies and meddlers—
have you come to terms with the Colossus, Prinz?"

Puzzlement appeared in Nikolauz's eyes. "Colossus,
Major? As in the legendary Colossus of Rhodes? I do not
understand."

"The Colossus of the North. Los Estados Unidos del
Norte. They are even worse meddlers than the British!"

Nikolauz relaxed visibly. "Come then. I'll explain to you
in the car."

They loaded their skis atop the ground car. Inside, Nikolauz sealed the vehicle and turned on the heater. He removed
his woolen mask; Perón followed suit. The Prinz opened a
compartment near the car's instrument panel and removed a
jug and two heavy cups.

"We will toast our new friendship, Major Perón. Our new
friendship, our alliance, and our future empire of two planets!"

Perón lifted his cup. The Prinz had forgot his plan to develop the moon as a tourist attraction and decided instead to
conquer two planets. Perón sighed. "To all of that, Your
Highness." He drained his cup. The hot rum was not as good

as that served in Italy. He turned to face Nikolauz. "You were going to explain to me your feelings about the United States of North America."

Nikolauz started the engine of the ground car. He shifted several levers. The drivers whirred and the tracks began to clank, carrying the car back toward the lunar pyramids.

"Major Perón, you must understand that I do not pay great attention to the politics of that nation."

"When titans struggle, mortals take heed."

"I take your meaning. Yes. We date the modern era from the events of 1927. We were very happy on our side of the planet, pursuing our goals and leaving the other side of the earth to pursue its own interests. Then the daredevils in their aircraft came crashing into our domain, and nothing has been the same.

"We had never even heard of most of the nations of your hemidisk, knew of others only as vague legends. Then, suddenly, we were plunged into a new reality."

He swung the levers of the ground car, careening it around a jagged outcropping of ancient lunar rock. "I think the president of what you referred to as the Colossus was, at the time, someone named Walker. They keep changing leaders there—it's very disconcerting, Major. We don't elect a new king every four years. How do they ever get anything done? They're always getting ready for a new election, or holding an election, or busy changing government.

"Well, let's see, in the year 1928 that fellow Walker was in trouble over some money he had taken from the public treasury and given to his friends. I don't understand why that is frowned upon either—they must be a very strange nation. Then there was a business crisis and everybody got very poor, so by 1932 they threw out the man they had put in to replace Walker. I think he was called something like Alfried Schmidt. Then came a Mellon. He was supposed to fix everything and he couldn't do it, so they threw him out. Am I boring you, Major?"

Perón shook his head.

"Are you certain?"

"Really. I love politics, Prinz."

"How odd. I find it sublimely boring. I only keep up because it's part of my job. Besides, I think I might be able to knock off old Otto and take my rightful throne one day.''

''Yes.'' Perón grunted in alarm and pointed to a fissure that cut across the ground car's path.

Nikolauz swung the car ninety degrees, paralleled the fissure for one hundred yards, then swung again toward the pyramids.

''After Mellon,'' Perón prompted.

''Well, if we must. Now let me see, was it Baldwin? Churchmound? No, they were in Europe somewhere. Pacelli? No!'' He released the ground car's levers to snap the fingers of both hands. ''I remember! Mellon couldn't make everybody rich again, so they threw him out and put in somebody with two first names. I can never remember which is right. Thomas Thomas. Norman Norman. Whichever. He was going to fix it all up and make everybody rich, but instead he made everybody poor. Something like that.

''So then—I am *so* weary of this, Major, I can't tell you just how weary I am—they threw Thomas Norman out and put in something called the National Renaissance Party. The head of the country is called something like Pulley. Does that sound right? Dudley Pulley?

''Anyway, he's supposed to be a good fellow. Old Otto thinks Pulley is just marvelous. Our friends in Prussia seem to think the world of him, too. Maybe I'll meet him someday, if I ever get off this boondocks of a moon and get a decent job. Maybe I'll be a bigtime real estate mogul, or maybe I'll still get to be King of Svartalheim. I think I'd really like to be king.''

A day later, *Patrilandia* was serviced, resupplied, and ready for launching to Counter-Earth. Prinz Nikolauz personally visited the ship and her crew as launch time drew near.

The Prinz was in close conversation with Reimar Horten. The bond of language drew them together; Nikolauz told Horten stories of his experiences during the fateful year of 1927.

''I was a youngster then, Herr Horten, just a youngster. If I'd been more mature, if I'd known better how to conduct myself, well, history might have been different.''

''Indeed, Your Highness.'' Horten nervously removed his glasses, polished their lenses, and returned them to his face.

His eyes grew and shrank alternately as he moved the glasses. "I have made a study of the events of that year. I believe they were largely the same on both of our planets, although there remains much to be learned."

"You're right, Horten. I might be king today!"

"And Prussia might dominate Europe and the world, and I should be the head of the *Reich Aeronautik* instead of exiled to a country like Argentina. Pah!"

Nikolauz looked into Horten's mismatched eyes. He said, "You are not fond of your companions, *mein Herr.*"

"Is it so obvious, Your Highness?"

Nikolauz laughed. "Herr Horten, come with me if you please. Your ship will remain here safely. Your companions are otherwise engaged. I would speak with you in private."

The Prinz led Horten to a private office. He placed a large flagon and two goblets on an ornate desk.

Horten stood facing him, his body in a rigid posture.

"Sit, sit, my friend!" Nikolauz motioned Horten into his chair. "And have a drop of schnapps with me."

"As Your Highness wishes."

"Horten, how important is your business with those others?"

"We are here to make contact. To cement an alliance. To assist in necessary actions."

"Yes, yes. But what do you think of those three?"

Horten hesitated.

"Don't you find that Argentine major a bit of a windbag?" the Prinz asked. "And the lady—well, a fading rose, I fear. Nor do I quite trust her. Believe me, Herr Horten, a lifetime devoted to survival against court intrigues teaches one a few things. I don't like the way that lady behaves. I would not turn my back on her."

Horten sipped at his schnapps.

"And as for the English, never trust an English, Horten. Never! They are born deceivers, liars, and seducers. Bad—a branch of our Nordic race, Horten, that seems to have gone wrong. They should be rooted out in my opinion. Of course, I'm just a poor Prinz stuck off here on the moon, so what do I know?

"But look here, you!" He leaned across his desk. His

elbow knocked the liquor flagon off the desk. Horten managed to catch it in midair and return it to the desk.

"Very good, Horten, very good. Thank you." The Prinz leaned back, closed his eyes to gather himself, then began over. "Look here. My military commander here on the moon is a bit of a dunce. Why don't you let your friends go on down to earth. They're just going to muck about in local politics anyway. Your Major Perón was pumping me for information all during our little skiing expedition yesterday. I thought I'd met a true sportsman, someone to join me in a day of recreation, and all he wanted to do was talk politics!

"We're going to move, Herr Horten!" He thumped a beefy fist on the desk top. The flagon jumped. Horten caught it again. The two goblets tipped over and rolled, but both were empty.

"We're going to move," Nikolauz repeated, "and I want you at my side. I want you as my chief of liaison with the other earth. I don't trust that English and I don't like those Argentines. What are they, anyway—some sort of polyglot human mongrels, Siwash and Wop and Odin knows what all else, all mixed up."

Horten studied the Prinz. The man was appealing for his help. He was obviously a weakling and a fool. But he was well positioned politically and even better positioned militarily. The Svartalheimers might regard Counter-Luna as a boondocks assignment, someplace where they sent an incompetent princeling to keep him out of trouble—and out of their hair—but it was an ideal gun platform. From Counter-Luna a smart military man could call his own shots, dictate his own terms, form his own alliances.

He could keep the Prinz around as figurehead, as front man. But Reimar Horten would run the show.

"Your offer appeals to me strongly, Prinz. But I will need to know just what is available to us here on the moon—what troops, their level of training, their equipment. Especially, what weapons and equipment are available."

Nikolauz's hooded eyes may have flashed for the merest fraction of a second before resuming their look of tipsiness. "Of course, Herr Horten. Whatever you want. Say"—he leaned forward, elbows on his desk; they slipped and he caught his balance in time to push himself upright again—

"say, I think we could toast this little partnership with just a drop of good schnapps, don't you, Horten old boy? Sure you do, sure you do. I can tell!"

Horten lifted his goblet and the Prinz reached for the flagon.

Oswald Mosley muscled *Patrilandia* into the thin air over the Svartalheimer-occupied pyramids. He gunned the nuclear-powered engines, sent the bat-winged craft skimming away from the central lunar fissure. There was no need to traverse the tricky region. *Patrilandia* needed neither to gain nor lose speed; the craft could boost away from Counter-Luna on minimum power, coast down the gravity slope to Counter-Earth, then lose speed again in the planet's upper atmosphere and fly in as a normal aircraft.

Mosley turned to his copilot. "We're fortunate men to live in this century, don't you think, Perón? Why, just thirty years ago I was struggling to get a crate into the air. Bedsheets and baling wire—that's what they were made of. And here we are, flying from planet to planet, all in one lifetime. What do you think of that, eh?"

Perón sat, his chin resting on one fist, his eyes slitted.

Mosley nudged him with his elbow.

Perón started. *"¿Qué pasa?"* He peered around, shook his head. "I am sorry, Sir Oswald. I was distracted. You asked me something."

"No matter, Perón. Merely making conversation. You are worried about Miss Duarte."

Perón grunted an affirmative. "She is so weak. She looks . . ." He shook his head.

"An ambulance will meet us at the aerodrome. It was all arranged from the moon, you know."

Perón looked around. Behind the passenger seats, Evita was resting on a makeshift bed. Her eyes were open, looking half dazed. But she saw Perón watching her and managed a wan smile.

He responded with a grin of his own. He hoped that his worry was not apparent to her.

Evita closed her eyes. Her breathing, although clearly shallow, remained steady.

Perón left his seat, touched Evita's cheek, then moved to peer from *Patrilandia*'s bubble.

As on their own earth and its moon, the Egyptian city on Counter-Luna lay on the long-fabled, so-called dark side of the satellite. In all the complex motions of the two bodies, the pyramids had never been seen from the surface of the planet. Radio communication existed between the bodies; a system of relays already in place when the Svartalheimer troops arrived had been maintained. By this means messages could be sent from the pyramids along relays to the lunar edge, then beamed to earth. Replies followed the same path.

Mosley had been following the path of the radio-relay stations. The last in the series loomed ahead; beyond it, Counter-Luna's curving edge fell away. Empty space lay beyond.

"Here we go," Mosley called from the controls. "Best strap in, old boy!"

Perón remained at the bubble, but steadied himself against a projecting surface.

Mosley executed a skillful wing-over.

The lip of the moon dropped away suddenly beneath them. The illusion that *Patrilandia* had been a land vehicle rolling across the lunar surface left her passengers in a momentary state of vertigo; where pumice and rocks had passed close beneath their craft, there was now a drop of a quarter million miles to the majestically turning Counter-Earth.

"Perhaps I should have let her go," Perón mused aloud.

Mosley said nothing. Counter-Earth was in full edge, its gleaming white ice rim a dazzling diagonal cutting the sky in half dead ahead of *Patrilandia*.

"She wanted to go back to the Temple of Isis. Or to the Temple of Isis here, as she had done on our moon. I was afraid for her, Mosley. I wouldn't let her go."

He crossed the cabin again, knelt beside the sleeping Evita. He took one of her hands in his, held the almost transparent flesh to his cheek. "She was too weak. I was afraid." He released the hand and stood. "You were with her the first time, Mosley. What happened? You never told me all that happened. I want to know."

Mosley looked over his shoulder, then back toward the instruments.

Perón joined him so Mosley could speak to him without turning away from his piloting duties.

"I've told you all I know, Perón. All that I saw. There was an altar, there was an idol. Miss Duarte disappeared beneath the altar. I tried to follow her but I lost her trail. She came out by herself."

"And in the mist region? The time that Evita rescued you. You have not spoken much of that, either."

Mosley became flushed and pale by turns. "I passed out, that's all, old boy, that's really all that happened. There must have been something in that mist, some sort of gas. It's bad stuff."

"Evita found you and carried you back."

Mosley nodded. "A remarkable feat for a frail female."

"She did other things. In the ship. Changes. And her appearance. I think that something happened to her on the moon. She has abnormal powers, but she pays for them— each time she exerts her extraordinary powers, she grows older and weaker. Is she going to die, Mosley? Has she become a witch? Or a saint? I should have let her go back, but I was afraid."

He prepared a cup of broth and carried it to Evita. He had to hold her up as she drank, but it made her a little stronger. *Patrilandia* skimmed over Counter-Earth's ice rim. Mosley's skill and his confidence as pilot rose with each passing hour. Perón alternated with the Englishman at the controls. His touch was heavier than Mosley's, showing less sensitivity to the ship's feel but greater strength in his responses. They were both superb pilots, but their styles were unalike.

At last the ship circled in for a landing. The designated airfield was Washington National Airport. The ultimate source of the radio transmissions that had summoned *Patrilandia* from earth had been here, and here the travelers would meet with the leaders of the struggle on Counter-Earth.

Oswald Mosley conducted the needed communication with National's control tower. *Patrilandia* was piloted by Juan Perón. Eva Duarte, half comatose, lay covered with every available quilt. It was late afternoon. The sky above Washington was a dark gray; a wet sleet had moved in off Chesapeake Bay, producing an early dusk. The lights of the city and streams of automobile headlamps marked a shifting pattern beneath *Patrilandia*.

Even above the sound of *Patrilandia*'s nuclear-powered engines came the roar of a squadron of sleek Seversky fighter planes powered by Pratt and Whitney radial engines. "Fall in with them," Mosley told Perón. "The tower says they'll escort us to the aerodrome."

Surrounded by Severskys, *Patrilandia* made a pass above the night-illuminated Capitol dome, then roared low over the airport. Perón exclaimed in surprise, "I thought this was a civil installation!"

The runways were brightly lit. Perón saw a row of huge Boeing B-15 bombers parked along one runway, their silver skins partially obscured by accumulating sleet. On another, even more remarkably, Perón recognized a contingent of European-built Junkers model 52 trimotors. He could not tell because of the weather, but he suspected that they bore military markings.

He maneuvered *Patrilandia* even lower, approaching the runway Mosley had pointed out. Snowplows had cleared a strip down the center of the tarmac. As *Patrilandia* dropped in to make her landing, Perón spotted an ambulance standing by, headlights blazing, white exhaust rising from its tailpipe.

Minutes later he watched bleakly as Evita was transferred via stretcher to the ambulance. The vehicle roared away from the runway and disappeared.

An officer wearing a Sam Browne belt and sidearm greeted Perón and Mosley. His uniform resembled the *Yanqui* army garb familiar to Perón—with minor changes. The officer's shirt was an odd silvery color. He wore a brassard bearing an unfamiliar red and black device. His officer's insignia denoted a major of the United States Army.

He treated Perón and Mosley with brusque correctness. With a minimum of conversation they followed him to a Pitcairn autogyro. Once they were inside, the officer left them. The pilot whipped the 'gyro's blades to a screaming whirl, then jumped the craft into the sleet-laden air. He gunned the puller prop and sped across the city.

They slid through the evening air over the hideously ugly Smithsonian Institution, over the Mall, and dropped softly onto the White House lawn itself.

The autogyro pilot had not spoken a single word. He leaned across the cabin and undogged the aircraft's door.

Perón and Mosley clambered out and followed more waiting guards into the White House itself.

A Presidential aide in the now-familiar olive and silver uniform ushered them through the White House. He wore a similar brassard on his sleeve, and on his epaulets, the single silver bars of a lieutenant.

The President awaited them in the famous Red Room. The room was dominated by a huge banner bearing the same device as the officers' brassards: a circle half of red, half of black, slashed by a bolt of silver-colored lightning.

The lieutenant presented Perón and Mosley to the President. He was a long-faced individual with graying reddish hair. He wore a civilian suit and the increasingly familiar silver shirt and armband. The lieutenant said, "The President of the United States and leader of the National Renaissance Party, Mr. William Dudley Pelley."

Pelley stood up to shake hands with Perón and Mosley. "We receive many visitors here at the White House." He spoke in a peculiarly dry, harsh-voiced manner. "But I think you beat all for coming a long way to see me. Well, sit yourselves down. I want you to meet my secretary of state, Joe McWilliams; secretary of war, Mrs. Elizabeth Maude Dilling; and attorney general, Mr. Lawrence Dennis."

Perón and Mosley shook hands with the others.

"You've got here at a wonderful time, a glorious time for the whole world, gentlemen! We're at a turning point in the history of civilization, nothing less. And you are going to help us make that turn!"

CHAPTER
15

Fighting to keep control of *Manta* in the sudden vacuum of the ship's crew bubble, Jack Northrop swerved through the meteor shower. Each speck of rock momentarily illuminated by the ship's external lights might be an inert bit of mineral or a potentially deadly foe, a barnaclelike parasite eager to attach itself to the yellow craft and bore into its skin with potentially catastrophic results.

Northrop felt a weight on his shoulder. Prepared for the worst, he turned and saw Albert Einstein thrusting a sheet of paper toward him. The savant had sketched a mathematical model of the distribution of meteors in the shower. He had plotted a circuitous course through the rocks; by following it, *Manta* would encounter the fewest possible collisions.

In the cabin's vacuum, speech was impossible, but Northrop nodded understanding as Einstein ran his finger over the chart. Northrop looked from the chart to the meteors outside. He oriented himself, then swung the ship into the first of the series of maneuvers Einstein's chart dictated.

Miraculously, the repeated impacts of meteorites dropped almost to zero. But something far larger, something the size of a huge man, was creeping over the transparent bubble, blotting out the sky, waving its extremities.

Through the thickly padded altitude suit and breathing apparatus, Northrop recognized Josh Gibson. He swung open the crew hatch and extended his arm to Gibson.

Gibson caught Northrop's arm; with the engineer's help he was able to crawl back into the cabin. He gestured frantically, pointing to the rear of the ship.

Didrikson!

No word was exchanged. Northrop realized instantly what must have happened. Standing on *Manta*'s wing, trying to keep a grasp on the craft with one hand while wielding the iron crowbar against the attacking parasites, Babe had been tossed from the wing. She was drifting now. If they didn't get her back in, and get her fast, she would surely die.

Northrop kicked *Manta* through a tight inside loop. Since up and down were purely arbitrary, there was no need to add the roll that would complete the Immelmann. He drove back through the meteor swarm. As if angered by *Manta*'s repeated disturbance, the rocklike creatures increased the ferocity of their attack.

Northrop knotted a lifeline to the belt of Gibson's suit. He should have done this to start with, with both athletes, he realized. But there was nothing to be gained by self-castigation. He peered ahead of *Manta*. There, as far ahead as the ship's lights could pick her out, Babe Didrikson twisted, desperately struggling to pluck the ugly parasites from her suit.

Without a word being spoken, Josh Gibson crawled through the hatch again. While Northrop maneuvered the ship toward Babe, Gibson determinedly worked with his crowbar, picking space barnacles from *Manta*. He had developed a method of smashing one against another, using his crowbar like the bat that had terrified a generation of pitchers.

When *Manta* swept past Babe Didrikson, Josh gauged the distance to the stranded athlete. He couldn't reach her. Instead, he launched himself from *Manta*'s wing, using the muscles of his spring-steel legs to send himself hurtling toward Babe.

He held his crowbar in one hand. With the other he had grasped the lifeline before launching himself, and now he paid it out as he swung toward Babe.

They collided, managed to hold for a moment, then he was tugged away, past her, by *Manta*'s continuing motion. He could feel *Manta* swinging again in her course. He was whipped behind the ship like that tail of her namesake.

Northrop headed back toward Didrikson again.

Gibson forced down his bile as he realized that she had been almost covered with parasites. His own padded suit was slashed where the sharp, rocklike exoskeletons of the barnacles had struck.

He swept up on Didrikson again. *Manta's* yellow shape had barely missed her as Northrop canted past. Josh could see that Didrikson had managed to grab at his lifeline, but it was moving too fast for her to get a firm grip. Instead, the line was slipping through her gloved hands, or she was sliding down the line toward Gibson.

He braced himself for the impact he couldn't avoid. It was like blocking homeplate and having Buck Leonard barrel in from third, arms pumping and spikes high.

Wham!

He couldn't be knocked off the lifeline, but he could lose his crowbar—and Babe Didrikson could go careening off once more, probably knocked unconscious, and they might not be able to reach her again in time to save her life. Once those parasites had bored through her padded suit, her life was up for grabs.

But he was able to hold her. He was knocked half unconscious himself, but he wrapped his arms and legs around her, clutched his iron crowbar across her back.

Northrop began hauling them back toward *Manta*. Even as the lifeline was drawn in, Gibson resumed working on the barnacles, prying them off Babe's altitude suit with frantic speed.

Inside the transparent bubble Northrop and Gibson stripped Babe of her padded altitude suit. They got it through the hatch and away from *Manta* as fast as they could. Northrop had already managed to get a patch onto the holed bubble, and atmosphere was pumping back into the cabin.

Einstein had broken out the ship's first aid kit. He swabbed the wounds on Didrikson's body. None were deep; still, by the time Einstein had finished applying tincture of Mercurochrome, Didrikson's tanned skin looked like an Expression-ist's nightmare. Gently, the scientist helped her into a set of soft clothing.

"We're out of the things," Northrop announced. "That course you plotted saved us, Doc."

"It was like planning a tack," Einstein said. "When you sail, you have to learn."

Josh Gibson said, "I got one more task to tend do." He still wore his heavy suit. He hefted his crowbar and made his way to *Manta*'s wing. Behind him, the others could be seen inside the bubble. Didrikson was recovering from her narrow escape from death in the meteor swarm. Einstein and Northrop pored over papers, referring to the ship's instruments and to Einstein's computations.

Gibson set to work freeing *Manta* of the barnacles that had attached themselves to her during the ship's transit through the swarm. He kept his lifeline attached to his suit, but did not need it. The most difficult part of his task was working around from the craft's upper surface to her lower—there was no up or down, few handholds on *Manta*'s surfaces, and Gibson's heavily padded hands had difficulty in keeping their grip.

Still, he dislodged every parasite he could find.

When he finished the task, he was arm-weary and drenched in sweat. He made his way back to the bubble, negotiated the hatch, and threw himself onto the deck to rest.

Einstein explained their situation to the two athletes. *Manta* had completed most of her journey. Counter-Earth and Counter-Luna were growing objects ahead of the ship, spinning about each other as well as maintaining their own motions.

Didrikson had recovered her alertness and regained much of her strength. She asked, "What about the other ship?"

"Horten?" Northrop looked at her. "I don't know. Probably, they're way ahead of us. May have landed already."

"What about the radio?"

"I've been trying. In fact, it's been a while. Time for another attempt."

Babe propped herself up on her elbows. She took a deep breath, pushed herself to her feet, and stood over Northrop. "I don't understand what those Egyptians were up to, Jack. I know we've been over this and over it, but were they from

Egypt to start with or not? And why did they leave earth? And what are they doing now?''

Northrop shook his head. ''They don't know themselves where they originated. They left earth because they were so horrified by what they had done, they couldn't stay any longer. And they're not doing *anything* now, just staying on Ceres and watching the worlds go by. The two earths that they're responsible for, where there had only been one.''

''Then they won't help us. That's what I'm after. They won't, eh? We're strictly on our own!''

''That's right. But let me see what I can get here.''

He worked with the ship's radio. ''I think I can hear something, but I can't understand it. I'm going to head in for Counter-Earth. Dr. Einstein is plotting a course for us to use Counter-Luna as a braking force and fly in gently to the planet itself.''

Counter-Luna and Counter-Earth lined up like concentric rings on an archer's target, with *Manta* the arrow.

''That hole in the moon gave us a big boost comin' up, won't it do the same thing going back?'' Gibson asked.

Northrop said, ''It will do just the opposite. What I'm going to try is to whip through there, lose momentum in the fissure, then swing around the earth and back to the moon and do the whole thing over again. We can lose enough speed that way to make a nice gentle landing. Otherwise, we'd burn up or auger in, one or the other.''

Counter-Luna grew until it filled most of the sky ahead of *Manta*. Northrop angled away to avoid the straight-on shot. He kicked *Manta* into an angular dive, headed for the fissure. As the ship approached Counter-Luna, the pyramids and sphinxes near the fissure came into view.

Gibson watched. ''Land of Pharaoh again!''

The dancing electromagnetic glow within the fissure became visible.

Manta's radio crackled. An unfamiliar voice came over the ship's speaker. Einstein raised his face to peer at Counter-Luna. ''They speak German here?'' he said.

''Is that it?'' Northrop asked. ''I speak a little of the stuff, but I couldn't understand that.''

''Old German. Very old, and strange. But German, yes.''

Northrop passed the handmike to Einstein. "See who it is. It can't be the Horten bunch—they'd speak modern German."

Einstein took the microphone. He fumbled with the switch on its side, turned the thing over and back, then spoke into it.

The alien voice came crackling back, but before the message was complete, *Manta* had entered the electromagnetic field at the satellite's center.

The radio blacked out as *Manta* rushed into the fissure. Once more electrical fields flowed, lightning crackled. The ship shuddered and slowed perceptibly, then moved out of the channel and dropped away from Counter-Luna. The second earth stood in dazzling full disk beneath the four travelers' eyes.

Manta flashed toward Counter-Earth. Although the ship's speed had been reduced by its passage through the moon, it was still moving at a dangerous pace. A direct approach to Counter-Earth could still be disastrous. The ship might, with luck, survive a quick trip through the atmosphere: its clean design minimized drag and friction.

But the speed with which it was moving was far beyond its capacity to absorb in a landing. An attempt to bring *Manta* in at any airport would leave only a pile of smoldering rubble.

"Something's wrong!" Northrop yelled. "We're off course."

Gibson said, "But we're headed right in there."

"That's just the problem! We're supposed to approach at a glancing angle."

Einstein peered at his scribbled figures. "Another mistake I made, I think."

Northrop shook his head. "I don't think so. There's something wrong with the ship. God knows, she's been through enough—the storm, the Einstein layer, two attacks by Horten and his bunch."

"I don't think it's any of those," Gibson said. He shook his head slowly. "When those meteor things were chewing away at us, at the end there, after Babe was safe, I went back out. I tried to get 'em all, but if I missed one and it got inside . . ." He shook his head again.

"That could be it," said Northrop. "Anyway, she's not responding right. If I try to swerve now and get us back on course, we could start tumbling. That would mean a sure crash.''

Einstein said softly, "Then what are you going to do?"

"We only have one chance." Northrop narrowed his eyes as he gazed at the dangerous target thousands of miles ahead of *Manta*. He set his jaw; a look came into his eyes that his companions had not seen before. They had faced perils aplenty, but not one such as this, one in which the lives of four human beings and the fate of two planets rested squarely on Jack Northrop's shoulders.

"Everybody strap in!"

The sun glinted off the icy seas that surrounded Counter-Earth's North Hole. Glaciers moving slowly across the northernmost stretches of Spitzbergen and Siberia, Alaska's north slope and Greenland. Beyond them the grinding ice floes and roaring maelstroms of the legendary Symmes' Hole.

Only fifteen years had passed since Charles Augustus Lindbergh, Amelia Earhart, and Howard Hughes had come roaring back from the far side of the disk, completing a successful circuit of the hole-rim course between the earth's two sides. Mere days before the European team of Manfred and Lothar von Richthofen and the Russian Princess Irina Lvova had traversed the Hole from the European side to the legendary realm of Muvia and Svartalheim and Hai Brasil.

Their huge Udet *Kondor* had weathered the Hole successfully, but had failed to complete the journey via the South Rim.

The Lindbergh-Earhart-Hughes party in their specially crafted *Spirit of San Diego* had completed the journey via Rim and Hole, and had thereby opened the modern era of commerce and mutual exploration between earth's two hemidisks.

And on Counter-Earth—had similar events transpired?

Soon the answer would be known!

Had the great circumpolar air race taken place prior to the fateful date of October 4, 1912, there would be no question. Prior to that date the history of the two earths was identical, for the two earths had been one. But any event dating from that moment onward was a mystery.

Manta plunged Counter-Earthward. The planetary disk filled all of the sky, all of the view of the travelers. Behind them the Counter-Lunar disk was perfectly aligned with the sun.

"We arrive in a time of eclipse," Einstein commented. "The astronomers will be out in force, observing the shadows and the sun. I wonder, will they see us?"

No one had an answer for that.

Counter-Luna's shadow was moving across the planetary disk, making a black circle that moved across the landscape. In the center of the shadow, a seeming point of illumination blazed, drawing a white line over mountain, forest, ocean.

At the moment that the shadow crossed the North Hole, *Manta* plunged into the circular chasm of ice.

The roar of the North Hole's eternal maelstrom blotted out the sound of *Manta*'s magnetic engines.

The skyship herself plunged down the center of the opening. Her only hope of avoiding a fatal plunge into roaring brine or a disastrous collision with a mountainous shard of ice was to hold just this course.

The edges of the Hole were cloaked in darkness, a depressing contrast to the brilliant illuminations of *Manta*. Even as the craft plunged onward into blackness, the shaft of light moved from her graceful wings. The ship was in midnight darkness.

The shaft of light glanced off the rushing brine. In a moment of frozen reality, the travelers—all of them save Jack Northrop, whose attention was riveted on *Manta*'s controls—caught sight of a centuries-old square-rigged ship, her sails in tatters, her crew long reduced to skeletons or less, swirling in an endless, solitary minuet.

Then the shaft of light was gone.

Through the blackness of the Hole, Jack Northrop caught sight of a distant star. He bore in on it, praying beneath his breath that *Manta* would not be destroyed.

Now with an almost audible rush full daylight swept back into the Hole.

Northrop reacted with lightninglike reflexes. *Manta* had come within inches of smashing a wingtip against a floating iceberg.

On the surface of the berg a hunting pack of monstrous white worms rose and waved dripping mandibles in futile rage at the loss of their prey.

Manta swerved crazily back toward the center of the fissure. Northrop swallowed, wiped at his face with one hand, then went back to concentrating on his work.

When *Manta* emerged from the farside opening, it was into deep night. Counter-Luna was providing afternoon companionship to the sun on the familiar side of Counter-Earth, and the unknown side slept in darkness.

"Which direction now, Jack?" Josh Gibson asked.

Einstein replied before Northrop could. "They are all south from here, Joshua!"

"But our compass will catch," Northrop added. "And we have maps of this side."

"So you do have a plan!" Babe Didrikson was almost her old self.

Northrop asked Josh Gibson to take the controls. "Just keep her on this course." He drew a deep breath, then let it out. "You see, we don't really know who sent the request for assistance on Counter-Earth, and we don't know what conditions are here. There's been a top-secret government study going on, ever since the signals were first detected. Dr. Einstein has been our chief consultant. We've had teams at top universities working on this thing.

"What Colonel Selk said about 1912 clarified the situation a lot. We didn't know what conditions we'd find here on Counter-Earth, and we had no idea why there even were two earths. Selk answered that one all right!

"The big threat that we *think* we're facing comes from the Svartalheimers on this side of the disk, and their relatives in Europe. That's an alliance that we faced on our own earth. The involvement of Horten supports that theory. Who else they're tied in with—almost certainly forces operating out of Argentina—we'll find out."

"Then, where are we headed?"

Northrop looked into the darkness outside *Manta*. "Muvia. The Muvians are the most advanced people on their side of the disk. They were also the target of Svartalheimer aggression at the time of the Lindbergh expedition. We've kept tabs on the situation in our own world. We don't know what may be going on on Counter-Earth."

Didrikson said, "Do we have any agents in Muvia?"

Northrop spread his hands. "On our earth, yes. On

Counter-Earth, do our counterparts in America have a presence in Muvia—¿quien sabe?''

Josh Gibson turned from the controls for a moment. ''I don't see why we don't just head for America. Your orders came from Washington, didn't they?''

Northrop agreed that they had. ''But we can get there in a day or two. I'd rather err on the side of caution than take an unneeded risk.''

''You mean, Washington doesn't know we're coming?''

''That—or worse. We don't really know the history of this planet after October 1912. That's almost thirty years. What might have happened in that time?''

There was no answer to the question. But Gibson had another. ''What about Jack Northrop? I mean, if this is another earth, don't they have another one of you around here? Where is he? What's he doing?''

When Northrop failed to respond, Gibson pushed on. ''How about another Einstein? Another Didrikson? Another Josh Gibson?''

Einstein supplied the response that Northrop did not. ''Mr. Joshua, I have spoken with my young friend Werner Heisenberg many times about his so-called uncertainty principle. He holds that in a sense the ultimate truth of the universe is not subject to our knowing. But if this is so, it does not mean that there is no objective reality—merely that nature places a barrier between ourselves and this ultimate truth.''

Gibson shook his head and turned back to Manta's controls. ''Whatever you say, Doc. But I'm not sure if I understood you. Did you answer what I asked?''

Einstein laughed. ''My good friend, you illustrate my point beautifully. Well, but we may learn some answers; God gives us that much. Soon we will be there, and then we shall see if there is for us each a doppelgänger.''

Gibson was still at Manta's controls when the magnificent ziggurats of Muvia loomed ahead of them. It was dawn on this hemidisk. The sun's rays burned through night mist; columns of vaporizing fog rose over the red-tinted city. Silent Muvian air platforms drifted between the huge structures. Farther away the buildings were of more modest dimensions. Quays extended from the island's shoreline into natural harbors. Sailing ships competed with giant magnetic platforms for cargoes of foodstuffs and manufactured goods.

On the roofs of the nearer ziggurats, Muvian ray projectors focused on approaching and departing platforms. Huge botanical enterprises dominated the roofs and broad steps of the pyramidlike ziggurats.

"The hanging gardens," Josh Gibson whispered. "I've been to the land of Pharaoh and now I see the hanging gardens of Babylon. Nebuchadnezzar will be here. Doctor, do they worship Baal? Will we walk in the fiery furnace?"

"I think these are a kindly people, Joshua. And this is not really Babylon, although I must agree with you that it looks like it."

Ray projectors turned toward *Manta*. "Jack, they're taking us over," Josh exclaimed. "I can't control us at all!"

Northrop slid into place beside Gibson. "Don't fight it. The Lindbergh expedition reported the same thing. They'll bring us in."

A broad tarmac had been cleared on the roof of the city's largest ziggurat. Magnificent flowering shrubs surrounded it; palm trees stretched their graceful trunks above the flat roof.

Manta dropped gracefully onto the tarmac.

The four travelers stirred. Babe Didrikson was already at the exit hatch, ready to leave the craft. "Let me go first," she said to the others. "If there's any danger—damn it, I've been the least useful on this expedition. Let me take the risk."

She didn't wait for a response. She undogged the hatch and jumped down from *Manta*'s yellow wing onto the tarmac. She drew a deep breath of sparkling morning air. Although it was summer, the early hour and the altitude of the ziggurat kept the air cool.

Free of the confinement of the little ship, recovered from her wounds, Babe wanted to jump, to dance, to whoop with sheer exuberance.

She did! She let out a single happy yell.

She had not seen the opening in the mazelike gardens.

The woman who stepped from the opening was slim, taller than Babe. She wore breeches and a soft blouse. Her light hair was done in a short, graceful bob—a fashion some ten years out of date. She wore boots. Her skin was deeply tanned, and showed the lines of middle age.

As the woman advanced toward her, Babe stared. Her mind raced. The woman looked familiar to her; she had seen pictures of her, newsreels in fact. She had been one of the most famous persons in the world some years before. She'd been one of Babe's girlhood heroines. Older now, but that was natural. She had disappeared half a dozen years ago.

Her fate had been subject of endless conjecture and wild rumors. She was one of the great mysteries of history, one of the famous disappearances. And now she advanced toward Babe Didrikson across the roof of the hanging gardens of Babylon—alone, unarmed, unafraid, welcoming the strange skyship.

"Amelia Earhart," Babe cried.

A frown creased Amelia Earhart's forehead—which smoothed again as she held both hands out in greeting. Babe responded in kind. Amelia said, "I know you from the newsreels. I saw you in the Olympic Games. What an honor to meet you! Welcome to Muvia, Babe Didrikson!"

CHAPTER
16

Their horses snorting loudly, the breath of animals and riders alike steaming in the frigid Andean air, Peroni and his guest galloped their mounts toward the stony redoubt. The steel-gray granite of the Andean peaks alternated with patches of snow. Although the snow was old, its purity sparkled as it had when new-fallen, here in the crystalline mountain air.

Peroni grinned the wide smile that had won him friends and favor throughout the Argentine army. It had also won him the trust of his hosts in a series of foreign postings. He had served as his government's military attaché in Vienna, Rome, Madrid, and in Santiago. In each city he had charmed the ladies despite—or perhaps because of—his being a happily and thoroughly married man.

His famed charms had also won him access to an amazing series of closely guarded state papers in each nation. His charm and the network of agents he commanded in behalf of his government had served both the major and the Republic of Argentina well. It was only in Chile that his path had been discovered, and then only after his departure from Santiago, wife and horse safely in tow, that the Chileans had discovered the extent of his work. And then they had laid the blame squarely in the lap of Peroni's successor, the hapless and innocent Lonardi!

Now, back in Argentina, Major Giovanni Peroni had been posted *Comandante* of the army's winter warfare school at San Carlos de Bariloche. He missed the blond, musical Aurelia, now mistress of the Peroni *estancia* in remote Chank Aike in southern Patagonia. But in a few months he would receive a few weeks' leave and return to the *estancia* and the bosom of his family.

For now, he was content with his assignment and more than content with his life.

He slowed his magnificent dapple gray to a gentle canter. His guest did the same with his borrowed chestnut gelding.

"Your President Ramírez was correct, Major. The landscape here is very much like the Alps! The sights fill my heart with beauty—and yet I long to see my home again!"

"I knew you would love it," Peroni said. "When I was in Italy, the Admiral himself told me that the Alps would make me homesick for Argentina. Our nations are alike in many ways—perhaps that is why so many Italians have come to make their homes in Argentina!"

"It could be." The visitor would have said more, but the two horsemen had reined in at the entryway of the school itself. They walked their horses beneath a portcullis. Major Peroni took the salute of the gate guard—the guard whose duties were more ceremonial than real. Who would want to enter such a school except one authorized to be there?

The school was housed in an ancient building, one that predated the independence of the Republic. Its thick walls and heavy battlements, its towers and turrets, made it resemble a castle that would not have been out of place in the Europe of half a millennium before.

In fact, it was fully 300 years old, built by a half-mad millionaire who had emigrated from Thuringia. He had dreamed of building for himself an empire in South America incorporating Araucanian Indians, Thuringian immigrants, and a priesthood of his own choice, their posts to be confirmed by the Pope.

Forces of the Spanish Empire had surrounded the mad Emperor Wotan's castle and held him at bay until in a fit of despair he had flung himself from a tower, disappearing into an Andean abyss. Wotan's body had never been found, and his restless spirit was believed by some to haunt his castle—

now the army's mountain warfare school—pleading with his followers to repulse the Spanish and establish his reign.

A pair of orderly-grooms led the two horses away to be curried. The *Comandante* and his guest made their way to Peroni's private suite. A fire had been laid in the sitting room. The major showed his guest to a comfortable armchair facing the fireplace. Peroni opened a wooden cabinet, removed a bottle of brandy, and brought it with fine glasses to the fireplace.

"To your leader, Admiral Balbo," Peroni said.

"And to yours, the equally splendid President Ramírez." They drank.

Peroni said, "Dinner will be served in an hour. An orderly will summon us. In the meanwhile, I think we can talk some serious business, Signore Mussolini."

The Italian smiled. His broad face and lantern jaw contrasted with Peroni's flashing teeth, as his balding pate contrasted with Peroni's heavy, black hair.

"It's been a long while since you were in Italy, Major."

"It has," Peroni agreed, "but I have not wasted my time since then. I trust that you have not, either."

Mussolini shook his head. "I have sounded out the king as to his feelings. He wants nothing but to be left alone. He calls it staying above politics. The English model. Let the little ministers and the military popinjays strut and squabble as they will.

"I think what happened, he saw the trouble that Wilhelm and Nicholas got themselves into in 1912. Lucky to escape with their heads, both of them. Willy lost his crown at that, the Bismarcks have turned into Mikados. And Nicholas—well, he won't be missed. Not by the Russians and not by anyone else."

Peroni grunted. He had been staring into the fireplace, perhaps seeing visions of Aurelia, perhaps seeing visions of her and of himself, not as a humble field officer and army wife, but as something far more splendid, riding through the streets of Buenos Aires in a Duesenberg or a Rolls, waving to a multitude and returning to the Casa Rosada to preside over a glittering state ball.

"You really believe you can displace Balbo, then?" he asked.

"With no doubt whatsoever. The fool tells me everything—I'm his tame journalist, you know, trumpeting every
little pronouncement that the grand Admiral chooses to make.
But I need the help of *Italia Diaspora*. You are such an Italian
yourself, Signore Peroni."

"Not quite," Peroni demurred. "My father was Sardi-
nian. My mother was half-Araucanian. I am a native-born
Argentine."

"But you carry the blood of the noble Roman." Mussolini's prognathous jaw jutted when he spoke the phrase. "And
the new Rome shall outshine in glory the old!"

Peroni turned his back to the fireplace. He faced Mussolini
but in fact he was gazing beyond the Italian journalist, pondering on the eternal paradox of Argentina, a paradox em-
bodied in his own heritage and one that he perceived every
time he observed his Araucanian-tinctured features in a
looking glass.

He raised his snifter and peered over its rim. Behind Mussolini, on his own, Peroni's, desk, stood a modern radio-
telephone linked with relay stations that could carry his voice
all the way to Buenos Aires and beyond. Yet behind that desk
there hung on the stone wall erected by the mad Wotan a pair
of dueling sabers, and beside the sabers a stone-framed window—now double-glassed to keep out the eternal mountain
chill—the Andes. Beautiful and cruel, their razor-sharp ridges
had felt the padded feet of gentle guanacos and given nest to
the huge Andean condors for tens of thousands of years. They
had stood here not only before the Spanish invaders arrived,
but before even the Indians had made their way down the
spine of the continent, before the legendary sailors of Rapa
Nui or the ancient Asian explorers had set foot in Chile.

He tried to imagine what Argentina—in fact the whole of
the New World—had been like in those ancient days. Egypt
and Babylonia, at least, and possibly also the ancient Empire
of the Han, had existed by then. Civilizations long extinct
and forgotten might have held sway in the Mediterranean, in
Africa, in India. Certainly the peoples of the far side of the
earth were in place—some of them, at least.

But in all of South and North America, no human foot had
ever strode. No human eye had ever seen the tropical jungle
of the Amazon or the bleak gray plains of Patagonia. No boat

had sailed the great lakes of South America. No human had ever confronted the magnificent cats that roamed the southern land, the wolves that roamed the distant north. No man had beheld the wonderful birds that populated the continent: toucan, macaw, eagle, condor, penguin.

And someday the vain human enterprise would disappear, leaving the majestic Andes and the teeming wildlife as if mankind had never intruded.

"Signore! Major Peroni!"

He blinked and put down his glass, withdrew a pair of oversized rimless spectacles from his desk drawer. "Forgive me. I was distracted. You were saying . . . ?"

Mussolini smiled his tight-lipped smile. "Merely that we might return to Buenos Aires in the morning. My tour here has been both enlightening and enjoyable, but I must continue my work."

Peroni assented. "I will accompany you. We can take the railroad at Jacobacci. It's a long trip to Buenos Aires. You'll see some of our spectacular countryside."

Two days later their train pulled into a dusty village. The journey had indeed been spectacular, crossing Argentina's Mesa Volcanica de Somungura after descending from the Andes, reaching the ocean at San Antonio Oestres, crossing the Río Negro at its mouth near Punta Rasa. . . .

The village was developed enough to support a wooden railroad station. There was a rough platform, a crude shed, a sign with the name of the village painted in letters that had long since faded. Through their coating of grime they were barely legible: "Junín."

Mussolini and Peroni had shared a first-class compartment all the way from Jocobacci. The cramped quarters dictated by railroad travel were beginning to cause friction between them, despite their mutual esteem. Each, however, for his own reason saw fit to maintain cordial relations.

Mussolini was just finishing an elaborate meal. The sun had risen not long before, and the two men had shared a breakfast of eggs and *biftec asada* accompanied by heavy, black coffee. "Why are we stopping here, Peroni?"

The major bent and peered from the window. "Junín? What a lousy burg! It's beyond me!"

The train inched forward. The two men could see a magnificent private railroad car being readied on a siding.

"I've got it now," Peroni said. "You see that car? Recognize it? That's the most famous private railroad car in Argentina. President Ramírez himself doesn't travel in that kind of style!"

Mussolini put down an unfinished morsel of *asada* and craned his neck. "Whose is it then? The British ambassador's?"

"You do not understand Argentina, Señor Mussolini. That car belongs to Agustín Magaldi, the most famous tango singer of the nation. Whenever he tours the countryside, he travels by private car. *Ho-ho!* Come have a look at this!"

A young girl had apparently stowed away in Magaldi's car. She was being evicted by one of his entourage.

She tumbled backward from the iron steps and landed on her derriere in the rocks and cinders of the railroad siding. She jumped to her feet, brushing herself off. She was barefoot, scrawny, dark-haired. Her hair was coiffured in a clumsy imitation of the elaborate upsweep pictured in the magazines of the day. Her dress was short, its skimpy skirt revealing dirt-smeared legs and scabby knees.

She started to jump up and down, shaking her fists at the private car. She was screaming at the top of her lungs.

"Can you hear what she's saying?" Mussolini asked.

Peroni laughed again. "Not a syllable, but I can read her lips just a little bit." He studied the girl in silence for a minute. He laughed again. "Señor Mussolini, I grew up among gauchos and I have spent my life among soldiers, and I'll tell you something. Never in my forty-seven years on this planet have I witnessed an exhibition of cursing to match that girl's!"

The girl flung herself at the guard of the private car. She was repulsed with more violence than she had met the first time. Her face turned crimson. She picked up a fist-sized rock from the railroad bed and flung it at the nearest window of the car. The rock bounced away, leaving a webwork of cracks where it had struck.

A second guard appeared on the car's platform. The two guards grasped the screaming girl by her arms and pulled her into the car. Shortly it was attached to the train and the journey to Buenos Aires resumed.

The two men found their spirits revived by the girl's spunky performance and its unexpected finale. Mussolini reached inside his frock coat and pulled out a tortoiseshell cigar case. He extended the case to Peroni, then extracted a smoke for himself.

Still chuckling, they lit up. "Well," Mussolini said with a sigh, "I guess you never can tell how things are going to come out. Young girls throw themselves at famous men the world over—I've seen it on three continents now. You ought to see the women who cluster around all the Caponi brothers in Chicago. They use every kind of allure known to their gender: beauty, silken gowns, fine perfumes.

"But this one tops them all! Tattered dress, filthy bare feet, screaming curses, and throwing rocks. But it worked. One must give her credit for that—it worked!"

Peroni joined him in his laughter.

Mosley sat in the rear compartment of his hired Cooper saloon, sunk in a dark blue funk. He had obtained the agreement of Major Perón and the Washington group to his proposal that he visit Britain and establish contact with his own followers. The Washington people—Pelley, McWilliams, Mrs. Dilling—had resisted the idea at first. They would know his British organization, certainly, if he had one. They knew of no such organization, therefore . . .

Therefore, what?

Therefore, he must be a fake, a poseur.

What, then, could be his motive?

They trusted Perón well enough, and Eva Duarte had proved a grand winner with them. The Pelley group had experienced major problems with the press and radio in the States. Despite Pelley's overwhelming election victory in the Presidential race of 1940—certainly a violent reaction to the failure of the previous Norman Thomas regime—he had failed to win the support of influential newspapers and magazines, radio commentators and motion-picture newsreel producers.

They all too often opposed Presidential policies, and the more Pelley tried to bring them to heel, the more they attacked him before the public.

Eva Duarte had spent a long session alone with the chief executive. Following this she was with him every day, sometimes alone and sometimes in company with other advisers. She imparted to him her own skill in manipulating and controlling the broadcasters and the journalists. Her suggestions, backed up by Pelley's squads of uniformed volunteers, were beginning to take effect.

But why did Mosley's own British Legion of Blackshirts fail to register when mentioned in the White House? Why was Mosley's own name unfamiliar?

On his own stamping grounds, he had sworn to find out.

And in London, at the War Office, he had!

Second Lieutenant Oswald Mosley, Royal Flying Corps, had been killed over Vimy Ridge, France, 1 January 1913.

The Cooper saloon purred along the back roads of Staffordshire, winter-bare beech trees stretching skeletal branches overhead, fields of winter-dead grass stretching to the rolling hills on either side, patches of unmelted snow punctuating the brown fields with grayish white.

The Cooper pulled through tall swinging gates at Wooten Manor. Black marble globes surmounted the portals of the spacious grounds.

Looking up from the cushioned seat, Mosley allowed himself a bitter smile. The four-story house loomed against the dark gray January sky, a darker gray monstrosity. Mother had refused to put in central heating, and the dozens of fireplaces scattered through the Manor's fifty rooms expelled their smoke through dozens of tiny chimneys that gave the roof of the Manor a ragged, unfinished look, as if the builders had contemplated a fifth story and started to lay down its framework, only to lose interest and leave their work in this messy state of incompletion.

He had never cared much for Mother. It was only a peculiar sense of obligation to his dead father that made Mosley keep up contact with the old woman. Once she was gone, he could install whatever friends and associates he chose at the Manor. Things would be different then: better.

He wasn't even sure why he was making this visit. If the Oswald Mosley of Counter-Earth had been dead for more than twenty-nine years, he certainly could not walk in on the old woman and introduce himself as her long-lost son, back from those decades in the grave.

The gravel of the circular driveway crunched beneath the wheels of the Cooper. The sound was oddly pleasant to Mosley, almost hypnotic. When the car halted before the broad stairway leading to the main entrance, he felt a moment of inexplicable sadness. He told the driver to wait for him. His visit would not be a long one. He would require transportation back to town.

He let himself in at the Manor's main entrance. Jenkins the footman, startled, moved toward Mosley. Jenkins! Still here after all these years! On Mosley's earth he had died of influenza in 1921!

The old man peered at Mosley with pale, watery eyes. His mouth gaped. "Sir Os—" the old man started.

Mosley frowned at him. He held his hat for the old man to take. "I'll keep my stick, thank you." He let the old man take his coat.

Jenkins was staring at him. This was the moment he had to survive, he knew. If he succeeded with the old man, then he thought he could do well with Mother also. First, Jenkins. "Is something the matter, my man? Stop staring!"

"I'm very sorry, sir." The old man shook his head. "I thought for a moment"—he paused—"that I knew you, sir. That you were someone else, sir. I'm sorry, sir."

"I am here to see Lady Mosley."

The old man said, "Yes, sir." He held out a silver tray.

What a fool, Mosley thought. What a fool I am! In no way could he send in his card. Instead, he found a blank in his case, unscrewed the cap of his pen, then hesitated. His mind was vacant. He needed a name. He scribbled.

The old man thanked him and hobbled away.

Soon he was back. He led Mosley into Mother's sitting room as if he were a stranger. The old lady sat stiffly erect on her favorite chair. When Mosley entered the room, she pushed herself stiffly to her feet, leaning on a stick. She wore an old-style floor-length black dress, a single strand of pearls around her high-collared throat. Her hair was white and piled atop her head.

She stared as Mosley entered. She cast a quick look over

her shoulder, then returned to gaze at him. She trembled visibly.

Behind her hung the object she had looked at fleetingly, a huge painting, stretching very nearly from ceiling to floor. It was a larger than life-size portrait of himself as a boy just out of Sandhurst. He wore the uniform of the Royal Flying Corps marked with the Sam Browne belt and cocked cap and single golden pip of a second lieutenant. A sidearm hung in its holster.

The boy stood before a Bristol Scout. Behind him a wind sock hung limp before a camouflage-painted hangar.

"You must forgive me, Captain," the woman said. She looked down at the hand-written card that she held now. "Captain Jenkins. Or do you prefer Sir Aubrey?"

"Either, Mo—Madame." He stepped toward her, leaning on his stick. And here we stand, he thought, each of us leaning on a piece of polished wood, staring at each other.

"You must forgive me," she repeated. "My son was killed on New Year's Day, 1913. It is my custom to spend the first week of each year in mourning. Perhaps younger persons do not understand such conduct. I realize that customs have changed, but I have not."

"I understand, Madame. That is why I have come. I hope you will forgive *me* for arriving uninvited. I have been in Washington until very recently and had not the time to write to you."

"Of course." She stared at him again. "I see that you are looking at the picture of my son. It was made after his death, of course. But I think it a very good likeness. If you will pardon my saying so, Kip would have been about your age had he lived. There is even a strong resemblance to your features."

Mosley looked at the shadowy moustache on the lip of the boy in the painting. He found himself involuntarily fingering his own black moustache.

"Perhaps," he admitted. "It's hard for me to say."

Lady Mosley lowered herself once more to her chair. "I do not wish to appear inhospitable, Captain Jenkins. But one does not normally receive casual callers during the annual period of mourning for one's eldest son. May I inquire as to your purpose in coming to Wooten Manor?"

Mosley cursed himself for choosing the name Jenkins. It was the first to come to mind, but he had taken the name of Lady Mosley's footman as his own! "May I be seated, Lady Mosley? An old war injury. Hardly even a wound. But in damp weather . . ."

She motioned him to a chair. It was one he had occupied a thousand times; the same, or its indistinguishable twin. "As I mentioned, I have recently returned to England. I have been away from this island for many years—in America, and elsewhere. I should have visited you long since."

He waited for a response, but she instead waited for him to resume. "It is about your son that I have come here."

She merely nodded.

Mosley found himself perspiring. He drew his handkerchief and wiped his forehead. "We were together, Kip and I." She reacted when he used the name Kip. He knew it was one kept for family, but he was damned if he would refrain from using his own name for himself, even to sustain this ruse. "We were together at Sandhurst, and at flying school, and—at Vimy Ridge."

Now she responded at last. He could see tears trembling in her eyes. He gave no indication of seeing them.

"Your name is—" she read his card yet again—"Group Captain Sir Aubrey Jenkins. I fail to recognize the name. Kip wrote to me until the end, you know." She hesitated. Then, "Just which Jenkinses are your people, Captain? Do I know them?"

"Cumberland, Madame."

She did not question the assertion.

"I came because I remember Kip each New Year's, too. I felt . . . that I ought to."

She offered him tea. He accepted. It was as it had always been at Wooten Manor.

"Please tell me, Captain, about Kip. I received only the official dispatch. There was a letter from his commanding officer also, but one could tell that it was merely a formality. Tell me how Kip . . . died."

Mosley smiled inwardly.

"It was dawn. We were sent out on patrol. Our Bristols were unarmed, you understand. We carried sidearms when we flew. Webley revolvers. Peach-cheeked boys with Webley revolvers against Richthofen's Fokkers! Would you believe it!

"And we didn't know any better, or care any better. We thought we'd live forever, you see. Or die gloriously for King and Country. We were children playing."

"Was it Fokkers, then?" she asked. "I had thought—"

"It was Fokkers, Madame. Richthofen's *Staffel*. They were far in advance of our aircraft. Faster, more maneuverable. And they were equipped with machine guns! We were thrown to them, just thrown to them. I was one of the few lucky ones, Lady Mosley. I came away with this." He rapped his stick against the side of his shoe. The sound it made gave the impression that he had a wooden leg.

"New Year's Day. Fog and sleet. Bitter cold on the ground and worse by far in the air." His eyes grew misty, distant. He made himself stare, out of focus, at the huge, idealized portrait. He didn't even have to suppress a smile. "I remember it as if it were yesterday, after all these twenty-nine years.

"Richthofen came over in his scarlet triplane, challenging, taunting. I'll say this much for the old man—*our* old man— he didn't want to sacrifice us. He didn't want to send us against those odds, against a foe we knew we couldn't match. He'd told us to restrict ourselves to reconnaissance duty only, to avoid combat until we were equipped with better planes, with planes that could match the Baron's.

"Those red wings waggled. Richthofen flew so low over our field we could see his face, even through the sleet.

"He dropped something.

"Kip was the first to retrieve it. He tore open the package right there on the field. It was a beautifully crafted jeweler's box, the sort of case a military decoration comes in. Kip opened it. I leaned over his shoulder. I saw it. There against the black jeweler's velvet lay a single white feather."

He looked into the old woman's eyes.

"Kip became a madman. There was no holding him. He ran to his Bristol, climbed into the cockpit. Everyone was shouting. There was pandemonium on the tarmac. Richthofen and his Hun legion were circling overhead. It was madness, madness! Kip flew into the middle of them. I'll credit Richthofen this—he held his killers back. They didn't gun Kip down before he could reach them and fight.

"But once he was up there, what could he do? One boy with a Webley revolver in his hand, against Richthofen's Flying Circus! He flew like a genius that day, Kip did! I stood on the landing field, cold sleet and hot tears mixing on my cheeks! We had our orders! The old man ran onto the field himself. He made the mechanics roll our planes back into their hangars and he personally locked them up! It was Kip against the Circus—alone!

"He would pursue one Fokker, three would follow him, guns blazing! He was firing a revolver, Lady Mosley! He was riddled with bullets. I hate to say this, to say this to you, but I must. When we found him, his body and his plane were both positively riddled with German lead! There's no way he could not have known that he was mortally wounded. A Fokker was coming straight at him—we all saw it, every one of us. Kip knew he was dying. Still he fired his Webley. The Fokker was firing both machine guns. They were on a death course, a collision course! The German must have thought that Kip would veer at the last moment, but Kip bore in to the end. The two planes collided with a flash of flame and a cloud of smoke unlike any other on earth. Kip knew he was dying, but he took his enemy with him."

He stopped, trying to gauge his effect. One more touch . . .

"Madame, Richthofen flew over our base again the next day. He came alone in his scarlet triplane, flew low, waggled his wings, and threw something out of his plane. I was the first to reach it this time. Madame, it was a hero's funeral wreath."

Lady Mosley stood. "Jenkins will show you out, Captain. One does not know why you have told this absurd story. Of any other flier, one might have believed it. But my son was a craven from the day of his birth. He lived a coward and he died a coward. I wish you a swift journey back to London or America or wherever it is that you make your nest."

CHAPTER
17

"But you died! You—"

"What on earth are you talking about? Here I am." She took Didrikson's hand between hers and rubbed it. "Do you think I'm a ghost?"

Seldom at a loss for words, Babe found herself stammering. "After the big race—you know, 1927—"

"Of course."

"I was just a kid then. You were my heroine. I used to listen to the radio every night, to hear about you."

They were standing together, midway between *Manta* and the entrance to the garden maze. The others had followed Didrikson from the skyship. The ship was now secured. Einstein and Gibson and Northrop stood in a group, letting the two women speak privately.

"I remember all the stories of the air battles you were in, how you saved your partners in the sky over San Diego, and then you were nearly killed yourself and Eugene Bullard saved you—Howard Hughes's old flying instructor."

"I'm flattered. I know you, too—or I know of you. I saw you in newsreels of the '32 Olympics."

"But you had gone back to Muvia by then. It was in all the papers, I saw it in the Beaumont *Post* at home, and then we were on the road and it was in the *Graphic*, I saw it—I remember so vividly, Amelia! I was sitting in the clubhouse. Somebody brought in an early edition between games of a doubleheader with the Brooklyns. I was supposed to start the second game. The *Graphic* had a photo of your plane; you and Charles Lindbergh were killed in the crash. You were flying a Grumman biplane and you disappeared and the *Graphic* found the wreckage!"

Earhart burst into laughter. "You don't know much about newspapers. The *Graphic* was famous for that. They used to make up photos to sell papers. They'd cut up stock shots and have models pose and put all the parts together and run them in the paper!"

"You mean, you and Lindbergh have been here all the time?"

The older woman grew serious. "I've been here. Charles is not here. He—he was never a patient man. He always had his ideas of what was right, of how things should be done. I'm afraid that he's working for the wrong side now. I shouldn't say this—I'm not really sure of it. But he's not here anyway. No one is quite sure where he is.

"But come along!" She brightened again, took the younger woman by the arm, and marched her back to the others. Didrikson introduced them all. Earhart knew of Einstein, of course. And she had heard of Northrop's pioneering work in aviation. She had never heard of Josh Gibson. He thought that a little strange, but said nothing.

They traveled through the ziggurat by a maze of lifts and ramps.

Earhart led them to an arched doorway that let onto one of the roofs of the ziggurat. Tropical trees rose above them. Vines connected them; birds flashed brilliant colors as they swooped from tree to tree. A monkey appeared on one branch, stared at the humans, then deliberately picked a fist-sized fruit and threw it.

Babe Didrikson caught the missile with a diving effort, regained her feet, and threw it back at the monkey. The monkey, startled, caught the fruit in its paws and disappeared into green shadows.

"You see what life is like in Muvia," Earhart said. "These people are an amazing paradox. They have a magnificently advanced science, yet they live with nature. They take it into their homes. They work with the forests and the beasts, they don't conquer them. They're peaceful, they're gentle—and they're prey for others who don't share their values. You must meet some people. At least two. They're waiting for us.''

She led them along forest trails. Babe kept reminding herself that she was not in the wilderness, she was walking through gardens planted on the broad deckings of a monstrous step-pyramid rising thousands of feet into the air. But tree trunks rose a hundred feet or more above her. She could hear the call of tropical birds and the cough and moan of big cats somewhere in the gloom. A green-bodied snake hung calmly watching them as they walked past it; Earhart said, ''Don't worry—that one is harmless.''

A spider the size of a house cat scurried across their trail. Before disappearing, it halted and studied them with eight eyes that glowed like rubies.

They emerged onto a strip of sand fifty yards across. Beyond it lay a sizable lake. The sun was bright; there was a fair breeze blowing. A small wooden-hulled sailboat, one of dozens dotting the water, was tacking back toward the shore.

Einstein's eyes watered.

Earhart spotted him dabbing them. ''Is the sunlight too bright, Dr. Einstein? Would you rather stay in the shade?''

The savant shook his head. ''You are too kind. No. It is only that I love sailing. This lovely sight—it makes me long for my little boat, my *Tinef*. You know, my little terrier Chico loves to sail as much as I do. We go out in *Tinef* and sail, and only God sees us or hears what we say to each other. And Chico and I—we tell no one.''

He laughed at himself. ''Well, maybe Chico tells our tomcat. I do not know the secrets of the animals.'' He shook his head.

The boat pulled up on the beach. Two men climbed from it. One was bronzed, black-haired, muscular, squarely made. The other was taller and thin. He wore casual whites and a soft white hat; pince-nez perched incongruously on his nose. They walked over to the party of newcomers.

Amelia Earhart introduced them. ''Sisquoc, chief librarian of Muvia. Muvia has no government in exactly the sense we know. Sisquoc is as close to a ruler as the Muvians possess. And the representative of our desperate forces in America—

our last hope is that you'll be able to help us!—Franklin Roosevelt.''

Sisquoc bowed his head in a gesture of greeting.

Roosevelt offered a hearty handshake to each newcomer.

They had moved back indoors. They had seen the Muvian radio lab that had sent the messages picked up on earth.

"You knew, then, that there are two earths?" Einstein questioned a Muvian engineer. "You knew about the twinning of our world, and about the field that my friends have foolishly named the Einstein layer?"

"I'm not an astronomer, sir. Or a physicist." The Muvian engineer was a woman of middle years, slim, the kind of woman who is ordinary in appearance at twenty, pretty by thirty, handsome by forty, and beautiful at fifty. Einstein watched her face as she spoke. She was approaching the age of beauty.

"I'm just a radio technician," she said. "But we suspected the existence of a second earth."

"The ephemerides!" Jack Northrop asserted.

The engineer laughed. "The sailors were the first to complain. They said the constellations were in the wrong place. They were the same constellations, but they were six months out of position. And you're right, Mr. Northrop, all the ephemerides were wrong. But when they were recomputed, the errors were perfectly consistent—not random! Everything was six months off.

"At first, we thought that time was out of joint. Somehow the clock had jumped half a year ahead—or behind.

"Then our astronomers started checking the positions of the other planets. They were wrong, too. But not just six months off schedule. They were exactly where they belonged, we figured that out. We found out that *we* were out of position. It was still the right date, but the whole planet had been transported to the opposite side of its orbit."

"Which is just where you would be six months earlier or later," Northrop supplied.

"Yes! But the displacement was not of time—it was only of position. The displacement of time was an illusion created by the displacement of space."

Einstein had lit his pipe and closed his eyes meditatively

as he puffed at it. *"Alles das selbe,"* he muttered, *"alles das selbe.* It is all the same."

"And the Einstein layer? How did you know about that?"

"Why, Professor Einstein had established that long before we knew about the twin earths. It was our bouncing of radio waves off the layer that established that he was correct. But he said he was not surprised. He knew it all along."

"He? He?" Northrop was growing excited. "But *he* was with us. That means there's an Einstein of Counter-Earth!"

The savant smiled gently. "With a life identical to mine until 1912—and since then, how different?"

"Don't you want to meet him? Don't you want to know each other?"

Einstein frowned in concentration. "About that I must have a little think." He rose and strolled away, pipe smoke trailing in a blue-gray wake. Hands clasped behind his back, eyes cast down, he wandered in a drunkard's walk until he returned to the others. "Well," he said, "I would not want to interrupt this man. He must be very busy. But if he can spare me a little time, maybe together we should talk. Maybe we should."

He looked up, startled by a new idea. His face was wreathed in a smile. "We could play duets! *That* I would enjoy very much."

Franklin Roosevelt cleared his throat. "We have a more immediate problem, my friends. Our scientists have long known of the existence of Counter-Earth—your world. I suppose you call ours Counter-Earth, don't you? But in any case, we've hoped that conditions might be somewhat different there. We traced the discrepancies in our skycharts and ephemerides back to a specific date."

"October 4, 1912," Gibson volunteered.

"Precisely. Maybe the WD came out differently on your planet, maybe the events—"

"Hold it. What's a WD?" Babe Didrikson demanded.

"Oh. The letters—it's an abbreviation. The War of the Dynasties. The greatest disaster of modern times. Don't tell me you never had it in your world!"

"I don't know. Is it what we called the One Year War? It broke out in December of 1912. The Kaiser was—"

"One Year War!"

Einstein said, "You had no such war?"

"It began in 1912. Yes, the Kaiser was involved. But—one year! You're sure it lasted only one year?"

The four travelers exchanged nods. "Almost to the day."

Roosevelt removed his pince-nez. With thumb and forefinger he rubbed the bridge of his nose. He threw back his shoulders and inhaled deeply.

"Are you all right, Mr. Roosevelt?" Babe asked.

He nodded. "Yes, I—thank you, yes." He carefully placed the armless spectacles back on his nose. "Only a year," he breathed. "Your world must be a paradise."

"You think so, yes?" Einstein said. "It could be worse. But what of this War of the Dynasties? It lasted more than a year, yes?"

Roosevelt gazed at him bleakly. "Almost twelve years, Professor. The war began in 1912. The German Empire and the Kingdom of France attacked the decadent monarchies of the East. At least, that was what they called them—Russia, Austria-Hungary, the Ottoman Empire. The Tsar appealed for help to his cousin in England. England sent arms and supplies to help Russia, shipped them via the Mediterranean and the Black Sea. Of course, the Ottoman Turks controlled the Dardanelles, so that portion of the route was protected."

He heaved a great sigh. "Britain controlled Gibraltar. Neutral Spain controlled Tangier. The French tried to stop Britain from shipping arms; they began to attack British ships, then British ports. The result was inevitable. Britain was drawn into the war on the side of the Eastern empires.

"Both sides tried to draw the United States into the war. Their efforts offset each other. America remained neutral, selling guns, airplanes, tanks, to anyone who could pay—provided they picked up the war goods at an American port.

"When the Atlantic struggle became too severe, the U.S. announced a new policy. Al Smith was President by then. He embargoed all shipping to belligerent powers from American ports. But shipments for the British and Eastern empires were sent to Canada, and British ships picked them up from Canadian ports. Shipments for the Central Axis were sent into Mexico, and picked up there by French or German ships.

"It was awful—awful! I was secretary of the navy then. President Smith had been my hero. But the conniving, the ruthless maneuvering for advantage! The war was good for us, you see!" He looked around the group, his face twisted in a rictus of grief that made a parody of joy. "The more the European powers ground themselves down, the more they became dependent upon American industry for the tools of war.

"We became the arsenal of despondency! American technology advanced as never before. Each more powerful gun, each more deadly chemical, each more destructive bomb, each more invulnerable airplane—they had to have it! Their own industries lay in ruins. Their youth lay dying by the tens of millions! Their treasuries were empty.

"Our bankers and industrialists danced in glee! The Europeans mortgaged their futures to buy our explosives. They sold us their colonies to pay for poison!"

Sisquoc stopped him. "Please," he said. "It is all over now. It cannot be undone. And your friends are here. We will yet be saved, Franklin."

Roosevelt shook himself. "I've been governor of a state, served in the cabinet—my cousin Theodore was President. A few friends even mentioned my own name as that of a potential President. But those dozen years of war, while the world bled and America grew rich—I don't know if I can ever hold office again!"

Jack Northrop said, "You summoned us from our earth to yours. Why?" He looked from Roosevelt to Sisquoc to Earhart. Again, "Why?"

Earhart said, "The world never recovered from that war. There are revenge seekers on every side. The old order was destroyed. It was a bad order. I don't defend it. The monarchies of Europe, their ever-shifting alliances and balances of power—it was not a proper system. The people suffered. Progress was stifled. But there was hope for betterment." She shook her head.

"After the War of the Dynasties, things went from bad to worse. One crown toppled after another. The republicans who replaced the old royal families meant well, but they were weak. Government succeeded government, each more radical than the last. Europe is now a congeries of militarists, more bloodthirsty than in 1912. And better armed, with far deadlier weapons. Oh, the research that went on during the War of the Dynasties was marvelous! They have bigger and deadlier arsenals today than they ever have."

She stopped.

Roosevelt had regained his composure. "An old man," he said. "I should stick to my sailboat, and let others run the world."

Northrop asked, "What are conditions in the United States?"

"We are on the brink of disaster. Our own electorate has followed demagogues. The latest is a monster—and he is the legally elected President of the United States: William Dudley Pelley. Do you know how he was elected? The last President was Norman Thomas—a Socialist. A good man, an honest man. A brilliant man. Socialism was a poor answer for the nation's problems. We weren't ready for it. But he was a good man.

"Pelley didn't attack Thomas's politics. He didn't say that his policies were wrong, or impractical. He accused poor Thomas of being an intellectual! Mencken loved it! Pelley pointed his finger at President Thomas and accused him of studying! He said he was reading big books when he should be in the field with the workers turning the soil! Pelley's campaign slogan was a wonder! 'Just Plain Bill!' That was all—no program, no principles. The people were desperate. Europe is preparing for war again. The economy is in a shambles. Everything was geared to selling war goods to the nations of Europe, and once the War of the Dynasties ended, the United States went into a massive depression.

"Now Pelley is doing everything he can to promote another war in Europe, to get America rolling again. But the arms are too advanced this time, and we're too caught up in it all. It will be a catastrophe. And enough people know it, and have spoken out against Pelley's mad policies, that he's trying to stifle all opposition.

"Do you know what that man has done? He's appointed six new Supreme Court justices, at a time when there are no vacancies on the Court! His police-state tactics have been overturned by the Court, so he wants to pack it with justices who will vote his way! The next thing he'll try is to rig the congressional elections this November, and then make himself President for life!"

Einstein laid his pipe aside. "Mr. Roosevelt, what can we do? What can anyone do?"

Roosevelt's tone was steadier now. He had delivered his attack on William Dudley Pelley in one furious outburst. In a lower voice he said, "The dictator controls the executive branch and he has seized the judiciary. Congress cannot stop him—he has too many votes there, and by this November it may be too late to vote in a new majority.

"People who want to regain some sanity in our nation's politics have started moving through the state legislatures. They're working to pass a set of constitutional amendments to unpack the Court, to reinforce the Bill of Rights, to reduce Pelley's bullying so we can restore liberty and avoid war."

"A very tall order." Northrop shook his head.

"We can do it—if we can stop him from crushing opposition and making himself a monarch!"

"And what is our role in this drama?" Einstein asked.

"We cannot overwhelm Pelley by massive force," Roosevelt said. "But we can restore liberty by peaceful means if he can simply be prevented from riding over the law of the land. Everything he's done so far he has done by perfectly legal means—that's the most maddening part of it! Even the packing of the Court—the number of justices is set by custom, not by law. And the limit on Presidential terms to two is also a custom, not a law.

"Pelley rode over the one, and he'll ride over the other."

"Yes, yes," Einstein persisted. "But what is it that you want us to do?"

"All we'll need is a diversion. Some event in Washington to draw the attention of Pelley and his henchmen: a false attack, a natural disaster, anything. Good men and women are sitting in state houses every day, prepared to act at the signal. Everyone must act at once, and it must be at a moment when Pelley is distracted, off his guard. The new amendments will be passed, the law will be changed. We know that he'll still try to resist, but we believe that the people will prevent that. He'll have to accept the *fait accompli* or he'll be overthrown."

"And for this, from another world you summoned us," Einstein said. He nodded his head sadly, the soft white nimbus of his hair bobbing.

"Yes." Although Roosevelt was only a few years younger than the scientist, his physique was dramatically different. Roosevelt was tall, broad-shouldered, well-muscled but with no suggestion of beefiness to him. Einstein was ethereal: his white hair, pale eyes, wrinkled face, and abstracted air conveyed a sense of unworldliness. "Will you help us?" Roosevelt asked.

"For myself," Einstein said, "I must say yes. For the others, I cannot speak."

Roosevelt looked from one to another of Einstein's companions. Each in turn nodded assent. Northrop's gesture was the most emphatic of the three. "When do we start?" Northrop asked.

"We need to do some planning. And I suspect you'll want to rest up for a little while. There's no time to waste, but we can hold off for a couple of days anyway. The various state legislatures are in session. They're awaiting my signal. They'll be in place for weeks anyway. We just don't want to tip our hand—if Pelley scents what's in the wind, he may decide to strike first."

"You don't think that he has agents among your supporters?"

"That's worried us a lot. All we can do is exercise care in selecting our people. And keep the key information in the fewest places possible. The fewest people possible. I don't think any of our key people are unreliable. If some of the small fry are, that simply cannot be helped."

Einstein heaved a sigh. "We are finished, then? For the moment, I mean? Yes? Then I may make a request of you please, Mr. Roosevelt."

"Of course, anything."

"I would so love to sail a little. If you are not too busy, or you could lend me your boat."

"With the greatest pleasure, Professor! I would love for us to go sailing."

Jack Northrop said to Sisquoc, "Could you have some of your mechanics help me service *Manta*, my ship? And then, if I could arrange to meet some of your aircraft designers."

Sisquoc turned him over to the radio technician who had sat in on their meeting.

Amelia Earhart asked Babe Didrikson and Josh Gibson if they would like a guided tour of the city. They accepted.

As they strolled the broad boulevard that ran between the rows of ziggurats, Earhart turned to Didrikson. "You said something before—about sitting in the dugout between games. That was in Brooklyn?"

"Sure. We were playing the Robbies."

"Playing what?"

Babe was startled. "Baseball."

"But—you're a woman."

Babe laughed. "Have been for years. Kind of like it."

Earhart reddened. "I mean—but what kind of baseball? Women's baseball?"

"No. What do you mean? National League baseball. You know, the Brooklyns, the Boston Bees, and Cubs. What baseball did you think?"

"There are no women in the National League."

"You're looking at one."

"But what do you do? How did you get into the pros?"

"Listen, I'm the best pitcher in baseball. I'm the best pitcher since Babe Ruth—that's why they call me Babe. Well, except maybe for Satchel Paige. No, I'm better than Satchel, don't you think, Josh?"

"Satch is a little faster, I think. You have a better spitter. Just about even."

"You creep!" She punched him in the arm. "Don't believe him, Amelia. He just tries to get me mad. I'll get even with you next season, Gibson, I swear it! I'm the best in the business! Paige is a great pitcher but I'm better."

"I've caught you both, Babe. Don't I know?"

"Yaah! What about the '40 All-Star Game? Who got the win? Come on, didn't I get the win?"

"You didn't beat Satch. He did fine. The other guy got the loss."

"I didn't give up a single hit in three innings!"

"Yeah, but you gave up fly balls and grounders. Satch got more strikeouts." He was having trouble suppressing his laughter.

Amelia Earhart watched the dialogue in astonishment. "What do you mean, you caught them both?"

"Well, I caught Satchel on the Senators in the American

League, and then I got traded to the Brooklyns and I catch
Babe for Robbie.''

"But you're black!"

Gibson held his hand before his eyes. Slowly those eyes
widened. He held his hand in front of Didrikson. "Oh, Lord!
Look at my hand, look at my hand! She's right! What's happening, Babe, I'm black all over!"

He roared with laughter.

"All right," Earhart said. "I forgot you're from Counter-
Earth. Things are different there, is that what you're telling
me? Is that it?"

Gibson stopped laughing. "Only some things, Amelia."

Later they held another strategy conference. Jack Northrop
raised a nettlesome question. "Your enemies are in the United
States, is that correct?"

Sisquoc said, "Mr. Roosevelt's main concern is in the
United States. We've been raided by forces from Svartalheim.
We're worried by them. In fact, my predecessor was a casu-
alty in such a raid. They've kept no territory of ours, but they
have got many of our machines."

"And," Roosevelt added, "we know that Svartalheim is
tied in with Prussia and Thuringia. And through them, we
suspect, with Argentina."

Northrop grunted. "I'm afraid I have some further news
for you. Bad news. I'll put it in one word: luna."

The conversation grew more somber.

CHAPTER
18

Reimar Horten sealed his new partnership with Prinz Nikolauz by toasting the peoples involved. "To the true Teutons, the ancient and future great race—Thuringians, Prussians, Bavarians, and Svartalheimers!"

He downed his schnapps.

"And *Hölle* take the rest of them!" Nikolauz added.

They hurled their goblets into the fire.

"Now," Horten said, "I will need to get a few people up here, people of the utmost importance."

"How do you know they live in this world?"

"We will have to find out. History here is different. We will have to make radio contact. First is my brother, Heinrich."

"Did he come with you? Is he not home on your other earth, Reimar?"

"Of course he is. I mean the Heinrich Horten of *your* earth!"

Nikolauz looked confused. Horten waited impatiently until the Prinz had worked out his puzzlement. "*Ach, ja.* I but forgot."

Reimar Horten sighed.

"But just a minute," the Prinz resumed. "If your brother—Heinrich you say his name is?—if your brother Heinrich you left at home on your earth, but also there is a Henrich Horten on my earth . . ."

"*Ja?*"

Nikolauz shook his head as if to clear it of cobwebs. ". . . will there not also be another Reimar Horten here?"

Reimar nodded. "I have no need for him. Anything he can do, I also can do. *Verstehen Sie?* You understand this? One Reimar Horten, two Reimar Hortens, there is no advantage. But Heinrich is very talented. Together we worked many times. To locate him, if we succeed, can bring us help."

Nikolauz's expression betrayed his dubious acceptance of Reimar Horten's notion. Still, he was willing to make the attempt. "And where would we find this Heinrich Horten?"

"You have agents on Counter-Earth?"

"*Ja.*"

"In all parts of Germany? In the *Kanzler's* office? In the ministries?"

"*Ja.*"

"You know we are a thorough people, Prinz. I would try even our old family home. In Greifswald. You know Greifswald? No? In Mecklenburg, near the Baltic. A wonderful town. Very cold. I like Argentina better. But try there."

"We can send a message by radio. Very easily."

"Good! And if Heinrich is not in Greifswald, then please place an inquiry through the Ministry of Munitions. He must be found."

"You do not want me to try Argentina?"

"Absolutely not! If he is there, let him stay there! But if the other Reimar is there, we must not make him aware of my presence on the moon!"

"But, Reimar!" The Prinz was growing distressed. "What about Major Perón? And Miss Duarte? What about the English Mosley?"

"What about them?" Horten snapped. "They have gone on to your earth. They are safe in Washington, no?"

"Yes, but—"

"But what?"

"Are there not also a Perón, a Mosley, a Miss Duarte, on our earth? I mean, another of each, ones born here? If there is another of you, would there not be another also of each of them?"

"Prinz Nikolauz, you asked for my assistance. More, you asked for my alliance. You must trust me. Leave my companions to carry out their assigned tasks. Your friends control in Washington, is this correct?"

Nikolauz said it was.

"Leave my Perón and Mosley and Duarte in the hands of your good friends in Washington. Leave alone their equivalents in your world. If you do not know of them, that tells us that they do not exist—or that they are persons of no value to us."

"But if they are of importance in your world, would they not be also in mine?"

Horten shook his head. "The smallest difference between the two earths can grow to the greatest. 'Cleopatra's nose, had it been shorter, the whole face of the world would have been changed.' "

Nikolauz looked dazed. He lifted the flagon of schnapps and peered into it as if an answer might be contained there. "Herr Horten, I am just a simple military man. I do not see what Cleopatra has to do with this."

Horten removed his spectacles, folded them, and slipped them into his pocket. He shut his eyes and spoke into the blackness; it seemed the best way to deal with the Prinz. "A mere figure of speech. It means—it means a little change to start can grow to a big difference. What little differences there are between your earth and ours, you see, may have grown. Maybe there is no Reimar Horten on this planet. Maybe there is, but he failed an examination at the *Gymnasium* or the *Technische Hochschule* and is today a cobbler or an armorer. You see? We do not need this Horten. But Heinrich I want!

"Also, the armaments designer Ronald Richter. An expert he is at nuclear matters. Propulsion systems, and also weapons.

"And a good pilot. The best pilot. Through Heinrich we should reach her. Hanna Reitsch."

"*Hanna?* Reach *her*?"

"*Ja!*"

"But—a woman?"

"A pilot!"

Nikolauz muttered to himself. "Valkyrie, yes. In Untersvartalheim. But a pilot to fly to luna? Such a thing."

"You will get them for me?" Reimar Horten drew his spectacles from his pocket, unfolded them, slipped them on. He blinked his unmatched eyes at the Prinz. He had found over many years that doing this disconcerted people. He liked to do it.

Nikolauz rummaged until he produced another goblet for himself. He asked Horten if he wanted one also, but the wiry man refused. "You won't mind if I have another little sip, then, Herr Horten." Nikolauz collapsed into his chair. He poured a healthy drink for himself, downed it, then poured another and gazed into it with slightly unfocused eyes. "Luna's a lonely posting," he said. "I used to complain about my life on earth. You know, there's an old Svartalheim with wondrous cities and machines. Lots of comforts. Lots of pleasures."

He grunted.

"Lots of pleasures," he repeated, "if you know what I mean." He looked at Horten for acknowledgment but received only bland attention.

"I was hoping for a shot at the crown," Nikolauz said. "Never figured I really had much chance at it. Too many princes in the family. The first one is a joy to one and all. Couple more come in handy, too. Besides, people who worry about line of succession don't like to put all their eggs in one basket. Only one prince, you know, and all it takes is an unfortunate hunting accident, a duel against the wrong opponent, a piece of spoiled meat, some lady of the night who takes a bribe—oh, anything can happen.

"And then where are you? Sending out the call for some prince from another land, some remote cousin who doesn't even speak the language and whose loyalties are never quite certain. It's no fun. So they like to have a couple of younger princes around the palace. Can always send 'em off to become bishops or admirals or marry 'em off to overweight princesses from strategic neighbors."

He sipped at his schnapps. "But you get too many princes around and they start getting in the way, so you post 'em off to remote provinces as governors, or you make 'em petty diplomats, or you send 'em to command garrisons in godforsaken places like this." He waved his hand, indicating not merely the room but the entire satellite.

"Skiing, Horten. Pumice skiing on lunar caldera. What a way to spend your life!"

Horten stood up. "Will you send the messages I requested, Prinz?"

Nikolauz sighed. "All right, all right. You're an awfully impatient fellow, but I'll do it."

The Attorney General of the United States of America was a huge man. He stood six feet six inches tall. His shoulders were those of a former fullback. His face suggested the appearance of an old-style battlewagon. a tall pompadour of curly steel-gray hair; a broad, sloping brow; a Roman nose; a heavy, underslung jaw.

He looked as if he could kill you with his bare hands, and rumors held that he had done so on more than one occasion in his early days as a professional rabble-rouser.

His name was Lawrence Dennis.

He wore a double-breasted brown suit with bold pinstripes. His shirt was patterned white on white; his tie, broad and boldly painted. His arm showed a brassard bearing the disk and lightning of the National Renaissance Party.

He shook Perón's hand in a bone-crushing grip, then Mosley's. "You back from England, Ozzie? How're things going over there?"

Mosley winced at "Ozzie," but he said, "Lovely. For all that England has fallen from power and grace, she is still a beautiful country. And I believe in her people. Under the proper leadership, Britain will regain her place in the sun."

"You had a good time, hey?"

"Indeed, I—"

"Don't mean to cut you off, Ozzie. But business first." He turned away from Mosley and faced the President of the United States. "Here it is, Bill."

William Dudley Pelley leaned across his desk to accept the sheaf of papers Dennis had brought to the White House. He leaned back and studied the top sheet. He looked up and told Dennis that he was satisfied.

"Sure you are. I don't see why you want to do it this way, but if this is what you want, you can have it. What kind of lawyer do you think I am?"

Pelley managed a chilly snicker. He continued working his

way through the papers. As he neared the end, he looked up, letting his gaze wander from face to face among the people surrounding his huge desk. In addition to the Attorney General, Juan Perón, and Oswald Mosley, there were four others: Joseph McWilliams, slim, bespectacled, and dapper, Secretary of State; Elizabeth Maude Dilling, round-faced, overdressed, and perfumed, Secretary of War; Huey Long, red-cheeked, rumpled, redolent of alcohol, Vice President of the United States; and Eva Duarte, perfectly coiffured and smartly tailored. But thin, frighteningly thin and pale.

"You want to go over it for 'em once more, Bill?" Long asked. His distinctive manner of speech, part backwoods Louisiana, part Cajun, poked through the alcoholic slur. "You're one hell of an explainer. Didn't he explain this to you before, Larry?"

Dennis shot a look of fury at Long. "The next one I work on, Huey, is an amendment to abolish the Vice Presidency."

Long cackled gleefully. "Come on, Bill, why don't we just tell the people that we're doing it, and not bother with all of this paperwork? You know you hate paperwork, and it's . . . it'll . . . it's'll all be the same anyhow."

"We have our program," Pelley said. "And there's been too much obstruction and foot dragging already. The states— the majority of them are still under control of the old parties. They don't like our plans for financial reform, they don't like our plans for reorganization of the military. Larry, they don't like the way you've been running the Justice Department at all. Not at all."

He leaned back and gazed up at the red, black, and silver banner that hung above his desk, dominating the Red Room.

"Every time one of the troublemaking politicians starts screaming, we hear echoes from forty-eight state capitols. Every time we manage to shut down a libel-spreading newspaper or lift the license of some obscenity-spouting, God-defying radio station, they fill the land with screams. Every time some patriotic red-blooded proud Americans try to stop one of those movie studios from putting out treasonous propaganda, the forces of reaction want to tear us down!"

"And your solution to this?" Mosley asked.

"The states that formed this nation were a band of wonderful, liberty-loving heroes, Sir Oswald. They fought for their independence and won it.''

"I know that all too well, Mr. President.''

"Just plain Bill, please.''

Mosley reddened. "As you wish, sir. Uh, Bill.''

"Thank you.'' Pelley smiled thinly. "Of course you know all about our revolution. But it's time for a second revolution in this country. The states are now anachronistic. They serve no purpose. They impede the effective administration of the law. They promote division and disunity. We already fought one Civil War in this country; we don't want another.''

"And they're interfering with your program now.'' Mosley fingered his moustache.

"Not for long. We're going to build a new empire in this land. More than that. In all the lands of the earth. And with you fighting at our side, eventually we will rule both earths! What a challenge! What an achievement! Not Alexander, not Napoleon, not Bismarck, could dream of uniting two entire worlds under the sway of a single master! We're going to do it! *We are going to do it*!''

Mosley smiled. "Not Alexander, not Napoleon, not Bismarck. But Caesar, perhaps?''

Pelley leaned back in his leather swivel chair. "Caesar?'' He steepled his fingers and rested his chin atop their apex. "An interesting notion. But Julius, not Augustus. Everything by legal means. I don't want a crown, Sir Oswald. Crowns aren't the order of the day. I don't even think I'll wear a uniform.''

"Your silver shirt?''

Pelley laughed. "People love the feeling of *belonging*. The average man feels little, he feels helpless. He's lonely—even in the middle of a throng, he feels lonely. But give him some kind of badge or sign that he's one of a special group and he's happy. He'll lay down his life for you. Just make him feel he belongs, Sir Oswald. That he counts. That he's one of the elect.''

He beamed around the room. It was the first time he had done that; he did it very rarely. But now he did it. "We are the elect!''

"The Chosen People?'' Mosley said with a grin.

Lawrence Dennis's hamlike fist crashed onto President Pelley's massive desk. "That ain't funny!" he growled.

Elizabeth Dilling said, "And it is not in good taste, either, Sir Oswald. I should think that a person of noble blood . . ." She let her statement trail off, permitting him to fill in the rest of the words for himself.

Mosley flushed. He had overstepped himself, he decided. A change of subject was in order. "Mr. President—Bill. You plan to abolish the forty-eight states?"

Pelley leaned forward. "With all of those governors and state legislatures out of the way, I can do anything. I already control the Congress. Those mossbacks in the Court kept knocking my program down, so I sent up some more justices, and now the Court does as it's told."

"A very pretty tactic," Perón approved.

"But one state is controlled by the Democrats, the next by the Republicans. There are still some of that fool Thomas's Socialists running around, even though they've been discredited from top to bottom. A single Republic, soon a single Party. A single President who will soon be a single Leader. It's coming, Major Perón. It's coming!"

Mosley asked, "How long will it take you to do this?"

Pelley smiled. "Mr. Attorney General?"

Dennis growled. "I still think Mrs. Dilling ought to send in troops with bayonets."

"Into forty-eight state houses?"

"What do we have National Guards for? Call 'em up, put 'em under federal control, march 'em into every state capitol and assembly in the country. Put the regular army into Congress if they make any trouble."

"They won't."

"And send troops into the Supreme Court if they squawk."

"They won't either. It's just the states."

"Okay then."

Elizabeth Dilling made an odd noise, not quite a simper nor exactly a coo. "We could do that, Bill. Some of the generals would rather do it that way anyway, I'm sure. Not that I've talked it over with them yet."

"I should hope not!"

"Oh, no!"

"No," Pelley said. "We'll send these bills over to the

House and Senate in the morning. Let the boys go through
all the motions, send 'em to committees, call 'em back up,
take their votes. All of it nice and legal. You don't understand, do you, that this is important. We don't want to go
down in history as a band of thugs who destroyed democracy
in this country. We're operating by democratic means! We're
just embodying the will of the people!

"Take a lesson from history! Napoleon was elected, did
you know that? So was Julius Caesar!

"Why do you think Russia went the way she did? All of
those bomb throwers and fire setters and assassins—ha! Then
when the Tsar had enough of them locked up or hanged, he
had his scare, and they wound up with democracy after all.
But we have democracy already!

"It's a sad fact that the government in our country gets in
the way of democracy instead of doing what the people want.
We're going to make democracy work! Give us a week, Sir
Oswald." He turned back and addressed one man. "Give us
a week to push this through. Then we'll have our stumbling
blocks knocked aside. Then you'll see how a country ought
to be run!"

The craft rose from a field in Württemberg and followed
a course determined by her pilot's personality rather than
matters of economy, efficiency, or expediency. Hanna Reitsch
was the most brilliant of German's test pilots. She had won
this position despite her sex; she had been fought every step
of the way. She had demanded, she had persisted, she had
bullied, threatened, and on two occasions fought duels to get
her fair chance as an aviator.

She won both duels, and proudly wore the scar of the second of them. Her opponents, both of them men, both of them
powerful, both of them scornful at first of her challenge, now
wore shrouds.

She boosted her craft from its launching ramp at the Gotha
Werke in Schramberg. As the G.229—Hanna had no time for
such foolishness as giving names to machinery—rose toward
cruising speed, she peered down at the rolling countryside.
The green meadows of Württemberg gave way to the darker
hues of the Black Forest. Hanna's childhood had been filled

with romantic tales of the castles and trolls, princesses and wizards, goblins and knights, who filled the forest.

She had rejected all of this to pursue her passion of flight.

Sharing the G.229 with her were Hilde Horten and Ronald Richter. Hilde had been the chief designer of G.229; Ronald Richter was the world's leading developer of miniaturized nuclear weapons.

G.229 carried a small supply of Richter's creations—hand-launched, self-propelled explosives that rendered any previous bombs puny by comparison.

Hanna swung the G.229 into a swooping climb. The monowing was built like a dart—pointed nose, triangular air-foils negatively dihedraled, a vertical tail rising behind the cockpit. The dartlike craft swung into a steeper path as it coursed northward over Karlsruhe, Mannheim, Darmstadt, Hanau. By the time it reached Marburg, it was no longer moving northward at all—it was in a blazing, vertical climb.

A door opened in an ancient building, now in use as a bank. A woman stepped from the bank and halted. The street was lightly dusted with a January snowfall; the woman wore heavy boots, thick woolens, and a fur coat. She heard a booming sound from above and stared open-mouthed as what appeared to be a miniature sun flared, then shrank as it rose into the clear sky.

The woman shook her head and walked to her waiting lim-ousine.

Hanna Reitsch pushed the G.229 to its limits, and the craft responded. The dartlike ship was enameled a matte black; only the transparent bubble and a few markings in gloss-finish Chinese red would be visible against a black sky. Those fea-tures, and the craft's angry red exhaust glow.

The pilot turned toward Hilde Horten. "A perfect day for a test, Hilde. A perfect flight. You designed well, *Liebling*." She reached and put her hand over Hilde's. Hanna's hand was chunky, her fingertips square, the flesh hardened. Hilde's was soft and pink.

G.229 accelerated until it had come within 24,000 miles of the moon. Now Hanna Reitsch reversed the ship's course and applied maximum power; the ship's engines acted as brakes. Hanna approached the moon with her ship screaming, its attitude vertical toward the earth, nose pointed back toward the planet.

Luna stood edge-on. Hanna brought G.229 screaming over the edge of the lunar disk, still decelerating. Craters and mountain ranges flashed beneath the ship, brilliant daylight and black shadows alternating. Hanna had avoided the lunar fissure approach.

Because the ship was still traveling at immense speed when it passed over the lunar pyramids, Hanna swung once again, still traveling tailfirst. She pointed the ship's streamlined nose at the greatest of the pyramids, exchanging the now horizontal momentum for vertical.

The ship rose tailfirst over the pyramid, using its engines to reduce speed. Before the ship's vertical momentum was wholly expended, Hanna flipped the ship nose-for-tail. It reached apogee, hung for an infinitesimal moment, then began to settle back toward the moon. Hanna applied the engines carefully, balancing their upward impulse against the pull of lunar gravity. G.229 balanced delicately, drifting ever so slowly toward the Svartalheimer base.

The ship's radio had been squawking unattended ever since G.229's first dazzling pass over the pyramids. Now Hanna lifted the hand microphone and responded to the desperate sputtering that came from the speaker. "We will land as directed. Yes." She peered outward and downward. "Yes," she resumed. "I can see the olive-colored ship. I think I recognize the designer's touch." She laughed. "Yes, they are with me, as requested, Your Highness. Yes. Horten and Richter. Yes, both. Yes, Your Highness."

She clicked off the radio.

Just before G.229 would have settled on its tail, Hanna Reitsch applied thrusters and gyroscopes, turning the craft into a horizontal attitude once again. Reitsch, Horten, and Richter scrambled from the ship even before its exhaust glow had faded.

They assembled in Prinz Nikolauz's suite.

Reimar Horten stood awaiting the arrival of the newcomers, while Prinz Nikolauz sat contemplating a goblet of schnapps as he lounged behind his desk. Horten greeted the newcomers by name.

"Hanna!"

"Ronald!"

He stopped, stunned.

The third newcomer he expected to be his brother and sometime collaborator, Heinrich. Instead it was a stranger. A woman. A stranger . . .

Reimar's eyes popped. The woman resembled his brother, yet the thin, pallid Heinrich Horten seemed to have been transformed. He—she had added flesh. Her blond hair curved gently around a soft-featured, pink-cheeked face. Her eyes were a lovely blue.

"Reimar," the woman cried. Even her voice carried suggestions of Heinrich's. "Reimar!" She dashed across the room, ignoring the presence of Prinz Nikolauz and the others. She threw herself on Horten's neck, threw her arms around him, buried her face in his shoulder, weeping loudly. Her sobs shook not only her body but his as well.

She rubbed her tear-wet cheek against his. "*Ach*, Reimar! I could not believe it! You were dead! I saw your body, there in the ruins of G.228. Only because we had both promised to continue the work if the other died, did I go on with G.229. But you are alive! I don't understand! I buried you! I threw dirt in the grave, with my own hands I did this!

"But yet you live, my brother, yet you live!"

Reimar Horten staggered back and collapsed into a chair. He covered his eyes with his hands.

CHAPTER
19

Roosevelt sank into his seat. "Luna? What about it?"

"You have no idea what's there?" Northrop said.

"Why, I suppose I know as much about it as the average man in the street. You know—craters, mountains, hole in the center like any other cold body in space. Everyone has seen the near side. No one has seen the far side."

"I'm afraid you're in for a shock, Franklin. Maybe for several. The moon is inhabited—or at least it has been in fairly recent times."

"You're joking."

"I assure you, I am not."

Roosevelt removed his pince-nez and rubbed his nose in the way that was characteristic when he was pondering. He looked at the others, settled his glance on Einstein. "Professor, do you know what Mr. Northrop is talking about? I suppose we've all seen the books of Mr. Wells and his associates. Are there, what did he call them, Selenites and Moon-Calves up there?"

"Nothing like that," Einstein told him. "The truth is both more remarkable and more frightening than any fairy tale."

"I don't understand. We can see the moon through our telescopes. There is no one there. Wouldn't we see them?"

"They're on the so-called dark side," Northrop told him.

"When we left our own earth, we passed by its moon. We passed through its central fissure—there's an electromagnetic effect there; you can use it either to boost a craft into higher speed at the beginning of a journey or to brake your speed at the end."

"Yes, yes. I'm sure our engineers and scientists will want to learn all about that. But that has nothing to do with these Selenites."

"Not Selenites, Franklin. Egyptians."

"What? Now you must be joking. Modern Egyptians or the ancient variety? I thought the King Tut craze had died out fifteen years ago!"

Northrop looked at his companions. Einstein seemed to be half in a daze; he must be "having a think"—about what, Northrop could barely even guess. Josh Gibson was listening intently to the conversation between Northrop and Roosevelt. Babe Didrikson had quickly formed a bond with Amelia Earhart; they seemed more interested in hearing each other's life stories than in dealing with the problem of the moment.

"My friends will support me if you doubt my word," Northrop told Roosevelt.

"I'm sorry. It isn't that. It's just so farfetched, man. But go on. Tell me about these Egyptians."

"Very well. This is going to be a lot of information, and it's going to come at you fast. Try to trust me. If you want any more explanations, I'll do my best."

Roosevelt agreed.

"All right then. First of all, you understand the theory of the twin earths. Each has its own moon as well."

"Of course. That was why we sent our signal. We were hoping for help from Counter-Earth. Or, if you consider us Counter-Earth, we were calling for help from the first earth—from our twin."

"Good. We heard the call. We left earth, passed through the lunar fissure hoping to get that boost as we passed through the electrical field there.

"Now—" Northrop gestured with both hands—"as we came through the fissure, we caught a glimpse of the far side of the moon. There is a city, a classical Egyptian city, surrounding the fissure. The works, Franklin—pyramids, temples—you've seen it in Egypt. Everyone has seen the photos."

"And you're telling me that the ancient Egyptians built a city on the moon? Do they live there still?"

"Well, first of all, we're not sure that the Egyptians built the city on the moon. Maybe it was moon people—humans, not Mr. Wells's Selenites—who built the pyramids in Egypt."

Roosevelt nodded.

"But they're not on the moon anymore," Northrop resumed. "They've left. It was their blunder, a scientific error, that caused the twinning of the earth. There was only one earth prior to the year 1912. Then the inhabitants—call them Egyptians—used a weapon that had unexpected results. It created the second earth. And the Egyptians were so horrified that they abandoned both the moon and their secret installations on the planet itself, and withdrew to the asteroid belt. We stopped there on our way from our earth. We saw them.

"But there was someone else on the moon! On *our* moon! We have our own would-be world conquerors, and they picked up the same call for help that we did. They have ships as good as ours, maybe better. They beat us to the moon. They attacked us there, and again as we passed the Einstein layer—never mind what that is—on our way here.

"Franklin, I can't guarantee this, but I'm damned well convinced that your enemies from this earth and our rivals from the other have made an alliance. And that they are on this earth's moon right now.

"I don't know what they're doing, I don't know what moves they're planning, but I'm sure that it spells trouble for us all—for me and my companions, for you and your allies here in Muvia and at home in the United States."

Roosevelt shoved himself from his chair and paced the room. "Is this true?" he asked Einstein. The savant nodded.

Roosevelt put his hand to his forehead, leaning his elbow against the wall beside an ornate window frame. Through the window, the Muvian sun was bright; the creeping lianas that covered the wall of the ziggurat at this point filtered its light into a beautiful weave of yellow and green. Roosevelt watched a gigantic beetle crawl up the vine. Its wing cases were marked with an intricate pattern resembling a Greek theater mask of tragedy.

"You and I, brother," Roosevelt murmured, "you and I!" He flicked the insect gently with his fingernail. It opened its wing cases and flew into the outdoor garden, buzzing loudly. As the beetle opened its carapace, Roosevelt could see, in a moment of time sliced into tiny increments and stretched to offer him supernormal clarity, the tragic mask melt into one of comedy.

"You and I, brother," he said yet again. Then he turned back to face Northrop and the others. "This information is important, surely. But I ask you—what would you have us do? We're ready to act. Our allies are waiting in every state house in America. The longer we delay, I'm afraid, the more Pelley will have consolidated his control over the country and the less chance we will have to succeed.

"Mr. Northrop—what do you suggest I do?"

"I am your brother, yes—but not in the manner you think!" Reimar Horten said.

Hilde's eyes widened. She took Hanna Reitsch's strong, blunt hand. Her soft fingers twined through Hanna's rough ones. "Reimar, what do you mean?"

He explained the existence of the second earth to her. This information was not widely held among the populace of Counter-Earth. At the time of earth's twinning in 1912, the surprising disruption of world commerce that resulted from the invalidation of the ephemerides was a topic of widespread interest.

But once tables of tides and astronomical data were corrected, the great majority of humankind returned to its business as usual. Corporations operated for their profits, wars were fought, novels written, symphonies performed, and races run.

But even a microscopic difference, perhaps the change in the tide-propelled course of a single planktonic microcrustacean, could cascade through the food chain, could change the behavior of a larger sea denizen, could cause a swimming vacationer who would otherwise have returned to a crucial occupation to be devoured by a marauding shark (or cause one who would otherwise have been devoured to escape, thence to return to his occupation and make a decision that would alter the course of the world).

On Counter-Earth, the Horten siblings, brother Reimar and sister Hilde, had remained in Europe. They had worked to develop craft that could outperform anything previously seen on the planet. These craft could lead their country and its allies in Svartalheim to travel to Counter-Luna, to rediscover the abandoned city of pyramids and sphinxes that had stood there from time immemorial, to reoccupy the facilities and plan their attack on their planet-bound enemies.

At the same time on the original earth, the Horten siblings, brother Reimar and brother Heinrich, had fled the war-ravaged continent and settled in the more salubrious climate of Argentina. There they had developed their nuclear-powered ship but had held it in abeyance until called upon by Juan Perón and his associates to participate in the desperate race to the far side of the sun.

On that other world, Heinrich Horten awaited word of the success of his work, work that he had entrusted to his brother Reimar.

On Counter-Earth, Hilde Horten had seen her brother Reimar die in the wreckage of G.228; yet now she beheld him in company of the Svartalheimer Prinz Nikolauz, commandant of the military installations on Counter-Luna.

"I see." Hilde lowered her gaze from her brother's—or not brother's—face. Alone in this world, she was not disconcerted by the sight of his mismatched eyes; she had known this all her life and to her it was a natural part of her brother's appearance. "And in this case, *Bruder* Reimar—may I call you *Bruder*—what are our plans? Why did you summon us from Schramberg?"

"*Schwester*—sister—how oddly that rings in the ear! Our ally the Prinz and I have made a plan. That was why we had Herr Richter accompany you."

"Richter!" He addressed the hitherto silent individual. "You have brought with you your weapons? You are ready to use them?"

Richter assented.

"And how many weapons do you have?"

"Four dozen," the nuclear scientist told him.

Behind his thick glasses, Horten's eyes showed his pleasure, as did the rest of his face. "Four dozen. Very good. A total of forty-eight nuclear devices. And each one is very small, yes?"

Richter held his hands as if preparing to drop a football at the beginning of a scrum.

Horten's smile broadened. He turned to Prinz Nikolauz. "This is perfect, do you agree?"

Nikolauz did agree. "But we will need more, will we not, *mein Herr*? For—afterwards?"

"Oh, yes," Horten conceded. "Richter, you can build more of these—once we have used the four dozen—when the need arises for more?"

"Of course. Materials may be slightly difficult to obtain, but they can be had. Surely they can be had. And more devices can be built most easily."

Hanna Reitsch asked, "Are we to use G.229 as a bomber? To deliver these devices?"

"Only in a sense, Fraulein. Each must be aimed with the utmost of precision. Each will be delivered to the state house of one of the American United States. Our friends have achieved power in Washington, but they are opposed in the forty-eight capitols. They are not smart enough—ruthless enough—to do what needs to be done in their own country."

He had retreated to take a seat beside Prinz Nikolauz. The two men now sat side by side behind Nikolauz's desk. Horten's thin lips pulled back from clenched teeth making the rictus of a half-mad grin. A giggle escaped his lips.

"We are going to do President Pelley a favor," he tittered. "There are political problems on the other earth, but on this one, well, things are going swimmingly! Swimmingly! Swimmingly! When the time arrives—and it is very soon, very soon—each of the forty-eight capitols will disappear. *Boom! Whoosh! Gone!* You understand?"

Horten flung his hands into the air, dropped them back into his lap and flung them upward once again, as if throwing piles of sand into the air.

"*Boom!*

"*Whoosh!*

"*Gone!*"

Nikolauz grasped Horten's wrist. Horten ignored the prince. He grabbed both wrists. Horten pulled away, began capering about the room, cackling over and over, "*Boom! Whoosh! Gone! Boom! Whoosh! Gone!*"

His sister, Hilde, took him by the elbow and led him to an

antechamber. She got him to lie down. She sat beside him, stroking his face, murmuring, "Reimar, *mein Bruder, mein Bruder.*"

The flush gradually left his face. His rapid, shallow breathing slowed and grew deeper. His staring eyes lowered and then closed.

She leaned over and kissed him on the cheek.

He opened his eyes again. Now they were calm and his manner was rational. "Sister," he whispered.

"*Ja.*"

"I never had a sister. Never before." He started to giggle, then caught himself and lay still, eyes squeezed shut until the spasm had passed. "I never had a sister before, and now I find that I've had one all my life. How very strange. Sister— Hilde—tell me, you are lovers with Hanna?"

She lowered her eyes, then made a tiny nod. "Do not hate me, Reimar. You knew. My—other—Reimar knew. He would only speak to me or to Hanna about technical matters. You would never let us visit your home, never let your wife and children talk to me. You never let me visit my nieces and nephews, never since you . . . knew."

"That was not I, Hilde."

"Yes, I understand. It is so hard to believe. Two Reimars— one dead, one living."

"And you say I have a wife? Children?"

She smiled. "I have seen them—only from far away. You— I mean, the other Reimar, never let me visit. Only if I would give up Hanna, he said. I couldn't do that, Reimar. You cannot understand. You with your home, with your family. You could never understand."

He smiled bitterly. "I have no home, Hilde." He held her two hands between his own—her soft, pink hands between his thin, gray ones. "I have never been with a woman. Or a man. Always with my slide rule, with my drafting tools. I only worked with my brother, Heinrich." He gave a single gasping sound, half cough, half laugh.

"Something is wrong with me, Hilde." He pressed one fist against his chest. "Maybe when the other Reimar died, something happened also to me. I don't know."

She leaned closer to him. She put one hand against his

cheek and pressed her own face against the other. She whispered his name in his ear.

He struggled to sit up. "We must do our work. I must talk with Richter. There are two Ronald Richters, yes. And two Hanna Reitsches. Yes, two of each. We can rig bombs, we can make them hover. Do you know that, Hilde? We can make them hover! Four dozen of them, one for each state of the United States. All in place, all at once, waiting, counting, and when comes the time, all of them—four dozen of them—*Boom! Whoosh! Gone!*"

Hilde was crying. Reimar saw her tears. Somehow they made him calmer. He reached with his hand and wiped away the salty wetness. "Gone," he whispered.

"Reimar, after—after all of this. Come back with us. Your wife and children—go home to them. Let me come and be the auntie, also. *Tante* Hilde. How I long to be *Tante* Hilde to your children!"

Reimar Horten lay back, his eyes closed. *Schwester. Tante.* It was all so very strange. He tried to picture himself as husband and father. Awakening with a woman every morning. Coming home each evening to a household of children.

Unfamiliar sensations ran through his body. He could not understand what it meant to him. *Ehemann. Vater.* He listened as the words rang in his head. *Husband. Father.*

He saw Ronald Richter's devices hovering, hovering. Four dozen of them, over four dozen cities. He heard the sand slithering through four dozen hourglasses, sounding like the anaconda slithering through the tropical rain forest of Argentina's Salta Province.

Hissing.

Sliding.

Then four dozen devices flaring, blaring. Four dozen cities utterly destroyed. Pelley triumphant. And soon Svartalheim triumphant. Perón triumphant. Reimar Horten triumphant. How could he compare that with Reimar Horten, husband and father?

He sat bolt upright, eyes open wide, a snarl distorting his features. He saw the face of his sister; then Hilde disappeared and was replaced by row upon row of flaring devices.

Reimar Horten fell over, into Hilde's arms.

• • •

"Now, Perón, I must go *now*!" Evita had regained a portion of her strength. She had managed, with the help of carefully applied cosmetics, the assistance of hairdressers, a proper wardrobe, to regain much of the appearance of a smart and rapidly ascending actress. A closer look would reveal that all was not as it had been only days ago.

She must return to her homeland and seek out her Counter-Earth twin, her other self. She must see the degree of success this other Evita had achieved. Her life had been one of close chances, of near-misses and narrow achievements. If this other earth differed from her own in tiny ways, might not the other Evita have walked a different path?

Perhaps the so respectable Duarte had married the mother of Eva María Ibarguren on this earth, and left his other household to the shame of whoredom and bastardy. Perhaps the other Evita had claimed the surname Duarte by right rather than by will.

Perhaps the other Evita had triumphed where she still struggled.

But if not . . .

Since her hour in the Temple of Isis, Evita knew that she was a woman changed. The goddess had given her necromantic powers. But in exchange she had exacted a cruel price. Each time Evita called upon the abilities given her by the goddess, part of her own life was drawn from her. Each exercise of her abilities aged her by years.

She would appear her counterpart's elder sister already. In time she might become a withered crone while the other Evita remained fresh and young.

This was the price she must pay, if she were to accomplish her goal. She was determined that it was a price worth paying.

What could she do? Evita was afraid to put her powers too much to the test, for if each use of those powers aged her, then she must exercise them most sparingly. The beauty that she had striven so hard to perfect was slipping away from her: this she knew.

And yet, she had walked unprotected outside *Patrilandia*. She had lifted the English Mosley like a child and carried him across billowing clouds. When she utilized the powers granted her by the goddess, she seemed to become the goddess. She had not only Isis' supernatural strength but also her supernatural beauty.

Her hair, her gown, her flawless skin and glorious body— men would fall at her feet, begging for the right to serve her! Women would seethe with envy and wither with despair!

But then . . .

But then Evita would return to herself. The goddess would fly to whatever realm she called her own. And Evita would be left with wrinkled skin, withered flesh, gray hair.

She covered her face with her hands, then dropped her hands to her sides. She stood with her feet spread, drew her shoulders back, inhaled deeply. She would be strong. She let out her breath in a hiss, watching her protector's movements.

Juan Perón paced the hotel suite, his impatience manifest in every movement, every pause. "You can go, of course you can go. I will go with you. But can't you wait just a little while? We have to be here when the blow is delivered or we lose all advantage!"

"No! Now!" She wore a tailored suit, its shoulders broad and lightly padded, pointed lapels crossing over her silk blouse, tan over white. The skirt reached just past her knees. Her stiletto-heeled shoes were set to one side and her silk-stockinged feet nestled warmly in the sitting room's thick carpet. "You don't understand why it must be now, why I cannot wait!"

Perón shook his head. He had affected civilian garb also. His suit jacket hung casually on the back of a Louis XIV chair. His broad, hand-painted tie hung almost to his waist, covering the front of his white-on-white shirt. His gold cuff links, a present from the President of the United States, bore the disk and lightning symbol of the National Renaissance Party.

"I know why you should wait, *querida*. Even I, a mere man, am capable of understanding that much. We are on the brink of victory. Our colleague Reimar Horten—"

"The little pig!" she interrupted him. "*Maricón!* He hit me, Perón, do you know that? *He—hit—me!* He is going to pay for that!"

"He was wrong to do that, *querida*, wrong. Of course. But still, the man is a mechanical genius. When he arrives from luna with the weapons, these absurd states will be destroyed. Pelley will have his total power in this country. But he's a fool—he has no idea what the destruction of the forty-eight capitols will mean. This country will be in chaos. The threat of the Colossus will disappear, and we will be in position to move northward!

"Think of it, *querida*! Ramírez will be no problem—we will sweep him out of the way. Together we will lead Argentina in a grand march to the north! Montevideo and Asunción will fall into line or be ground underfoot! Then we will turn our attention to the Chileans. They won't last long! After that—"

"Lovely, Juan. You go ahead and conquer the world. I have business in Buenos Aires and I cannot wait for this fairy tale to come true. Are you coming with me?" She made a move as if to rise from her gilt-covered chair.

Perón said, "I cannot come now. That is the end of it."

"Very well. Help me to the aerodrome. Oswald will pilot me, now that he is back from visiting his mama in England."

Perón shook his head. "If you must go, my dear, why not travel by commercial means? An ocean voyage—"

"Too slow!"

"Then by air."

"Yes."

"The new Constellations—"

"No! *Patrilandia* must take me. *Patrilandia* alone is fast enough! I cannot delay, Perón!"

"But we need Oswald here."

She laughed scornfully. "You don't need him here. You are so transparent, Perón! You would be nowhere without me—and you *will* be nowhere without me if you don't do as I wish. You think I'd prefer that simpering English with his silly moustache and his cultivated limp to my Perón? You make me laugh. So does Mosley! He'll be my chauffeur, that's all. Oh, your tender male ego is all aquiver, my little major! You can relax on that score. I'll keep you as long as you're useful to me, and as long as I stay with you, your star will continue to rise.

"But now—get me Mosley, and get me *Patrilandia*!"

• • •

Furious with rage and humiliation, Eva María Ibarguren climbed down the iron steps from Agustín Magaldi's private railroad car.

A fairy! A milksop! A mama's boy! That's all that he was! Who would have thought it! And she, Eva María, had moved heaven and earth, had humiliated herself to gain entry to his private car.

And she had succeeded!

It had taken every weapon in her armory—blandishment, bribery, promises and tears. To get into the great tango singer's room backstage at the Palacio Cristal, Junín's best and only theater—only to be thrown out without ever laying eyes on the great Magaldi. To get into his limousine as it waited to take him from the theater to his waiting railroad car—and be thrown out by the chauffeur without ever laying eyes on the great Magaldi.

To get into his railroad car and be thrown out again—and then, when only her rage had compelled her to hurl a rock and smash a window in the car, had she been ushered into the presence of the great Magaldi!

He was a shorter man than she had expected, and portly. His hair in a net! And makeup around his eyes! It must be for the stage, of course—that was the explanation.

Magaldi smiled at her, asked her name (she gave it), her age (she lied), her intentions (she would go to Buenos Aires and become an actress on the radio and on the screen). Agustín Magaldi smiled and offered her a brandy and a cigarette. She took both. The brandy burned and the cigarette—wrapped in lavender paper, with a gold-paper mouthpiece!—made her dizzy.

The great Magaldi seemed more kindly than she had feared. He invited her to sit beside him on his velvet plush settee. With his own hands (pale and fleshy, with clear polish on carefully manicured nails) he poured her another brandy. He pushed a button and a steward appeared. Magaldi asked Eva María if she had eaten dinner—it was after midnight. She had not. He ordered cold langouste with mayonnaise, a small salad, maté tea for them both.

She sat, picking at the langouste, sipping the bitter maté through a solid silver tube. The great man seemed more interested in her with each passing minute. He encouraged her plans, he asked her more questions. He went out of his way, it seemed to Eva María, to touch her hand with his own, to press his velvet-trousered leg against her threadbare skirt and the thigh within. He wore a perfume that cloyed in her nostrils.

Again he summoned the steward, this time to order flan for them—and a bottle of champagne! María's heart soared. Hope flared inside her chest like a banked fire rising into flame.

The steward opened the champagne, poured a small amount for Magaldi's approval, then discreetly disappeared.

Steadying himself against the rattling of the train by placing a soft hand on María's knee, Magaldi raised the bottle and started to pour for them both.

The door opened and an overdressed, heavyset woman with obviously dyed blue-black curls stormed into the compartment.

"Agustín!" she screamed at the singer. "Take your hand from that filth! What are you doing?"

Magaldi grasped the champagne bottle with both hands and sat trembling, his lips pressed together, his face pale beneath its makeup.

"Whore!" the woman yelled at María. She lumbered across the compartment, slapped María's face once, twice, forehand and back. María burst into tears. "Small-town trash. Filthy *grasita*! You *puta*! Get out of here! Get out of this car before I have the conductor stop the train and leave you in the dirt where you belong. Agustín! Go to your room!"

The singer ducked his head so he would not have to look at María again. He slunk from the compartment and through a hanging curtain. María found herself burning with humiliation, tears pouring like hot rain from her eyes.

"In every town they try," the older woman said. "Every little village whore thinks she can steal my son. Ha, ha, ha! None of them can! None ever will! Never, never!

"Well, little whore, we'll let you ride to Buenos Aires. Let's see you ply your trade with the sailors and the *descamisados*. You'll see how you like the big city after you've spread your legs for a hundred or a thousand of them! You'll be sorry you ever left Junín! Sorry!"

I will not be sorry, María whispered fiercely to herself. *I'll do what I must, but I will be a star. I'll show the old bitch! I'll spread for every* porteño *in pants if that's what it takes! I'll be bigger than her pansy-boy someday. May the Holy Virgin help me, I'll do it!*

CHAPTER
20

"Tot! Wieder tot!" Hanna Reitsch leaped to her feet and pounded across the room. Hilde Horten stood in the doorway, tears running down her face, wailing the news again and again to Hanna. Reimar Horten was dead—again!

They clustered around the body. Hanna Reitsch, Hilde Horten, Ronald Richter, Prinz Nikolauz himself. "What happened?" the Prinz demanded, swaying in the doorway. "He was all right. He was my new friend. My partner!"

Hilde managed to sob the story.

"There could not be any connection," Hanna told her firmly. "This whole fantastic tale of two earths, of every living person having a doppelgänger on the other world—if it's true, then each of us lives her own life. It one's double dies, there is no connection. We each live on as long as we can!"

"Then why did he die? My brother—I lost him, I got him back, and now I've lost him again!" Hilde threw herself on Reimar's body, weeping, plucking at the material of his tunic with her soft fingers.

Hanna laid her heavy arm across the other woman's shoulders—not to try to pull her away from Reimar's body, merely to offer her comfort and to guide her when she was ready to leave the body.

Ronald Richter drew Prinz Nikolauz aside, moving back toward the Prinz's private chamber. Speaking softly so as not to interrupt the grieving communion of the two women, he engaged the Prinz in conversation.

"We are still going ahead, Prinz?"

"I have not thought—"

"Why not?"

"I don't know, Herr Richter. I mean—"

"What options are available?"

"I . . . Come, we'll talk." He drew Richter back into the other room. He poured them each a glass of schnapps.

Richter held his glass carefully, looking into the firelight through the translucent goblet and its contents. "I'm a very trusting man, Your Highness."

"So?"

"Poor Horten—he drank with you, then . . ." He tilted his head toward the doorway. Through it came softly the sounds of the two women—one still weeping, the other whispering words of encouragement.

Prinz Nikolauz looked at Richter with puzzlement. Then his eyebrows rose. "You don't think, *mein Herr*—"

Richter said, "Of course not, Your Highness." But he put his glass carefully on the prince's desk.

Nikolauz said, "I'm not offended, *mein Herr*. You don't know me. I suppose we Svartalheimers are a little mystery to you Europeans. We are all true Nordics, of course. Our languages are the same—a few words differ, a pronunciation or an idiom, that's all. But still—still I don't blame you. So I'll prove my good faith to you."

He picked up the two goblets and downed their contents, one after the other, holding one in each hand. Then he poured schnapps into the goblets again and set them out so Richter could select one.

The engineer smiled. "We have our masters and our allies. In Europe, Svartalheim, Argentina. The unfortunate death of this fellow from the other earth—there is no reason to let it deter us. We shall proceed as planned."

"To destroy the opposition in North America, to President Pelley." The prince gazed out the window of his establishment. The earth rode high in Counter-Luna's black sky. Turning majestically in three-quarter disk, it presented a magnificent pattern of gleaming ice rim, blue oceans, white clouds, brown and green continents.

The North American continent was visible. Ronald Richter gazed at it with narrowed eyes. He pointed a finger, moved it slightly to the side, then again, again, again, then dropped it a fraction and began moving it back, as if ticking off a set of figures beneath the first row of his movement. With each tug of the finger he made a soft clucking sound with his tongue.

"And what is my role?" the prince asked.

"What have your superiors dictated?" Richter was astonished the Prinz Nikolauz would address such a question to him. But if the man was such a weakling as he appeared, if he needed to ask for advice, approval before every little move—then Ronald Richter would be more than willing to assume the role of leadership.

The prince said, "They just tell me to stay here on luna. To take action against any enemy who tries to land here, to provide support for the work of our side."

"Good! Do that! Prince, I need Fraulein Reitsch to pilot G.229 on this mission. I myself must go to deliver the devices I have built. Each is provided with a hovering unit. Each can be placed in position above its target—we will travel in G.229 to do this. When the time arrives, every device will detonate. Every one! One for the capitol of each state of the United States! But I do not want Fraulein Horten along! She is a genius in the field of aircraft design, but she is soft and womanly and she is doubly bereaved by the death of her brother and his doppelgänger. She is to remain here. She and Herr Horten's body. You will take charge of her, and of the body. Fraulein Reitsch and I will perform the mission."

Nikolauz waved his hands in front of his face. "If you're sure it will be all right with the people, uh, at home. My career, you understand, *mein Herr*. A lot of people, they think, well, he's of royal blood, this fellow, he's got everything laid out for him, he has nothing to worry about, he's set for life. But it isn't true, Herr Richter, you know it isn't true. I hope you understand that."

He wiped a hand across his brow. "That fellow Perón who was just here—he came with poor old Horten. In fact, he and an English lord and a lovely young lady, a lovely, lovely young

lady, but there was something wrong with her, she seemed
quite ill to me. Anyway, this Major Perón—all he wanted
from me was information. Tell me this, Prinz, tell me that,
Your Highness. Who did thus, Nikolauz? What happened
then? No end to it, no end at all.

"How's a fellow to have any fun? I mean, stuck away here
on this godforsaken satellite, what's there to do anyway? Invite a chap up to the caldera for a little skiing and he still
wants to talk about history, talk about politics. The man was
obsessed!''

"If Your Highness pleases!'' Hanna Reitsch stood in front
of his desk. "Herr Richter and I will be on our way.''

Nikolauz waved one hand as he turned away. He put his
feet up on the windowsill and gazed out. "That's the greatest
irony,'' he said. "I can see the earth, every friend, every
enemy. As if they were at my fingertips. But they are not. I
am barred from them as if by an impenetrable barrier. The
barrier of distance. That's the crowning blow to an old military man stuck away up here in the sky. Surely, Fraulein
Reitsch. You and Richter, eh? What about Fraulein Horten,
you going to abandon her here, eh? Well, we'll make her
welcome. Little feminine companionship won't be amiss.
Look here!''

He swung around, bootheels making a thump as they hit
the carpeted floor. "Look here, you two.'' He fixed Hanna
Reitsch with a moderately clear eye, then shifted his attention
to Ronald Richter. "Don't mess up the planet too badly, will
you? It's a nice place, you know, or it was the last time I was
home on leave. I'd still like to get back there sometime. Do
what you have to do but don't mess it up too much. That's
all I ask!''

Patrilandia approached the Palomar aerodrome via the
Plata estuary. By the time the bat-winged craft came skimming over the water, the Argentine aircraft carrier *López Rega*
had scrambled a flight of Italian-built Macchi C.202 fighters.
Patrilandia whooshed over the carrier and past the fighter
planes as if they were standing still.

At the aerodrome itself a squadron of cadets was aloft in
Bücker Jungmeister biplanes. At the approach of *Patrilandia*
the flight panicked. Most of the young pilots escaped, some

by crash-landing their planes in open fields. Others managed
to parachute. Two of the trainers collided in midair; no para-
chutes were seen as the flaming biplanes spiraled down to
explode on the earth.

A German pilot, in Palomar to demonstrate the new Heinkel propellerless monoplane for the Argentine air force,
scrambled his aircraft. He was not able to catch *Patrilandia*
but he chased the bat-wing and rolled to a safe landing alongside it on the tarmac. The German pilot, *Überleutnant* Erich
Hartmann, was the first to reach *Patrilandia*.

Oswald Mosley climbed from the aircraft, helping Eva
Duarte to alight. Hartmann stood staring at *Patrilandia*.
"What is it?" he asked. He studied the bat-wing's camou-
flage coloration, its armament, its Argentine markings.

"We need a car. At once. Are you an Argentine officer?"

"I represent Germany. I'm here to show them the Heinkel." Hartmann jerked a thumb over his shoulder at his aircraft. "But if Argentina has the likes of your craft, I don't
see why they're purchasing fighters in Europe!"

"Never mind." Mosley could feel that he was doing well.
He was in command of the situation. The Argentines were
distracted by the confusion of their training flight. Mechanics, military officers, medical personnel, were dashing around
on foot and in vehicles. Now was the time to get what he and
Eva Duarte needed.

With Hartmann's assistance they made their way to the city.
Mosley was relieved not to deal with Argentine officialdom—
his status in the country was not exactly illegal, but in the ab-
sence of his patron, Juan Perón, he had little influence. For Eva
Duarte also, there came the chilling realization that she wielded
only the borrowed power of the military aide to the President
of the Republic. In her own right she was . . . an actress, a
performer—nothing more.

Hartmann's car, a Horch roadster, was parked inside the
hangar where the Heinkel was serviced. His ground crew had
raced onto the tarmac to tow the aircraft back to the hangar.
Now he helped Eva Duarte and Oswald Mosley into the roadster and tore from the aerodrome. Evita, again showing signs
of age and fatigue despite her smart tailoring and careful
makeup, directed Hartmann to Radio Belgrano.

In the lobby she halted, shocked. The receptionist on duty

was a young woman she had joked with a hundred times. Today she showed no recognition of Evita.

"But I am Señorita Duarte. Everyone knows me. I have starred in one production after another."

"I'm sorry, madame." The receptionist was impressed, obviously, by Eva's appearance: only a woman of wealth and power would arrive in a Horch, escorted by so well dressed a man as Mosley and by a uniformed officer of the *Luftwaffe*. But she did not know Señorita Duarte, nor was the lady's name familiar to her.

"Who is here then?" Evita demanded. "Is Yankelevich in his office?"

The receptionist pressed a switch on her panel, spoke into a telephone briefly. She looked up at Evita. "Señor Yankelevich is engaged at the moment. If madame would care to tell me her business, perhaps I—"

"Perhaps you could get a job scrubbing latrines!" Evita snarled.

The receptionist shrank from the unexpected crudity.

"Now tell me at once! Where is Yankelevich?"

"He's sitting in on a rehearsal. Señor Blomberg is starting a whole new series on the *Oro Blanco* show. He—" She leaped to her feet but she was not fast enough to block Evita's path as she swept past the lobby, into the corridor that led to Radio Belgrano's largest rehearsal theater. She stopped for a moment, peering through the double glass into the studio.

Blomberg was there, tie loosened, shirt rumpled, script in hand.

Yankelevich sat behind him, watching from the control booth, *Oro Blanco*'s regular engineer at his side.

The sound-effects man was at his table, surrounded by the equipment that would create the reality of a space rocket, a sizzling death ray, a humming super machine, an exploding galaxy.

And in the cast, beautifully turned out, her dark hair contrasted against a broad-brimmed picture hat, her suit as smart as the latest that the shops of Calle Florída could provide, Evita Duarte's arch-enemy Libertad Lamarque!

Evita felt herself tingling in every cell. She heard Oswald Mosley and *Überleutnant* Hartmann gasp; they drew away from her. She was enveloped in a column of energy. She could not tell whether her body was coated in flame or sheathed in ice. Pressure pulsed through her veins.

She could see Libertad Lamarque's face redden, her eyes bulge. The *ramera* clutched at her throat. Slowly she sank to her knees, gripping the microphone stand, letting the pages of her script flutter crazily to the floor like giant flakes in a snowstorm.

Evita grasped Hartmann and Mosley by their elbows. She was suddenly weak, exhausted. She could barely stand. But she knew what she must do. She knew where she must go. She managed to steer her two escorts from the station, again leaving behind havoc and confusion to distract any who might try to stop her.

They reached Hartmann's roadster and she gasped her instructions to him. As if he were piloting his propellerless fighter plane in pursuit of *Patrilandia*, *Überleutnant* Hartmann sent his roadster barreling down the highway and through the city streets to the *Estación Central Ferrocarril*. He braked the Horch to a halt. Eva was desperate to get out of the Horch, but she was so weak she could hardly move.

Hartmann half carried her from the roadster. Mosley hovered uncertainly—he had brought off *Patrilandia*'s landing at Palomar and got them away from the aerodrome, but he was now at a loss. He was here at Juan Perón's behest to assist Miss Duarte in whatever enterprise she wished. But *Überleutnant* Hartmann seemed to be providing all the help Miss Duarte required, and Mosley was suddenly a wallflower at the dance.

Hartmann aided Evita as she made her way through the station. She had to reach the gate, the very track where she had first set foot in Buenos Aires a decade before as a scrawny, filthy, barefoot child of thirteen. She knew—somehow she simply *knew*—that her twin on this Counter-Earth had failed in that first attempt to conquer the *porteños*.

The hiss of steam, the thump of couplers, the sounds of announcements over loudspeakers, the smell of the great machines and the thousands of rushing bodies, brought back to her the moments of her arrival in the metropolis. Still using her mother's name then rather than that of the father who had maintained two households in two cities, she had arrived in the private car of the touring tango singer Carlos Gardel. How he had used her—and then cast her aside to be used by others! She alone had wept for joy at word of Gardel's death two years later, while the rest of the nation had wept for grief!

Eva Duarte by then, no longer Eva María Ibarguren, she had clawed, scratched, bit, worked her way from one minor role to another, from protector to protector, from walk-on to supporting actress to featured player to star!

But what if she had failed to obtain that original ride from Junín to Buenos Aires? How she had begged Gardel, how she had flattered, how she had offered to do anything, anything, anything in exchange for a ride to Buenos Aires in his private railroad car! And the great singer had played with her, raised her hopes then dashed them, then raised them again only to dash them again—until finally he had permitted her to travel to Buenos Aires huddled in a corner of his palatial rolling home!

If he had denied her at the last moment? If he had used her, degraded her, abused her, and then ordered his underlings to throw her onto the cinders? Would she have given up her hopes and lived a life of drab servitude in the dusty town? Or would she have tried again, again, and still again until she succeeded in reaching the great city?

She leaned on *Überleutnant* Hartmann's arm. She saw Oswald Mosley limping along beside them. Ahead she could see Augustín Magaldi's gorgeous coach. Agustín Magaldi— the greatest tango singer alive, successor to the dead Carlos Gardel in the hearts of Argentina's millions of women.

But before they reached Magaldi's car she saw Mosley hobbling ahead, leaning on his polished walking stick. ''Perón!'' she heard him cry. ''Major Perón!''

A uniformed officer was climbing from the car ahead of Magaldi's. With him was a man in civilian garb. The officer bore an uncanny resemblance to Juan Perón. If Evita had not left him in Washington, more than 5,000 miles to the north, busily plotting with the American *Presidente*, Pelley, she would have taken him in fact for Perón. But that she knew was impossible.

The civilian with this officer was shaven-headed, lantern-jawed. He spoke rapidly, moving his hands in excitement. He carried a dispatch folder tucked beneath one arm. He and the Argentine officer chattered to each other in rapid-fire Italian.

The officer stopped and stared at Mosley.

"*¿Perdón?*" the officer said.

"Aren't you Major Perón?"

"Almost." The officer laughed. His English was heavily accented but perfectly clear. "I am Major Giovanni Peroni, at your service, good sir."

"But you are Juan Perón! You were just in Washington!"

The officer turned to his companion, "Tell him, Mussolini," he said good-naturedly, "am I this Perón fellow? Have I come from this place in the Colossus of the North?"

In English even more heavily accented than the army man's, Mussolini said, "No, Giovanni. You are Peroni not Perón. And you and I come from the mountains near Chile, not from the United States." He shook his head at Mosley. "No, mister. He's not your friend. You made some mistake. Now we must go."

The two men brushed past Mosley, disappeared into the *Estación*.

Evita nudged Hartmann. He helped her past the car, past the immobilized Mosley. A girl was climbing from the private coach that brought up the end of the train. There was no sign of Augustín Magaldi or any of his entourage. Just the young girl, her dress dirty, her hair disheveled, her face flaming with humiliation and rage. From the car behind her could be heard the voice of an older woman, screaming imprecations at the girl.

She turned and shook her fist angrily at the railroad coach, then started up the platform for the *Estación*.

Evita stopped her, grasping her arms with hands made strong by sheer will. "María," she whispered.

The girl halted and stared into Evita's eyes. Watching her, Evita could see herself, see herself as a younger girl, one as smart and as angry as life in the dirt of Junín could make her, yet laughably ignorant. And touchingly, strangely innocent. Did she see herself in Evita's face, as Evita could see herself in the girl's? Did she see an older, wiser version of herself—sophisticated, graced, made wise and aged by her struggle in Buenos Aires?

And yet, Evita realized, they were the same age. This

childlike creature was her double here on Counter-Earth. They had been born the same day, probably at the same moment. Each of them was just twenty-two years old. Twenty-two—and one was like a child, and the other was like . . . She choked back a sob.

"I am yourself, María. And you are I. We are both of us Eva María Ibarguren de Duarte, both of us in Buenos Aires, both of us from the dust of our mother's house in Junín!"

María looked at her. Barefoot as she was, and with Evita standing in her spike-heeled pumps, the child had to peer up into her face. But she recognized that which Evita prayed she would recognize there.

"Myself? I don't understand, señora."

"Not yet, María. But you shall. And I can see that you feel the bond between us. I am from another world."

"*¿Una fantasma? ¡Ay, no, tú eres una santa! ¡Una santa!* Thou art a saint!" She started to sink to her knees, but Evita caught her by her dirty hands and embraced her.

"*¡No soy una santa, queridísima!* The last thing I would be is a saint. No, I am a woman like yourself. More like yourself than you can yet imagine, but you shall understand. You have no place to live in Buenos Aires. You have nowhere to go."

"No."

"We will take care of that. You shall have the best. You shall wear fine clothing and sleep on satin. You shall have tutors and coaches and you shall be the grandest star in all of Argentina. Augustín Magaldi himself will beg you to appear as his leading lady, and you shall grant his wishes or you shall turn him down, at your own whim."

Her arm around Eva María, leaning on her other self for strength but lending her the hard-gained knowledge of Buenos Aires and the world, Evita turned to Oswald Mosley and Erich Hartmann. "Go get your automobile, *Teniente*. Sir Oswald, we will need some money. We are going to the Hotel Excelsior. We will need a suite for now. Later we will move to an apartment, perhaps on Calle Casa Posadas, or perhaps in the Barrio Norte. And we will need cash. I am taking Eva María shopping on the Calle Florída. She will need everything—beauty treatment, hair-do, manicure, and pedicure.

And of course, a complete wardrobe. Everything from hats to shoes. Everything. Everything!''

Mosley tugged at his moustache. "But, Miss Duarte, don't forget that I'm a visitor in this world, myself! The Oswald Mosley of this world was killed thirty years ago! I spoke with my mother—his mother, I mean—just days ago. She knows he is dead. She—''

"You will work that out, Oswald. A mother whose son comes back will not reject him.''

"But she did! She—''

"You'll go back, Oswald. You will convince her! You have every childhood recollection, your fingerprints will even match. Did they record your fingerprints when you served your king? There will be a way. *There will be a way!*''

Mosley accompanied Hartmann back to Palomar. The German officer was ebullient, bragging of his aerial accomplishments and the virtues of his propellerless fighter, besieging Mosley with questions about *Patrilandia*: its unconventional configuration, its fuel and its engines, the base from which *Patrilandia* had flown, its rated speed and range.

Mosley answered in monosyllables, ultimately feigning inability to understand Hartmann's heavily accented Spanish and English, hiding his own knowledge of the German language. He was more concerned with his own future. He was sunk in a cold gray fog.

He had returned to England and confronted his mother, and she had seen through his imposture. Except it was not really imposture. It was—what? He could not even define his own act.

Could he travel to the Flanders graveyard where the Counter-Earth Mosley lay—had lain for three decades—and claim to be himself, risen from the earth? They would exhume the other Mosley, perhaps. They would find bones, yes, and what other artifacts? Could he claim that the corpse in his grave was that of another, some unknown sacrifice for King and Crown, lying these years beneath Oswald Mosley's tombstone?

Then what?

What would Mother say, what could she do? She had despised her son all these years—but all these years she had thought him dead. What grief, what guilt, lay in the old woman's heart? If he could convince her that he was truly her son—and he was certain, in time, that he could—she would be forced to take him back.

Or if not, if she remained adamant and unconvinced, how many more years did she have? Old and unwell, add the strain of his own badgering, she couldn't live for long. And then he could go into court, could hire solicitor and barrister, claim his title, demand his cruelly withheld patrimony.

He stiffened his back, raised his chin, ran a finger along his dark moustache. "Yes, Lieutenant Hartmann. If you will drop me, please, where I can board my aircraft."

Over Topeka they appeared, and over Oklahoma City. Over Little Rock and Jefferson City, Des Moines, Lincoln and Denver. One glowed and hovered above Santa Fe. One gold spheroid no larger than a grapefruit, over Austin. Another, over Baton Rouge. Another, over Jackson. Nashville next, then Springfield. One after another after another, until forty-eight golden spheroids hovered and glowed and hummed malevolently, almost invisibly, high above the capitol of each of the United States of America.

Hanna Reitsch piloted G.229 skillfully from the center of the country, moving carefully in a spiral, moving ever outward toward the oceans and the borders. The ship was small and it moved quietly.

Even if it had not, no federal aircraft would have risen to challenge it, no eager fighter pilot would have been permitted to scramble his Seversky P-35 or his Curtiss Hawk. No, for word had come from Washington, from the Secretary of War herself, Elizabeth Maude Dilling, that the entire Army Air Corps was to place itself on a one-day stand-down while every piece of aerial hardware, from the flimsiest trainer and observation scout to the heaviest and mightiest of bombers, was examined for possible sabotage.

Yes—word had reached the War Department in Washington that agents of a foreign power had infiltrated the Air Corps and had tampered with the aircraft that made up America's first and last line of defense!

Thus G.229 moved silently, swiftly, from capitol to capitol, leaving over each a golden spheroid containing a timer, a detonator, and an explosive charge that would utterly destroy the building over which it hung—and most of the surrounding city as well!

The last device was in place. Its target: Augusta, Maine.

Ronald Richter heaved a sigh of satisfaction. "We may leave now. And thank you, Fraulein, for your excellent piloting. You will receive commendation when we get home."

"You do not wish to stay here and see the outcome of your handiwork, Herr Richter?"

"*Ach, nein!*" Richter snorted. "I certainly do not wish to remain here, or anywhere near here, when my little toys perform their tricks. No, Hanna."

"Well, then. I for one have no interest in returning to the moon."

"Not even for Hilde?"

She paused before answering. "Perhaps I will see Hilde again some time. But then again, there are many pink-cheeked *Mädchens* to be found. Many, Ronald, I assure you."

"To Europe, then. I surely have no interest in the moon. Let that fool of a princeling sit there with his precious schnapps and his crazy dreams. Skiing down volcanic slopes! Come visit luna, spend your marks! Ha! Once America goes down, the other fool, Pelley, will be drawn down with it. Earth is the planet of opportunity, Hanna, and America is the land whose streets will be paved with gold—for those who know how to pick it up!"

The little ship, G.229, disappeared into bright sunlight above the Atlantic Ocean, headed eastward. Far below, an ocean liner drew a wake, like a white chalk line across a dark gray slate, headed for Liverpool from New York.

"Still," Richter yielded, "it would be interesting to see my toys perform."

Hanna Reitsch lifted an eyebrow. "So, *mein Herr*?"

"It should be a spectacular sight." Richter smiled. "Best seen, and most safely, I think, from a very great height."

Hanna smiled in return. "My buggy bounces high." She returned to G.229's controls. She swung the sleek craft toward a soaring suborbital path. Around the craft the sky turned black and stars appeared.

CHAPTER
21

It was one of the strangest performances imaginable, yet the two participants—they were their own entire audience, save for some wildlife in the surrounding gardens—were more than pleased with the outcome. Albert Einstein played his violin for some selections; for others, a battered piano that had somehow made its way from the far side of the world and come to rest in Muvia. When he played violin, he was accompanied on piano by Babe Didrikson. When she played her harmonica, he accompanied her on piano.

He taught her Mozart, Bach, Scarlatti.

She taught him Chester Burnett, Willie Dixon, Robert Johnson.

After he matched a Mozart fantasia to Tommy Duncan's "Bubbles in My Beer," Babe jumped up and down. "You're almost as good a fiddler as Bob Wills himself!"

Einstein smiled. "I am very pleased, very flattered. Now I wonder if we could try just one more piece."

"Sure, Professor! This is the most fun I've had in years."

Einstein sat with his bow in his hand, his chin resting on his knuckles, having "a little think." "Very nice." He set the violin and bow to one side and seated himself at the piano. "This you will like, I think. This your harmonica will go with very nicely, I think."

He leaned back, turned his eyes to the foliage and the sunlight, and began feeling his way into the first of Bach's Twelve Little Preludes.

Babe listened, held her harmonica silently against her mouth.

When Einstein finished the prelude, he said, "You see? Do you think you can join this?"

"Perfect," said Babe.

Einstein signaled with his head and they began to play. As they worked through the piece, a stillness settled over the garden. Through it the music could be heard. The spirits of the two musicians were no longer in the garden; they were in the music.

Einstein sensed something other than his surroundings and Bach's prelude. He was becoming aware of events thousands of miles away, events in the other hemisphere and on the other hemidisk. His expression became more intense and his playing more powerful. The playfulness of the piece disappeared. Something overwhelming took its place.

Josh Gibson held the bat just as he held his Louisville Slugger to terrorize the pitchers of the National League.

The Muvian children who surrounded him watched, excited. They had played ball games for hundreds of years, but baseball was a mystery to them. Josh had improvised a bat from a tapered dowel, a field had been laid out, and the children had taken to the game at first sight.

When Babe Didrikson and Dr. Einstein finished their recital, Josh hoped that Babe would come and pitch to him. They could give some exhibition for these kids! Right now, there was no way Josh would bat seriously against a Muvian youngster, but he could show them the way to hold a bat, the way to swing one, the way to plant their feet.

He made sure that no one was standing close by; he didn't want to risk hitting a kid. He had their best thrower toss a few over the improvised plate, then signaled that he was ready to demonstrate batting form.

The kid reared back—he had a first class arm! He let go a high, fast one.

Josh swung the improvised bat. It was of a dark, local wood, almost like ebony. Hard and heavy.

He found himself high in the air, standing as solidly as if on the ground but hundreds of feet over a city. He was already halfway into the swing. Where the Muvian ball should have been was a strange object. It was big, as big as a softball, and it was golden-colored. It seemed to pulse and flare with an evil light.

There was nothing to do: Josh finished his swing. As he followed through, he felt the satisfying impact of hardwood on ball, heard the sharp crack that nothing else in the world could duplicate: The golden sphere sailed high and far. It disappeared.

What had happened?

He looked down. He was still suspended in the air, but the city beneath him was a different one. He blinked, hefted his bat, looked around, and another golden sphere hummed and pulsed in front of him. He swung his bat. He felt the impact, heard the oddly melodic crack, watched the golden sphere sail out of sight.

It happened again.

And again.

Josh was beginning to sweat.

Swing!

Crack!

Swing!

Crack!

His arms were starting to ache. It didn't matter. He'd been getting out of shape—this would help him get back in condition.

Swing!

Crack!

Each time there was another city beneath his feet, each time the golden sphere sailed high and far and disappeared in the distance.

He lost count of how many swings he took; there must have been dozens. He didn't know what had happened, he didn't know why he had to hit the golden spheres, but something told him that he must. Told him that there were no three strikes in this game. Every swing must be perfect, every impact absolutely solid.

Another!

Another!

And he was in Muvia again, surrounded by children. The local talent had released the ball, Josh was halfway through his swing. He felt the satisfying impact and heard the inimitable crack of hardwood against ball.

He watched the ball sail high over the heads of the Muvian children who had hoped—vainly—to be able to flag it down.

Josh dropped his bat and sank to the ground. Remotely he could hear the children's exclamations of amazement at his hit turning to cries of alarm. He tried to sit up and reassure them that he was unhurt. He was only tired. But so tired, so very, very tired.

He wondered where he had been, what he had done. It was like a dream, like one of the dreams his teammates had told him about when they returned from a den they had visited in Havana after a game against the Sugar Kings. It was like nothing else, they'd said. It was like floating in the air, and time slowed, and they could do anything.

Had he really stood in the air and swung at forty-eight golden baseballs? He had known somehow that there were no three strikes, no foul tips or Texas Leaguers. It was a home run every swing or—or what? He didn't know. He simply didn't know.

But he had not failed. He'd given every shred of skill and strength that he possessed. He had nothing left, but that was all right. It was all right. He'd done what he had to do. His conscience was clean. His soul was free. He closed his eyes and rested.

The first glowing golden spheroid appeared before G.229's windscreen. Hanna Reitsch gasped aloud.

Ronald Richter had been sitting beside Hanna, eyes closed as he contemplated his future. With the United States of America plunged into chaos, luna under control of the fool Nikolauz, the continent of Europe might explode into warfare at any moment; and this time there would be no overwhelming forces from across the Atlantic Ocean to tip the scale against Germany and its friends.

Richter had taken little part in political affairs. Up to now his role had been that of the scientist ready to obey his employer: the good soldier who did as he was told and let others, whose job it was to make decisions, make them.

But these things were changing now. From this day onward—

The exclamation of the pilot startled Richter from his rev-
erie.

"What is it?"

Even as Hanna Reitsch pointed, another golden sphere
popped into sight, dancing and pulsing near the first. In a
moment there was another, then still another.

"What did you do?" Hanna demanded.

"I? I did nothing! I placed these over the forty-eight cities
that were designated. The capitals of the United States!"

"But look, Ronald!" She drew her finger in an arc. The
spheres were continuing to appear, one after another. Within
minutes, G.229 was surrounded by a polyhedron, its imaginary surface defined by forty-eight equally spaced pulsing
golden spheres.

G.229 was racing eastward, high over the North Atlantic.

Below the aircraft, the great ship *Titanic* plowed a steady
course on the easterly half of its circuit between England and
America. Despite the bitterness of the January air, a few hardy
passengers sat bundled in wooden deck chairs. Of these, a
handful had noticed the silvery speck moving from the west,
flashing directly overhead, and obviously intending to make
a landing on the other side of the ocean long before *Titanic*
could make port.

"That spells the end for ocean liners," an American
businessman commented to his wife. He wore a woolen cap
and an overcoat turned up against the cold; she, a knitted
scarf pulled over her hair and a mackinaw lined with Argentine sheepskin. "It's too fast, too easy to fly."

"But ships are so much more *fun*," his wife challenged.
"Who would want to cross the ocean in a few hours when you
can have the luxury of a stateroom, the gracious dining . . ."

In G.229 Richter had burst into a cold sweat. "I have to
stop them! I have to shut them off!"

Hanna Reitsch tried to maneuver away from the gold
spheres. She banked, climbed, dived—all to no avail. The
polyhedron duplicated every shift of G.229's attitude, every
increase or decrease in her speed.

"When will they explode?" she demanded.

"We have no time!" Richter answered. "I'll do it myself!'' He reached for the bolts that held G.229's bubble in place.

"You can't! Not at this altitude! We—''

"Then we'll get out! We can't stay here! They're going to—''

"What's that?'' the woman in the deck chair exclaimed. "It's like—another sun!'' She blinked. Her eyes smarted, began to tear painfully. The afterimage of the blinding glare refused to fade. She groped for her husband's arm, found it. He held her hand.

"I can't see,'' he said. "Are you all right? It was—I never saw anything like—'' He kept his eyes shut a little longer, then opened them again. The world was bathed in a painful glare that he realized was the afterimage of the explosion rather than an external phenomenon.

Only now did the sound of the detonation come, and with it the shockwave that rocked *Titanic* in her path despite the efforts of gyroscopes designed to steady her against the North Atlantic's seas.

"Did the plane explode?'' the woman asked.

"It must have. But even so—even so, what kind of fuel could it have been carrying?''

Titanic was slowing as Captain Davidson ordered his men to search for wreckage, to search for survivors of the terrible explosion, even though they knew from the outset that there could never be survivors of such a disaster.

"Get on the air,'' Davidson ordered his signal officer. "Get word to New York what has happened. Get word to the military. They have to be involved. Even that monster President Pelley has to feel something when he learns about this. No, we'll do better! Get on the wireless to London! There's more sanity there!''

Juan Domingo Perón sat upon his horse Mancha, surveying the bleak countryside of southern Patagonia. His civilian clothing was more comfortable than his major's uniform; the baggy trousers and broad-brimmed, flat-crowned hat of the gaucho were practical enough, and the sheepskin coat kept out the cold that penetrated this southerly land even in the height of summer.

It could have been far worse, he told himself. Furloughed for his role in the Counter-Earth affair, he had still made it back to his home world safely, something that Reimar Horten had failed to do. Reimar Horten or Perón's poor Evita!

Horten was dead.

Evita had found her doppelgänger in that other Argentina, that country so much like this, yet so remote across the cosmic void!

Oswald Mosley had brought *Patrilandia* back to Washington when Evita adamantly refused to leave that other Argentina. The Colossus was in a state of turmoil, but not as President Pelley and his cronies had planned. Somehow their plan to destroy the capitols of the separate states had backfired. The legislatures of the states, acting in concert, had amended the nation's constitution and sent Pelley fleeing from the White House one skip ahead of impeachment.

How strange was fate! Mosley had remained on the other earth, throwing in his lot with the deposed Pelley. They would find their followers somewhere. They would manage, perhaps even find their way to power again. Or perhaps not.

He alone had returned to tell the tale. He alone. Evita and Mosley were even now seeking their fates on the other earth. Reimar Horten had found his!

And Perón had singlehandedly flown *Patrilandia* back across the millions of miles only to find himself dismissed from his position of prestige and influence, exiled to his holdings in Patagonia. All for the crime of deserting the President of the Republic in the midst of a Gene Autry film!

A bitter rictus curled the corners of his mouth. It was far different from the grin of *Teniente* Toothpaste.

Perón wheeled his horse about.

"Where were you, just now?"

Perón looked at Ronald Richter, seated on a nondescript nag that the major had cut out of the remuda for him. "Counter-Earth," the officer admitted.

"Still?"

"I will not forget the experience, señor."

"Of course not."

The German looked at his wristwatch. "It's almost time to get back." In all directions save one the flat pampa stretched away until it was lost in gray mist. An immigrant shepherd who had brought the beginnings of his flock all the way from Wales, and who now rented rangeland from Perón, waved from a tiny hillock. Perón waved back.

To the southwest of Perón and Richter a low building of raw concrete blocks blended inconspicuously into the bleak landscape. No sign advertised the activities that took place within. Only those directly engaged in Richter's research projects entered the building, and they knew well what went on there.

As Richter and Perón walked their horses across low, grayish vegetation, Richter said, "I wonder what it would be like to meet oneself. The other Ronald Richter—now I will never know him, eh?"

Perón shrugged. "Richter and his pilot were lost along with their aircraft. A ship reported a flash of light over the Atlantic just at the hour that Richter's devices were due to become active. But why over the Atlantic rather than over their targets? ¿Quién sabe?"

"And the other Juan Perón? Surely you looked for him."

"There was hardly time. I tried to find him, via the Argentine embassy in Washington, but there was such turmoil, there was no result."

"But there is another Perón, is there not? Just as there was another Richter?"

The major shrugged. "Who knows? The earths are not identical, Herr Richter. Alike, oh so very alike, yes. But not identical. Why was Oswald Mosley injured in the One Year War on our earth, but recovered and lives to this day, when on Counter-earth he died three decades ago? ¿Quién sabe? Another Perón? Perhaps yes, perhaps no. If there is, he may one day become President of the Republic. I had hoped to do so, but . . ." He moved his hand in a gesture that took in the estancia but excluded the vast territory of the remainder of the nation.

"I will continue my work," Richter vowed. "I will develop the weapon that I believe that other Ronald Richter built. I will find out where he went wrong, what error he made that destroyed him."

"For whom?" Perón asked. "For President Ramírez? Let the fool sit in the Casa Rosada, Richter. Let him sit there and watch Gene Autry movies. He's a harmless old man. Don't stir him up.''

"He will not be there forever," Richter said. "He will be replaced, and when he is replaced, I will be at the side of his replacement. Are you sure it will not be you, Major Perón?''

"Am I sure?" Perón halted his horse and sat ramrod straight in the saddle. "Am I sure?" He studied the heavy gray clouds that hovered low over the pampa. The Welshman's sheep clustered together as if to protect themselves against the sky. Perón held his silence until Richter began impatiently to move away on his mount. He was nearly out of earshot before Perón said softly, for the last time, ''¿Quién sabe?''

The White House rose garden was not at its best in January, but President Cordell Hull chose to walk there every day. Summer or winter, rain or shine, he walked in the rose garden. He met there with aides, he walked there alone when he had problems to ponder.

Today the Washington sky was heavily overcast. A previous snowfall still showed in the garden. The gravel paths had been cleared, however.

Now a few vagrant flakes were falling. Another hour or less might reveal a major storm, and Hull would be driven inside to conduct Presidential business, but for now he led his secretary of the navy and his two distinguished guests through the mazelike garden, their heavy shoes crunching the gravel with each step.

"William Dudley Pelley, President of the United States," Hull exclaimed. "Believe it or not, that's the part I find hardest to accept. Two earths, Egyptian pyramids on the moon, people living out there in the asteroid belt—I suppose it's all so fantastic, I can't mount an argument against it."

"It's all quite true, Mr. President." Albert Einstein, alone of the party, was not attired in suit and tie. Beneath his heavy overcoat the savant wore a sweater and baggy trousers. Beneath his heavy winter shoes he wore no socks.

"I believe you, Professor Einstein. I'm grateful for what you and your companions did for us all. Jack''—he faced Jack Northrop—"where are those other two, Miss Didrikson and that Gibson fellow?''

"They were waylaid by members of the White House staff, Mr. President. They're inside signing autographs and talking baseball."

"You hear that, Franklin?"

Franklin Roosevelt, secretary of the navy, said "Yes, Mr. President."

"Well, good for them." President Hull chuckled. His soft Virginia accent sweetened the words. "And, as I said, it's Pelley that I find hardest to believe. That slimy little reptile— can you imagine it? President! What can possibly have gone wrong with the people in that country? To elect a creature like that to the highest office in the land! What can I have done to win him as an opposite number?

"Never mind," he went on. "Roosevelt, I want you to get me a confidential report on that fellow. I mean, on *our* Pelley. From chief Silver Shirt to President—what a surprise!"

The President exhaled a great lungful of air and watched it vaporize before him. "Perhaps we'd best get back inside." He led the way through the rear entrance of the White House and led the others from the rose garden into the Red Room. In a few minutes they were seated comfortably. A fire crackled at one side of the room beneath a portrait of onetime President Samuel J. Tilden. Coffee and brandy were served all around.

Josh Gibson and Babe Didrikson had joined the group: Josh wore an impeccably tailored suit and tie; Babe, a fashionable skirt and high heels.

President Hull had thanked them for their service to the nation. "I don't know when we'll be able to speak of this publicly," the President told them, "or how much we will be able to reveal. For the time being, I hope I can rely on you to remain silent with regard to the entire matter."

Babe said, "Not a word, Mr. President. Not one."

Josh merely nodded in agreement.

President Hull said, "I thank you. On behalf of the entire nation. Perhaps the entire planet—or two!" The President smiled. He turned toward Jack Northrop. "Now, these, uh, Counter-Earthly Americans—do they need our help, do you think?"

Northrop said, "I think they're all right now, sir. It was a near call for them. Pelley had taken over the government and

was trying to push through an amendment that would abolish
the forty-eight state governments. He'd already packed the
Supreme Court with obedient followers. He was establishing
himself as a full-fledged dictator. But the folks there put a
stop to it. They didn't even need much help from us—they
called for help, and we went there to provide it, but in the
end they wound up solving their own problems for themselves."

"Huh," the President interpolated. "So often things work
out that way, Jack! And what's the situation now?"

"They've a provisional government, and there are going to
be a full set of elections in 1942—this November—for a new
Congress and for a temporary President to fill out Pelley's
term."

"Any idea who'll be chosen?" Hull inquired.

Northrop's brow furrowed. "My guess, they'll keep the
fellow who masterminded the strategy of having the forty-
eight states amend the Constitution and get rid of that foul-
ness in the White House. He certainly proved his leadership,
and he's got the Constitution in his heart."

"And who was that?"

"Well, sir"—Northrop reddened—"it was Franklin Roosevelt."

The Secretary of the Navy joined the President in peals of
laughter. "Franklin Roosevelt as President. Why, I suppose
anything's possible," the President finally gasped. "But still,
Jack, still! First you tell me Silver Shirt Pelley is President.
Then you tell me Frank Roosevelt is going to be in there next!
Ha! But then, I suppose, anything can happen. What do you
think, Franklin?"

Roosevelt shook his head. "I'm getting a little long in the
tooth to think of a Presidential run, Mr. President. I'm going
to invite my good friend Dr. Einstein to go sailing with me
when the weather warms. I'd rather be a fisherman. Thanks
all the same."

"And I also," Einstein chuckled. "Yes, very well put. I
would rather be a fisherman! Yes, I also would!"

For a moment President Hull grew serious again. "There's
a lot to be done, though, even if our counterparts on the twin
planet have come out on top.

"We need to get to the moon before those malefactors

who nearly blew you fellows up can take it over for good.
Lord knows what treasures and what secrets rest on that old
cheese ring! And as for those fellows on the planetoid
Ceres, you're sure they don't want anything to do with
us?"

"I received that very clear impression, Mr. President."
Jack Northrop was emphatic.

"Maybe we can do something about that, too. We'll send
some charmer up to try and make peace with them."

"It isn't that they're angry with us," Northrop explained.
"They feel that we're blameless—well, all except a few
nations on earth, such as Svartalheim. The, uh, Khemites feel
that they are the guilty ones, and they've placed themselves
into a sort of voluntary quarantine to keep from doing more
harm."

Hull rubbed his jaw. "Well, we'll have to see about that.
Will you take the job, Jack? As a personal favor to me, and
as a service to the nation?"

Northrop said, "I still want to get home in time for the
Four-Hundredth Anniversary celebration at Santa Barbara,
sir."

"That's a few months off, isn't it?"

"Yes, sir."

"Thank you, Jack. Then you've got a job." He had a sip
of brandy laced with coffee. "Ah. Now that's something really good for a chilly winter's day.

"Now"—Hull rubbed his hands, extending them toward
the cheerful fire. He peered up at Samuel J. Tilden's lemony
expression and winked—"there remains just one question that
I would like to ask. I think that Professor Einstein might be
the one to help with this."

The savant had been gazing into the flames himself, "having a little think" about something he did not reveal to the
others.

"You hit this thing," the President said, "this so-called
Einstein layer out beyond this thing you call the plane of the
ecliptic—is that right, Doctor?"

"Yes," Einstein nodded, "that is correct."

"And you saw what lies beyond this layer, and you actually, uh, *fell* through it and walked around on the other side?
Is that correct, Professor?"

Einstein assented.

"Well, tell me," the President said, "just what did you see there? What was it like? Is it true, as I've heard, that you saw God? That you met the deity, actually and literally met God?"

"It was a very private experience, Mr. President. I do not wish to be secretive, but I'm not sure I can talk about it. Please, if you will forgive me for that."

"I understand." The President nodded. "I really do understand. It's just—well, sir, if there's anything at all that you think you might be able to tell us."

Einstein turned his gaze from the fireplace to the tall window that opened out onto the White House rose garden. He looked up. The heavy clouds had finally released their burden, and a thick fall of sparkling, floating snowflakes was descending from the sky. "I saw wonderful things, Mr. President. And I saw terrible things. I must tell you first of the terrible things. The atom, Mr. President—you know something about the atom?"

"No more than any layman, Dr. Einstein. Oh, a little about protons and neutrons—Sunday paper science."

The scientist smiled wistfully. "The atom is a great source of power, Mr. President. Perhaps even greater, potentially, than the Muvian magnetic engine. But it can also be turned to the work of destruction. A bomb can be made, no bigger than this." He held his hands as if cradling a large cantaloupe.

The President waited for Einstein to continue.

Einstein sighed. "Such a bomb, Mr. President—it could destroy a city. This city, or Rome, or Peking. One little bomb, Mr. President. And it could leave behind poison that would make the survivors sicken and die before their time, and their children be monsters, and their grandchildren be weak and sickly. Unto the seventh generation, Mr. President."

Hull stood by the fire staring into its heart. "Do we wish to build this weapon, Mr. Einstein?"

"You must decide that, Mr. President. If we build it, it may spell our final doom. If we do not build it and another nation—say, Svartalheim—does, it may also spell our final doom. I do not know what to tell you, Mr. President. I do not know.''

Hull turned to face the others. Each of them felt the strength and goodwill that had brought him to the highest office in the land. "Let us discuss something more cheerful for a while.'' He looked from one face to another.

"For the moment—gladly, sir.''

Hull managed a small smile. "Your story makes me wonder. You see, there may well be a Babe Didrikson and a Joshua Gibson on that other earth, and they may well be athletes, just as you two are. A trifle different. The customs there, being what they are, Miss Earhart having told you the things that she did. But it is hard for me to understand your not having met the Einstein of that other world. Or even the Northrop.

"Do they not exist there?'' The President took a turn around the Red Room, pausing to stand at the window. He watched snowflakes drifting gently onto the dead and empty rose garden. Even in the depths of winter, he looked forward to the spring. The White House staff included gardeners, of course, but when he could escape his duties, the President would be in the garden, come April, on his knees, wearing padded gloves to protect his hands from the thorns, working to bring life and beauty back to his favorite place.

He turned back to his guests. They had not answered his question, waiting for his moment of contemplation to pass. Now they spoke.

"If there is a Counter-Earthly Jack Northrop, I expect he's doing what I would most love to do. He's working with the Santa Barbara Anniversary Day Committee, preparing for the big fiesta and parade. I know his great ambition in this life— to ride down State Street in Spanish garb, Grand Marshal of the anniversary parade, waving to the crowd.''

President Hull nodded. "I wonder if you envy that other Jack Northrop. Don't answer, Jack. I don't want to know. But I'll tell you that I envy him. I truly envy him. And you, Dr. Einstein. Is there another Einstein on that other earth?''

The scientist smiled gently. "I don't know. Maybe there is. There must have been, I know, until the year 1912. After that, anything could happen. If I went to look for him, I would start in Switzerland. At the Patent Office. He might be there yet, maybe even a technical expert, first class.

"But what I hope, ah, what I hope is that he is in Vienna, a musician."

The Red Room fell silent save for the soft crackling of the fire and the even softer whisper of snowflakes falling against window panes.

"And you cannot tell us about meeting the deity," President Hull said. "I return to the subject, Doctor, and I apologize for intruding on your privacy. But a matter of such profound importance . . ."

"I cannot tell you about that, Mr. President." Einstein looked at Cordell Hull, peering into the President's face. "I cannot tell you about God. Only listen, Mr. President, listen to God. In this room, at this moment. Listen to the flames. Listen to the falling snow, so soft a sound, so beautiful a sound. Be still and listen to the beating of your heart."